THE VILLAGE
OF
LONGING

and

DANCEHALL DAYS

George O'Brien

VIKING
in association with The Lilliput Press

VIKING

Published by the Penguin Group
27 Wrights Lane, London w8 5tz, England
Viking Penguin Inc., 40 West 23rd Street, New York, New York 10010, USA
Penguin Books Australia Ltd, Ringwood, Victoria, Australia
Penguin Books Canada Ltd, 2801 John Street, Markham, Ontario, Canada l3r 1b4
Penguin Books (NZ) Ltd, 182–190 Wairau Road, Auckland 10, New Zealand

Penguin Books Ltd, Registered Offices: Harmondsworth, Middlesex, England

The Village of Longing first published in Ireland by The Lilliput Press 1987,
and simultaneously in England by The Sixth Chamber Press, with a limited edition
of twenty-five copies
Dancehall Days first published in Ireland by The Lilliput Press 1988
First published as one volume by Viking 1989
3 5 7 9 10 8 6 4 2

Copyright © George O'Brien, 1987, 1988

Printed in Great Britain by
Richard Clay Ltd, Bungay, Suffolk
Filmset in 10 on 12pt Palatino

A CIP catalogue record for this book is available from the British Library

ISBN 0-670-82366-x

for Ben and Nick: 'two fine boys'

CONTENTS

THE VILLAGE OF LONGING

DANCEHALL DAYS

I

MY THREE PARENTS

1

It's teatime.

Chrissy, my aunt, is slicing a cottage loaf with a crackle and spray of delicious black crust. She's humming a song-hit, 'Shrimp Boats', or maybe the new Rosemary Clooney, 'Mambo Italiano'. Her brother George - Georgie, we call him, or often, 'Geo': 'jaw' – will be in from work soon. The meaty tang of his dinner sits in the steamy kitchen air, heavy male aroma (Geo is all smells: paint, putty, sawdust, Brylcreem, booze). At the sink, Mam, my grandmother, is in the posture I will see her in forever, crouched slightly, head bent over some chore, wisps of grey hair bothersomely hanging around her hard, handsome face.

I wonder if she's going to Lyons's tonight.

For a year or more when I was nine or ten (in the pages that follow I'm seven going on twelve) she regularly visited Bid and Willy Lyons after the chapel. The chapel came first, needless to say. Mam wouldn't dream of missing morning mass at the convent or of closing the day without 'paying a visit'. Off with the apron and dull grey skirt, on with the cloche hat and kid gloves, and away with her, hail, rain or snow, her crisp gait and erect bearing announcing to Lismore at large the uprightness and quiet implacability of her faith.

Handily enough, the Lyonses lived in Chapel Street, just opposite the chapel's tall, white, ever-open gates. Too near, in my view. Wouldn't the Angelus, funeral and mass bells deafen them? (Joe Kelly, who lived next door, *was* deaf.) And then, living so close, they wouldn't be able to feel what I thought was the best part of going. Being just-on-the-verge-of, feeling just-about-to-be. Voluptuous anticipation: a feeling finer than any offered by the services, which for all their other-

3

worldly overtures, were predictable down to the congregation's last cough.

Chapel Street was dull and poor and quiet. I didn't care for
it. It looked lonesome. Few youngsters lived there. Mam loved
Chapel Street, though. Proud as she was to have married into
Main Street and a fine, detached house like Swiss Cottage, she
never denied the cabin she was born in. From her loyalty to
the street she could even speak with pride about Tim Healy,
the noted turncoat of Parnell's time, though she never knew
him and despised his unprincipled politicking. But his father
ran the Union (poor-house), as the hospital was called in her
young day, and it pleased her to think that through that
connection, less than ideal though it was, Chapel Street
silently, surreptitiously but nevertheless indelibly, was borne
beyond itself into the world of affairs and men. Mam was an
embodiment of the extraordinary powers and accuracy of the
appeal in the words *sinn féin*: ourselves. And it was her fierce,
pleasure-giving fidelity that brought her to Lyons's: Willy
was one of the old stock.

The same could not be said for Bid. No-neck Bid was coarse,
outspoken, ill-mannered and unpredictable. She was not
altogether 'no class', a term Mam used to pigeon-hole and at
the same time explain boorish uppityness. But she'd 'read the
riot act', 'leaving nothing unsaid' to an antagonist, and 'live
where another would die' (of embarrassment) – delighted in
doing so. Mam detested such letting of bad blood, and Bid's
reveli̇ ng in it. She was a suppressor, and desired others to be
the same.

But Mam had an excuse for Bid and her red-faced choler. She
wasn't from Lismore, a place which was, for Mam, a moral
Switzerland, where decorum had been the order of the day
since the Blackwater River first carved out its somnolent,
deeply wooded valley and offered a crossing-point for the
town to settle on. Bid wasn't even from County Waterford, but
from the river valley on the far side of the Knockmealdowns
(our mountains), from the garrison town of Clonmel, or rather
from Irishtown, whence she'd arrived with her raucous ways
to serve in the scullery of one of the numerous big houses that
made our valley a colony more enduring and elaborate than
anything merely military.

4   And now, here was this pugilist married to someone who

was, Mam assured me solemnly, 'every inch a gentleman'. He certainly looked the part. Being retired, Willy never wore work-clothes. I knew few men of any age of whom that was true, and hardly any that the family was on first-name terms with. Willy carried a walking-cane whose varnish glistened – not for him the grimy ash-plant of local old-stagers like Marsh Reagan and Pike Parker, Willy's childhood playmates, who unlike him had not retired but were too old and sore to work. Another thing that impressed me: unlike those contemporaries of his, Willy didn't have a nickname, which placed him in the exclusive 'Mister' category, making him virtually a Protestant. And, finally, for me the finishing touch, he had a moustache, that ribbon of venerability which all the most imposing adults wore. My late grandfather (Mam's gifted George) had one. The toffs who came to the door with jobs for him and Georgie – Colonel Foster, I remember, and Captain Jameson – wore them, thin silvery ones against plump, pink complexions: cirrus at sunset. (Priests never had them, but we never regarded them as rich, grand or special. They were just poor boys, raised far away from town and comfort, peasants doing the best they could without presence or polish.)

Despite Willy's impressive appearance, however, not quite every inch of him, I thought, lived up to Mam's assurance. The eyes were wrong. Bloodshot, watery, slightly exophthalmic, they gave him a wounded, fugitive, startled look. I watched him pass by on the other side and out the convent road on his daily constitutional, shuffling slowly, breathing heavily, his look exerting a fearful fascination on me. What gave him that?

'He', said Mam, 'was a high-up in the Post Office over in England; the right-hand man of some big-bug. Worked his way up. One of the cleverest boys ever to leave the town of Lismore.'

Mam's lips just smacked, she so relished the authority with which she made such statements, and the classiness of the achievement.

'How did he work himself up?' I wanted to know.

'He wanted to get on,' said Mam, 'so he studied by night, and passed his exams, and sure enough in no time he was sitting pretty in London West Central.'

London West Central, studying by night, getting on: enchanting universe of potential! That picture in Georgie's

5

old geography book: 'Cheapside', tall loaf-like buildings, ungainly trolley buses, and the caption 'Centre of World Commerce'. Post-office exams! The idea of them settled in my mind as an archetype of obscurity, hardship and delicious challenge.

And Willy had triumphed. He was of the same calibre as my Uncle Frank who got a university scholarship, was a Bachelor of Civil Engineering, and now was building a railway in Tanganyika. On Sundays he drove forty miles through dust to hear mass from a German priest. Or Kathleen, B.Sc. (another scholarship, this time the prestigious Earl of Cork, no less). She was making 'planes in Bristol. But did their going mean they might come back like Willy, broken somehow, wheezing, needing strange partners to see them through? It could. Look at my father. He went away to be a teacher and then his only love, my mother, died. Or was that different?

Perhaps Willy himself could have told me. As things turned out I had plenty of opportunities to ask him. But I never did. I never asked him anything. To the end he remained for me an icon of the world's inscrutable ways.

The questions Mam had answered about Willy were prompted by my seeing him out walking. The period of her visits, and then mine, was later, when he became bedridden.

I can't remember now exactly how my visits started. Maybe I was going through one of my bouts of self-imposed piety and felt that practising one of the corporal works of mercy – visiting the sick – would be a suitable expression of my pretensions. Or it might have been that, under the task of the Passionist father who came to conduct the Easter observances (my visits began, I remember, in silky-aired April), I thought I should volunteer for a spell of self-denial, and thereby improve myself even beyond their ambitions for me. At any rate, I'm sure I made my offer freely (no prompting from Mam; she dealt in righteousness, not piety), and judging by the kind of offer it was – I would read to the invalid – showing off figured prominently in my motivation.

Not that my offer was all ego. When I was sick, being read to was really the best bit, better even than warm lemonade. I remember Chrissy sitting in her overcoat in my freezing bedroom rattling off reams of *Treasure Island* to me, while I snuggled up to the hot-water bottle, drugged to the eyeballs by the pleasures of weakness.

I wasn't all altruism, either, of course. The thought of sampling Bid's temperament at first hand was alarming. Mightn't she eat me if I did something wrong (and childhood, I'd learned, was a phase of inevitable wrong-doing)? And I didn't know how I would handle coming face-to-face with Willy, or how he would take to me (would I cry if he wheeled his baleful eyes towards me? – I always cried at home when I couldn't understand). But then there was the attraction of going into someone else's house. I loved other people's strange air and the different ways they found to arrange familiarity. I loved their quirky trinkets, their mottoes in pokerwork, the placid grey of their ghostly old photos.

Willy's room was at the back of the house, downstairs, at the end of the cramped hall, overlooking the deranged and fruitless garden, where Bid's cats prowled. Bid's mother was foster-mother to at least half a dozen menacing toms, and took pride in reciting their complex genealogy: 'This fella's that fella's uncle. Go on ya vagabond!' her endearment accompanied by strong blows to the place lately vacated by the mother-wise moggy. 'The óinseach,' said Mam harshly, back home. 'Fit her better to air the house.' True, the house stank of cat, and the stench mingled with the smells of Willy's room, sweat, pee, and vinegary medical essences arrayed in amber bottles and ruby phials on the nightstand. Mam always let the window down a crack before I began the evening's read. But I felt it was inappropriate to expect Bid to keep house, now that I'd seen close up the spiky ginger of her manner and heard her harangue the neighbourhood in the language of green-eyed suspicion. Out prowling around, looking for fight and staking out territory, is what she really should have been doing, it seemed, leaving steadfast, concentrated Mam to abide the alternative life of the sick-room.

Besides smells, Willy's room was smothered in holiness. An *Infant de Prague* stood pertly to attention in his tight-fitting tunic on a ledge by the door, the cross-topped globe in his hand no more a burden to him than a ping-pong ball. The holy-water font hanging from a nail by the light switch was a memento of Lourdes. The figure on the heavily varnished crucifix at the head of the bed was as naked and as abject as a scavenged bone. And from the wall at the foot of the bed a fully

7

bearded Saviour in a purplish frock looked down, his bosom wounded. This was the Sacred Heart. He wore a slightly anxious look, profferring his velvety valentine with its accessories of flame and fletched arrows. Willy stared at him a lot, inert in the big brass bed, forbidden to move, all his energy consumed by breathing.

My reading started with *Seven Years in Tibet* by Heinrích Harrer, a choice of which I was extremely proud, since it was a grown-up's book in every sense of the word. It was a far cry from Enid Blyton, Patricia Lynch and the Hardy Boys, for one thing. That's not to say that Noddy, Longears the turf-cutter's donkey and Franklin W. Dixon were by then beneath me. But they were only stories, and *Seven Years in Tibet* was true, and had photos to prove it. The stony places and flattened faces fascinated me. The shaggy yaks, the prayer-wheels, the windy emptiness of the Roof of the World, the tea with butter, the bright saffron of the monks' habits. . . . The idea of being on the same planet as such strangeness was as powerful to me as something from the Gospels.

As well as that, and also very pleasing, this book was our own, not borrowed from the library, like most of what was read in Swiss Cottage. Someone, possibly my Aunt Elizabeth (a nurse in England), thought we could do with belonging to a book-club, so World Books plied us with its choices, mainly stories for big people by authors with remote, unlikely names – Rumer Godden, Nevil Shute, Pamela Frankau. From time to time something really foreign turned up, like the Harrer (Lorenz's *King Solomon's Ring* was another), which meant that I too could join in, savour at home the schoolroom scents of new paper and fresh ink, hear the crackle of gummy joints as the spine stretched, admire the livery – forthcoming titles surrounded by signs of the zodiac on the back of the dust-wrapper and the vivid splash of colour on the front, butter yellow for *Seven Years in Tibet*.

I remember the jacket better than I do the contents. In those days, and for too many years after, I read for speed, not thought. My only substantial recollection is of how the Dalai Lama came to be, of how a child of parents humbler than Christ's in an out-of-the-way place like one of the mountainy townlands around Lismore, was sanctified by being found and properly identified. That part stuck only because it aggravated my own incurable desire to be claimed and elevated, meaning not that I wanted to rule the world but that I ached to go to Dublin and live with my father.

The reading consisted of rattling on regardless. I'd arrive about half-seven and charge ahead with hardly a civil word to the invalid, my headlong canter competing with the chatter of the women in the kitchen. At about half-nine I'd stop because of failing light (Bid didn't think the act of mercy worth using electricity for). My idea was to perform, not to embody, to let the words fall where they may and be applauded afterwards. I was all spray and no tide. As far as I knew, that was the way to be. Depth was not something I was used to. Slogan, joke, curse, song, proverb: these were our parts of speech. The reply churlish, the counter-check quarrelsome. But I never knew anyone who could explain, or appear calmly and without defence to think about something. Priests, teachers and adults just told whoever was in earshot what to do and what not – all assertion, no questioning.

Passive Willy was not the one to challenge my behaviour. Played-out as he was, if anything he merely confirmed it as appropriate, the rubble of pebbles (which was as much as my verbalizing amounted to) making a fragile causeway to something broader than the bed. And I was delighted to prate away: I never got restless or bored or tired of the sound of my own voice. Willy sang dumb throughout, offering only a few words in parting to Mam when the session ended. But I didn't need him to say anything: I firmly believed that he had to be enjoying it because I was doing it for him.

I demolished *Seven Years in Tibet* in next to no time, and with hardly a pause for breath jumped to the next selection, *Annapurna*. Excellent choice, I thought smugly: another true story, another World Book, another grand jacket, this time in piercing ice-blue. But *Annapurna* was my downfall. I liked the bit about the man losing some of his toes due to cold: that made the flesh tingle pleasurably. But I had to labour to get that far, had to barge and hack my way as best I could through stretches infested with 'rendezvous', 'bivouac' and the dreaded 'cwm'. I cursed the English language for having kept such barbed tripwires to itself until now. I sat in the upright kitchen chair, sweating and slurring and palpably losing face.

But *Annapurna* is memorable for another reason too. It   9 brought about the only conversation that's remained with me from those evenings. Willy's breath was in such short supply that it may have been our only one, and besides, part of his novelty was his total lack of interest in me and my child's life, an indifference unique among adults of my acquaintance. So, I was most surprised when, quite out of the blue, Willy interrupted my assault to ask what part of the world were we in now.

'The Himalayas,' said I.

He seemed to brighten. 'Isn't that India?' he said.

I told him it was.

'Tell me,' he said, 'what about –' And he rolled off a list of names I'd never heard of, Baluchistan, Gujarat, Rajaishan. . . . I was struck dumb. Clueless. 'Rendezvous' and its fellow-travellers were nursery slopes compared to these! All I could think was that I'd never come across any of these names in my stamp-album. If Stanley Gibbons & Co. had no place for them . . .

'They're gone,' I said.

'Ayeh,' said Willy, with a wondering sigh. 'Gone?'

'There's only India now,' I said, with bold finality. 'And Pakistan.'

'Pakistan,' Willy repeated, as though he caught an echo of something in the name. Then he fell silent again.

'Yes,' I said, confident now (philately hadn't let me down: I'd been told it would be good for me). 'The places you're talking about all are gone.' I dare say I even knew what 'gone' meant. It never occurred to me what Willy's echo might have contained, what exotic telegraphy might have passed along those fading nerves, what inkling of an old, deep-burning yen. I never thought. I returned to *Annapurna*, all the better equipped to tackle it with smugness my fuel.

As things turned out, however, I didn't get much further with it or any other book. Summer grew strong and I wanted to be out in the air. Then, as happened every school holiday, either my father came down or I went up to Dublin – either this dream personage (tolerant, unfussy, playful) appeared and I forsook everyone and everything to devote all my time to him, or I was transported to a more vital realm where, seeing myself as a mixture of sophisticated princeling and rehabilitated prodigal, I believed I belonged only to find, year after year, the belief turn to hunger.

At any rate I was not to return to Lyons's for in the autumn Willy was removed to Dungarvan (where the nearest full-scale hospital was).

We were in the kitchen when Chrissy brought in the news, adding in the plain, clipped tone she used to convey a particularly notable item of gossip, 'Bid ran after the ambulance going "Willy – Willy – Willy".'

'The blasted foolah,' said Mam harshly. The response was predictable. Mam detested displays. When her man went she just sat in the parlour, hour after hour, staring at air, mute as a severed limb. But why was her tone like a lash?

Maybe it was easier to attack Bid instead of to think about Willy. After all, someone his age only went to hospital to die. And there he was now, stretched out as a case, enfolded in linen premonitorily starched. The bright boy. The gentleman. Her oldest man-friend. Maybe she was trying not to be reminded of her dead George, and of how Willy had reminded her that she'd been young. Springtime evening strolls down the Green Road, skating on the flooded 'inch' (the riverbank) in hardy January, strong arms to be held in dancing the lancers and schottische to a crisp military band in the Courthouse.

Maybe. If Willy's going caused any pang or hankering in Mam, she didn't show it. All that followed her remark was a minute or two of stillness before the cups were cleared. I fell back on my own thoughts: the room, the words, the summer air freighted with the hoarse breath of dying.

2

Impressed as I was with myself for taking on all that reading and amassing all that merit, the evenings I really lived for were those when Mam went to Lyons's alone, and I had what I most wanted in the world, Chrissy's undivided attention.

Mam was principle and steadfastness, duty and its long-suffering sister, self-denial. Chrissy was pure enjoyment. 11

Mam was the long haul. Chrissy was the moment; Mam the speech from the dock, Chris the tune on the wireless. We had fine times, we two – music, warm fires and gusts of giggling.

We wrote stories, or maybe it was just one long story that we made several attempts at. It was about Pat and Mag, two tramps, on their way to Drumshambo. Pat and Mag were real people, real tramps, who turned up in Lismore every so often. Pat had the cut of an ex-soldier about him. He was fairly tall, wiry, had close-cropped foxy hair and carried himself with a brash stride. Also, he had a moustache. Mag, though, was a dolt. Shapeless, moon-faced, with a shuffle not a walk, she looked totally downtrodden. She wore a man's gaberdine coat a couple of sizes too big for her, buttoned from neck to calf. She always went in her hair, hail, rain or snow. And winter or summer she only wore wellingtons.

These really were the lowest of the low, much worse than tinkers, not that we regarded tinkers favourably – far from it, begging was treated most uncharitably in our house, being thought of as, quite simply, a blatant deficiency in self-respect. But tinkers were something. Their shawls, ponies, caravans, squads of children, added up to a style and an identity. They even had names – Hogan, Connors, Sheridan. They flung their washing gaily on the bushes to dry. None of this was true of Pat and Mag.

'Where do they sleep, Chris?' I remember asking.

'Out the road under a hedge,' she replied, off-hand, matter-of-fact, and for a minute I thrilled to my own good fortune.

They never did get to Drumshambo. Just as well for them. Once there I'd have had to abandon them, anyway, since I knew nothing whatever about that town, only that it was far, far away in a part of the country I had no connection with and, therefore, not the slightest interest in. I only thought of it for the story because it sounded funny. (It made me feel superior not to be from funny-sounding places such as Ballydehob, Knocknagopall, Ringaskiddy and, the village nearest Lismore, Cappoquin.)

The reason Pat and Mag never got anywhere was not because I, for all my tender years, subconsciously appreciated that their tramps' existence should exemplify an inherent, Beckettian incompleteness, but because I wanted to play the drums. Writing was a chore, and gave very poor returns for the amount of time spent on it. All too few of the moments, in the moment-by-moment activity of writing, were ink-filled. Rather than passing time, writing seemed an exposure to the possibility of being overrun by time. Kneeling on a chair at the Swiss Cottage kitchen table, bent over a copy-book, crude, wooden-shafted pen poised, pleading, 'What'll I put now, Chrissy?' – that's how I think of writing, a desire not to be stuck.

Drumming had no such problems, especially when I had such a receptive instrument as an oil-stove and such pliable sticks as the axles of a defunct toy truck complete with rubberized wheels. With the amount of bounce they gave I could roll and flim-flam away to my heart's content, Chrissy's light soprano wafting gamely above the uproar.

I never thought of drumming as keeping time – any fool could do that – but as embellishing the time signature to the point of sublimation, if not downright suppression. The beat could be carried by the merest tapping of a foot. What I wanted was the spray and rumble that filled the intervals. I kicked the side of the heater just as a metronomical matter of course, not because I thought there was a chance of losing my footing.

My barrage caused problems, though. The heater – a Rippingille Fyreside, a much classier item than the upright Valor favoured by most families – was newfangled and temperamental. It operated by allowing the paraffin to drip slowly into the wick, and needed a totally flat surface in order to behave properly, as an aid to which it had adjustable legs. Needless to say, my time-keeping resulted in substantial maladjustment, which let in poor Fyreside for more beating, this time from Mam, who hammered it with the side of her fist and muttered bitter criticism of Chrissy, whom she suspected of having been soft-talked into recommending the paraffin prima donna by Joe Wall of the Co-op. Beating objects could improve their behaviour: Georgie often went a few rounds with the radio and sobered it of static. People were not beaten (only once did Mam hit me a clatter across the face); frosty looks and icy silences invariably proved to be lash enough.

Instead of an oil-heater I should have had a Trinidadian oil-drum, but as things stood I rattled away, as happy as Larry. I favoured martial airs: two half-Emperor rolls to start, and I

13

was off, my mind a gaudy parade. And sometimes for good measure I twirled my axles in the air (once a wheel flew off and landed – *plop!* – in Chrissy's tea: such laughs . . .), as I'd seen the side-drummers of the Mellary pipers do. Easy for them, though; their sticks had loops. Too bad Lismore didn't have a band like that, a band that offered me an immediate future by playing in daylight. The band it did have was for adults and the night.

The Marino was a fox-trot, slow-waltz, quick-step kind of band, strict tempo in the Victor Sylvester manner. The sound was Sylvesterish, as well: Frank Sweeney on mellow tenor-sax, Gandhi Colbert, the ultra-thin station-master, on violin. I don't know who thought up the band's name. I assume, though, that it wasn't the Dublin working-class suburb that was being conjured up but something vaguely Rivierean – balmy evenings, Latin lovers, verandas. . . . They played all the latest, hits by Johnny Ray, Guy Mitchell, Frankie Laine. Their 'Jezebel' was a study in inanition compared to the iron-larynxed tempest of the original, but their 'Roaming round the world / Looking for the sunshine / That never seems to come my way' was definitely *con moto*, and 'The Blue Tango' made a hothouse of many a labourer's brain. They played hops and hurling-club benefits in Cappoquin, Ballyduff, Mocollop, Kilworth, Araglen, and at least once broke the twenty-mile barrier for a date at Watergrasshill.

Chrissy was the pianist, which meant that not only could I take pride in her appearing in public but also that the band sometimes came to Swiss Cottage for rehearsal. And when that happened – usually on the Friday evening before a Sunday date – I was allowed to stay up late. I watched, agog, the instruments being uncased – the golden burnish of the sax rising from its snug, plush groove; the umber varnish of the slender fiddle. And of course, above all, the sacramental assembly of drums and cymbals, the cold gleam of their fixtures, the nipple-headed sticks and chrome brushes, the rap and thud of preparation. How Frankie Walsh tolerated me under his feet, pleading incessantly, 'Can I've a go?' I can't imagine. But he was tolerant to a fault. He'd smile at my desperation, swing me onto his circular, official seat, and try to teach me the crossways grip, all wrist and fingers, that he said was the proper way to play. I was too excited to learn. As

14

far as I was concerned, there was no proper way, there was just playing. My foot couldn't reach the bass-drum pedal, nor my arms all the cymbals, but I didn't care. I bounced up and down on the seat, beat without rhyme or reason those soiled, worn skins that were the colour of a shabby sheep, and felt my whole person turn into a beam.

Once or twice, I remember, I was allowed up extra late – to as unnatural an hour as nine-thirty, perhaps – to sit in on a few numbers. Needless to say, the heater was barred. Obviously I couldn't play it because it was too noisy, but, more important, the heater was a secret between Chrissy and me, and it felt great to have something to keep from Mam. But I was happy to whack a box until Mam poked her head around the parlour door with her, 'Now, Seoirse.'

'Did you hear me?' I demanded, turning to go up the stairs.

'I did, boy,' said Mam: was that a smile in her voice? 'Off with you now.'

And up I scampered, because bed offered more pleasure. I sensed the poor boys of the lane tapping their feet and rhythmically shrugging their shoulders under the street light on the corner opposite. I heard their coarse encomia. I lay safe and warm, humming, and felt delightfully superior to them. And I wanted to shout down to them did they know that was my aunt down there, carrying the melody with airy assurance, plunging into the deep, dark notes with laughing abandon – did they realize that these thoughtless, ticklesome, instantaneous pieces were the real her, my Chrissy? And didn't they glory in it?

I never did shout down, of course. I much preferred to think I had it all to myself, digging my heel into the mattress without ever missing a beat, crooning tune after tune with never, never a stammer over lyrics, waking up after ten the next morning to find the resonance of those brittle, sparkling keys inside me, jitterbugging in my veins like thrilling ichor.

Music could be treacherous too, though. I'd already found that out, thanks to the wireless. There was a programme on Athlone (as we called Radio Éireann) every Wednesday lunchtime, 'Hospital Requests'. It was ushered in by a syrupy treatment of Gershwin's 'Someone to Watch Over Me', and, unlike lunchtime listening on other days, had no sponsors and was not introduced by a 'personality' such as Joe Linnane or 15

Dennis Brennan, but by a staff announcer. The show consisted of messages from the well to the ill, accompanied by a piece of music. It was a morbid accessory to our meal, no doubt, but we all enjoyed it, especially when a hospital known to us was mentioned, such as Ardkeen in Waterford City or the Bon Secours in Cork, though Chrissy and Mam often objected that Dublin bias was shown and that if you weren't in Peamount Sanatorium you hadn't a chance of being mentioned. Chrissy and Mam also liked guessing from the name of a far-off hospital, unknown to them, what the patient might be in for. TB always seemed a safe bet.

Sometimes a child would be mentioned, and the women would look lovingly across the table at me and tell me how lucky I was.

'Poor little devil,' they'd say to the radio. 'Think of that, Seoirse; how'd you like to have your birthday in hospital?'

I did think of it. It was horrible. It made me feel very pleased with myself. And – since that was what they seemed to need of me – I felt grateful to my guardians as well: who knows, I thought, only for them I might be stretched out in Ward Z, Pavilion B, this very minute. Then, slap bang in the middle of my complacency, some upsetting song would break through, and I'd burst into tears.

Various singers got to me, and various idioms. Burl Ives doing 'Jimmy Crack Corn', especially the line, 'The master's gone away'. Anything by Kathleen Ferrier struck me as the acme of melancholy (and, as I was often told, she died young). And – the moisturiser *non pareil* – Paul Robeson. He gave me a hell of a time, particularly with 'My Old Kentucky Home'.

That unforgettable song had all the ingredients of definitive water music. 'My Old Kentucky home far away', 'I'm coming', 'Weep no more, my lady', these, combined with the profound lugubriousness of the incomparable Paul, had me howling in no time, howling so inconsolably that there was nothing for it but to turn the thing off until I came to my senses and saw what Chrissy kept telling me was maybe right after all: 'Sure, Seoirse, you're not poor old Joe or anything like it . . .'

If 'My Old Kentucky Home' had been the height of musical treachery, things wouldn't have been so bad. But music had depths of perfidy beyond the range of even Paul Robeson and Stephen Foster, and possessed a power to upset whose sources were much closer to home. In a word, Chrissy was to teach me the piano.

At first I was very excited, imagining that by imitating Chrissy's accomplishments I'd be more like her – carefree, capable, playful, musical: the perfect combination of child and adult, the combination which I longed to perfect. It was good too that Mam considered piano-playing a natural inclination for me, since her encouragement came in terms I could easily identify with. She kept saying how glad I'd be afterwards, and sure a pianist would be welcome anywhere: wouldn't it be grand when, later on, I was 'in company somewhere' (Dublin, of course, that best of all possible worlds) and someone asked if anyone could play. Through the French windows I'd stride, doctors and teachers stepping back to give me access, and out of my head I'd play till dawn – the Cary Grant of Ballsbridge! Simple stardom, that's all I wanted.

I knew the piano was a treasured instrument, and not just because of Chrissy's exploits with the Marino. Not everybody had one, by any means, and ours was kept in the parlour, along with all the other things we didn't really live with: the picture of my father as a baby, the cups, flasks, plates and butter-cooler that Georgie had won running and cycling, the bizarre round table of solid teak, each of whose three curved legs was marked like elephant trunks and faces, minus ears but complete with protruding ivory tusks. And finally, as though in definition of the piano's classiness, we had John Scott-Allen, the organist at the Protestant church, to come and tune ours, the sense of quality deriving from the extreme unusualness of engaging and paying a Protestant to perform a service. Well worth it, though, all agreed, especially when John rewarded us with a five-minute concert when the tuning was done. 'Oh, the light touch of him,' Mam'd exclaim, rapturously. 'By gor, he's another Charlie Kunz.'

So – I had everything going for me. Except myself. I simply couldn't do it. Left hand ingloriously sparred with right, and refused to be reconciled. Melody charmed, bass distracted. Adult coaxed, child sulked. Adult lost patience, child lost temper. Chrissy didn't love me, I *hated* her. I became, on certain grey afternoons, quite simply and unabashedly hysterical. Having to practise, making mistakes, going back over, concentrating. . . . It was all too much for me, too tense,

17

too definitive, too humiliating. I never had to put up with this kind of exposure in school, why should I be subjected to it in pursuit of what was supposed to be a grace and a pleasure? Why had discipline so much to do with it, the lessons so rigorously devoted to limiting options? All the piano had given me before was spontaneity, effervescence, joy: what made the piecemeal approach the one true way?

I had perhaps as many as a dozen lessons in all before my terror and loathing of feeling so vulnerable, so inchoate, so unco-ordinated, won through. Maybe if we'd started with numbers I knew instead of the child's first fingering book – 'bought specially', as I was frequently reminded – and containing tunes which I'd never heard played and which I considered vaguely English and prissy and dull – what was I to 'Baa-baa Black Sheep', or it to me? We should have started, maybe, with the great song my father taught me, 'The Big Rock Candy Mountain'. (But my father was in Dublin.) Or perhaps if we'd been in a less precious room, a place that was less of a shrine and more of a kitchen. . . . Or maybe we should have been a family of Eskimos. . . .

Of all my many tearful tempests, those brought on by the piano lessons bore out best Mam's most frequent criticism of me – 'He can't bear correction.' All the charmless inadequacy of my vanity, impatience and excitability was revealed. The lessons confirmed that I was the cripple that my mother's death and father's absence had made me. I wasn't special, I was hampered. If I was special I'd have been able to sit down and play like Chrissy. Like Chrissy. I didn't want to be myself (the self I might have been had been deferred, uncalled for, by my parents' misfortune); I wanted to be the person who amused me. And now that the main amusement – the airy grace and effortlessness of my beloved's fingers – had grotesquely given way to an implacable logic requiring total selfless surrender, all I could do was sit slumped on the revolving stool in the airless, camphor-tainted parlour and feel music's treason, my face a river of distress, my mind a frenzy of jangling, echoing chords.

So, the lessons were noisily dropped, and not too long afterwards, so were the expressions of disappointment. Chrissy and I were able to be real playmates again. This meant that the drumming and writing resumed, and also that after school we could, every so often, go for walks together.

It was Chrissy who called them walks, and they really were for her benefit, even though we seldom got very far and she had to justify them by saying to Mam, 'It'll give the child an appetite for his tea.' What happened was that Chrissy would saunter down the town, meet someone, or more usually go into some shop (business was always slack on weekday afternoons) and stand there gossiping. Sometimes we'd go farther afield, down the bridge and into the country a little way. Invariably, Chrissy would bump into a boy on these excursions and stand chatting and laughing with him, an unmerciful bore to me, needless to say, much worse than hanging around in Bríd Linneen's or Teasie Meade's where at least I had the chance of getting a sweet to keep me quiet, the sweet accompanied by the warning, 'But don't tell Mam!'

Naturally, it was nice for her to talk to boys, and even I could sense there was an air of getting away with something about those meetings – the speaking in low voices, the half-shocked sound of the giggles. Yet Chrissy seemed more at ease sharing a cigarette and discussing the latest with one of her cronies. And even though she loved a good gossip, I think what she needed from those little outings was not just news. I think she was simply drawn to people who earned their living. She was happy to be in their ambit because it was public, something might happen. Those who stood behind the counter had continuous, varied, socially necessary contact with the world. They weren't exactly subject to the peculiar form of frustration known as being 'at home', twenty-six years old and a mother's help still – the lot of many an unmarried, ill-schooled contemporary of Chrissy's. I would be very sad to think that Chris might ever have felt bitter, or superfluous, or disabled because she couldn't cut soap or draw a cork or, like her friend Alice Luby, be surrounded in the Co-op manager's office with dockets, invoices and Bible-sized ledgers. But it must have been hard for her, day after day, relying for sustenance on domesticity alone (chapel only supervening), deprived of the rewards and distractions of daily life in its social forms, having to ask for the price of a smoke, for money for clothes, having to ask – for all I know – if she could go out with Joe Wall tonight.

Joe Wall. Black hair, dark eyes. Swarthy. Slender. He was 19 from 'down the county', meaning some townland east of Cappoquin, some place we in Lismore didn't have to take seriously: Ballinamult, Modeligo, Affane, some place with just a crossroads, a church and a pub, untouched by rail and only recently electrified. And Joe spoke with the French r's and tormented vowels of his people. We delighted in imitating that accent, Chrissy especially. (She was a mimic of genius. My father, not given to hearty laughter, had tears roll down his cheeks from Chrissy taking off the locals.) 'Deyhre a fayhre in Dun-geayhrvan', we'd say, and convulse with giggles. We felt wonderfully superior: Lismore was *the* place to live. 'Dungarvan is the pisspot of Ireland and Abbeyside the handle', we'd say; and, 'Tallow: the last place God made, and forgot to finish'; and when a thing was crooked it was 'all to one side, like the town of Fermoy'. Better Lismore than any of those places was a widely shared sentiment. But within Lismore, who was at peace, who felt unyearningly at home? Nobody I knew.

Although Joe Wall had the accent of his locality, unlike most people from that part of the world, he didn't screech. His speech was more of a purr. I liked that. It seemed to go with his dark features, and enlarged my sense of his foreignness. And he worked behind the hardware counter in the Co-op. I loved that.

The Co-op was one of my favourite places in the whole town. Georgie bought his Uno paints there, and every Saturday morning I was told to run down to the Co-op for a pound of Clover Meats' best back rashers. As well as the grocery and hardware there was a bar and a yard full of farmers' feedstuffs, and in the yard a cool, tiled room storing eggs and salty homemade butter, a purchase of which Paddy Flynn would slap into shape with the two butter-paddles – silvery motes of salt jumped in the air with every slap. And in the passage leading to the yard there was the barrel.

The barrel frightened and fascinated me. It contained half-heads, pigs' heads split in two. Toothy, prognathous, leering, grey, they floated in thick, unclean-looking brine. The idea of people eating such things alarmed me. No doubt I'm diminished, am somehow less of the people, for never having acquainted my digestion with those salty gargoyles. At Swiss Cottage, the roast beef of old England was our typical Sunday dinner, not jelly and gristle, and proud Mam was to put it on the table, though every so often Geo expressed tiredness of it and called for swine-parts. The fact that people did eat it, though, was fascinating. Many Saturdays I watched in wonder as unknown, untowny women in black shawls descended on the barrel from outlying townlands and hauled out a series of samples, scrutinizing each selection with canny eyes, discerning who knows what succulent potential in the line of a jaw or the flap of a cloven snout. When they were satisfied, they carried their choice, dripping, by the ear into the grocery counter where it was wrapped in a couple of sheets of *The Cork Examiner* and stowed under the purchaser's shawl in a deep, dirty bag.

The hardware was much more sophisticated, to my mind, and I felt more at home there because I associated its turps-tainted air with Georgie. But, as things turned out, I would have been better off trying to talk to those strange pig-fanciers, or getting in the way of the men in the yard and their maledictions. Because what I had to put up with from Joe and Chris was more than I could bear, made me feel as furious and undone as any piano lesson had.

There I'd be, poring over an Uno chart, absorbed by the alleged tonal differences between vermilion and siren-red (I couldn't rightly see; like every other commercial interior of my acquaintance, the hardware was dark). Or I'd be fiddling with hinges or locks or a box of screws, empty-mindedly pleasured by their oily newness. And there'd be this cough. I'd look up. There Chrissy and Joe would be, arms around each other, humming, swaying elaborately in a dance.

Saboteurs! He the dark one, the foreigner, the snake in the grass, impersonator of the Marino's tawdry associations. And she, unspeakably worse, slipping silently into a self beyond me altogether, there in the consummate ordinariness of a slow weekday afternoon.

How dare they! Why did I have to see? And why do it repeatedly? What were they trying to prove?

Time after time I flew at them, puny fists flailing indiscriminately. But I might as well have burst into tears, for all the good my attacks did. 'O!' went Chris and Joe, 'Ow!' – and off they sidled out of range into the dark corner by the never-opened street-door, clutching each other, laughing. And when the laughter stopped I'd hear the scratching of the feet on the shop's coarse floor, and the subtler scratching of cloth on cloth, and the humming – damn music, insufferable signature of all that I was not.

3

'Tottenham Hotspur nil, Aston Vílla nil. Sheffield Wednesday two, Wolverhampton Wanderers one.'

It's Saturday afternoon, and 'Sports Report' is coming in loud and clear on the BBC Light Programme. After the results all the familiar voices will be on hand, gravelly Geoffrey Green, hectic Harold Abrahams, J. Barrington Dalby of the *Daily Mail* on boxing, and of course our host Eamonn Andrews of whom we're all so proud, none more so than Mam (though she hates 'foreign games'): 'Imagine an Irish boy getting on so well in England,' she remarks, hearing his soft Dublin burr, as if he's not doing a job but performing a miracle; as if England for the first generation emigrant is bound to be a loss of public face.

The announcer's litany goes on. 'Scottish League Division Two. Cowdenbeath two, Hamilton Academicals one. Forfar four, Stenhousemuir nil.' The voice is supercilious, unexcitable, giving the impression that its owner didn't give a tinker's curse what happened, and if everyone else did (as they must, otherwise why broadcast?), the more fools they. But in one way it was an ideal voice: it suited the vaguely ecclesiastical design of the wireless, a Philco, its rounded top, circular dial and curved strips of wood across the cloth of the speaker making it look like a little tabernacle. What more appropriate voice could come out of it than one sounding at least as well trained as a Redemptorist's?

The Philco suffered horribly from static, though, for which incontinence – as involuntary, unmalicious and unpredictable as bedwetting – it received traditional treatment: beating. 'East Fife five--kraak!' Mouthing a selection of oaths Georgie sprang up from the newspaper, into which he'd been studiously copying the scores, and with the broad of his palm, lambasted the hapless instrument.

'Thunder in the air,' I said (my father told me that).

'Thunder my arse,' said Geo in a low growl, not looking at me, readjusting his spectacles and returning to the paper. How could I contradict him? He was as much father to me as Chrissy was mother.

Besides, I knew better than to talk to him during 'Sports Report'. Being stymied by static was one thing, but the distraction of a know-nothing child was much more than he should be asked to bear. Interrupting an abstruse discussion about Walter Winterbottom's next Eleven or the fate of the All Blacks with some uncontainable irrelevance about my day's doings, elicited a roar which froze me.

Silence was a mortifying condition for me at the best of times, as I firmly believed that whatever crossed my mind had to be aired immediately, if not sooner. Moreover, I belonged to a household where there was continual clamour for free speech, and for free speech in its definitive· form at that, namely, the last word. So, why shouldn't I be able to put in my spoke when I wanted? I had such good questions, too. How would you get a job on the wireless? Why had the teams such funny names (Accrington Stanley, Crewe Alexandra)? And above all – one to which I still don't have a good answer – why did Geo take down all the results?

There were two sorts of results, soccer and racing. The soccer ones were easy to record, because the fixtures were set out in the papers with spaces for the numbers to be entered. I was even allowed to do it sometimes. Georgie would ferret out the butt of a pencil from his overalls and bark at me to carry on. But the racing results – more exotic names: Uttoxeter, Haydock Park, Doncaster, Goodwood – were much more difficult, and were one of the reasons Geo so fiercely insisted that I sing dumb.

The runners and riders were set out in the paper according to no pattern that I could discern. Hedged around by form numbers, weights, trainers' and owners' names, Georgie had to look sharp to mark those who figured at the finish. His pencil would chase up and down the list, trying to keep pace with the announcer, a game of concentrated co-ordination in

itself, its impatient and slightly obsessive character high-
lighted and preserved by being conducted in silence.

It has occurred to me since that George noted the vagaries of
horseflesh to inform and console the chronic punters whom
he'd certainly run into later on, drinking at Madden's. Maybe
they gambled on the Football Pools too, though I think the
Pools were outlawed in Ireland. Still, with so much coming
and going between England and Lismore I suppose enrolment
in one would be easy to arrange. But if the Pools were illegal
why did the national dailies provide space to record the
scores? I have no answer. It's one of those things that belongs
truly in the past, beyond interpretation and intractably its
useless, undiminished self.

The results were not the only, or even the main, reason for
the rule of silence, however. The main reason was that Georgie
loved to argue. I've never met a man to relish disagreeing like
him. It wasn't so much that he believed everyone else to be
wrong and he alone right, though that was part of his irrepres-
sible yen to wrangle. In addition, his arguing desired to
demonstrate that he was more authoritative than anyone else.
If an illustrious cross-channel pundit mentioned the genius of
Marciano, Georgie would snap back with, 'What about Tony
Zale? He'd Louis on the ropes in the twelfth. Only for a lucky
punch . . .' He'd flare up in defence of Dr Pat Callaghan
whenever the latest feat in the field was discussed. Gordon
Richards had his good points no doubt, but no jockey could
compare to Charlie Smirke.

In all the cries of 'Bunkum!' and 'Arra, what ails you!' that
punctuated those radio hours there was a very complex
reaction. First of all, obviously, Georgie was an insatiable
sports fan. If it ran, walked, drove, swam or cycled, it was
Georgie's friend. As well as that, and perhaps this is where the
results'-noting comes in, he absolutely loved to be up to the
minute, ahead of tomorrow's papers, in the know. I think, too,
that he often despised the dispassionate clubland tones of
some radio 'personalities', annoyed at the thought of their soft
money and cushy jobs, and by the fact that though they'd seen
so much, their outlook and perspective wasn't worth a curse.
Those plausible, ineffectual voices lacked all that Georgie's
possessed – ardour, passion, faith – but with which it could
accomplish so little. Over and above the need to top every

received opinion and reported occasion with one of his own, there seemed to be a more powerful, less articulate desire for voice itself. His arguing was an assertion of the legitimacy of arguing, of telling it straight, of extolling the legend and affronting the hack, of disagreeing without the air heaving with tension and rancour as it did in the kitchen when he and Mam went at it.

Compared to how petrified I felt during those personal set-to's, sharing 'Sports Report' in silence wasn't too bad at all. Georgie and I were on our own, in the dining-room (that's where the radio was kept, along with the good china, my parents' wedding-picture, the photo of me in my First Communion suit by Stritch of Fermoy, and the oleograph of a slant-eyed Lady of Perpetual Succour). Geo covered the table with the daily papers, a gesture both business-like and anarchic – and impossible in the kitchen. He pushed his battered soft hat, speckled with paint and plaster, back off his forehead, and his pipe smouldered sweetly. The women were in the kitchen getting tea ready, but we were men together, attending to men's business, which of course sport exclusively was, as much so as, if not more than, going out to work. And naturally once I knew silence was obligatory I made sure not to break it, not wanting to be shouted at, obviously, but also indulging in the narcissistic satisfaction of deliberately being good.

It seems now that the easiest thing would have been for Georgie simply to forbid me the room because of his craving to hear. 'Run away out and play;' everybody said it. But he didn't, not at five on Saturday afternoons, anyhow. Maybe he too thought of us as men together. Or did he imagine that exposure to world sports headlines would fill me with the desire to feature among them one day? Alas, I became a fan, not an athlete, and a hollow fan what's more, my mind full of trivia. Unlike George, I haven't been able to create a world-view from statistics and affections. I'm too watchful of myself to be so idiosyncratic, so outspoken.

As to maleness, well, Georgie was erratically interested in making a man of me. He made me climb to the crest of the roof of the Presbyterian church once (by ladder: he was working up there). All I could see as I clung to the ridge-tiles were trees. I felt cheated. A better idea of his was to call me 'Mike'. I was

25

very pleased by this. The name I was known by in those days was 'Seoirse' ('Shore-sha'), which I disliked enormously. Nobody in Lismore could pronounce it: 'Shosho' was the best they could do. And the gratings over the holes into which rain from the gutters drained were called shores. And I was called it for what I considered to be the wrong reasons – as the first male grandchild, I had to be named for my father's father; and with two Georges already in the house ahead of me I had to be different to prevent confusion. Tradition and convenience did not provide the basis I needed for identifying with what I was called.

So, I found it ticklesome to speculate about what being a Mike would be. Stocky. Hard as nails. Filthy. Poorly dressed. Reared on the street. A child of the people. His house was a warm cabin in Botany or Church Lane. And of course he was great at games. I liked him a lot. But the more I thought about him the more I realized how well Seoirse suited me – obscure, uncommon, unfamiliar. That, I felt sure, was me *really*. I couldn't be a Mike, even for Georgie. I don't know if he ever accepted this: he did, I feel, in a desperate, inarticulate way want me to be his little boy – a way which I now crystallized in our silent camaraderie, a condition of legitimacy then, of true fracture now.

To breathe Georgie's smoke, to practise perfect obedience, to be – however vaguely and uncomprehendingly – abreast of the latest, gave me a delightful sense of attachment. But by far the best thing was that it was only a preamble to the evening ahead, when the same sense would, thanks to Geo, come fully into its own for an hour or two.

From 'Sports Report' onwards, everything went according to a different pattern from that of other days. Tea wasn't the same because Geo wasn't late in from work and needing his main meal. And instead of the usual bread, butter and homemade jam of workaday evenings, on Saturdays we had a selection of buns by Thompson's of Cork, delivered fresh to Noey Greehy's just a few hours before. Buns with cream in the middle, jam doughnuts that leaked deliciously when least expected, and a strange suety raisiny species of gingerbread called Chester-cake. We'd have one each, and maybe Geo would be offered a boiled egg and a slab of Golden Vale processed cheddar as well.

'Quite a party!' our expressions exclaimed, smirking through the sugar and smears. And indeed those teas were about as relaxed as we ever managed to be together. It was the buns that did it. We were all perfectly conscious of what a concession to irresponsibility they represented. To pay good money for what you should be able to make yourself at quarter the cost was an immense affront to Mam's idea of domestic economy. We never went in for cakes by Gateaux or such frivolity. Make what you need was Mam's philosophy. She mistrusted the readymade – the machine-knit sweater and the tinned vegetable were anathema to her. How could anyone be a decent housewife and avail of such costly and labour-saving items? I asked her once why we couldn't have some of the relishes that seemed to flow freely through the meals my playmates had. She was horrified. 'Them old things are only to cover up bad cooking,' she told me. And, later, having thought more about it: 'It's only drunkards like them, the spicy taste makes 'em mad for another drink, and that's all they want.' This I couldn't dispute. I'd noticed that whenever Geo brought home a jar of mixed pickles there were blunders and mumbles late on the stairs for several nights afterwards. Of course, the telling-off he received for buying something 'out of his own pocket' instead of from Mam's well-watched kitty – for, in effect, pleasing himself – might well have contributed to the making of his step-missing gait.

That kitty, which came from Georgie's weekly earnings, often caused Saturday evening squalls. Mam used to get it into her head every once in a while to challenge the size of it. Georgie would be accused of keeping more back for himself than was right. He'd counter-attack that he was being begrudged a drink now, what would it be next, tobacco? These skirmishes always ended by his storming off, slamming doors.

They're more upsetting to think of now than they were to witness then. George could contradict the BBC and all belonging to it, but he never managed to outface his mother. It was as though her widowhood gave her a moral strength, a power over him, that he couldn't withstand. Her manlessness was a constant, unspoken taunt, reminding him that, in her eyes, he would never be the man his father was. Never the tradesman, never the provider, never the authority. Her George had only

27

one equal: herself. And not all the shouting and slamming in the world could infuse Geo with an antidote to her view and reassure him that he was real enough as he stood.

What annoyed me at the time about these wrangles is that they occurred at the worst possible moment, just as Saturday evening was about to reach the climax of its specialness. Everything so far had been building nicely. After tea, Georgie shaved. A kettle was boiled specially, the kitchen sink was placed entirely at his disposal, down with the wooden razor-case and its delicate petal-shaped snap, out with the razor from its velvet nest. An intricate twirl, sheer steel gleaming in evening light, and a new blade was inserted. Then the shaving mug, the face santa-claused with lather, the head immobilized in a succession of odd poses, and snick, snick, snick . . .

A radio-knob, a mass-produced bun, the glint of a razor: the workaday surrendered itself to, begat, an alternative, restorative pace and idiom. That's what made Saturday so special, those hours of recuperation, as though peace was being made with the week's toil. Much better than Sunday, when rest was official: secular adequacy insinuated itself more naturally than compulsory worship. Mam's challenge to shiny-cheeked, clean-shirted Georgie was a refusal to believe in the minuscule, delightful heresy of a kitchen miracle. And just when he and I were about to set off on our delicious pilgrimage to the library, too!

Georgie was a terror to read. During Lent once, in a spirit of exquisite satire, he gave up everything – smoking, drinking, going to the cinema, sugar in his tea – and sat in evening after evening reading. The women resented it, being unused to not having the house to themselves, but Geo read on remorselessly, a book a night for forty nights.

This was not usual, though, sitting in our midst reading, placing himself in a kind of purdah which we had to admit but felt to be untrue. There was no need to be so pointedly 'good'; it wasn't being good at all, it was only a response to Mam's criticisms of what a derelict Christian he was. A pity he didn't have as well thought out a reponse to her other criticisms.

Typically, Georgie was a closet reader. He read in bed. No matter how late it was, he told me once, when he got home he couldn't sleep without reading. He read by flashlight, or rather by bicycle lamp. Exhausted batteries accumulated on the dressing-table until Chrissy, the bedmaker, threw them all out, fresh ones included, causing great ructions, Georgie being extremely sensitive to the idea of being tampered with. (He really raised the roof if one of his newspapers was mislaid and unavailable when he came in from work.)

I don't know why he didn't use the electric light. My sense of Mam suggests that she complained to him once about running up the light bill. Her strength, her reality, consisted in being prepared not to bend about issues of this kind, causing the objects of her criticism to invent very elaborate rationales and self-justifications in order to assimilate what was pure, unmitigated, small-mindedness.) His response, along the lines of his Lenten demonstration, was to deny her for ever after the basis for such an accusation, making her inflexibility his own, attaining (like a true Irishman) freedom through deprivation.

On the other hand, my sense of Georgie suggests that he used the lamp so's not to have to get out of bed to switch off the ceiling light. Getting up again was a nuisance to be sure; but better to have poor light and awkward position than undergo a fifteen-second dash across freezing lino to the switch and back? Yes: Because this was the way he decided to do it, the way (for all I know) he may have hit on as a youngster, when lights out meant something. A way nobody else would dream of, so how dare anyone criticize it?

And what didn't Geo read? Well, first of all, newspapers. Three dailies, *Press*, *Independent*, *Cork Examiner*. Two weeklies, *Dungarvan Observer* and *Waterford Star*. Eight Sundays! Two Irish, *Press* and *Independent*. Six English: *Graphic*, *Empire News*, *People*, *Sunday Express*, *Dispatch* and *Chronicle*. These he devoured after first mass and breakfast, as though starving for them. He loved to read out juicy morsels to us, savouring the gossip of the stars, grunting 'Good God' at the 'human goat' type of bizzarerie which, according to Fleet Street, constituted life in the English provinces.

What else did he read? *Wide World*, which had pictures of crocodile-eating Eurasians, or vice-versa, on the cover. *Ring Magazine* – bearish Archie Moore, squat Hogan Bassey, Carmen Basilio's eye, like a blue-red orange, after lithe Sugar Ray had finished with it. Don Cockle, thrashed in California. He read Nat Gould, Edgar Wallace, Leslie Charteris, Peter 29

Cheyney. Westerns by the dozen. War books: *Two Eggs on My Plate*, *The White Rabbit*, *They Have Their Exits* by Airey Neave. Geo's taste a lust for action in a world of talk. With my hand in his thick calloused hand – down by the dim lights of Main Street's stores, past the gaggle of old men and boys gossiping around the Monument, up Gallow's Hill – I felt my face aglow with the thought of being in this strong man's keeping, safe and sound in the feeling that he, at least, belonged in the world beyond the home.

The library was on Gallow's Hill (locals said 'Gallus'). It looked like it was on the edge of town because, apart from the National Bank opposite, there was nothing near it. In front, the road sloped off to Tallow, westwards. Behind, some of the Castle Farm ran away to the river, protected by a tall stone wall: private – keep out. Botany was close by, of course, and came out onto the main road farther west, but it was largely obscured by the bank and bank garden, and besides, it and the library had little in common.

Officially New Street, Botany was a straggle of cabins built when transportation to Australia was the judicial rage. Apparently moving – or being moved – into them struck a contemporary wit as joke exile. Now the street was anything but new, its homes wan and world-weary where they weren't dilapidated. They didn't look quite as bad as the ones in the poverty zone at our end of town, Church Lane, but it was only a matter of time till they did.

From such façades – and indeed from the peeling, washed-out fronts of Main Street – the library seemed a world away. It was neat and trim: red brick and white painting. It sat above street level, on top of steps, behind a gate and railings. It had parquet floors and leaded windows. It enjoined quiet. I had no trouble thinking of it ecclesiastically, though its size made it closer kin to that other mainstay of national architectural ambition, the bungalow.

I was very impressed, in addition, by the fact that the library had a special status independent of the one I conferred on it. (As usual, if something pleased me it had to be special. Pleasure, the satisfaction of desire, the matching of world to need: these were not to be thought of as commonplace.) The library was the headquarters of the County Library service, and to prove it had a large, green, lumbering Bedford van which Andy Drohan drove out to the branches, reminding them of Lismore's superiority.

The idea of siting the County Librarian's office in Lismore has, for me now, a peculiar period feel. I can see some ardent civil servant in the early days of the Free State deciding on it. And it was an imaginative decision, though I find it sad as well as endearing. Lismore is one of those special Irish places to have its own book (like Kells or Durrow). Therefore, shouldn't such a place, sanctified by learning and culture in the days when your average Brit was still attempting to master the bow and arrow (or so we were encouraged to believe), be the town of the Book once more?

Indeed, what could be more appropriate? It's debatable, however, if the people of the town were able to see themselves and their birthplace as others saw them. They all were aware of Lismore's ancient history, knew of the Book, the Crozier, the fact that the immediate spiritual satrap was Bishop of Waterford *and Lismore*. But you can't eat ancient history. Let the civil servant be as imaginative as bedamned. Let his gesture be a perfect embodiment of the prevailing cultural orthodoxy. What did it profit the man on the corner? Sweet damn-all. He and his countless brothers would have much preferred a future instead of a past; if possible one that didn't start with the boat to England. Sadly what Dublin sent down was a gesture, a posture, a notion – not a daily wage out of which the man on the corner could evolve his own cultural vocabulary.

To make matters worse, there was nothing in the library that might make me relish what lay behind officialdom's nod in our direction. There weren't any children's books in stock that I remember about the legendary heroes, their derring-do and sexiness. All I was interested in was the action-packed latest, doing my best to mimic Georgie's tastes. If a book didn't contain an aeroplane or a launch, I wouldn't go near it. I did choke down some of the classics – *Kidnapped, Martin Rattler* – and grudgingly acknowledged their story-interest. But as a general principle I rejected reading chosen for me by adults. That principle, as well as my craving for contemporaneity, must account for my lack of interest in the heroic-past-in-pictures books that my father brought down to me for Christmas once or twice. At any rate, their larger-than-life figures 31 never really appealed to me then. The life-sized took my fancy. If I had to have heroes, let them be legitimate heroes, like Biggles, or the Yank who floated down the Amazon on balsa wood in *The Seven Little Sisters*, a great book made even better by the fact that I got it from the library to keep, a tattered treasure, withdrawn from circulation, which Georgie brought home for me one time he was renovating one of the inner rooms. As long as the library provided a steady flow of latter-day heroics, I was content, and when Georgie said approvingly, 'Looks like a good one' (*Tiger Mountain* by Angus MacVicar), my Saturday was complete.

I found it hard to accept that Georgie's wasn't. Whereas I could now float home and sink myself pleasurably into some hotbed of foreign intrigue (the best thing about evil was that it always took place in a good climate – subliminal acknowledgement of the devil's omnipotence: he brought his normal working conditions with him on his terrestrial visits), Georgie's Saturday evening was just beginning. I suppose I didn't feel entirely comfortable with the thought that he was grown up, and wanted to be out and about doing grown-up things. All the more so since going drinking, which is what he did, was the cause of so much ill-feeling, Mam objecting bitterly to his keeping the company of the spongers, bums and leeches who, in her dreadful vision of Lismore's night-life, infested the bars of the town.

In one literal sense, Mam's objection was all too accurate. Apart from the shopkeepers, who didn't drink or if they did lost their shops, and the professional people, who kept their drinking to themselves, pickling their livers while they preserved their status, there weren't all that many with enough in their pockets to drink whenever they wanted. Some, perhaps, didn't have the stomach to defy their mothers week in, week out. But for the most part, there weren't that many common citizens with regular work. A few postmen, a handful working at the Castle, a very small number of tradesmen: these were the regular earners. As for the rest, grave-digging, clearing up after a storm, helping out at threshing and beet-snagging, a day here, a day there, filling in their time with Public Assistance and begetting children on wives shaped like steamrollered mattresses . . .

Georgie bewailed the lack of work, too. Only for the

32

goodwill his father had created among the gentry, he might well have found the going harder. Not that it was easy. The gentry were dying out. And Georgie could be heard complaining loud and long that shopkeepers couldn't be relied on for sixpence. He redecorated their nameboards, repointed their chimneys, resashed the windows of their heavily furnished, under-used upstairs apartments. But getting them to pay was like getting blood from a turnip. And as for farmers: they were as bad, if not worse. What they couldn't botch together themselves had to be paid for in bags of potatoes or maybe a goose at Christmas. At least the gentry, whatever else about them, paid cash on the nail.

So Mam was right. There were a lot of men in the town in need of a drink, and in need of the price of one. But she was wrong too. The very companions that she named as the biggest spongers were the ones Georgie needed most, the old stagers of the town, waiting out their time in some married daughter's houseful of squally nippers or alone in unkempt, cold-hearthed cottages. If they couldn't sit down for a drink and a chat at this hour of their lives, the world was a dead loss altogether, was Geo's attitude. It pleased him to know he could please these old lads: as he told me afterwards, he felt at home with them. Mam was wrong because she refused to admit this, refused to see that Georgie had needs which only he could satisfy – or if she saw that, didn't want the choice of forms to be at his discretion.

Geo's aim was not just to please, however. He wasn't sly enough to patronize people. He needed not approval, but talk. In the low, smoky, sour-smelling room the old codgers' moist voices reminisced away. Experiences were resurrected and opinions dusted down. They became men again, tearing and dragging for some toff's steward, poaching the Duke's salmon under a sovereign-coloured springtime moon. Nutty Keating, Geo's favourite, a stone-mason with a belly like a sandbag, gave tips about granite and told stories of travelling the country raising churches. His finest hour was the time he spent on the cathedral at Queenstown, as he still called it, looking out over the droves of youngsters like himself setting sail for America, thinking how lucky he was to have a chisel for an anchor.

But everyone in Lismore had been lucky 'in them days', 33

before the Great War, 1916 and all that. There was lashings of work, and porter was only a ha'penny a pint. Miss Curry shipped out flowers from the town that bedecked the breasts of London debutantes. Paxton had his butter factory. The clogmill was going strong. You could hardly cross the street for the bustle and jam of horses and carts.

'Ah Jesus, there was some life in it then.' Even I, doing nothing to seek out old-timers' musings, was familiar to yawning-point with this refrain. What it meant to Georgie to pursue and absorb its most stirring settings and minutest variations I can only guess. But pursue them he did. He would no more dream of neglecting Nutty or Cuggar Whelan or Marsh Reagan or John the Bird than he would the library or me. Perhaps we were all mixed up together in his mind.

Or was it that he was patiently piecing together memory, impression, animus and fact in order to get precisely right the lineaments of the limbo into which the town had declined? Or was the insufficiency of the present softened by the continual review of the amount of life that had gone into making it? No doubt he loved the old lore for its own sake, the romance of other days unrehearsed and vivid on the tongue – who had threatened bloodshed for a half-acre of hillside, whose daughters had never married and why? Was it true that the big-shots down the river used to hold Orange conclaves? Loved it, yes, but did he make anything of it? Or is to love not to make anything more, but to rest in a state of indiscriminate, unadulterated acceptance, each story sufficient to the evening of its telling? All I know is that he flew in Mam's face more flagrantly for the sake of those pensioners that he did for many an ostensibly more personal cause. With a son's ache, he seemed to lust after what he couldn't live.

'G'night, Mike!' he'd cry.

But before I'd raised my head from my new book to shout my own glad, thankful, 'Night, Mike!', the front door was slammed, and he was off into the adult night, headlong and hungering.

II
CORNERS

1

A great thing happened when I was ten: I stopped sleeping in the same room as Chrissy and Mam and got a room of my own. 'The girls' room,' it was called, and it was also the room in which Dad (my grandfather, that is) had had his final illness. But these associations didn't bother me. I was too busy acting independent.

I got the room after my bad dreams died down, maybe as a reward, or maybe as an expression of relief on the part of Mam and Chris. Although I haven't had them since, I remember those dreams very vividly, and I remember they went on for a long time, not every night, but very often, for well over a month. Nightmares about my legs being cut off alternated with a truly terrifying sensation of being upside-down in bed. I can't see now why a sense of having head and heels reversed should be so awful. At the time, however, it gave me feelings of dreadful molestation, as though I was the sport of incomprehensible forces.

I know my crying out and quivering caused disquiet because Mam eventually came up with something to blame for it. According to her, my condition was the result of a seaside holiday I spent with Granny Royce (my mother's mother), my father, and one of my Wexford cousins, Patrick Askins. We spent three weeks together in a bungalow belonging to other cousins, the Morans, at a place called Ballyvaldan, near Blackwater, County Wexford.

'That lonesome ould place,' said Mam, reprovingly, having never been within fifty miles of it.

She had a point, though. I wasn't happy there. I felt I was being cheated out of three weeks of my father's exclusive attention in bustling Dublin. But I never thought it so bad that 37 nightmares should be my principal souvenir. Even if I was afraid of the water (and had my fear shown up by Patrick, who was not only braver but younger), Blackwater was interesting. There was its name, for one thing: the same name as the river in Lismore, yet it didn't have a river in it. Strange. There was a shop there that sold ice-cream, owned by a family named Fortune, and when the daughter of the house served us, my father always said, 'Was that Miss Fortune?' and I laughed and laughed. And there was Dempsey, whose car we hired to take us back to Enniscorthy, where Granny Royce and Patrick lived. He had a habit of saying, 'Be the gob o' man!' whatever you said to him, and he whirled his Consul round the unpaved backroads with a flourish. I loved him.

So, I don't know what got on my nerves. Maybe whatever it was didn't emerge till I got back to Lismore, because I wouldn't have been able to trust anyone except Mam with it. Or perhaps what upset me was returning itself. The holiday household – father, (grand) mother, brotherly cousin – was a closer facsimile of what I wanted. But it turned out, after all, to be only a rehearsal, a game of happy families, and shockingly short-lived.

But I got the room. And very proud I was of it as well. It was mine, mine! Before long, whenever the atmosphere in the kitchen disagreed with me, I threatened to withdraw upstairs, completely, to live alone as much as possible, to become in fact what history and fortune had fashioned me, a man apart.

It wasn't until years later, when I was fourteen or fifteen and home from boarding-school (by which time both Georgie and Chrissie had at last left home and – since I was seeing less of my father – I had Mam all to myself more or less all summer long), that the room really did become a retreat. In the early days of my occupancy, however, the best thing about it was that I now had my own window on the world. On the lean uplands of furzey Shrough sun and cloud composed a child's painting of green, brown and yellow. Farther up, a blue shoulder of Knockmealdowns sloped westward in shy hurry. Every so often I'd spend an hour lost in those far-off colours.

There was such scenery around Lismore, though, that I took it for granted. The pride of mountains and the massiveness of woods was not what overawed me. The street opposite my window sufficed for that, supplying as much as I desired of mystery, sympathy, terror and play. Church Lane. When I think of it now I think not only of a lost playground and all the poor people whose poor homes were there (that's what overawed me, really, their nothingness); I think too that it was the town in essence, Lismore in its bare bones. And with my room facing directly onto it I came to believe that the view contained, or illustrated, something about myself, and that I'd been appointed to the room in order to find out what that was. Something along those lines must have crossed my mind. I spent so many rainy afternoons staring down that mean street. I could look straight down and see everything. Often I felt as melancholy at the sight as if I'd been looking down a ward in a hospital.

The lane was L-shaped, skirting around behind the north side of East Main Street and coming out at the gates of the Protestant church, hence the name – officially Church Street, christened no doubt by the man who owned it, and most of the town besides, the Duke of Devonshire. I could only see the long arm of the L, down as far as Dunne's, the ball-alley, and Doherty's, though as I gazed I had the whole of the lane in mind. The right-hand side, going down, consisted of a row of one-storey cabins (in the lower lane, out of sight, these were fronted by square, squat, slate-roofed porticoes). On the left there were some cabins too, to start with, and then a gap where some two-storey houses had stood when I was small. They had been condemned, though (a term which had put me in mind of disease), and knocked down. All that remained was a hole in the side of the street, a pile of yellowish rubble speckled with scraps of paint and burgeoning colonies of nettles and dockleaves.

'An eyesore.'

'Well, 'tis true for you, it is an eyesore.'

Adult opinion was unanimous. But nobody did anything about it. We youngsters were glad the rubble remained, because it made great cowboy country, the finest network of gulches and passes around.

Opposite that pile of failed housing stood the tap. There was only one in the lane (and the same was true in Botany and Chapel Street). Early and late, whenever I looked, some woman could be seen staggering off with a brimming bucket in each hand, arms wavering slightly in inarticulate semaphore. Everyone else in the town had piped water. Only poor people had to fetch and carry in order to wash and eat. It was strange. I couldn't imagine how money and water mixed.

It was the same way with electricity. The town transformer was down the street from the tap in Boyle's field, just by the ball-alley. Its clean, silent energy was a wonder to me, and I liked its abstract hum. Raised above us, resplendent in coils and condensers, it struck me that it could well be an idol for a tribe that didn't have one – the English, maybe; I was always hearing at home how godless they were. But marvellous as electricity might be, there was many a household in the lane and elsewhere whose kitchens it never brightened, and where candle and oil-lamp shone on uneclipsed.

No doubt I felt drawn to the lane because of the strange state of its light and water. Such conditions made the place seem another country, hardly Ireland at all, but some dilapidated, unrenewable zone quite out of touch and out of keeping with the place the risen people called their own. I must have wondered idly what kind of people these cabin-dwellers were, really: how they bore being so different from Main Street? It was impossible not to be struck by the unbridgeable, inscrutable gulf which the mere turn of a corner could evidently create. But to be drawn thus was only to be vaguely drawn, the product of solitary upstairs musings, those moods in which I saw more clearly than anything else the strangeness of the world and the arbitrary formulae of its dispositions. Usually I was too busy playing down the lane, with the lads of the lane, to bother my head about differences.

We played in the ball-alley. That was the lane's greatest draw. A rectangular court with a front wall perhaps twenty foot high, and side walls sloping down from it until they levelled off at say seven feet, the alley was undoubtedly one of Lismore's great amenities. It was built before the Great War, when the lane was a far different place (as Mam made sure I knew). I imagine the idea was to anticipate or deflect the work that the devil is said to make for idle hands. But partly, too, the alley represented a piece of cultural assertion typical of its generation. It must have taken a certain amount of guts (a virtually incalculable amount to those in my day whom the low state of the town's morale left feeling high and dry) to erect a Gaelic games facility right in the town on land which presumably had to be bought, land which might well have been earmarked for a couple more rent-yielding cabins. The inspiration to build it was possibly supplied by the Ramblers, Lismore's football team of the day, who (I quote Mam's attitude) were just about world-famous and beat the best of them. Yet to find a field to play on they had to settle for a thistly semi-hill some miles along the Ballyduff road. So, I suppose, now that I think of it, we played our ball in an historical monument.

The Gaelic game we played was handball. We didn't play it properly – I was about to add, automatically, 'of course'; what was there in the town that didn't leave something to be desired? There was no club. Normally, handball affairs would be under the same aegis as those of hurling and football. Nobody doubted that it was a Gaelic game, of course. It wouldn't surprise me to learn that some nationalist ideologue has traced its Indo-European roots, noting along the way handball's similarity to the Basques' *pelote* (and, wasn't it from that part of the world the Tuatha de Danaan came north to fashion us), not to mention Pakistani expertise at squash – those are the lads from the Indus valley, aren't they, the cradle of Celtdom itself. But, for once, national wasn't synonymous with seriousness and organization. Not the least pleasure of the alley was that we were left to carry on as best we could, and had only ourselves to please. In this one case, neglect was enlightened.

There being no club, we had no way of acquiring the proper balls to play with, the standards, as they were called: there was a softball standard, which merely stung the palm off your hand, and a hardball, a small rock about the size of a squash ball which, when struck, jarred every tissue between wrist and fingertip. Not only did nobody have the money to buy these official projectiles, the shopkeepers of the town knew it and never bothered to stock them. Though, even if we had them to play with it wouldn't have done us much good, since they would have been too lively for an alley without a back wall. For, as though designed with a view to articulate incompleteness, that's what our alley lacked. A ball with the life of a standard in it would have ended up among the porticoes every toss. So, since nobody was going to provide us with a wall to confine the bounce, we made do happily with superannuated   41 tennis balls and lumps of sponge as lively as brick.

Once, I remember, an effort was made to put handball on a more public footing. It was always acknowledged that we would never produce anyone like the Ryans and Doyles of Wexford, or Kirby of Clare. But couldn't we, for God's sake, try to make the game less of a hand-to-mouth thing, with maybe a town tournament and neutral markers. And why not usher in the new age with an exhibition match, a proper singles challenge, best-of-five . . . . The planning and anticipation had the anxiety of a prayer about them. I don't know who the two who played the exhibition were, strangers from down the county, probably (there was a beautiful alley in Loughmore, the poor quarter of Dungarvan; it had a *glass* back wall so the people in the adjoining stand – *a stand*! – didn't miss a move). But I remember that they paraded up the main street and down the lane, followed by a large throng, and led, strange to behold, by the massed melodeons of the three Keatings, Pad Tierney, I think, drumming, and beating the shine off a triangle, an old soak from Botany who went by the name of Jim Slog. The melodeons' suspirations had a sarcastic drawl to them, the crowd was beery and rambunctious, and I would like to think that there was a jeer at respectable, do-nothing Main Street in the whole thing.

We all enjoyed the exhibition, but nothing ever came of it. Either we needed a more exalted inspiration, or were too set in our informal ways to bother with leagues and the like, or perhaps there was a question of who would supply the shorts and singlets which were necessary if we were to become official, judging by what the two imported contestants wore. The lads I played with hardly had a shoe to their foot or a seat to their trousers. And when I hear again, now, the slap of running feet in rainy streets, or see the white of private flesh, I realize that it wasn't really the alley that I was drawn to, much as I enjoyed handball (not least the discovery that there was a game I could play), but crossing the line to consort with the impoverished, sharing for a couple of hours their looser, unstylized, more dangerous life.

I envied them. I had the beige, hand-knit sweaters and the cotton socks. But they had strength and fury and staying-power. Nobody told them they had to do homework or to sit

quiet and read a book – sensibly, since where would stillness get them? So they had plenty of time to develop their prowess at handball and catapulting and soccer, attraction to which was inspired by all the brothers and neighbours who came home from England. It made good sense to favour soccer. Sooner or later – and usually sooner – every youngster in the lane was bound for the boat. And they never made the grade hurling, largely because so few of them could afford to buy a stick. (A rubber soccer ball was a lot cheaper and lasted a lot longer.)

And could those boys play handball? Day after day, game after game, they flammed ball against wall with untiring ease. They always ran me ragged when I played against them, and when I played with them, in doubles, I hardly got a shot, because their timing and alley-sense enabled them to antici-pate whatever might come my way. But I accepted that they were streets ahead of me, admired them for it, thought of them as stars (the brightness of their vigour, their inexhaustibility). Often I went down to the alley just to look on.

A summer afternoon. I've placed myself gingerly – afraid of my life that I'll dirty my trousers – on the bald hillock opposite the alley. The players toss, for serve. At once I'm lost to – immersed in, stupefied by – this paupers' ballet. Blur of arm and ball, disputatious call ('Short!', 'Hinder!'), slap and smack of rubber rifled against stone. Except it's hard to think of poverty. (Afternoon inches by, bodies whirl undimmed.) Are these the lesser orders, the ones, who, I've been told, must live on only bread and tea, whose mothers scurry sheepishly up to the convent with a tin to ask for the charity of leavings, whose fathers will do no work heavier than elbow-exercises at Grock Foley's bar? They were not indeed! They were light, blithe, vivid – *life*!

Nor was this experience of them confined to the ball-alley. It was there when Eddy Cooney showed me how to make a bird-lime (make a paste from the pith of alder, smear it on a twig; when the bird lands there, he sticks, so you can catch him). It was there watching them shoulder home a limb after a storm, or a *brusna* (a bundle of brambles and deadwood typically the size of a miniature haystack). The leavings of the Duke's plantations; sole means of keeping the home fires burning. It was there when I saw Des Callaghan or Tom   43

Lenane trudging down Main Street with their overflowing buckets of whorts and blackberries, grinning at the spoils of the day, at the cash Bob Nolan was going to give them, at the sixpenny ice-cream that was to be their main reward, the rest being required for bread.

And above all it came to me on Stephen's day when the poor boys of the whole parish – and most prominently to me, of course, my lane buddies – took to the streets as wren boys.

Stephen's morning was one of the few times of the year when the whole household in Swiss Cottage stayed in bed late. Mam didn't get up for mass, nobody worked, and the house conveyed a delicious air of somnolence as I settled into one of my Christmas books, partly no doubt because it held more people – Peggy and my father down from Dublin, Frankie or Elizabeth home from England. But then – smash – right in the middle of the heavy-lidded peace – Bang, Bang, Bang! – the wren boys at the door.

They knocked and knocked, blowing their new tin whistles, harmonicas and kazoos, pausing only to deliver their chant:

> The wren, the wren, the king of all birds,
> St Stephen's Day he was caught in the furze.
> Up with the kettle and down with the pan;
> Tuppence or thruppence to bury the wren.
> All silver and no brass,
> Give us our answer and let us pass.

Bang, Bang, Bang!

Groans and maledictions from annoyed adults were all they ever got at our house. But no matter how comfortable I was, or how cold I thought it might be up, I had to rush down and peep out at each troupe in its regalia.

There were usually four or five members to each bunch – boys and girls, not necessarily members of the same family, generally not, in fact. One piece of regalia was compulsory, a bush, festooned with sprigs of holly, shreds of ribbon and coloured paper. 'Ah, they don't do it right at all,' Mam complained once; 'I remember when you'd have to have a wren tied to the bush.' A dead one? 'What else?' her tone seemed to say. 'The lads of the town'd be out all day Christmas Eve hunting them down.' I squirmed. Gay tatters were a lot better.

Naturally all wren-people wore make-up and fancy-dress. Lads with big sisters did best here, sporting cheeks of hectic rouge and cast-off dresses. But the girls were synonymous with cleanliness in my book. And their fathers' shirts, sweat-soiled soft hats and clumpy wellingtons looked good too. Often I didn't recognize who was there, though this is probably less a tribute to wardrobe and make-up than a statement of my own excitement – the daring fun of the participants, the ticklesome knowledge that they were going to get money for riling a townful of sleepy-headed big people.

I wished I was with them. It made me sad and mad to know that the closest I'd get to them was later on when they'd counted their take and told, with relish, how some farmer – John Farrell, perhaps – had not only given them two bob but had sat them down to a fine feed of duck-eggs and hot soda bread.

But not for me, or for any of the heirs of Main Street, the iron-hard, early-morning road, or bright rags under a wintry sky. Besides, what need had we to bring Christmas into the streets? Weren't our own homes good enough for us? Respectability: a door that stayed shut, no matter how clamant the visitors.

2

Yet the lane was part of me, and would have been even if I'd never known an alley or a pauper. This was thanks to Dad, my grandfather; he was born down the lane. The house was just a stone's throw from Swiss Cottage, and fortunately for family pride was the best-kept in the lane; it had yellow ochre trim just like ours. But I'd been told time out of mind that any resemblance between the two dwellings absolutely stopped there. It was all right to come from the lane in Mam's youth (in Mam's youth everything was different), when German bands came oompahing through the town and the Jewish shirt-pedlar went from door to door repeating, 'Von shilling von veek.' 'Ah, God be with old times': that phrase still rings down the years, dragging behind it all its intimidating implications, like a ghost and its chains. People were happy long ago, it implied, and wasn't it the past that put the seal of integrity on all we were and all we should be, and how could you expect God to be with the times that were in it now, with all them Communists and everything.

Looking from my window at Dad's old house and the barn-like structure attached to it which was the family workshop, it intrigued me to think of him as a child looking up at the window and imagining himself Swiss Cottage's proud possessor. Did he need to promise himself a future, and did he see its shape in the high pitch of that roof and the mansard windows, in the very idea of an upstairs? I liked to think so, pleasured in the drift of my own mind by imputing the real drift to his.

I had to imagine, because we never talked, and the bits and scraps about him which I accumulated in the years after his death were less important for their information than for their tone, so that what I have now is not a grandfather but a legend, a genius, an archetype of the great man. All I can picture, however, is a hard-breathing old party with a pepper-and-salt moustache and twinkling eyes who treated me kindly. He'd draw pictures of birds and motorcars in the margin of his *Cork Examiner* while I was waiting to be sent to bed. And he gave me medicine: every day at eleven he'd come home for it, a bottle of porter, mulled. When it was ready he'd take me on his knee and give me some to 'make a man' of me. The closeness of his coarse, sawdust-smelling clothes. The sweet astringency of that warm, aromatic beer sipped from a sugar-coated spoon. I heard the breath whistle through his ravaged tubes; but I only smiled.

Whether or not Dad dreamt of attaining a fine house on Main Street, his rise from the lane has, to me, elements of a dream-journey, or even mythic translation, attached to it, since he had accomplished so much through action and by no other means, while when I thought of my inchoate self, action seemed a perishable option. My father definitely chose not to live on his father's terms, a decision which had the intermit-

tent effect of belittling him in my eyes. Whereas, and this is why he struck me as an enlarged presence, Dad was definitely the son of his father, prehistoric Johnny.

I say prehistoric because, to hear Mam tell it (and, Lord did I not!), family history began with Dad and herself. She had good reason to excise any preceeding O'Brien from the record. But I can't follow her example. Sketchy as my knowledge of it is, Johnny's is too good a story to obliterate.

Foxy Johnny (he had red hair) hailed from one of those stony parishes between the east bank of the Blackwater and the sea, down Aglish way. The native quarter, a place nobody ever comes from, an area at the far eastern end of which – around Ring, Old Parish and Helvick Head – people still speak Irish. Apparently Johnny had sparkling Irish; one of Mam's few boasts about him was that Brother Geary, one of my father's teachers, used to come down for advice about idiom and *blas*. And maybe the old native sang for the teacher, as well, pouring out, quite unabashed, by the kitchen fire, the rich, sad love songs of the Decies, his homeland. Sang for my father too, no doubt (my father loved Irish), and told him stories, but I can't be sure about that: nothing came down to me.

Despite Johnny's cultural hoard, however, I don't really see him as a folklorist's placid accomplice, or even as a remnant of a vanished race. My sense of him contains a good deal of fire and drive and hardness. To me he's not a mythic figure just because he survived, but because he survived in terms he set for himself: he succeeded.

The odds were daunting. First, he had to learn his trade. This meant walking the long, lonesome road, bare-footed into some carpenter in Cappoquin, to whom he served his time – living-in, probably, which saved his feet but made the workday longer; getting a taste of the town; setting his face, gradually but inexorably, against the riverbanks and the familiar fields which, just then (the 1860s), were coming back into their own after the famine-ridden forties. I don't know if his people paid for his apprenticeship, as was the custom then; if so, I can't imagine how they managed. I've never even thought about it much, distracted from that aspect of the story by a more fundamental one which continues to amaze me: his people's foresight. It's just extraordinary to me that parents, 47 harried virtually to death's door by hunger, would have located the realization of a future (their son's security) in the same landscape. No America for them, and not for their Johnny a life on the land or a life in service, but the life of an independent tradesman: let strength of hand and certainty of eye suffice!

I'm assuming that young Johnny had the strong will of his parents behind him, but of course that's not necessarily so. But it did take an act of will on somebody's part to come into town, and not to be satisfied with Cappoquin, either, but to head for Lismore; where thanks to the Castle, the nobs and toffs were plentiful, and therefore so was work. As Johnny's marriage shows, however, he had will enough to make such moves without anyone's prompting.

His marriage is as unlikely as the rest of his saga. He married Nana. I believe my father was the first to call her that, but I never heard anyone call her anything else. I don't know her name. She was a servant in one of the big houses around Lismore, and was a Northerner, a Protestant, for all I know, an Orangewoman.

What's unlikely is not that she was in service two hundred odd miles from home. In those days, around Lismore at any rate, it was not uncommon for the gentry to hire servants of their own religious persuasion, thinking them more trustworthy, more entitled to have the opportunity of cultivation through service, and a more intimate – not to mention more desirable – embodiment of clean Christian living, than anything the local natives could produce. It was a policy with which Nana, obviously, identified. What she hoped to get out of it, I have no idea: something more, I hope, than the frigid satisfaction of doing her duty. But whatever it was, it's safe to assume, I think, that she never expected to find herself in the arms of that foxy teague, Johnny O'Brien.

How he must have wooed her! Surely nothing less than a mad mindless fling could have brought about a wedding as flagrant as theirs. What else would have made him persist? What else could have made her fly in the face of security and relinquish the keys of her master's meatsafe in favour of a cabinful of kids in Church Lane? I can almost feel the zest of Johnny's satisfaction. Knowing that he'd won that place-proud Northwoman must have made him feel he was going to prosper.

And so he did, working every hour God sent, and fathering a family betimes. No stopping him! Two girls and three boys, and all the boys were brilliant. Jim was the first man in the area to drive a car. Paddy was a miracle-working smith; such a damn shame the 'flu of 1917 took him. And there was George: what couldn't he do?

Mam had the answer to that question: nothing. When the Duchess of Devonshire herself (the Castle! My God; you could rise no higher than to be hired by her) wanted one of her private apartments decorated a special, duck-egg blue, and failed to find the paint either in Cork or London, who mixed it for her? Dad.

Then again: he was out at Colonel Jameson's one time seeing about a job, Mam told me, 'and the girl showed him into the room to wait. When the Colonel came in, he stopped and looked around like there was something odd: "Is that a clock I hear ticking?" says he. "It is, Sir," says Dad. "But that clock hasn't worked for years," said the Colonel. "I'm not surprised," said Dad, "your mantelpiece is out of plumb. I just wound it and put it there on the table." The Colonel nearly dropped,' said Mam, grinning like a girl at such cleverness.

And he saved a man from jail. In those days if your walk wavered by a fraction of an inch a policeman'd be down on you, and you'd be handed thirty days without the option. 'No, but', as Mam went on to explain, 'on top of that, your character was ruined, of course, because no one'd give work to a drunkard.' Anyhow, one Saturday evening Dad was coming up Main Street and just at Ferry Lane corner some fellow from the lane staggered out more or less on top of him. There was an RIC man at the corner, hoping for that very thing. But Dad just caught the drunk by the arm, and held him severely upright the whole length of the street: Dad said he could feel the policeman's eyes looking into his back every step of the way. 'Oh them RIC,' said Mam. 'They were devils. But they got no soot that evening.'

Needless to say, I delighted in those anecdotes – doubly delighted in them, for not only were they marvellous to me in their own right, but the telling of them gave Mam an easeful air of satisfaction and serenity. These are my possessions, said her tone, I am pleased. When she sketched those little scenes, 49 the past was not oppressive. It was like going to the seaside on a weekday, a place with acres of open, idle space, and here a man with balloons, there a beach hut, and along the way a private party under a striped awning.

When I heard of Dad playing the concertina, it was a great relief to find no judgment being made. The memories of his talent as a mimic 'doing to pieces' the flutterings, barks and grufferies of the gentry who were his chief employers, came across as tributes to his independence. And all the time, obsessively, 'Such presence of mind. . . . Great presence of mind.' A tongue that never failed the wit that moved it, a hand that hardly moved less slowly than the eye that prompted it, a man supremely equipped for the life given him to lead, so fitted he must have believed that it was indeed his life, no accident, but an integrated entity. How rare that makes him seem.

None of this (none of what Mam told me, nothing in the pleasurable past) explained how it happened that Dad left the lane and installed himself in the nearest available big house – I wonder, by the way, what he thought of 'cottage' in that house's name: did it strike him that what to him was a mansion, compared to his own home, might to others be a plaything, a dainty architectural frivolity, a picturesque retreat 'from the real world'? I don't suppose he had the luxury or time for thoughts like that (and in any case his mind was too vigorous to dwell on irony). He must have been aware, however, that the house had symbolic value, since he came to it not through making a success of his father's business, but by being so successful in competition. In a word, Swiss Cottage was won in a fight.

Word of the eruption and split never passed Mam's lips, so my sense of what actually took place is hazy. I'd overhear a reference to it, then the following Christmas an obscure piece of information would volley round the dinner table, causing everyone to fall silent for a moment and to look fierce. And then, oddest of all, when I thought about it, there was the situation of Dad's sister, Alice, who lived in perfect normality with her man and children down the street from us. What was odd, though, was that we didn't seem very close to them; at least that was odd to me, because if I had cousins I'd always be down at their house or be having them up to mine. And then, on asking, I was told about Daigue, Alice's husband.

I daresay it was about his name I asked, ever anxiously on the *qui vive* for names stranger than my own. Daigue's name was an abbreviation of its Irish version, Déglán, Declan, the sainted prelate of Foxy Johnny's part of the world, from which Daigue hailed, from which indeed he had been sent into the town of Lismore to serve his time in the work-shop of his successful landsman. And, luckily for him, to marry the boss's daughter. May it not have been that as a result of the fight between Dad and his father, Daigue became heir apparent to the O'Brien family business, causing such a coolness in relations between brother and sister that the next generation would inevitably feel it? So then, it may well have been . . . . And then again, it may not have been that at all, which is what I'd prefer, since there's something devitalizing about making fast, making watertight, a tissue of a plot, as though that were all the past had to offer.

Yet, why was it that when Winny, Dad's other sister, came on a visit from Glasgow – she went there, I presume, because it was the true capital of Nana's kingdom – I had to go down to Alice's to see her; she didn't come next or near our door?

I sat in the overheated parlour, heard what a fine fellow I was turning out to be, and wondered what was that to them. Unfamiliar faces, strange accents, a roaring fire too early in the afternoon. I was given a peach, I remember, a Glasgow peach, for all I knew; another piece of unfamiliarity, oranges being the acme of local fruit treats. And a slobbery job I made of it, juice staining my trousers (*I'll be killed!*), juice congealing on my bare knees. Finished, I held the moist stone in my hand, not knowing how to get rid of it, as embarrassed as if I'd perpetrated some blasphemous *gaffe* or sexual delinquence. And all the time I knew – *I knew* – they were going to make me sing – it was standard practice in those days that when you visited you sung, and you being the child. (They didn't.)

The afternoon was a major piece of evidence that there had been some obscure but decisive explosion in the long ago. Otherwise why would there be strangers with the whimsical, tension-making notion that they and I had some connection? Why, indeed, would there be remote Alice, and the casual   51 cousins, and Daigue with his spectacles as thick as bottle-ends who looked straight through me, wordlessly, as though I was no more to him than a hole in a wall? A whole family, a whole tissue of ties, known indifferently, essentially not known. If that didn't imply an ancient flare-up, what did, I wonder? No doubt I was peculiarly sensitive to gulfs. And then, out of nowhere, people to see me, tender statements, strange fruits. Why? And would they have been strangers to me if there had been no rift?

That afternoon of obscure intentions and unrealistic claims seemed an inscrutable reduction of an unilluminated past (mystery enhanced, not allayed, by fruit and soft talk). This past was what Dad had risen above. He'd detached himself from father, sisters, lane, history, just as he'd secured Mam, a girl of twenty, from Miss O'Shea's workroom, installed her in Main Street (Swiss Cottage, no less), and filled her full of children.

The present was enough for him. That's why he seems so immense to me. He stamped himself on time as emphatically as he stamped his billheads with an inky image of Swiss Cottage. I see in him the drive that will not be detained by 'Why?' I feel from him inklings of understanding that not knowing admits.

3

Church Lane corner, the Mall seat, Ferry Lane corner, the Red House corner, the Monument. As long as it wasn't raining – and often when it was – knots of able-bodied, idle men took their silent ease at these five stations, without even a couple of keys to fiddle with in their noiseless pockets.

If England didn't exist, they would have had to invent it.

But it did exist, a fact of life which made quite a number of these men both happy and sad. Some of them were home from England to convalesce in native air from city life and damp lodgings. They'd be back in Hammersmith before the year was out. Others were home permanently, having tried 'across the pond' (emigration had an argot of its own too, like everything else) a couple of times and baulked at the trauma of it.

I knew one of the latter type fairly well, Cha. He lived in the cabin next door to the house Dad was born in, and where I often visited him, shilling-piece in hand, to have my hair cut. That dwelling was the one in the lane I knew best. It consisted of a hall running about twenty feet from front door to back, with, to the left as you went in, the kitchen, and to the right, two bedrooms. His parents, a brother and sister, originally occupied this space, but only Cha and his sister lived there now.

The kitchen had a table and a couple of chairs in one corner, a dresser with a few pieces of blue delft in another, and in a third, a tripod holding an enamel dish, in which Cha and his sister performed their daily ablutions. There was a larger, low-lintelled open hearth along one wall, with a crane and a few pitch-black, cast-iron utensils hanging from it – the same method of cooking, I noted with amazement, as that used in the depths of the country. (I had a habit of thinking *brusnas* – among other things – more picturesque than necessary. It unnerved me to find I was wrong.) Above the fireplace, a mirror, two-foot square, thick varnished frame, and stuck in its bottom left-hand corner, a picture.

Kneeling on a chair with a pillow-case around my neck while Cha clipped – I can still see him lifting the gleaming chrome shears out of its oiled-paper nest, as good as the day he'd bought it (but what moved him to buy it?) – I had plenty of time to study that picture. It was of Cha at a dance, a wonderfully pretty girl in his arms (in my memory she wears a white dress). In the shadows, other couples are having a large time, but nothing can possibly surpass the radiance of Cha's expression.

The picture, he tells me, was taken in England. I know it must be somewhere other than Lismore because its brightness and frank joy is in such contrast to the bleak space it now looks out on. I ask him why he didn't stay in England, and receive various answers: the work is slavery; Birmingham is a woeful dump – not a tree or a river in it, just smoke and dirt; 'I couldn't stick it, boy.' He'd rather be at home, working when he could, ambling from one corner to another when he 53 couldn't, drinking like a fish all the time. He was about thirty. Already his lips were drawing into a pinch, his jaws were hollowing, his eyes were losing their lustre. He'd probably had his finest hour, was lucky to have a photo commemorating it. And there were dozens like him, in whose long faces and sagging, corner-influenced shoulders I saw that poverty was only partly a financial matter.

It wasn't until years later, however, after I'd taken the Rosslare boat myself and worked and drank in Cricklewood and Paddington and Camberwell Green that I got some sense of how London could turn old neighbours into casualties. When I was a child, it wasn't sympathy I learned to offer them, but reproof. They were failures, I heard; they couldn't stick it over there and they couldn't settle down decent at home. They were corner-boys. ('Don't put your hands in your pockets,' I was admonished; 'you'll end up like one of them Sheridans.') They were drunkards; all they lived for was rolling home legless, stinko, senseless, lousy, blotto, blind and stocious, singing in voices that seemed to emerge from cavernous bottles, keeping decent people awake, pissing in the gutter – shameless tramps!

And to make matters worse, in the eyes of my loved ones, this kind of low, blackguarding carry-on, was very often subsidized by their tougher-minded brethren who had managed to stick it out 'over', and who came home for their fortnight's holiday with more money than sense, decked out in the fake finery of Fifty-shilling Tailors. They, in a sense, were worse for having succeeded, or so I inferred from Swiss Cottage kitchen critiques. Born to nothing, just like those who sponged off them, how could they have got on by the strength of their arms alone in a place where nothing thrived except smoke and godlessness? Well, of course, there was only one answer: what little moral fibre they had must have simply collapsed. Mind you, they were hardly Irish anyhow, to begin with (meaning they existed in ideological innocence, their allegedly offensive occasions immune from considerations of Church and State), so . . . . And the accents of them; honestly you'd swear it was a tin can being kicked around! Oh, and did you see the one that Kip Tobin has home with him – my God, talk about a masterpiece in oils! The adult urchins whom England had unnerved may not have had a ha'penny to scratch themselves with, but at least they didn't stoop *that* low. They'd remained elements of a recognizable world, where neither flesh nor devil found a footing. They were the poor who, as the Master promised, we'd have always with us. Demoralization was accepted as part of this plan, but fancy clobber was vanity of vanities . . . .

The thing to do really, the honourable and admirable way of dealing with the unfortunate necessity of England, was to go there and not change. Few indeed there were with the strength of character to do so, but thank God we had our own Lizzie as an example. That she was still 'natural', had no accent, dressed as a mirror of sober sense, came to us unencumbered by lover or even close friend, amounted to a body of law, from which judgments on those of more friable backbone could be drawn.

And it wasn't that Elizabeth had a soft job either, or was protected from the vicissitudes and temptations of an alien civilization. On the contrary, as a nurse, she was as exposed as anyone. Meal after meal, she dawdled over tea and cigarettes and told us the worst – vignettes from the children's wards, how Mr Evans had finally pulled through, the policeman who'd shot himself – grey brain weeping from his temple, 'and when they brought him in he was still alive!' And still Lizzie went to mass, went walking with her old pal Nora Willoughby, stayed in at night knitting. 'You'd swear she's never been a day away.' The refrain of friendly neighbours, the greatest compliment an emigrant could be paid. To journey unscathed. To remain true. Exile as a myth of stasis. Emigration as fidelity's enriching rite.

Elizabeth certainly had the air of a notary about her. She was terse, she was stern, she could be as scratchy as a starched uniform. She was thin, worn to the bone by nights of painful moaning and days of fighting her corner, the latter in defence of her professional judgment and her nationality. Woe betide anyone attempting to impugn either! Long stories recalling in detail the criticisms rebutted and the slurs denied stiffened our spines with every telling. They all concluded satisfactorily: 'I gave *them* their answer.' The colour would leave her face, then, and she'd reach for her Players. We all felt proud of her, but the stories unnerved us: they served to say, how distressing to be necessary to 'the English' (trans., the alien world) yet to be made feel unwanted at the same time. And we all thought, well aren't we better off here at home, after all?

Elizabeth, however, did not necessarily agree with that sentiment, and felt very irritated by the dead-and-alive character of Irish life. After a day or two at home she'd begin to get restless and would offer to wash down walls or dig the garden, requiring some light diversion of that kind to maintain her familiar output of energy. If some such outlet was not forthcoming she could get rather aggressive about the state of the country, and sometimes even about the attitudes of her nearest and dearest. I remember one hell of a political row in the course of which she called us all Communists, and scourged us verbally like a proper Dante Riordan. More Irish than the Irish themselves . . . . But I was afraid of her in those moods. I admired her guts, her tenacity, her utter belief in her own position. She had to be that way, I reasoned, to endure England. I just hated having to shake in my shoes because of it.

It was only in Elizabeth that I encountered such singleness. Other grown-ups home from England – men, respectable denizens of Main Street – never showed such fierce integrity. In them, there always seemed something blurred or softened, some minor addition to their original selves, a tiepin featuring the logo of London Transport, a trick of accent (Peadar Hickey used to say, 'How are *you*?' – his accent Lismore through and through, his emphasis pure Peckham Rye).

For men did go to England from Main Street. Emigration was never the prerogative of the lane, any more than it was that of the provinces, though it surprised me quite a bit to discover that Dubliners also crossed the water. Girls from Main Street also went, of course, girls like Chrissy and Elizabeth, exasperated finally by the nullity of home, striking out for independence with their twenties half-over, often never to be seen again. But it's the men I remember best, since their departure left their children in a state somewhat similar to my own, and I felt less unusual for a time, until the Daddy came back again for good or the whole family went to join him.

I remember one of my pals and his holidaying Da inviting me to go with them as they passed on a walk out the Deerpark Road. I accepted with pleasure, and a certain amount of excite-
56   ment. Since talk at home more often had Main Street doings as

its focus, rather than the lane or other paupers' quarters. I had a much more developed sense of the newsworthiness and novelty of Bill Egan's return. But I was sorry afterwards. Instead of hearing about bright lights and smart living in the great metropolis, as I thought I might from someone not related to me (my own people declining to for fear, I suppose, they'd feel guilty later for colouring my impressionable mind), Bill junior and I were treated to an avalanche of invective.

Never in all my listening days to lane-talk – and I listened to it close and long – had I heard such language; never had suspected that the father of a friend of mine, a man whom I myself knew to own a suit before he went to England, would curse and swear with such fluency and invention. And in front of children too! My own father, who was anything but square, spoke to me sharply when, in all innocence, I called one of the local mongrels a 'hoor', a term borrowed from Bocky Ford. Now here was Bill Egan scorching the ears off us with his terrible tongue.

He cursed the town and a lot of people in it; they were so stingy, he said, 'they wouldn't give their shit to the crows'. He denounced the countryside and all belonging to it, including not so veiled references to his wife's people. When we came to the cabins by the railway-gates, he fucked from a height the state of the country. 'God Christ Almighty!' he cried (a novel formulation to me, and I nearly laughed). Priests, brothers, and nuns came under the lash, everything and anything. The world consisted of cunts and fuckan eejits.

I never said anything about it, either at home or to my pal Billy. The whole performance was too amazing and too embarrassing to complain about. And of course I'd no idea what prompted it, apart from a vague sense that being forced to leave hearth, home and loved ones for icy digs in Kensal Rise must be a bitter pill to swallow. Next time I met him, though adult, Bill was, as the local expression has it, 'as game as paint', if anything, extra-jolly. I never happened onto his bitterness again, but that surprises me less than that one cloudburst of it when all we were doing was out walking, an activity that I'd hitherto understood adults to practise for the sake of their youngsters, not the other way around.

Compared to Mr Egan's shower of bile and Elizabeth's armour-plated defences, Church Lane's English contingent, so glibly condemned for their foolery, were the soul of harmlessness and honest-to-God good fun. The gaudy clothes, the speech dented by Cockney, the boastful street-corner bombast about drink and women (mostly, and more feelingly, about drink), seem now merely flesh wounds in the war of nerves in which every emigrant serves. Style and manner – some people even came home with new walks, rapid city struts; not always confined to girls in impossible (and surely sinful!) stiletto heels, either – were understandable blemishes, predictable deformities, tolerable insignia of altered lives.

Of course, they were 'shoving on', 'shaping', 'trying to cut a dash'. Why not? Even then, as I took in the criticism, I didn't see what fuelled it. I found myself more naturally drawn to the know-nothing exuberance of the temporarily returned, their longing to make a splash, their cultural anarchy. And this was only partly because I detested the asperity of our kitchen council, not for its lack of charity, since I had no moral self-consciousness then, but because its atmosphere made me feel intimidated, fearful, frail.

Besides, why shouldn't they have their holiday, their hullabaloo? Why shouldn't they feel cocky, now that they'd paid off the family debt to the town's hucksters? Everyone could eat sweet-cake now for a fortnight and real rashers too, not the customary handful of scraps from the bacon-slicer. Gin-and-limes could be consumed too, by the bucketful if needs be, though all the stay-at-home world would dispute its claim to be a proper drink. And, long after midnight, let the street resound to the cracked tenors and 'Hear my song, Violetta!'

If there was a deliberate undertow of *épater* to such carousing, so much the better, I thought. Because in one respect I knew Mam's criticisms to be true (Mam, source and inspiration of Swiss Cottage class-consciousness): these show-off visitors were nobodies. As soon as they turned Parks Road corner, making for the station with their flat, cardboard suitcases, they effectively resumed their anonymous lives: their hand-callousing, noisy, repetitive lives; their dirty, lonesome, well-paid lives. So weren't they right to act like somebodies when they could?

That's what the lane gave me, anyhow; a view of double-ness. I saw it in the place itself, in its active nullity, in the chronic incompleteness of poverty's finality. It was in my playmates too, in the uneven equilibrium between handball and hunger, debt and devilment that their lives represented. I learned that their lives were hectic, but its joy brittle. I learned that going out for the wren was a great gas, but that as sure as Confirmation or First Communion time came round, the same youngsters, just about as unrecognizable now in new clothes, would come knocking at our door again with, 'Me mother said you wanted to see me.' Only this time to meet with success; 'Oh, I do, child, sure aren't you looking lovely – here, now.' Silver coin pressed into pale, moist palm, immediate flight of recipient. (The new outfit had to be paid for somehow.)

With this abundance of otherness I freely identified, a glad act of psychic disobedience. And as for those gin-swilling, vowel-devouring peacocks in their British chain-store plumage, they became my archetypes of doubleness, embodiments of home's foreignness and the allure of the far away, specialists in longing and in longing mollified. Welcome aliens. Metropolitans. Brothers to whom in doubleness I felt my own life obscurely but enlargingly twinned.

III

THE DUCHY

1

'Picturesquely pitched on the banks of the Blackwater – ' Pat Lyons read, and there Brother Blake interrupted him: '"Picturesquely *pitched* . . . . " Well, sure that sounds like someone threw it there. You should say "picturesquely situated".'

Unabashed, Pat resumed. He was reading out his composition on Lismore Castle to the whole class. Blakey had asked him to. It had come first. I listened dully, alert only when the interruption came, though it was nowhere near admonishing enough to please me. I was mortified and cross. My effort had only come third.

I was upset because family, as well as personal, pride had been offended. The assignment excited me because it was so different from the usual 'A Wet Day' or 'A Bicycle Wheel Tells Its Own Story': it was a much more agreeable challenge to write about something substantial, familiar and famous. But I hadn't expected the grown-ups at home to join in. Usually they left me severely alone with my homework. Now, however, the novel opportunity arose to say something about the most dominant physical feature of their world. The Castle – Irish seat of the Duke of Devonshire – was the structure which denoted that the village belonged to a context larger than its own. Yet much as that belonging was cherished, the manner of it was hopelessly beyond the village's control. Everything connected with the Castle, besides the emotions it evinced, was pre-ordained, possessed, arbitrated over by 'others': nobles, superiors, employers. The Duke's dominion was a perfect and apparently indestructible embodiment of the soul of ownership: the dispossessed admiring the proprietor's fortress, the fleeced kissing the shears. I admired, too, not feeling particularly dispossessed. And so did Chrissy.

With an air of authority which clearly pleased her, she dictated, 'Built by King John in 1185 . . . ' and I bowed my head over the spotless copybook.

Assured by Chrissy's enthusiasm that this was going to be my finest literary hour to date, I was extremely concerned that the composition be a masterpiece of penmanship as well. Of all the attainments of primary school, the one I took most pride in was 'light writing'; script faint to the point of virtual illegibility, barely more prominent than the blankness of the paper it rested on, a film of whose perspiration it might be imagined to be: testament, in its fastidiousness, to superb nib control and delicacy of finger pressure! No easy accomplishment, given the equipment: the coarse, absorbent texture of the off-white, brown-flecked jotters, the wooden-shafted pen with a nib the size of a cockroach, and just as resistant to being toilet-trained, and school ink which came in powder form and had to be mixed; it evaporated leaving a sticky sludge at the bottom of the ceramic inkwells. Against such odds I pitted myself, anxious to acquire a skill which had, I perceived, overtones of decorum, care and ceremonial attention, a translation of colouring-book *politesse*.

There was a further not unimportant consideration. Over and above the satisfaction of calligraphic heroics for their own sake, a blot-free copybook could mean a slap-free start to the school day. At the very least it would spare me Blakey's jibes about how we shouldn't be trying to plant a row of turnips with our pens, though God knows maybe some of us'd be better off trucking in mud and dirt, because we just weren't able to tell A from B, and never would. 'So come out here.' Then would follow a list of names, a scraping of reluctant hobnailed boots as the victims advanced, the production of the length of seasoned ash. And *swish, swish*: four blows apiece. The tension, the moaning, the lads with their incompetent hands thrust under armpits and between knees, faces gargoyled to ward off tears, every ounce of their presence bent in wringing out the detestable ashen sting, the exposure, the affront.

'Third!' exclaimed Chrissy and Mam together, taken mightly aback. 'Who came first?' and when I told them, 'Humph!' ironically, as though detecting a design, 'Who got second?'

64   'John O'Connor.'

'Oh my God!' This surprised them so much that they had to turn to insults. 'John Butch, h'mm? Oul Mallet-skull . . . ?' Then, this attack of bile subsiding, 'What did he say?' (Blake, about mine).

'Too much history. He said I got it all out of a book.'

'Blasted cheek: does he take us for a parcel of know-nothings? What was Pat Lyons's like?'

I mentioned his alliterative indiscretion.

'Ha, picturesquely pitched, I'm sure. Where did he get that kind of language? Don't mind, boy; you're better than the whole lot of them put together.'

By this time I hardly minded at all, certainly not half as much as my elders and betters, with their mutterings about favouritism and mumbled explanations of how this blatant slight had come about. But Mam and Chrissy wouldn't rest until they'd arrived at a plausible salve for wounded self-respect. To do so was a sophisticated exercise in the hermeneutics of community attachments, requiring considerable imaginative and forensic skill, allowing intuition free play, invoking precedent and provenance and eking every last ounce of potential significance from the commonplace, until at length, slaked and satisfied by their thoroughness, they had nothing more to say but, 'That's it, surely.'

'Oh, that's it, now.'

Secure interpretation of the everyday was a must, so little else tolerated or responded to interpretation.

Perhaps one reason that Chrissy and Mam vented their frustration so vehemently was that they'd never expected an opportunity to express themselves formally about the Castle. To be sure, the form was adventitious, unforeseen, but at least they knew they were equal to its demands (more than equal, indeed, as Brother Blake's criticism pointed out). Maybe they thought my failure to come first a judgment on what they expressed. Or was it simply that, irrespective of the approach, the Castle maintained its distance from common life and thereby, passively and inscrutably, upheld its identity as an enigma – impenetrable, unapproachable, remote? It simply stood in our midst as an irreproachable monument to land, money, grandeur, supremacy and all the other trappings of Mammon, which were not for the likes of us (whose kingdom was not of this world). And yet, for all its difference, we   65 thought there was something of 'our own' about it, we extended to it a secret sympathy, an illicit intimacy, as though in spite of all appearances, we understood it. Tacitly, though without embarrassment, we gave the symbol psychic house-room (How could we not? Wasn't it a fact of life?); we domes-ticated the enigma, thereby making it enigmatic indeed – teasing, taunting, ticklesome. If Waterford City was known as *urbs intacta* (never penetrated by siege), what variety of virginity might describe our situation? Certainly some loftier, purer classification: perhaps we were the Holy Innocents, sanctified by our elimination from history, limbo's founding dynasty.

We were proud of our intimacy, but it was an intimacy with what lay beyond us, and we remained unrequited. So our pride was without hope. Our history – that chain of events in the first twenty years of this century which we could definitely call our own – discounted all the Castle stood for, yet had not installed in our awareness anything like so powerful or secular a symbol as the Castle. Nationalism's spiritual picturesque-ness was no match, on a day-to-day basis, with scenic ditto. Every time the Duke's standard – a corkscrew of green snake on a lime field – was raised, the victory of the Republic seemed more like the triumph of party instead of people, since we in Lismore were still attached to a remoteness; we were still experiencing decentredness of a sort, surrounded by a code of cordons and warnings to trespassers, involved in a species of psychological absenteeism. And not only psychological, either; the Duke was still the great landlord.

It even looked as if the Castle had its back to the town, because all we could see was the façade that fronted the river, the apartments contemplating the deep woods and haunches of mountain which it held in fee, averse to where we lived. The river was alive with salmon and trout, but not everyone could fish for them. Permission had to be sought 'from the office' (trans., from the bailiff) and very few could afford the permit or the tackle. All most locals had was the time to fish, not the material wherewithal. But a certain amount of poaching went on, especially downriver where lived a family bearing an Irish nickname, the Garabhánachs ('the coarse ones'). Blackwater *mafiosi*, masters of the night, dare-devils. Even on our highly respectable table a whole salmon would sometimes appear, payment for a funeral perhaps. At those dinners we would have rare silence, and savour, along with the delicate flesh (the colour and softness of mild twilight), the unfamiliar juices released by wrong-doing. It was like eating royalty.

Since everything about the Castle except its physical presence seemed tainted by abstractions, I suppose I shouldn't be surprised to find my knowledge of it so slight. But I am. Did I repress my curiosity about it in order to keep the reality of its 'difference' intact? Or did I just shun it, thinking that since the way of life it represented was not for the likes of me I would make a virtue of my disenfranchisement and seek a way of life that was?

Of course I know a certain amount about its history, but I know nothing at all about its life. I know that it has three hundred and sixty-five windows. . . . But is that true, really? I think not, now. I think that's just an example of the myth of the everyday which the Castle inspired, its presence attributing to the most trivial detail the possibility of being part of a system. A window is a purpose, an integer of vision. We lived in the duchy of synecdoche.

One good thing the Castle did, though: it gave work. There was the Castle farm, the sawmill, the hatchery where the salmon fry were incubated, and there were wood-rangers and water-bailiffs as well. I make no mention of the office, where rents were paid and complaints lodged. Two Protestants supervised it, one of them our neighbour, Mr Copley, the other a man by the name of Arthur King, remarkable to childish me, not for his name but for his car, a baby Fiat, which looked like the shell of a snail.

Yet even though the Castle's range of activities made it a going concern, and certainly diminished its picturesque properties for those employed there, still there seemed to be an elusive quality in its enterprise. It was as though the products of the work were not translated into the life of the town. And so even approaching the Castle from a practical standpoint it was still quite difficult for me to ascertain what really went on there. 'Lismore Castle is a Private Residence' a big sign proclaimed. It was simply beyond the bounds of possibility to enter one of its rooms, to sit on a seat, to breathe its atmosphere. The grounds were opened once a year for a garden fête to support the Jubilee Nurses Fund and Mam and

Chrissy delighted in examining the splendid hydrangeas and immaculate herbaceous borders, handiwork of Dave Montgomery, the Northern gardener. Otherwise, the only reason to venture within the Castle purlieu was business, purely business.

It may have been that its employees confused me, but I sensed most palpably the invisibility of Castle life because there seemed to be elements of ghostliness about them. John Noel Pollard was a butler there, and sometimes even (I heard it proudly said) went home to Chatsworth with His Grace. Morning and evening when the Duke was in residence one saw a glimpse of mackintosh, dickey and bow-tie gliding down Chapel Street to work. A quiet man, soul of discretion, a shadow of high living, a walking borderline.

There was the man called Pad the Bishop, a sawyer, dressed perpetually in black, with black eyes as deep-set and as fixed as rivets or as knots in oak, black-avis'd too, hefty mutton-chop whiskers unshorn, his face otherwise brownish, as though porter-soaked. He never said hello to anyone. He was too forbidding a sight even for us kids to shout after.

And there was Moss, Mam's brother, my friend, my mentor in melancholia, to whom a three-volume study would hardly begin to do justice, about the sorrow of whose life it is so difficult to speak. Pad the Bishop's colleague. Who lost the use of his left hand in that same sawmill – disguising the fact, and at the same time drawing attention to it, by always wearing a thumbless black glove. Who'd show me the scar sometimes, if I nagged him to: unnatural, metallic brightness of skin, wizened, hamstrung tendons. Who was just about deaf from the saws' callous singing. Whose voice was as low and slow-moving as a salmon in sunshine. He asked for nothing, refused nothing, married nothing, sired nothing. A true exile, standing at the Red House corner with his cronies in the evenings. He'd drink if it was offered, not otherwise. He'd smoke a pipe, go to Rosary. Placid to the point of anaesthesia, stoical as a boulder. Desire's enemy. Less ghost than ruin . . . Beckett-fodder. That the current of life should run so unobtrusively, so inexpressively, and still be truly life . . . .

The superiors were strange, too; but no doubt they were supposed to be, at least it was expected that they avail of the latitude which history and fortune had bestowed on them. Prilaux certainly did, but that wasn't thought strange, at least not to begin with. His behaviour conformed to a model of acceptability which was lost on me, but which I was unable to criticize seeing as how Mam approved of it ('Isn't he a fine figure of a young fella?') and Chrissy was captivated by his crinkly curls and his candid handsome face. None of the leathery labouring farmer about him – and I believe I heard in the women's tone, 'Thank God! At last, a gent, a swell, a toff . . . .'

I don't know exactly what Prilaux did. Steward, agent, overseer, under-secretary: the realms of influence and tiers of attainment were something I could only imagine. Besides, what mattered was his visibility. 'Morning. Fine day!' he klaxoned in his strangled, educated accent, trotting through the town on his immense chestnut hunter. Now that was class! In a series of delightfully casual gestures he'd dismount, tether the beast to a lamp-post and stroll into the Co-op. 'Morrow, Pat; say, be a good fellow . . . .' You could hear him all over the street. But what cared he who knew his business? His voice spoke of his station: powerful, tactless, carefree. And then one day he was gone – cavalry twill, ruddy complexion, chestnut mare and all. Where? 'Up the country, somewhere,' spoken resentfully, because nobody had any real means of knowing; because everybody found now that they didn't know Mr Prilaux at all. 'Must've got a better offer . . . .' Silence. Incredulity.

Mr Copley vanished too, which struck me as even stranger. He more or less lived with us, sure. And he wasn't young, he was a 'nice, natural being', in his middle-years now a bookkeeper, a bachelor, as mild as a clergyman, as kindhearted a neighbour as anyone could want – a lot better than one of our own crowd, whom in modesty and friendliness he sought to resemble. Plus, were more proof needed of his amiable heart, Mam repeated over and over how he would exclaim, seeing her dressed for the chapel, 'Oh isn't it fine for you!' He lived next door, and Minnie Foley with the whiskers was his cook and char.

No throwback he. Mr Copley was no hussar *manqué*, had no equine leanings, didn't in any way suggest those social archetypes of Anglo-Ireland, the buck, the youngest son, the feckless student, the subaltern, all of whom were evident in   69

Prilaux's make-up (which is probably why the town took to him; not only was he lively, he was recognizable). But few knew Mr Copley, who kept himself to himself, like a decent Christian. Only why in the name of goodness would someone as unencumbered as he, as self-effacing, as assimilated to the no-horse town, want to do anything to himself? It was a great shock when he did, however: we realized that there must have been a Mr Copley there that nobody saw. I wasn't told what happened, but I remember screening myself behind adult skirts and listening. 'Razor . . . bath water . . . police,' I heard. And I saw Mr Copley no more.

In view of such all-pervading poor visibility, it was no surprise to us that the Duke and all belonging to him had no presence, no vitality, no immediacy as far as we were concerned. We didn't expect him to impinge on us as a human being. Distance was ingrained in us. No doubt he and his retinue drove out in the shooting-break to inspect the far-flung estate, to bag pheasants, to condescend to their British brethren, whose homes and farms occupied all that fertile valley. Moss and the men of his time doffed their caps as he passed. But I didn't know him from Adam. Or his guests either, which occasionally proved frustrating. President Kennedy's sister, Kathleen, came to stay and 'insisted' (Mam proudly claimed) on walking up to early Sunday mass with the skivvies from the kitchen. The whole town was frustrated when Fred Astaire was one of the guests at the house-party. We could hardly contain ourselves. Aristocracy bedamned! Here was one of the new, more uplifting élite, someone to whom self-advertisement was, we believed, second-nature. So surely we'd catch a glimpse of him, latch on to the twentieth-century if only by the strength of an eye-lash, snap out of our familiar feudal shuffle and hit the high-spots, just for an instant, with the Tzar of Terpsichore! There was hardly a man, woman or child in the town who didn't, privately, surreptitiously, obsessively think of themselves as Ginger Rogers – speaking of whom, by J., she must be Irish; where else would she get that hair?

But sight or sound of Fred we never saw. What did we expect, though, really – that he climb to the top of the flag-tower and give an exhibition, the taps amplified for the edifi-

cation of the whole countryside, thereby proving his bodily
existence while ensuring that he kept his distance? I don't
know. What right had we to expect anything? The more daring
spirits of the town – Chrissy, for one – said when the visit was
over that it was a shame that the Duke didn't think of having
a dance in his guest's honour. But the Duke wasn't that sort:
private was as private did. And Fred remained in privacy as
well, a rumour of a person, image only; in our eyes, all his
being concentrated in the unique form of a celluloid dervish.
Still – we attempted not to feel offended – sure how could you
not take to a fellow by the name of Fred; such a candid, manly
kind of a name . . . . At the same time, it was a shame, we
agreed, that given the Duke's resources, all he could think of in
the way of diversion for the town was the garden fête. Didn't
he know as well as we did that the town was out on its feet,
that compared to our state, the paralysis of Joyce's Dublin was
a veritable St Vitus's dance? I don't know. But divil a Ritz did
the Duke encourage us to put on.

Here again, however, consistency was not the rule – mercifully, since inconsistency at least kept the state of things lifelike. The Duke did offer one notable stimulus to our cultural
edification. Whether this was what he had in mind, I have no
way of knowing. I would guess not, though, since if it was it
would mean that His Grace could hardly avoid the benevo-
lently satirical aspect of his gesture. And he was born to a
condition which immunized him from such game-playing.
Besides, he was only a plain man doing his duty. Selfless, in
his way. (And, as I keep wanting to say, invisible.)

His contribution to the mind of Lismore consisted of no less
than that Prince of the Turf, Royal Tan, whom the Duke purch-
ased not long after his triumph in the Grand National and
whom he retired to the lush grazing of County Waterford for
an old age of ease and admiration. The town was jubilant –
we'd been noticed! We were in the papers! Royal Tan was
used to such attention; we were not. Everyone went to pay
their respects to our famous guest, delighted to have such a
celebrated athlete to talk about, with whose exploits we could
all identify, a star we could understand as though he were one
of ourselves. And visible, too.

He arrived late in the year, October, I think. We'd go over to
see him after school. He had a paddock to himself behind

Dunne's cottage, and stayed at the far end of it, by the gate, a brown statue in the dank autumn air. We couldn't get close to him without wrecking our jackets, so we peeped over the brambles and waited for him to do something unprompted. He never did. Sometimes a couple of old-timers would come by to pay their visit. They'd stand apart from us, murmuring, reviewing the great stayer's career, caps pushed well back the better to scratch heads in amazement, envisaging the air full of divots and jockey's curses, fortunes changing hands, honour redounding and glory reflected – then, at last, sidling reluctantly away, unable to see more, and a final murmur: 'Wisha, God bless him, anyhow . . . . '

2

The Castle was the Duchy's centrepiece, of course, but up and down the valley, from Fermoy (fifteen miles west) to the sea at Youghal (fifteen miles south) there were establishments with mores and appurtenances just as difficult for me to visualize. Homes of the gentry: Glencairn, Salterbridge, Ballinwillin, Tourin, Dromana, Headborough . . . . Each within sight of the other (each its neighbour's sentry), but snug behind screens of beech and removed from the common thoroughfare by shady driveways, choosing custodianship of the slow, black, powerful river over the fellowship of the road.

No doubt it wasn't necessarily the case that these demesnes were deliberately installed as Castle satellites. It looked that way, though, all the more so since those who owned them had, with one or two outstanding exceptions (the Villiers-Stuarts of Dromana, for example), little or no truck with valley life. They were people who'd retired from imperial service and now were gentle-folk, meaning, as far as I could see, that they did nothing. Lilies of the field they were, neither siring children, nor tilling land, nor like the town's beached souls, making their peace with God. They seemed to have found in our valley simply a place to be, a place to wait out their time. Accustomed

72

to being abroad all their active lives, they retained the vestige of that condition to the end, just as they retained 'Major' and 'Captain'. Only now they served in the temperate zone and in a comatose district – inexpensive too; lusher and (being unfamiliar) less changed than the green and pleasant acres of their youth. Cultural refugees sharing a secret, shameful kinship with the men of no property whose labour they needed but whose existence they shunned. Yet still they stood to attention by the stately river, as though expecting the royal barge of another *Fidei Defensor* to appear, as though they had not been evacuated by history.

We knew them, a little; the family did, I mean. Mam knew them best, of course, had seen them in their Edwardian heyday. And she would have made it her business to know them in any case, being insatiable in her study of genealogy and the ways of rich-folk (perusing the *Sunday Express* for the latest doings of Billy Wallace . . .). She was able to think of these types as people. No wonder: Hadn't she and Dad danced the night away at Shane Jameson's twenty-first birthday party? The car was sent in for them. Dad let down any amount of whiskey, but it only made him dance the more. My eyes shone, listening, but not as brightly as hers, remembering.

Georgie generally had less contact with the gentry than Dad had. There were fewer gentry, of course. And I think the old guard looked very slightly askance at him, as though wondering if he *quite* had his father's winning combination of Edwardian *savoir faire* and Yankee know-how. Well, he didn't *quite*, because he was living in a world that didn't ask enough of him, a world in which it was impossible, and worse still, seemed irrelevant, to make the kind of break-through that his powerful forebears had.

Nevertheless, George could impress in his own way. Mam was fond of telling of how when he was working at Maxwell's, some woman, a guest, a writer, engaged him in spirited conversation about matters historical and professed herself, according to one of the hands who afterwards told Mam, to be most impressed by Geo's wide learning and sharp analyses. Forty years after Anglo-Ireland's swansong, Mam was not at all critical of the swanky guest's apparent surprise that a workman knew anything other than a few prayers and quaint phrases. She was too busy being proud of Georgie and point- 73 ing the lesson to me (*Read!*) to think like that.

It's also tempting to believe that Mam's critical powers were temporarily suspended because she needed to concentrate on organizing the story. The story seemed organized because of the air of composure and instruction which attended its telling. Mam didn't quite raise an index finger or stand forth as though sermonizing on a mount. But all that was there in the measured tone, the pauses, the teller's steady eye.

Not all Mam's stories were accompanied by these effects. But the one about being taken out to see Dromana by Mr Gorringe, the agent, was. And so were the tales of Chef and Madame (pronounced 'Madam' by Mam), a French couple, members of the Duke's entourage. Perhaps it was from them that she got the word which I never heard anyone else use – *cadet*, employed pejoratively as a verb as well as noun. So-and-so (from the lane, inevitably) was a useless *cadet*; he should be earning a living, not *cadeting* around. It means to idle, to affect gutter dandyism, to sponge drink. (For more, see Lenehan in Joyce's 'Two Gallants'.)

Other than that, which may well be totally wrong, I have no idea of what Chef and Madame said or did, which annoys me, as it's another door shut against my entering Castle life. All I remember is Mam's tone. But that's memory: if it were complete it would be difficult to contain, and redundant to exercise. And the tone is something. It gave the sense that what was being recounted was special. It lent the material wholeness, lifted it out of the common run of talk. I wasn't always able to appreciate the specialness because it seemed to have something to do with the influence and presence of the gentry, of which I had no direct experience. So I couldn't quite *see*, always . . . . Not that I minded: the stories' component of invisibility made them much more interesting – family folktales instead of history, parables instead of home truths.

It must have suited me to keep the gentry at a distance. I say this because I find it hard to believe now, that when I got my own bike – Georgie (of course) bought it for me from Simon Chute, Colonel Foster's grandnephew – and was able to visit any big house I wanted, I just didn't bother; I whizzed past their tall, green, frozen-looking gates without a second thought. Joe McDokes and The Three Stooges were what occupied my imagination, not colonization: my only ache was for a full present; the past was an accident, just one of those things.

And cycling was glorious, it brought me to enough places where I'd never been to make me not miss tentatively pedalling up lime-guarded avenues to places where I wasn't wanted. It wasn't just me either: we all learned to ride at the same time – Peter Hickey (who taught me), John O'Connor, Liam Murphy, Tommy Heffernan, Paddy Farrell. In those days traffic was so light – nothing apart from horse and donkey carts and an odd bus or creamery lorry – that we could freewheel with impunity, three abreast, arms across each others shoulders . . . . Flying down the Sweep, Bottle Hill, Corbett's Hill, the Kennel Heights. Never before was the mind so sated by the body's power, never since has air been so fresh and sweet.

We went to where the river Bride nuzzled swampily into the Blackwater, and tried to slither out to where the poachers' black skiffs lay up-ended on mud flats, beetles basking before nightwork stirred them again. We went to Kilahalla to the ship. A real ship, its appearance possible because the river was tidal as far inland as Cappoquin. A dirty old Dutch coaster, the *De Wadden* of Rotterdam, but wonderfully mysterious to us. We were in school when it carried on its business of loading pit-props for South Wales, so whenever we visited it silence and idleness wrapped it all around: spectral, gull-grey emissary from beyond the sea. Typically enough, it stood too far out in the water for us to get on board. But looking had its own satisfaction: it was something to see foreignness. What we didn't see, the big houses, we didn't care about. We sped through the whole of that land with never the slightest thought to who owned it. Any such consideration would have struck us as a massive irrelevance, for what bearing could it possibly have on the freedom of the road?

So removed were the gentry from us that it was almost possible to pretend they didn't exist, even on the day of the races, the Lismore point-to-point, their festival. The races were another mark of Lismore's distinctiveness; it was the only meeting within a fifteen-mile radius of the town. But it wasn't that so much that we kids were glad of, but the fact that we got the day off school and the knowledge that the whole town would be infected with a kind of Church Lane looseness.

Race day was usually around the start of spring ploughing, and in addition to Maiden Plates and Selling Handicaps had all kinds of peripheral novelties. A one-legged young man, with his head to one side like Christ in our oleographs, sat in the bushes by the gate and plucked his banjo lackadaisically. The man who lay on his bare back amid broken bottles came every year, and sometimes bent an iron bar over his upper arm for good measure. We watched his tattoos flinch in the intense torque of his muscles, and wondered if he'd learned the knack of bending in the Navy. The tattoos were so deep-dyed, so blue, it was as though the sea had imbued the strong man with something of itself.

There were stalls selling gaudy trinkets, and a marquee dispensing Murphy's stout, and there were swingboats containing little girls with bows in their hair clutching the white plastic handbags which were all they could still use from their First Communion trousseaus, and – uuUp went the boat! – puking all over their petulant Daddies.

The fortune-teller was there too, and around her tiny tent there was a vague group of men and women trying to look casual and not like a queue, but casting tense glances at each other to intimidate any prospective place-poachers. They appeared furtive not just becuse they were nervous about what awaited them within, not even because they were afraid some neighbour would see them and deride their longing, but because going to a fortune-teller was a sin. It broke, I think, the first commandment: 'I am the Lord, thy God, thou shalt not have strange gods before Me.' And as well as that, of course, it used in reverse one of the most familiar of Catholic formats: confession. I'm sure many a client found the reversal mighty pleasant. Instead of laying bare your past life to a punitive priest, all one had to do was listen to motherly tones providing instruction in danger and desire. For just five bob. It had to seem worth it.

The sober-suited punters awaiting of the mistress of fate's cards, ball or tea-leaves were the most discreet and serious gamblers on the field. But there were plenty of opportunities for those with less metaphysical wagers to place. There were swarthy women in charge of wheel-'em-in stalls. You ran a

coin down a groove onto a board of numbered squares; if your coin ended up in a square, not touching any of its borders, you won something – choice of stuffed toy, rubber ball or three glass marbles in a box. It was impossible, of course, but the first two or three pennies were a pleasure to throw away; one wheeled them in with a spendthrift's exuberance.

Then there was the three-card trick, all the more attractive for being illegal. The performer was as deft at shifting his little table (a cloth over a crate) as he was at switching the cards. The trick was made to look so easy, so enticing: any fool could do it. The cards moved with winning slowness, the queen virtually pausing for you to admire her sleek profile and sly, inward smile, so that you felt so absolutely, positively sure of her whereabouts that cupidity felt like a blessing. But just before you placed your hot little shilling on the sure thing some stranger in a black slouch hat would laconically throw down a quid, and collect handsomely. Well, maybe next time . . . . Then next time the trickster's hands flew among the cards with unprecedented finesse and stopped when least expected. Next time the befuddled bettor always lost.

It was strange the way that everything took its form from the occasion. Fortune-telling was gambling; the three-card trick was a compressed, exaggerated, hysterical version of racing. The stall-holders of the wheel-'em-ins and rifle range seemed the gentry's shady kin, reciprocal acts in the one circus, invisible save on this day of the sporting chance. We, the public, were the enticeable, naïve, unassertive world they dealt with.

And yes, it was impossible to ignore the gentry, finally. This was not just because the races were held on the Castle Farm, or because the voice that announced the runners and riders was posh and lofty. It wasn't even because race-day was the one day in the year that they revealed themselves as a community. I surreptitiously eyed them diving into hampers and swigging out of hip-flasks under the stand of beech by the road, well back from the common throng. They produced extraordinarily handy items, such as rugs to lounge on, field-glasses and shooting-sticks, which to me were the acme of class and common sense. They brayed and squawked to their hearts' content in their own lingo. They roared into view in shooting-brakes and Land-Rovers. Their women wore trousers. And of course they owned just about all the horses.

It wasn't even this last fact that impressed the gentry on me.

I was only interested in the horses inasmuch as they were the pretext for this saturnalia of jeopardy and cash. The racing itself was terrible. Mutinous animals being flogged over hedges and ditches: that's all it amounted to, as far as I could see. I much preferred the bookies, the syntax of their sign language, their outsized doctors' bags, their strange, energetic cries, 'Three-to-one, bar one! Five-to-one the field.'

I was too small to see much. And in any case the races took place mainly out in the country; most of the time all anyone could see were figures flitting beyond the branches of the naked trees. Still, it was possible to get a taste of the race if you stood by a jump. There one caught the sensational urgency of approaching hoofs and the moments of strained silence as, with a sound like fibre tearing, the snorting, airborne steeds had their bellies struck by the jump's mane of brushwood.

Standing by a jump had a couple of drawbacks, however. One was that it was impossible to get back to see the finish in time. The other was that every so often a horse fell and, as the official phrase went, had to be destroyed. The poor thing would strive to right itself, wild-eyed, frothing, whinnying with terror and pain. But all its efforts only made a shallow grave in the moist, spring earth. The vet went to his case. The slim, brass-barrelled humane-killer was applied to the temple. A last lurch and – .

Finishes frightened me too, though. Not the desperate striving of the hacks to be past the post and out of this; not the giant, bony figure of the great McLernan (champion jockey of all east Munster) stretched taut in the stirrups, welting his mount to glory; not the clash of rival tributes in the turbulent crowd. What frightened me, and forcefully reminded me that the gentry were no mere presence, but power, was the whipper-in. He too went on horseback and wore an official colour, though not the gay silks of jockeys, but the blood-red blazer of the huntsman (and, as I thought, the soldier). His job was to clear the way along the run-in to the winning-post, and he managed to press the crowd back quite simply: by riding as close to it as he possibly could and waving aloft, in threat, his riding-crop. 'Get back!' he barked. 'Make way!'

In his reckless policing and scarlet coat and horrid unenjoyment on his face, he seemed a hellish figure. He'd run you down as quick as he'd look at you. He's brute force, I thought, he doesn't give a damn; he's everything I heard about the English in the terrible days gone by. His presence suggested that I was quite wrong to think that race-day was all looseness, all squandering, all pleasure. He was purpose and order. He was alien, hostile. He charged at us with the force of a law, terrifying us for our own good.

I ran from him like a chastised whelp, and although, he was especially careful not to touch anyone and I realized, however inarticulately, that he was not a throw-back, not a symbol, not a force of destiny, but really only a jacket on a horse, my mind was turned into a tissue of painful smouldering, as though a branding-iron had touched it. I saw power without substance, force without salience, form without tact. For maybe twenty seconds I felt spurned and trodden down. Twenty seconds was plenty.

3

The whipper-in put the heart crossways on me, yet I felt free to repudiate him. His behaviour was hateful: I hated him right back. I don't think older people were quite able, or willing, to be so cut-and-dried in their reactions – and I mean not only in their reactions to the whipper-in, whose mode of discipline they seemed to approve, shouting commands of their own to support his, but also to the gentry at large. They seemed in some way tied psychologically to the gentry's presence.

The tie took various forms. For one thing, the valley had no history of rebelliousness: poaching was about the only form of local deviance – by no means a trivial one, to my mind, but one which has no place in the legends of the national struggle that were handed down to us (which may be unfortunate). And then when I saw those old lads admiring Royal Tan, or when I noticed Moss and his cronies doffing their caps as an elegant black roadster swished by, or even at the races looking at gaggles of elderly labourers leaning on the paddock fence and gazing in deep amaze at the steaming, exemplary creature now being fussed by the foulard fraternity (I wonder where they got those neckerchiefs, the ones with the pattern of amoeba swimming on a piss-yellow field) – simply being present in the particular theatre of gestures suggested to me that some principle of unity, or at least of implication, was at work.

I even saw it at home. Staunch though Mam was in her nationalist affections – none stauncher: she'd bite the head off anyone who dared murmur a demurral – she still bought a Poppy every year. There weren't many in the town who were invited to, either. But Miss Anson always came to our house and received a half-crown to remember the fallen of Flanders by. And if Geo objected he was soon made to desist. Of course, Mam had her own memories of the Great War, of the boys she knew who never came back from it (quite a number volunteered to go from loyal Lismore). Her first daughter was born on Armistice Day; she was christened Mary but known forever as Peace. And what did Georgie know?

It must have been hard for his generation. The patterns of close attachment between master and man had loosened considerably by the time George came into his manhood, and responsibility for moral exemplification had passed entirely to the officers of another empire, the clergy. No wonder he, my father and my father's Dublin friends had no time for priests. Yet there were elements of the whipper-in about Geo too, in his fiery temper, his unpredictable vitality, his ability to make me fear him. But it was all unwitting. The instrument on horseback acted deliberately, secure in his power for the time being. George struck out blindly, innocently, as though through the bars of a cage, as though to snap for good his real and imagined bands.

My generation, perhaps, is the first to be in a position to disregard loyalty either to Christ or to Caesar. It is tempting to think so – since I'd like to be proud of my generation. Besides, it makes excellent cultural sense to take the gentry's invisibility at face value, and to regard priests as simply religious functionaries. But I'm not in sufficiently close contact with my generation to know if it thinks along these lines. Maybe it's tempting to hope for the best, for a set of liberating loyalties, because it seems to me now that such a possibility existed when I was growing up. Though, of course, I may be able to say that only because possibility exalts every childhood; it's the hallmark of the child's openness and ignorance.

The vestiges of loyalty that I observed around me were hard to understand. I took them to be reminders of continuity, but the continuum to which the village's star had been hitched was, as far as I could see, going nowhere. Yet, I suppose when centuries of continuity stall, the mechanisms which kept it running smoothly for so long are bound to run on a little, fuelled by compulsiveness and uncertainty. No generation should ever take upon itself the task of undoing the work of a few hundred predecessors, though in order to achieve anything at all it probably has to believe it can. In Lismore, however, there was nobody equal to the job, no heroic consciousness to facilitate a return to the days before the Duchy.

Just as well, no doubt; complexity is more nourishing to the spirit than reverie. There was no concept of complexity, either, though. There was a landscape – a mindless, enduring litter of evidence.

Even before King John was a twinkle in his daddy's eye, the valley had been settled by monks and monastery. And even before that there must have been something going on at the Round Hill, a mound two miles east of town overlooking the river, from which the town takes its name. God only knows what such a druidic remnant really represents.

We know that Edmund Spenser knew the valley. So did Sir Walter Ralegh, and an impoverished Robert Boyle, afterwards Earl of Cork, and who knows who else of their contemporaries besides. The valley was a natural attraction for coast-hugging, westward-tending adventurers – I assume they hugged the coast as long as they could, for protection. And the Blackwater estuary was the first major one they would have come to without a sizeable fortified town at its mouth.

There is a town there now, of course, Youghal, but I don't think it was there to any extent before Ralegh came in from the ocean and built a jail on the site. The town in those parts long ago was Ardmore, home of a celebrated round tower, a much more impressive and more mystical edifice than Lismore Castle. It's easier for me to appreciate the tower for what it is, rather than for what it represents. Of course, it can

81

be made to stand for the solitary, embattled and enduring Church, beacon of the Dark Ages when only Irish monasticism stood between the Northmen and the lights going out all over Europe. But it's a strain to employ such terms; the struggle against darkness is no longer being waged on remote beach-heads in County Waterford. Unlike the Castle, the tower is historically complete: its meaning is bounded by the era of its service. And although still intact, in every other respect it's like all the other ruined abbeys and disused graveyards that dot the country from top to bottom – a placid, assimilated shell. An icon, the invisibility of whose inner life is entirely appropriate. But it wasn't on an estuary, and so Youghal was an ideal point of entry, wide, welcoming waterway. To express a thought too sacrilegious for nationalists, once again – in the wake of King John – nature was not on the side of the natives. The river was tidal. So, up came Gloriana's crew: nothing to stop them.

What did they see, those *conquistadores*, stealing up that still, accommodating river? Green slopes on either bank, rising gently, densely, as though they were the dark waters reproduced in an even more permanent form. Penumbrous, impenetrable. They met the river's unexpected, right-angle sweep west at Cappoquin, where there was nothing, nothing to attack or appropriate. Then, at last, Lismore, the Castle – the relief of seeing in that fastness something recognizably their own.

They sailed in clear and free. No people. If the forests harboured natives, they showed no sign. The land existed in a state of perfect integrity: aqueous, unmoving, arboreal, silent. A cathedral, a queen, a virgin. Like the James River, the Charles River, Potomac, Hudson – the penetrations without number later on. And it so little resembled property, being undefended. The urge to possess it, to seize it like a treasure, to treasure it so jealously that power became the sole metaphysic of occupancy . . . . That urge must have been as irresistible as an event in the subconscious. To pitch picturesquely, to shed blood, burn and starve in honour of possessions . . . . That lust to grasp this peace at all costs, this unmanned world, this kingdom without factions . . . . From what did such unstaunchable desire arise, this sacrilege-sized need to rupture the chaste greenery and husband it, this immense impulse to settle, as though the object of adventuring were anchorage, refuge, port after stormy sea?

And out of the husbandry grew a mind. The ardour of their lordships' eyes perceived the valley in a wholly new way. Their longing was secular, material. They freely thought the world their plaything; there was nobody to put a check on their avarice. The mind they fostered was called 'property'. Once mindfulness was installed, once a scale of values was introduced (whether consciously as an intellectual habit or just as a means of attempting to calibrate lust), once owner-ship became a synonym for living – then the beauty turned terrible. The place could never be just a place again. In addition, making immodest the whole accident of locality, there would be somebody's sense of it to cope with. The valley lost its nature and entered history. The appropriators, who retained the freedom of mind to do whatever they pleased, pretended that this didn't happen, or behaved as though history meant green reverie. Which was their undoing, requiring more freedom than they knew how to contain, eliminating challenge, corrupted by absolute power, their aftermath the mock-heroic present of my childhood with its stagnation, emigration and the new invaders, tourists.

Coming up from a swim in the strand we'd see them disem-barking, strange number plates, sometimes from remote parts of Ireland, oftener from England: BMD, VEX and GB stuck on the rear, which we translated with somewhat wistful sarcasm as 'going back'. The party usually consisted of Mum and Dad and an aged parent – the wife's mother, I always thought, having formed the impression from BBC comedy shows that she couldn't be kept out of anything. The women smoothed their frocks and Dad filled his pipe and they crossed the road to gaze blankly at the inscrutable Castle.

What did they make of it, those Magellans of the Morris Minor? I suppose for most of them it was just another roadside attraction, one more historical float in the procession of Ireland's eye-catching vistas and edifices. A five-minute stop could hardly allow for much experience, nor could the couple of lines in the AA book that might have influenced them to take the road through Lismore. And as for the semi-willed fortuit-ousness of their possessing the resources to be in our midst in the first place, the very fact that they lived with notions of mobility and choice, those were factors enabling them to view the Castle innocently, with wonder, as a prop in fairyland. Did they know how lucky they were to be savouring history without complexes, to gaze in restful amazement at what was so above and beyond them?

Who knows what they knew? Their gazetteers and handbooks gave them some information – quoting Thackeray on the Blackwater, 'the Irish Rhine', assuring them that the Castle was indeed a splendid example of something or other, but closed to the public. No information, apart from that regarding privacy, was available at the site. And the tourists never spoke: that is, sometimes they asked a question of the men sitting on the first arch, but they never even bothered to look at us. Usually instead of words, a camera was produced – one of the Castle, *snap*: one of the reach of river eastward to the hazy upland; one of the women, the Dad, to our envious approval, commemorating his presence by self-effacingly, though decisively, operating the machinery.

It didn't bother us in the slightest that we were ignored. That way we could observe at our ease Mum in her cotton-print and cardigan, bent-kneed Mother in tweed, spindly, shirt-sleeved Dad. In fact, it seemed appropriate now, picturing that endlessly repeated summer scene, that it largely consisted of a dumb-show, in which it wasn't clear who was looking at what and what exactly they were seeing – a pantomime of gesture and façade.

Besides we were too buoyant from our swim to feel anything one way or another about strangers. Where we swam, however, was not the Blackwater. What we called the Strand was the Abh' na Sead, a small tributary of the big black one which raced down the mountain, draining sheep-pastures. There was a pool there in which we splashed and floundered all summer long, and where later on (show-offs home from boarding-school) we learned to smoke and, much less rewardingly, hid in bushes on the girls' side. We could have swam in the Blackwater. Lads from Church Lane did, down at the rock. But it was only the likes of those reckless, unselfconscious ones that could give their all to fighting the terrible undertow. We weren't able: at least we were warned not to, as though our people knew that we hadn't the strength or heart for such disporting.

Tourists were not confined to family saloons, however, and in their other manifestation, the bus, we found them somewhat more of a tease. This was due to their arrival in force, partly: it really made us feel that the town was something and that the age of the horse-and-cart was surely doomed to see the bridge clogged with two or three tour-buses.

The buses themselves were a stimulus, being quite different from the common single-decker that made the thrice weekly run between Fermoy and Dungarvan. The tourers weren't even in green: they sported a greeny-yellow, rather insipid, livery, and the seats seemed to be raised up, and the high roof was in tinted glass.

The exotic aura of these roadsters was completed by the name of an Irish river festooned in scrollwork on the front, painted on a little more darkly than the livery, for all the world looking like weedroots under water, slant and entangled. How many of those names, to our chagrin, we never recognized at all! Funshion, Maigue, Fergus, Garavogue . . . . We recovered promptly from our embarrassing ignorance by telling our-selves that the strange names meant that Ireland was a real country, after all, containing unknowns of its own, vouchsafed to us by visiting Yanks.

In the normal course of events, Yanks were no big deal. Badger Crowley, for example, was a nice old guy, but he seemed just a little out of place – those nice lightweight check suits of his made him stand out, and his seersucker seemed a species of misjudgment. On the other hand, the old rip who lived out the country, Paddy the Gas, who spent every cent of his fat pension on drink for himself and his numerous buddies, seemed to be all the more a misfit from fitting in too well. It must have been that they just couldn't belong. When Billy Whelan from Massachusetts arrived one day in school we were told to call him 'Puncán' which we did with a will, exult-ing in the bastard freedom of prejudice.

But those three were returned Yanks, people who'd come home to stay. The tourists were real Yanks, just riding through. They fascinated us. We'd seen their movies, heard their songs, knew their twangy accents. Now we were getting to see them, live – inhabitants of the future we desired for ourselves (money, cars, blondes), war-winners, bulwarks against the red menace and the yellow peril. And a lot of them were good Catholics.

And they looked so healthy, these Yanks, tall, tan, plump: the only blemish we could see was that they all seemed to wear spectacles. Their clothes were great: devastating checks, shirts like postcards of a tropical paradise, big-butted matrons in cerise dungarees. You could tell by their appearance that they didn't give a damn what anyone thought of them. That was the kind of freedom we craved – to be able to tell the world to bugger off, to turn ourselves into sartorial Caesar's salads precisely as and when it pleased us, to stare vacantly into the middle distance with cigars the size of small trees clamped between jaws smooth as steel. They're children at heart, we thought, wishing that we could think of ourselves as half so gay and simple.

Sometimes they spoke – even to us kids, but more often to the group of elders who pitched their long afternoons in the vicinity of the bridge, half-hoping for a word from a stranger. 'Say now . . . ' and some historical question would follow. The natives would point fingers in uncharacteristically animated response, while the visitors nodded. Then, his thirst for knowledge temporarily slaked, he might say, 'I guess you men would take a drink', hand rummaging in a capacious pocket, carillon of loose change, forelocks touched, air thick with the sound of 'Sir'.

It happened too that every so often a bus would have an American 'young wan' on board, travelling with her parents, of course, but really (we knew) a true daughter of destiny in her own right. Destiny was pretty loosely defined, but we knew what we meant, a combination of economic ease and titillating peccadilloes. Usually, we seldom gave a girl a second look; that didn't come until we were fourteen or fifteen, by which time we found the girls at pains to ignore us. But glimpsing a blonde faun through the windows of a tour bus inspired us to manic antics. We'd race the bus as it dragged up the New Way and install ourselves, panting, at the Red House corner to watch her daintily alight – her blue-jeans the very robe of romance! – to take tea in the Devonshire Arms Hotel.

86   She'd look at us, of course she would, we hotly debated,

waiting till she completed her toothsome morsel (we saw cool fingers ply the cutlery, pearly incisors tear daintily at the cooked ham sandwich). Didn't she hail from where O'Brien and Murphy were as sound a name as any? But she never did look; neither eyebrow raised nor eyelash flickered. Demurely up the steps she climbed. The bus sprang to life. Our necks jerked forward, taut with the tense desire to speak, numb in ignorance of what the right approach was. Would shouting 'Elvis Presley' offend? How about whistling something by Pat Boone, 'Love Letters in the Sand', say?

No good, no good. She'd already gone, leaving us with just a haze of blue exhaust smoke to wave at. It was time for our own tea. We turned from one another to go. 'See ya,' we said, 'See ya', in laconic series. It felt as though a form of unity had been dispelled, as though we'd thought we were going somewhere, only to realize that indeed we were not.

IV

THE OTHER EMPIRE

1

'Confiteor Dei . . . ,' said Peter Hickey, and paused uncertainly.

'Go on, Seoirseen,' said Brother Murphy with snide impatience.

'Om-ni-po-ten-ti,' I managed.

'*Omnipotenti*,' the master repeated and, grabbing my pal Pete's arm, banged the point of his elbow sharp against the edge of the desk. We were going to be altar boys. One of the curates had come to school to talk it over with Brother Murphy, and a selection was made, mainly of lads like me and Pete, scions of Main Street, with a few make-weights from Botany and the country thrown in for the sake of appearances (Church Lane didn't make the grade).

Chrissy and Mam were overjoyed. So they had been when I graduated from the convent infant school and went to primary proper at the Brothers. And when I made my First Communion it was a miracle. They seemed to think there was something unlikely and very special about my arrival at such junctures, and regarded my having made it thus far with fond relief, my conforming to the common path a source of great reassurance to them.

An additional delight for Mam was that for each of these arrivals I had to dress the part, so she was able to express the seamstress in herself. Making something for me enabled her to see me simply as a child. Otherwise, she regarded me as a child-concept, the concept being that I was a responsibility which she was discharging not just on my father's behalf but on nature's. She was proud to discharge it, and needless to say I was very glad to have her – without her I believed I would be lost. But her awareness of her role was a constant reminder that I wasn't hers, a reminder reinforced by her seldom having time to play, her infrequent gestures of physical closeness, her never giving presents.

With Chrissy and George I felt I was theirs because they were so often ready to sing, to play, to draw me out. I still feel more theirs than anybodys, despite all the water that's between us, all the ink – despite, above all, my unconquerable urge to redeem and comprehend our deep life together in that small no-place.

Mam, though, was a lot warmer to me than to her own. She was forever harassing and reproving them. Their autonomy frustrated her. She criticized their behaviour as though its sole aim and object was to make her account to herself for it. Every so often there were complete breaks, during which the name of a certain aunt could not be mentioned. Some of these breaks lasted years.

But perhaps Mam could only see her world as a round of duty and responsibility. Her view expressed the onus of being flawless, unflinching, singular, which her generation assumed, for only in rigorous adherence to a militant faith could the victory of the people be assured and the soul of fecklessness, induced by the foreigner's psychic sway, be remade.

Dress-making, however, had nothing to do with this. It belonged to the days of her girlhood – an unmarried, unbloodied zone, before the Great War, before Tans burst in on sleep and made her children howl. So she took to fitting me for the altar with quiet, deep-seated glee.

The scarlet material for the soutane and the linen for the surplice were sent specially from Dublin. Peggy dashed into town to Clery's during her lunch-hour for them. (Peggy is another aunt; she lives with my father, cooks him dinner and plies the Hoover at weekends, reminds him in all innocence of what's missing. They don't get on too well.) And of course it was impossible to find a suitable length of lace to trim the surplice with anywhere else except the capital, so poor Peg had to spend two or three Saturdays trying to find what was right. Most boys' surplices had borders of stuff that looked like the first cousin to net-curtaining. That wouldn't do us, though. If God tolerated such inadequacy that was His business. O'Briens required more.

92   Meanwhile, Brother Murphy was rehearsing the Latin with

us – pinching and punching and pulling our hair to his heart's content – and acquainting us with the parts of the mass. It conferred an impressive sense of maturity to be on speaking terms with the priest's arcana. Collect, Epistle, Secret, Agnus Dei . . . I felt starry-eyed with insiderdom. And then there was the privileged tongue itself.

To some extent, of course, all of us at school were bi-lingual, thanks to compulsory Irish. But everyone thought Irish was useless. It didn't tell us anything we didn't know. The textbooks dealt with sheep, fields, hills and children. A world was depicted which we knew infinitely better through the medium of our first language, English, and from the everyday evidence of our own eyes. For reasons best known to our educational lords and masters the rattling old far-fetched stuff of the sagas was kept from us. So instead of the stampeding action of *An Táin*, imaginative nourishment came in the Palladium's diet of westerns, with Gabby Hayes and Walter Brennan on hand to make us proud of being Irish, in the unlikely event of anyone remembering, while partaking of the sagebrush, that he had a nationalist, or any other kind of, consciousness.

But Latin was different. Nobody spoke it, yet it underwrote a world which was much more coherent and imposing (a world of rank, of remote controls, of refulgent embodiments, of a ruler who held sway from beyond the sea) than anything the Gael possessed. There was no need to speak it, to apply it demotically. The repetition of sanctified, pre-ordained formulae accomplished more than common language could dream of. Its inutility was unquestioned, as though only through its uselessness could it uphold mystery and portend beauty. And there were its sounds. Even if the words themselves stuck like glue in our mouths, how could we resist their sonorities: 'Orate fratres', 'Sursum corda', 'Ad deam qui laetificat juventutem meam'?

And then, at last, the big day, my first serving. Neophytes were supposed only to make the responses and just watch while their more experienced colleagues served by deed. But in my case that didn't happen. Jim Linneen overslept, so Edmund Nugent and I had to go it alone. This was exactly what I wanted, of course, centre-stage from the start, and Edmund steered me kindly, giving me the water, which 93 according to rote would have meant my having the book as well, only I didn't, it being too heavy – and if I let it fall . . . !

It was lovely being so near the priest, the credence-table, the gem-studded chalice, the surreptitious colloquy ('Suscipe, Domine . . . ': 'Hic est enim corpus . . . '), the snap of the host being split for the priest's communion. Mam and Chrissy were loud in their praises and gave me an extra slice of fried bread for breakfast. By the end of the week – the serving stint began with first mass (8 a.m.) Sunday morning, followed by mass every morning at the same time and ending with second mass (11) the following Sunday – I had it all off pat.

Being an altar boy was the first experience I had of completeness. I was aware that it was possible, naturally; I knew that being in a state of grace promised it, and of course I had approached the communion rail with all my sins washed away, all my flaws annulled, and in a fit state to receive the body of Christ into my heart and into my mind. But all that, soothing though it could be, was insubstantial, temporary, abstract. It didn't lay its material under my hand. It wasn't complicated. It offered nothing to be mastered, no movement, no timing, no lifting, no utterance. Above all, no novelty. Sublime surrender as a member of the congregation was all very well, but it couldn't compare to the neophyte's élite officiating. The notion that the show couldn't go on without me gave rise to a feeling of integration as pleasurable as when, far less often, I got all my sums right.

As with fractions or decimals, however, once I knew the method I knew everything, and serving grew to resemble everything else, rote and reflex alone sufficing. The novelty palled. But not the taste for novelty, though, which had the effect of making us squabble for leading roles.

'You had the patten yesterday, boy!'

'I want the bell, Butch.'

'The book – you can have the book.'

'Shove it. I want the wine.'

'Who's on the water?'

The best to have was the patten. We had two kinds. The old one, shaped like a sauce-boat, was dull, straw-colour. The new one was as round and resplendently golden as the pendulum of a king's clock.

94   What was best about being 'on' the patten, however, was

that you saw people as they never saw themselves. Holding it under the chins of the faithful as the priest dipped into the ciborium and laid a host on their tongues was great fun. The poses people struck! Some held heads forward humbly, like turtles; others threw back shoulders as though manfully to receive a punch; faces turned into plates or canisters or footballs or chimney-pots or letter-boxes. And tongues came in every shape and size. They were round, ridged, thin, narrow, flat, pitted, cracked, tumescent and never, never smooth. They were brick, cerise, vermilion, ox-blood, speck-led, lathered, slithery, cindery, sponge. Sour Mr Burke had a pale, pointy one. Mrs O., the gossip's, was large and lolloping. When you came across a particularly fine specimen you could give its owner a sly look on the street afterwards and confuse him.

Fun though that was, nothing could beat the solemn pleasures, and I mean pleasure: a feeling of radiance and of being stirred, not just of being tickled. This feeling came from the quasi-sacramental condition in which everything connected with the church reposed. Everything was blessed – the candles, the pews, the table in the sacristy on which Tom Heelan the sacristan, totalled up Sunday's collection, maybe even the canvas bags in which he lugged the take to the National Bank. But a blessing was invisible, just as 'the sacrifice' in 'the sacrifice of the mass' was. And just as the sacrifice was carried out by the priest on the faithful's behalf, making him at one with and distinct from his flock, so a blessing was a statement about the quality of objects used in the priest's business which relieved them of their merely physical character, made them tributaries of glory, artefacts of divine purpose, remotenesses.

Moving in such an environment induced a good deal of headiness, leading me, for one, to think the priest's appurte-nances more numinous, more enthralling, than the occasions of their use. Alb and cincture caught my fancy more readily than 'Dominuş Vobiscum'. The colour, needlework and cut of chasuble and maniple impressed me more than the reception of the communion wafer by my stainless soul. Sacristy outweighed sanctuary; sacristan was as intriguing as celeb-rant. Tom bearing monstrance, ciborium or chalice from the safe to the robing-table, right hand clad in a special white glove, was as worthy as any priest.

Nothing would have been easier for me, I see, than to have become an out-and-out fetishist. But benediction saved me. Benediction had everything. And its diversions took place at exactly the right time, too, at the conclusion of tedious, inactive, repetitive Rosary. It was so good that those on the thurible or the candles for the altar didn't have to endure the whole Rosary but could go to light up around the fourth decade.

Both these jobs had certain drawbacks, however. One was that you were left out of the best bit of Rosary, the litany, the thrilling blazon – 'House of Gold', 'Tower of Ivory', 'Star of the Sea', 'Refuge of Sinners', and every type of Queen, Mother and Virgin besides. The dull voice of the congregation going 'Pray for us', 'Pray for us' couldn't dim the daring of those phrases.

Then, too, it was possible to get stuck with recalcitrant fire. Lighting the candles could be hell. Tom Heelan, possibly to torment us or (which is more likely) because it didn't occur to him, never set the candlewicks upright, so now and then it would be virtually impossible to apply the taper effectively. The wicks were too far above us to adjust manually, and for all we knew it might be a sin to do so, in front of the priest and everyone. So you just had to stand there, mortified, fuming, even praying for the cursed thing to ignite, arms aching from indecorously poking and craning at that measly, half-visible speck of black.

There was something to Mam's refrain: 'A wonder, now, the Canon wouldn't have a word with Tom about that.' But not one of us would hear a word said against Tom. That was mainly because he was so tolerant. He let us tie our soutanes around our necks by the top button, cloak-like, and horse around the headstones of the chapel yard – Batmen, Supermen, Phantoms. He told us stories about the Great War, in which he served. He even didn't mind Chainbreaker snapping off rivulets of candle-grease and chewing it, maintaining staunchly that there was nothing like it for curing warts (poor Chain had warts like the rest of us had dandruff).

Tom's war stories were remarkable. Here's a typical one.

'We were up there by the Siegried line,' said Tom, pointing his pipe towards the hurling field, 'and I was showing the top brass around, Churchill and them. They were over to see our defences, y'see, and the officer commanding was after asking me to do the honours. "Certainly, sir," says I, "anything to oblige." "Thanks awf'ly, Heelan," says he. Well there we were, the brains of the war, you might say, out beyond in no man's land, and I showed them this and that, answered their questions and all to that, when I let a bawl of "Duck, gentlemen!" out of me, like a shot out of a gun. Needless to say, they all thrun themselves on the ground and not a peep out of them. Five seconds later, not fifty feet away, up goes a grenade. Well, yer men got to their feet, brushed themselves down and, of course, were all over me. I could have had any medal I wanted. "But how on earth did you manage to do it?" says they. "A thing of nothing," says I, cool as a breeze. "I just happened to hear the Hun pull the pin."'

Evening after evening Tom regaled us with yarns like that, sitting on the stoop outside the sacristy, puffing judiciously on his acrid pipeful of Clark's Perfect Plug, a steady supply of which was the height of his ambition, a figure beyond the range of candles and devotions, a votary of quite a different sect, in fact, as he often gave us to believe, the British Army – let the gates of hell (Russia) try to prevail against it!

Another thing Tom never gave a hand with was lighting the thurible. If anything, this was a worse chore than the candles. Charcoal was used as thurible-fuel, and to get a piece going the flame of a match was held to its edge until some heat was retained (usually several matches later), at which point it was blown to a glow. Establishing the approved condition could be a nerve-wracking experience, and often, in desperation, pieces of taper were broken off and used as a base, with whole tablets of charcoal thrown on top of it. The result was a conflagration, the climax of which came when the priest sprinkled the incense on and, in a crackling gush, a billow of divine scent arose, the whole effect an imitation of what popping heavenly corn must be like.

My favourite thing to be on at benediction was the incense boat, but really anything would do. It was a struggle to detach the full-length, cloth-of-gold cope from its cruciform, cherrywood stand, and lift it onto the priest's shoulders, but I felt strong and manly from the struggle – proud, too: the stand was a piece of my grandfather's craftsmanship. Then there was the humeral veil, which had to be collected from the   97 credence table just before the priest raised the monstrance and which slithered richly round his shoulders. It too was cloth of gold, and on the back it bore a device, a lamb fashioned from little pearls, curled up in the shelter of a semi-circular sunburst. At the heart of the sun were the mysterious initials IHS. We fought over what they meant. 'I have suffered.' ''Tis not, boy. I have sinned!'

Even the bell was better at benediction, because the priest faced out, bearing aloft the magnificent monstrance, the spokes of gold surrounding its window suggestive of a sun which beamed down fair weather forever. And it was fun to time the three trills of the bell to occur between the three times the thurifer went *chock-chock-chock* as he rattled the pot on the chains, honouring the host with his home's supreme aroma.

In fact, it was possible to be on nothing at all and still get a great kick out of benediction. The smell, the light, the smoke, the glitter: these were intoxicants, thought-purgers, sweet-meats for the senses. Something as plain as standing for the final hymn had a deliciousness to it – Moll striving with the squally organ, the ragged voices of the congregation, the strange sensation of engenderment that the gold and smoke conveyed, Father Murphy's nasal tenor as he swayed back and forth, keeping time, everyone together: 'Oh Mother! / Tell me / What am I to do?'

Sometimes money changed hands. Priests home on holiday from America or the African missions tipped a shilling – enough for two glasses of ice-cream at Hogan's, three visits to the gods at the Palladium for the Sunday matinée, or one sixty-four page comic. Not bad. We felt we earned it for having been kept an extra half-hour from breakfast.

And there were weddings, which paid a little more, but which were rather more rare than visiting priests. A lot of people just didn't get married. Besides, England had claimed the majority of the town's eligible partners.

When somebody from Lismore did marry, the ceremony almost invariably took place outside the parish, sometimes because that was where the intended came from, often because the thought of having all the neighbours watching was unbearable. It was a great thrill for me to serve at the marriage of Billy Hogan and Kathleen Crowley, two people I knew well and was fond of. They made a smashing couple, I thought, all smiles (and I got a good tip). Usually, though, the couples were strangers, red-faced country fellows in blue suits, girls in bottle-green frocks with, as the papers used to say, matching accessories. I don't remember many of the strange brides being in white, and a non-white wedding traditionally means something tainted, so I suppose that's why they travelled with their small retinues to our church: to keep their secret intact.

It always surprised me that even after the ceremony, the nuptial mass and papal blessing ('all the trimmings', as people said, as they might of a meal), the principals of the party were still nervous. They didn't seem to know if they were coming or going when they adjourned to the sacristy to sign the parish register. I had plenty of opportunity to observe them, removing my surplice and soutane as slowly and deliberately as possible in order to give the tip as much time as it needed to materialize. It was while studiously folding my robes that the best-man at last made his sheepish approach, tugged at my sleeve, whispering, 'Now, boy', to which the correct response was 'Ah, no', while, quick as lightning, pocketing the half-crown.

In all, though, weddings struck me as basically fugitive affairs. Funerals, on the other hand . . . . Well, they were not exactly galas, like a hurling match or the Cappoquin Regatta. But from all I heard at home I knew it was much more important to have a good funeral than a fine wedding. A good funeral was a demonstration of esteem, prestige and charity, and in a way they were much more enjoyable or, more accurately, much more characteristic of the life of the town and the values – not to mention the rhythm – which dictated its course. And for us servers they were enjoyable because they were our only real opportunity for genuine public appearances.

At funerals, however, our special status was plain for all to see. We walked on either side of the priest, between the crowd and the coffin. One of us carried the cross and another the bucket of holy water and sprinkler, the latter with what I thought was the best name in the whole liturgy, the aspergillum. Not more than two servers, normally. We knew that burial wasn't a sacrament, really, but felt that it really was kind-of. It was accompanied by, or gave rise to, the combina- 99 tion of being at the same time pleasured and moved which, as far as I was concerned, was at the heart of holiness.

It wasn't the prayers that impressed me, though the 'De Profundis' had some rattling good lines – 'Et ipse redemit Israel ex omnibus iniquitatibus eis' fell from our mouths like a shovel of gravel. It wasn't even so much that the mechanics of burial intrigued me, although I was always relieved that interment went smoothly when Georgie had the arrangements, because he looked so flushed and uncomfortable in his suit. How things managed to go smoothly was, typically enough, beyond me: physical accomplishment and I were only rarely on speaking terms, and the interplay of boards and ropes as the coffin was being lowered seemed entirely a matter of touch and go, adding to the tension of relinquishing which gripped those standing impotently by.

What I liked was the unity. The six strong men, members of, or close to, the deceased's family, who stepped out of the crowd at the chapel and shouldered the coffin, arms intricately locked as they carried it slowly forth. The other men who came to take their place on the way to the graveyard, quietly insinuating their desire to honour. And behind us the silent crowd, the only sound the slur of footwear.

The dulled voice of subdued people praying. The hands of the bereaved being solemnly wrung again and again, and the layman's courtesy repeated and repeated: 'I'm sorry for your trouble . . . . ' Everyone was so genuinely present, so unreservedly committed to what was taking place.

'Et lux perpetua luciat eis', we responded, conscious of our own indifferent light, to be sure, but for once consoled by it, feeling that the deceased had the worst of it, and that we weren't too badly off at all the way we were.

2

Were we religious at home?

100   We should have been. Lismore was one of the original Holy

Places, a fact still commemorated by our diocese being known as Waterford and Lismore. When the world was a know-nothing place, Lismore was endowed with learning. A thousand years or so ago it had a flourishing monastery. Proud kings' sons from lands beyond the sea sat on the bank of the river spelling out their lessons, their purple tunics fluttering in the mild morning breeze, while from the round tower one of the servants kept an eye out for those curse-o'-God Northmen – so well he might; the river was tidal as far up as Cappoquin, a mere four miles away. But the picture of the noble youths studying was a powerful lure used to persuade me, during my fairly frequent bouts of hypochondria, to stop whining and go on to school like everyone else. I didn't know, then, naturally, that the images of holiness, serenity and composure associated with monastic Lismore were nineteenth-century hand-me-downs. Still, it's amusing to think that perhaps Alfred the Great studied there as a stripling, and that he failed cookery.

The man – how dare I say 'Man!' He was a saint, of course – who ran the settlement (which everybody refers to as a university) is commemorated in the Irish name of the town: Lios Mór Mochuda. For reasons entirely beyond me Mochuda has been translated into English as Carthage, so Lismore has a Protestant and a Catholic church bearing his name, and a parish hall, and a number of citizens, including myself. My name is Seoirse Carthage. Mouthful as it is, and much as I detest it, I was spared the option of using it, unlike some others who had to sport it as a forename, local usage abbreviating it to Ca.

The reason I hate Carthage is that it sounds totally phony. 'Oh, but I *like* it,' insist well-meaning idiots to whom, in moments of weakness, I've confided it; 'It's cute.' It is not cute and I don't want them to like it. I don't want to bear a name whose first association for most people is not that it's the original of a great Irish family name (McCarthy) but synonymous with classical ruination. I don't want to have to explain my names.

It's a real shame that Carthage didn't perform a few miracles and get himself known beyond west Waterford. Not only would he have eased the way for his namesakes, not just in the matter of moniker, but career-wise. The tourism potential of a miracle-working Irish saint would be tremendous, particularly as, in a body, the Irish elect aren't worth a damn as miracle-workers. If they'd spent less time buried in books we'd all have soft jobs now. I'd be a guide conducting the halt and the lame through the hallowed precincts, pointing out the well (every saint has to have a well), the place where the crozier was found (a treasure of the Golden Age, on view at the National Museum), and so on (I'd be sure to think of other things), and the gateway to the Castle (which for the last eight hundred years has stood on the site of the monastery) would be hung with the crutches of Christendom.

As things were, it was not our lot to make a fortune flogging relics to gullible foreigners. It was not our lot to do anything at all about St Carthage. He was just – well, there, like every other historical thing: a thread in the tapestry, neither exploited nor effaced, simply admitted. I remember once a priest of ours decided to do something to mark the saint's feast, which occurs some time in the first half of May. The well was located and bunting hung and a little pilgrimage took place. The exercise lacked conviction, however, partly, I think, because there was some dispute over the site of the well. That derelict hole in the ground at the foot of Dowd's garden was a definite anticlimax to the pilgrimage. A much more plausible siting would be the source of the water that poured for local use through a wall of the Castle grounds and known as The Spout. But since access to the Castle was prohibited, and it was beneath our dignity to request entry, the hole had to do. Besides, as I'm sure the adults realized, a procession to the spout was impossible in view of the amenity's phallic overtones.

The net result of the abortive *feria* was the recognition that St Carthage did not impinge significantly on the spiritual life of the town. But what did?

For Georgie the answer to that question was simple: nothing. He didn't want a spiritual life. He was confident he could tell the difference between right and wrong. A just reward for the work of his hands was all he aspired to. So he was anti-clerical and irreligious largely on the grounds of personal irrelevance. Nevertheless, he never missed Sunday mass, though he took care to stand just inside the door unaccoutred by beads or prayerbook and with cronies (other devout mothers' sons) to converse with when something sprang to mind. Having, apparently, no alternative but to go, it was necessary to treat being there inconsequentially. This attitude was sufficiently prevalent to be denounced from the pulpit every so often, not that that made a difference.

Professional animus fuelled Georgie's anti-clericalism too. The clergy never gave him work. Not that Georgie would have become a daily communicant if the parish priest contracted for him. But he did believe himself the best man for quality work, and justice as well as common sense surely dictated that the criterion of excellence, nothing else, made him worthy of his hire. After all, blast it, he was good enough to be hired by the toffs of the county, by Dean Stanley for work on the Protestant church, by Alec Ellis to attend to the Presbyterian church – but they were people who knew quality when they saw it, not like *pus mucha* Mike McGrath, who was still leaning over the half-door of the *bothán* he was born in . . . . Geo could rant an hour steady when he got going, the injustice of it all operating on him like a second mother.

The last straw for Geo was when the Canon decided to decorate the church. This was an unseemly decision in a general way, as Canon Walshe, his predecessor, was hardly cold in his grave before the new broom was produced. On top of that, a team of decorators was brought in from Cork, another county and another diocese, when it was giving work to the town he should be, not taking it away. And of course (it seemed fated), they didn't do much of a job, though admittedly they'd have their work cut out to please Georgie. The worst thing they did, in my view, was to efface most of the semicircular gallery of saints painted on the wall of the apse (the area behind the altar), leaving only St Patrick and St Carthage. None of the figures were named, but you could tell the national saint by the snakes, and if our own man wasn't left to us who else had a right to be? I don't know who exactly was painted out, but in all, four were. Surely St Declan of Ardmore was there, and St Colman of Fermoy, though his bailiwick was in the diocese of Cloyne. As for the other two I can only guess: St Otteran of Waterford City, St Finbarr of Cork? They were all fine, able-bodied men, anyhow, with lantern jaws and flowing, curly beards. Each was dressed in a full-length frock, grass green, ruby, violet or turquoise in colour. They had beady eyes. Hard men. Stern. They made a solemn distraction when mass dragged.

The work was as shoddy as the hiring principle, in Georgie's eyes. He must have remembered with some bitterness how freely his father had been called upon by canons and archdeacons of days gone by, and how his uncle Paddy, the smith, had fashioned the wrought-iron railings that separated the aisles. To be overlooked in favour of outsiders (and company men at that, not self-employed) must have felt like the confirmation of limbo.

Needless to say, had Georgie been contracted the glory reflected would have pleased me greatly. But the fact that he was virtually tradesmen-in-residence at the Protestant church was good compensation. I got to see things that none of the other lads did, except, of course, Tony Dowd and Har Allison, whose church it was. What going there in the devotional sense amounted to was impossible to say, attending alien service was a sin which only a bishop could expunge. But even empty and idle, the Protestant church was an intriguing place.

It was really ancient, much older than our church, indeed it had been our church until (so I was told) that sonovagun Cromwell stabled his horses in it – though, talk about an ill wind, that must have been when Mam's ancestor deserted, the man she had to thank for her posh maiden name, Willoughby (Georgie put it all together during wet days spent delving in the vestry). Inside, it wasn't a bit like ours. Not a lick of paint in the whole place, just walls of undressed stone which wept, scenting the air with clay. Not a holy picture, not a blessed statue, not a candle, not a station of the cross. If they were holy, they kept mighty quiet about it.

The best thing was the number of graves. They believed in burying indoors and out. Under shiny-smooth flagstones in the nave, soldiers and titled men reposed, indifferent to the world walking on them, which I found odd and eerie, especially when I was on my own. And there was a large area by the door to the belfry in which some vaults stood, containing the remains of bishops, I think; their ornate bulk deserved high-ranking tenants. These vaults unnerved me even more than the graves underfoot, partly because I wasn't used to thinking of the dead in terms of such edifices, and also because the stone they were built of contained traces of iron which had oxidized in the moist air, so that it seemed that the past was commemorating itself in its true, bloody, colour.

Dashing stealthily round the headstones in the yew-filled cemetery, wandering alone and small in the lofty, hollow interior, inspecting the skulls that Georgie's gravediggers brought up (orifices engorged with moist, yellow earth) – such interludes produced starts and shudders which undoubtedly had their delicious side (I was getting away with something). But, overall, the place oppressed me. Our church was richer, more colourful, more up-to-date. And, when I thought about it, that was only right. After all, weren't we, the Catholics, the bosses now? Let the Protestants be history if they liked: we were the present, and that was what I wanted. The melancholy Gothic of the lapsed overlord couldn't hold a candle to the brash red-brick of the people's choice. The very idea that it might be was, quite simply, unthinkable.

Much as Geo enjoyed working for Protestants – they let you get on with the job and paid promptly – he had no sense whatsoever of actually associating with them, any more than he felt that listening to the BBC day-in, day-out, might make him less of a nationalist. This strikes me now as another Irish cultural irony, Georgie's energetic, pragmatic style containing some of the cardinal qualities of the 'hard-riding country gentlemen' – quickness of eye, strength of hand, sureness of touch, vehemence of character. But, for all his excoriation of the ways of priestcraft, George acknowledged every year that he was born and bred a Catholic – that was all there was to it.

The acknowledgment was accentuated, though he wished it to be disguised, by its taking place just once annually, and not in Lismore. What happened was that every year around Easter, Geo and a carload of like-minded black sheep drove up into the Knockmealdowns to Mellary, Mount Mellary, the Cistercian monastery. There they'd 'scour the pot', make a clean breast of the year's excesses, such as they were – drink, temper tantrums, a fight or two, and if it was a good year a few quarter-hours of sex. To these he confessed, for them expressed himself truly sorry. He bent the knee, assuming – with, for once, no disagreement – the passivity of his people.

I never went to Mellary with George – the car always left too early in the morning – but I was there tons of times with Chrissy. Thursday was half-day in Lismore, so the girls who 105 served behind the counters of their brothers' shops were free. What better, then, than to don the rouge and powder, the navy-blue costume, and hire a car to go to confession. Chrissy and Mam joined in, I was squeezed between a couple of ample, happy penitents, and off we'd putter in Dinny Reagan's A40. These excursions took place quite regularly: they were a species of dating.

The Cistercians struck me as a strange lot. They got up at half-two in the morning to sing their office, they weren't allowed to speak (though they could smile), and they dug a bit of their graves, or so I was told, every day. Other orders came down to us, and preached. But we had to drive up to the men who, as a rule, kept mum. Naturally, confession proceeded as usual, and they did have a man in the bead shop selling holy trinkets, who talked enough for the whole community, bright chatter, a bird in a stone cage. And I suppose the man running the guest-house spoke – the guest-house was a strongly recommended retreat for people trying to kick the bottle. I'm sure it was very refreshing for adults to deal with clergy whose first concerns were neither prurient nor related to parochial funds. But I could never accept that anyone would volunteer for such a limited life, with only the blue, indifferent mountains for company.

The wedding principle of going away from home to feel at ease seemed to serve confessing, too. Maybe the thought of confiding in, of being vulnerable before, a perfect stranger was enticing. Not that it was felt that the confidentiality of the confessional at home would be violated. Just probably that peace of mind came more readily knowing you wouldn't meet the figure on the far side of the grille out walking his dog or at the Whist Drive. But what did these confessors know of the world of sin? And did ignorance make them severe, doling out sibilant chastisement and lengthy penances? Perhaps it was accepted that monks, being holier (being less in the toils of history and family, that is), would be wrathful. Besides, the more vividly the penitent felt the lash, the sweeter the accompanying salve seemed.

Or maybe the monks' greater proximity to God enabled them to see frailty through the eye of eternity, making them lenient. At any rate the women loved them. The mountains' cold shoulders, the narrow rule, the unknowable confidante –

did they subliminally identify with renunciation and its unspoken similarity to something in their own lives, and, were they thus temporarily appeased? I only know that everyone was happy going home: the car was full of 'Oh, a lovely man . . . a saintly man', and smug cigarette smoke.

Despite these trips, which she took quite as seriously as any of her companions, Chrissy stays in my mind as a sinner. I should hasten to add that Mellary afternoons were by no means the only indications of her commitment. Like most women of the town, and to a greater degree than a lot of them, Chrissy was involved in the Church's elaborate network of subsidiary devotional obligations, participation in which, as we were frequently reminded from the pulpit, was the true mark of a *real* Catholic.

Chris was a member of the women's branch of the Sacred Heart Confraternity and saw to it that the members of her guild were fully paid-up. (In everything connected with the Church, the hand in the pocket and the open purse were the inevitable accompaniment to the bent knee and the sign of the cross.) And Chrissy was a Child of Mary, meaning, as far as I could see, that she belonged to a secret society. The Children of Mary held their meetings in the convent, and appeared in public in blue cloaks and long white veils, singing. I suppose it was some sort of virginity action group.

Then there was the choir, if that's what the ailing organ and the handful of disheartened vocalists could be called. Nobody gave a damn about the choir, not even to the extent of declaring that we'd all be better off if it shut up. Chrissy's relationship with it was erratic. Sometimes when Kate, the regular organist, couldn't play, Chris would take charge. But it was too much for her, and it must have been thought impolite to practise, since she never bothered. Mainly she sang: 'Panis Angelicus' during the offertory at second mass, 'Ave Maria' (Gounod) on the Feast of the Immaculate Conception. A thin voice, but true, and so superior to anything else available that it seemed excessive, out of place.

Yet months could pass without her going near the choir. I preferred it that way. Her solos embarrassed me. One reason they did was my sense of Mam's lack of enthusiasm for them, which to me was tantamount to adverse judgment. Also, I believed that there was something obscurely sinful in being out on one's own in church, in exhibiting an extravagance of self, in sending shivers distractingly down the spines of the faithful (well, they went down mine and I didn't know what to do). It was much better when Chrissy came with Mam and me into the body of the congregation and I could observe her busy with her beads, head slightly tilted to the right, a preoccupied and semi-afflicted expression on her fine-boned face. No music. All self submerged in a welter of private prayer.

It wasn't because of the choir that I have my picture of Chris the sinner, even though I had been solemnly warned off the organ loft because it was an occasion of sin (people who were too respectable to stand inside the door with Georgie went up there for a chat), and even though I'd had experience of Chrissy's music sinning against me. But there was one thing that did influence my conception of her fallen condition: Lough Derg. St Patrick's Purgatory, a bleak island in the black north, was known as a place of pilgrimage since at least the time of Calderón de la Barca. Surely, I said to myself (a desire for justification my only perspective), nobody would go there unless he was made to.

The journey up was punishment enough for anyone, the way Chrissy told it. First, there was the trial by land, the bus. For people unused to venturing beyond their own parish, two hundred miles of twisty roads by bus was a right stomach-turner, especially since all aboard were smoking like chimneys, trying to get enough nicotine put by to survive the three smoke-starved days ahead. Then there was trial by water, taking the boat over to the island fastness. And finally the place itself, unalterably devoted to retaining the stars it had earned in medieval Michelins: dry bread, black tea, water.

It may have been just as well to arrive as sick as a dog, like Chris's group. That way the place's revenge on the flesh might not have seemed so drastic, having been unwittingly antici-pated. It may have been too, though, that no matter what condition you arrived in you couldn't really be prepared. The regimen punished everyone. Either the fasting did for them, or they couldn't stand the all-night prayer sessions, or they baulked on finding their feet in flitters from having to circle the stony surround of St Patrick's Basilica barefoot.

Only someone like Mam's friend Annie could relish that

sort of thing. She was what I called holy, much holier than Mam, even. They'd been friends since girlhood, their friendship surviving the years Annie spent in New York looking after rich children. 'You'd think she wasn't a day away,' said Mam proudly: Lismore *über alles*. Now Annie lived in Botany and had nothing but faded cotton frocks, a long, sensual, melancholy face, and a faith that lived like a flame.

She knelt in the front seat, gospel side of the centre aisle, underneath the pulpit, her head thrust forward with a leftward list, looking for all the world like St Teresa of Avila, St Catherine of Sienna, St Monica, Our Lady of Dolours . . . . At any rate, not like a local. Not like an Irishwoman. And certainly not like an Irish woman saint, because apart from the formidable Brigid and Dymphna, patroness of the insane, there aren't any – odd, in view of all the powerful women to be found in the sagas, Maeve, Deirdre, Grainne . . . .

Anyhow, there she'd be, morning and evening, hail, rain or snow, suffering and supplication written all over her face. When responses were called for – at Rosary, for example – she called out hers loud and long, savouring the throbbing tones every syllable: 'As / it / was / in / the / be / gin / ning / is / now / and / ever / shall / be; lead / us / not / in / to / temp / ta / tion; now / and / at / the / hour / of / our / death / A / men.' And during benediction she'd sing, an opulent, off-key contralto, dolefully belling:

> To-o Je-sus' heart all bu-hur-ning
> With fer-vent lo-hove fo-hor men.

That was it, for me, the real thing. Annie looked just like the pictures of those holy women, all stigmatized by the ache of their ardour. She had sailed the Atlantic, beheld the lights of Broadway, soothed infant heirs of Amagansett, and still she craved and cried out. And I knew there never was a saint who'd led a happy life.

That was the trouble with Chrissy: happiness. I couldn't understand how she could come home from Lough Derg and sit at the kitchen table lightheartedly telling us about it, mimicking this one and ridiculing that, as though nothing had happened. The descriptions of the penances were enough to frighten me, never mind trying to imagine what size of sin demanded such expiation. And thinking that she might have been guilty of some heinous enormity cast a shadow over her for me, made her seem lost to me a little. I saw her as having contracted the spiritual equivalent of the great fear of the day, a spot on the lung. From now on she'd have to be very careful.

But listening to her blithely continue (her *pièce de résistance* was an imitation of someone either sneaking a cigarette or cadging a drag), I became more concerned for her. It struck me that, for her, the whole experience was not a solemn sobering. Her laughter, I greatly feared, meant that her contrition was imperfect. Couldn't she see that to be sin-free was to be grave and constant? Surely she could. Even I could see that. The evidence was all around us. Look at Mam. Look at any woman. Didn't the whole town, Chris, make you realize that you were too true to be good?

3

Christmas was good, thanks to midnight mass, and it was fun to run through three dead masses in a row on the Feast of All Souls, but the best times for serving were Missions and Easter.

Although they had none of Easter's liturgical novelty, Missions were exciting. For the two weeks they were on the town felt more alert. The air was tense, as on the day of an important hurling match. There was an air of people going purposefully about their business, the way they did on fair-days. And it seemed that all around there was the clandestine sibilance of the turning over of new leaves.

A Mission drew as many country people into town as a good fair, especially men, which was a sure sign that there was something to be got from it, since farmers didn't come to town except from necessity and in the hope of gain. These glowering, heavy-booted men bargained with Providence, their sins beside them like so many fluke-ridden sheep or incontinent

calves.

It was because of the country people that services started at the annoying hour of eight in the evening. Missions being invariably summertime events – summer was the slackest time of the year, devotionally speaking – the people of the fields had to be given time to eat and spruce up before the three or four mile trek in. The annoying part was that for us youngsters, starting at eight meant there was no time to get a game going either before or afterwards.

To kill time we usually hung around the stalls. These were another way in which Missions resembled fairs. But fair-stalls were stocked with the best British padlocks and three-in-one penknives of brightest Ruhr streel, and were manned by apostles of Mammon, fast-talking Dubliners wearing signet rings and new-fangled nylon shirts who communicated such an air of modernity and confidence that you knew you couldn't trust them. Mission stallholders were quiet, unassuming men and women (the same as ourselves, as people liked to think), soberly dressed, serene smiles illuminating their simple faces as they waited impassively behind their little counters. This was another mark of their respectability, the fact that they had real stalls, with counters, canvas awnings and display shelves at the back, entirely different in tone and bearing from the fair-men's arrangement of battered crates in the back of a van.

Mission stalls did their best trade in holy pictures. There were two sizes, prayerbook and wall. St Joseph was easily the most popular subject. Usually he was depicted looking out over the viewer's shoulder (as though standing on a wall), a lily in his right hand. St Antony of Padua was popular too. He was one of the handiest of the saints: if you lost something and prayed to him, he'd find it for you. Youth had its own saints: Dominic Savio and Maria Goretti, both notorious for their purity.

Then there were statues. In this branch of business Our Lady led the field. Easy for her, of course, since she appeared in so many different liveries. Our Lady of Lourdes, of Guadeloupe, of Mount Carmel . . . . Runner-up in statue-sales was, surprisingly, Blessed Martin de Porres, the first Latin American to be beatified. The lesson of his status was, presumably, that there was hope for everyone – hence his popularity. Lastly there were the treasures, the rosaries that had crucifixes with relics in them, the miraculous medals, the white prayerbooks with ornate, gold-looking locks attached to their sides which were considered ideal for little girls.

It says something for the mood generated by the Mission that nobody showed any curiosity about the stallholders. Only now does it occur to me to wonder who they were and where they came from and how they knew where to come. Perhaps the various preaching orders issued a calendar of Missions according to which the pedlars planned itineraries. Maybe these camp-followers were members of some lay order, their plaster figures and oleographic images a subtle descent to the vivid inarticulacy of the faithful's creed, against which the power of the preacher (his licence to speak) could be measured to his advantage. Or could the portable store have been a penance – all that packing and unpacking – imposed by some vindictively imaginative confessor?

We invariably had Redemptorists for our Mission. Our own clergy, who hired them, wouldn't have any others. They were right, no doubt: Jesuits would have talked over our heads, and certainly wouldn't have roared enough at us, and probably were in any case much too expensive. I have no idea what three Redemptorists for a fortnight cost, but I assume financial considerations were, as ever, to the fore in the minds of our pastors.

It was the thing that irked people most about the Church – money. There were collections for the Pope ('Peter's Pence') and for the Church ('Propagation of the Faith'). There were the various drives for parochial funds – whist drives, 45 drives; the collections at both Sunday masses, payment for mass cards, fees for official functions (baptisms, weddings). And above all there were dues, collected at Christmas and Easter in order that the clergy might pay their way. This contribution was the most difficult to avoid for the simple, though bizarre, reason that a list of donors plus amounts was read from the pulpit during mass a few Sundays after the take. Anyone who wanted to know how you were fixed economically, or if you were trying to curry clerical favour, or if you were trying to get above your station by flashing the wad, was given plenty to chew on. So was anyone who couldn't give a damn one way or the other. (No prizes for guessing which of those two parties was more numerous.) Moreover, the litany of names and numbers (from 'Doctor Healy £5' down to the rank and file, lumped together according to amount, 'Two shillings: Billy Mulcahy, Moses Kennedy . . . '), was often followed by a harangue about the necessity of supporting God's anointed, and we should never forget it. That Sunday we were all publicans, and we were all sinners.

Well, perhaps not all. Georgie, for one, was given to speaking his exasperated and cynical mind in reaction to such crass expressions of clerical thanks, muttering, 'never satisfied', 'bloody spongers'. And, warming to his theme, what, time after time, Geo wanted to know was: why did the three priests have a car each? 'One'd be plenty,' for reasons Geo would spell out in detail. Trailing after his vigorous resentment, though, was a sad thought about all he might accomplish if he could afford a car – sad, because it only made matters worse to be jealous of men to whom he was entirely indifferent to begin with. Resentment wasn't exclusive to Georgie, however. When the harangue was particularly importunate, Mam got annoyed too. Sometimes she even went as far as cutting her next contribution by a whole half-crown, from ten bob to seven-and-six (more she could not do: people'd start thinking us paupers).

Not all the sermons from our own men were demands for money with menaces. Father McGrath (not the Canon, but sandy-haired Father Dinny from Clashmore, who once expressed a great *grá* for me to Mam) was fond of exhorting us to be 'up and doing', and derived many striking variations from the text concerning he who is in the field – 'let him not turn his back for his coat.' Canon Walshe, I dimly remember, performed interminable exegetical callisthenics on the Good Samaritan, and also displayed a fascination with Samaria, which he pronounced 'Sam-mar-eye-a', making God only knows what connection between the Marian and the Roman province. 'Oh blessed hour!' Mam exclaimed, bustling in to put the kettle on, 'I thought he'd never shut up.'

Needless to say, however, no performance by a local could compare to an evening with a Redemptorist. They were the boys to lay it on hot and heavy, and on whose account we shivered in our shoes. Yet, squirming under the lash, I for one took pleasure in my guilt because I felt equipped with a stable identity, that of a sinner. I found that it concentrated the mind 113 wonderfully to have one's satanic tail hanging limp and decidedly unbushy between one's legs.

The themes of the sermons were chosen to appeal to various sections of the congregation. For children there was 'He went down to Nazareth and was subject to them'; for mothers, the prophecy of Simeon: 'And thine own soul a sword shall pierce'; for the men of the town: 'Do you not know that I must be about my father's business?' There were a few general ones as well. 'The gates of hell shall not prevail against it' introduced vigorous Commie-bashing. And 'Thou hast made us for thyself, O Lord, and our hearts are restless until they rest with thee' ('words taken, my dear brethren, from the great St Augustine') prefaced an unmerciful onslaught on the vanities of the world, in particular that laboratory of evil and illusory joy, company keeping.

The Missioners had two styles of delivery, loud and deafening. The deafeners often started out deceptively, sometimes even deigning to soften us up with a joke if they detected tension (and some evenings even we altar-boys could feel the electric expectancy of, say, a thousand souls waiting to be chastised). Here's a Redemptorist joke. 'A workman was wheeling a barrow of manure to the local lunatic asylum, and one of the lunatics was watching and watching him. At last the lunatic said, 'What's that for?' 'Oh,' said the workman, 'that's for the rhubarb'. 'Wisha, God love you,' said the lunatic, 'We get custard on ours.' There'd be a smattering of titters and sniggers, and sometimes a *sotto voce* repeat of the punchline: 'custard on ours . . . . In the name of the Father and Son and the Holy Ghost. Amen.' With the sign of the cross the lull ended and the storm commenced. Five minutes after the final simper had subsided, the winds of rhetoric, to quote the Paycock, 'blowed and blowed', making the rigging and frail fretwork of our immortal souls groan.

Reclining on the steps of the altar, facing the congregation, we servers felt like smug, safe insiders as we surveyed the looks of the miserable sinners. The preacher could pound the pulpit and shake his fist, his spittle could spray the front seat, but thanks to our position and our uniforms we knew ourselves to be basically on his side and immune from confrontation. The guilt I felt was inspired by loyalty to the occasion, not by any feeling of wrong-doing. Naturally we were closer to the

Missioners than anyone else in the town was – who attended to them in the first act of the day, after all?

And sometimes closeness didn't stop at serving their masses. I, for one, was fortunate enough to spend what I thought at the time was a perfectly wonderful afternoon in the company of a Father Carroll CSSR. It was great because we went on a walk together and I was able to assume my second-favourite role in the whole world, that of a guide – I used to drive my father mad in Dublin shouting out the names of the streets our bus was passing through. (My favourite role of all time was, of course, that of obedient child. But my assumption of it wasn't always voluntary or deliberate.) So for a while we strolled along and Father Carroll – my memory is of a somewhat fleshy man in his late twenties – asked me the usual boring questions about school, and was I a good boy at home, and was I better at football or hurling, to which I replied 'Yes, Father' and 'No, Father,' venturing such information as I imagined might interest him.

I'd have been quite satisfied if our walk had continued in this placid way. It wasn't what we said that mattered. The very idea of being in the exclusive company of such a holy man – a man so obviously superior to our own clergy, since he'd given up his whole life to wrestling the devil for souls and didn't own a car or anything – was plenty for impressionable me. But it made our afternoon really great when he told me that he might be going out foreign soon. Now that was *really* the thing . . . . It was all very well to fight the devil on your home ground. But to go out there looking for him in places where, from all I'd heard of pagany, he felt a lot more welcome – Boy!

Where was he going? I wanted to know, suddenly bold and free in my responses. Father Carroll didn't rightly know, but he thought they had the Philippines in mind for him. 'They're an awful long way away,' he said.

I know, I thought, aren't you lucky! I saw round-headed, oval-eyed children looking in awe at a man with a book. I saw a body of water filled with sampans and junks (vessels which I knew existed from the cover of *The Far East*, a periodical put out by another missionary order). I saw myself and Father Carroll cycling out from our adjoining parishes, all in white on shiny new bikes, sunlight and cool fronds beguiling us.

I ran home to tea with my head full of dreams. Georgie came

in from work as I was blurting it all out and asked what was up with me. Starting all over again, which I was only happy to do, wanting everyone to partake in my joy. I was taken aback only to get as far as, 'I was out for a walk with the Missioner', before Geo broke in roughly: 'Did you tell him about me?'

'Oh, I did,' said I, innocently.

'You'd a right to keep your bloody trap *shut*!' George cried.

'And so had you,' put in Mam, swiftly. 'Mouth almighty!'

I cried, of course, and cried again later when, tucking me in, Chrissy told me Geo thought I'd told how bad a Catholic he was. The second bout of tears was worse because I hated George to think I'd let him down, and because it was awful to imagine his soul in jeopardy (what if he fell from a ladder in the morning?).

But neither tears nor Geo could eclipse entirely my new all-white image of myself. Radiant with resolve, I wondered why I hadn't thought of the foreign missions before. Was it because I was weak and a cry-baby, and because I knew that God did not require the services of somebody who was always falling down and making his knees bleed? To love God as he deserved demanded stamina – look at how healthy all the priests I knew were. None of them looked like finicks with their food. But now, fortified by the attentions of Filipinos, I'd blossom forth in all sorts of exuberant, heroic ways. I'd be the indefatigable instrument of the will of God, the eternal altar-boy in unceasing attendance on my beloved, invisible celebrant. I'd suffer the little picaninnies to come unto me, as well, and would only beat them if they were *very* saucy in school.

My vocation had me feeling extremely thankful, strangely cleaned, and that nothing further would happen now to damage me. I don't know how long these feelings would have lasted in the normal course of events. But, as it happened, I received a rude awakening, and from none other than the man who'd converted me, Father Carroll himself.

Ever since our encounter I naturally absorbed his every gesture, drank down his every word, and looked up to him as much as I dared, which was nothing like as much as I wanted. Less than a week later, however, we parted company. It was lipstick that did it.

I forget now what text he used, probably Paul to the Corin-
thians: 'Your body is a temple of the Holy Ghost', but I

remember very well how scalding his remarks were. His main point struck me as pretty elementary: he objected to getting lipstick on his fingertips when he gave out communion. But why didn't he speak on mouth-opening as a prerequisite for wafer-reception? Because, no doubt, that would not have provided enough to rant and rave about. And did he ever! Women who composed themselves for the reception of their Lord and Saviour by wearing make-up were the worst in the world. How dare they improve their God-given features with powder and paint! They were no better than the leavings of London streets. Whited sepulchres, that's what they were. But God isn't fooled . . . .

He railed for a good hour, and long before he finished I was squirming. I thought of Chrissy. Sure she meant no harm with those creams and colourings. She only wanted to look nice and to be happy. There was no reason for Father Carroll to lose his temper with her, I said to myself – and then it dawned on me where my loyalties lay. Someone else could have the new bike and white soutane.

Now Passionists would never give a sermon like that. Of course they were different in every respect. They came from Mount Argus, in Dublin, pretty near where my father and Peggy lived in Sundrive Road, whereas the Redemptorists came from Limerick only (any place except Dublin and Cork was regarded as an enlarged and unimpressive Lismore). They looked different. Redemptorists dressed like the secular clergy. Passionists, however, while not going to the extreme of the sockless Cistercians, seemed definitely that way inclined. They never wore suits, only soutanes, they never appeared without their birettas, and they had big cloaks with Latin-inscribed, white pasteboard valentines stuck over their hearts: I always thought there was a touch of Zorro about them, and I laughed when Peggy said once, flippantly (to my ears, like a city person), 'Oh, the Passionate fathers with the loose habits'. But nobody else laughed. Everyone believed that the Passionists were the real thing. 'Saintly men,' said Mam, somewhat unctuously.

No doubt the reason why they were taken with a sizeable pinch of awe was because their narrow, intense mission – to preach the passion and death of Our Lord Jesus Christ. And   117

then they came at a very special time of the year, Easter –
though, with what seemed peculiar tact and self-denial, they
left the Resurrection alone. It was easier to take preachers
seriously at Easter, because it sounded like what they were
trying to do was normalize the extraordinary, not (like the
Redemptorists) lift up the mundane. They had great material
too – all that blood . . . .

And Easter was undoubtedly the best time in an altar-boy's
year. True we no longer had *Tenebrae*, as Mam boasted they
did in her day. (I listened, intrigued, as she described the
pitch-dark church and the clapping congregation – mimicry of
the chaos and ruin which were the immediate aftermath of the
Saviour's passing.) Still, we did all right as we were. There was
the shrouding of the statues in purple cerements; there was
the distribution of cool, chemical-smelling palm-leaves (actually sprigs of pine); there was the ordeal of lighting the thick,
naked-looking Paschal candle. We had no bell to ring, instead
we smacked a book. The tabernacle was vacated and left open,
so we had its cloth-of-gold lining to fascinate us. Devotions
took place at odd hours of the day (3 p.m. on Good Friday).
And we were off school.

The whole difference of it – the whole sense of the Church
putting itself out– seemed a reward for all the raw times of
Lent, when everyone tried to give things up and were grumpy
whether they succeeded or not, and adults were only allowed,
in the words of the bishop's instructions, 'One meal and two
collations' – a dietary prescription which was an indefensible
attack on the working man, according to Georgie. The names
of Easter – Pontius Pilate, Judas Iscariot, Annas and Caiphas,
Simon of Cyrene, Barabbas, the Sanhedrin – seemed some sort
of climax, coming all together, of the strange names of Lent:
Ash Wednesday, Quinquagesima, Rogation Days. And Easter
obliged us to live our faith in real time. Every day meant
something vital now – Spy Wednesday, Holy Thursday . . . .
None of the usual ticking-over from Sunday to Sunday. Faith
was a matter of concentration, intensity, cataclysm. For four
days Lismore was no longer a place where nothing ever
happened. It was a small world in a huge constellation bearing
witness to an agony which was its sole salvation. It was
eschatology, paradise for a people to whom a blend of politics,
law and bloodshed was mothers' milk.

The Passionists' sermons certainly helped to concentrate the mind wonderfully on redemptive agony. I don't remember very clearly the generalized exhortations and symbolical transformations with which the sermons concluded, possibly because they were pretty familiar. I knew already that every sin I committed was another thorn in the crown, another blow from 'the rude and scoffing soldiery'. And Peter's cock-crow denials didn't interest me a bit. What really got me involved were the thoroughly visceral sermons, the ones that went through the passion blow by blow, from Gethsemane to Golgotha, describing the medical pathology of the events. 'Did you ever hit your fingernail a blow with a hammer? (And did you ever take the name of Our Lord Jesus Christ in vain at the pain and shock of it?) Well consider, dearly beloved, what it might be like to hammer a nail into your hand. Not just a tack, but a big six-inch nail.' Or the hand would be described, its nerves, its moving parts, its delicate, God-designed tissue. 'Think what it would be to do that to your worst enemy. Then THINK what it was to PUNISH the SON OF GOD, who LOVES you!' There was another one too about the perversion of everyday things – timber and tools, for example – which struck me as highly ingenious, though it was no match for the technicolor gore efforts. There was nothing like them for instilling pity and awe, for reminding us (as our history so often tried to do) that the ultimate – or maybe even sole – test of good faith is self-abnegation. We don't stand a chance until we embody or articulate the nothingness that either our enemies or our own misdeeds have made of us. Talk about 'a terrible beauty . . . '.

What I understand even less, though, are the Easter Sundays. How it never rained on them. And, coming home from first mass, how mild as milk the air seemed, as gentle and beneficent as the breath of the risen Lord himself, wavering spring grown strong at last. Now there would be sugar in tea again, and cigarette packets snappily unwrapped. My father was here, and a week of walks with him lay delightfully in wait (I'd be able to tell him, for the umpteenth time, the story of my favourite picture, *The Crimson Pirate* – Burt Lancaster and Nicky Cravat: maybe this time he'll be impressed). In the wings, of course, were profound miracles which I never took the slightest bit of notice of – birdsong, daffodils. And trifle for afters.

119

V

THE CLASH OF THE ASH

1

'Look at that, Seoirse,' said Chrissy. 'Show him, George.'

Painfully, Georgie rolled up a leg of his trousers.

'Look.'

I saw a mass of bruise, blue, black, smoke-yellow, red-edged.

'What happened?' I said, alarmed, but I already knew. Indeed, without realizing it, I'd seen it happen. Georgie had been hurling.

It was a junior match between ourselves and Kilgobnet, a crowd of savages from down the county (the opposition always consisted of savages). Georgie was our full-back. Every time the ball came into the square their full forward pulled across him, hit him with the boss of the hurley. He was a ruffianly, dirty scut, so he was, as the spectators' growls confirmed. But what he was doing was entirely commonplace. Lismore's poor record in the county championship during those years was partly due to our not having enough players prepared to 'stick into' their opposite numbers. I was not surprised by what I'd seen on the field. What startled me was the sight of the mottled leg and the realization that hurling had an aftermath. Before then I'd always imagined that whatever happened, even the blood that I'd frequently seen flow, was all play and was absorbed by, or abandoned to, the field when the match ended. Sunday's exploits were in a class of their own, to me; it was unsettling to learn that they might be accompanied by Monday's aches.

George squirmed as he rolled down his trouser-leg. 'That sonofabitch,' he said. 'I'll get him the next time.' And he stumped off out to work.

I felt sorry for him. It wasn't right. The ref was a louser. 123

Nobody was for Lismore. But underneath my sympathy I felt relief. Maybe it was all for the best that I was a useless hurler.

I wanted to be a star, of course. I yearned to tear away on a blistering solo-run, to send bullets into the back of the net, to exemplify 'the finer points of the game' and the art of 'bending, lifting and striking' which brought headlong Michael O'Hehir to hysteria on the radio. And some cheering crowds, a gold medal or two, and my picture in the paper would, I believed, have done me no harm at all.

Being by birth a Wexford-man (a 'yellow-belly'; Georgie used to tease me with the Wexford nickname, which I found very upsetting, feeling that I was being made a stranger), I had plenty to nourish my dreams of derring-do. At that time, Wexford had a wonderful team – though typical of one that I supported it never won as much as it should have. It had the three Rackards – powerful Nick up front, staunch Bobby defending, subtle Billy in mid-field. It had Ned Wheeler with the blond hair, Art Foley the goalie who stopped raspers with a minimum of show, Padge Kehoe who was either the son or nephew of some famous friend of my Uncle Seamus. A few of these heroes were even from my birth-place, Enniscorthy, a fact I found very thrilling, it being more proof of my specialness.

Neither my own appetite nor the achievements of my mother's county made a hurler of me, however. I was, unalterably, all fantasy and no execution. I had no stomach whatsoever for taking the field, stick in hand – and so lightly clad! On the contrary, I knew all too well that I was too frail and too afraid for the hue-and-cry of it all.

My frailty was something I was much more aware of than my fear. Mam told me all about it: how pale and peaky I'd been, how for nights on end she'd be by my bedside, how there was always a nice drop of Scotch broth simmering in case I unexpectedly found an appetite.

'Ah,' she'd reminisce fondly, 'Dad [my grandfather] used to say, You'll never do it. He'll never last. Oh, he will, I'd say. I'll pull him through. And I did.'

Her talk gave me a typical picture of myself. I was in a narrow bed; my face was as white as a sheet; my wan smile is struggling gamely against listlessness; adults are whispering together in a corner. I am pitiable and unlikely. I have been chosen by the same imponderable agencies as those to which my poor mother succumbed. I am being tested by God. The metaphysics of my complaint were more enervating than the complaint itself. I must have been the world's worst patient. Illness made me frail, no doubt, but so too did the long bouts of convalescence which followed. Even after the merest quinsy Mam and Chrissy watched me as though I was on the point of evaporating.

With such great care being taken of me, I was extra careful to take good care of myself. In the playground I hung well back from the rough and tumble. When anyone came near me I fell down and cut my knee and had a bandage, lint and boric powder applied to it as soon as I got home. (I fell down at the hint of roughness as promptly as I cried at the sound of harsh words. It was an excellent stratagem, releasing me from numerous nervous situations for the expense of just a little blood. But as with the tears, the falls came unplanned.) When I played hurling I stood with my stick around mid-field near the sideline, and prayed the ball wouldn't come near me. It usually didn't, thank God; it whizzed by, pursued by a thunder of big-fellows, gasping and snorting, pulling and hooking. 'The clash of the ash!' That was a sound (and a phrase) meant to kindle the spirits of all right-thinking Irishmen, but it left me cowering.

It was some consolation to realize that I didn't have to be a Cuchullain with stick and ball to prove my Irishness. In fact, I firmly believe that Irishness was my one unimpeachable attribute, which no amount of mere personal incompetence could diminish. The reason for this unwonted security was my mother. Thanks to her I had a splendidly patriotic lineage, one so pristine that it totally outshone anything Lismore could boast of. I didn't boast, of course: I just felt smug.

My mother's father, Liam Royce, had fought in 1916, not in Dublin, but even more abortively in Enniscorthy. Her mother served in Cumann na mBan. They were married in traditional dress, he in a kilt and tunic, she in green with *brat* attached by a Tara brooch, and a piper had played at the wedding. They learned Irish. They studied manuals of cavalry warfare. They were going to change the world. And two young men who were to become Mammy's uncles were with them, and rose out as well, when the time came. All Uncle Mike got for his 125 efforts was a bit of his thumb shot off. But Uncle Seamus did better. When I knew him he was a morose man who wanted nothing more from life than the power to eliminate black spot, green fly and all the other natural shocks which beset roses. A far cry from the time when he was an insurance clerk by day and a conspirator at night. (My sense of him is that the piquant paradox of that combination never crossed his mind.)

He was fairly famous, though. I could never quite understand why. The achievement of anybody who hadn't been executed was obscure to me. But I know that, along with his comrades, he suffered in Frongoch Camp. And when he was released from there he became a member of the first Dáil, and a lifelong friend of de Valera.

The last bit was what impressed Mam, herself 'mad Dev' (as she said) 'ever and always'. This was not a popular position in Lismore, but Mam prided herself on it. She admired Dev's stiffness, his ability at sums, his answer to Churchill at the end of the last war, his guts for sticking to his guns with his back to the wall. She also admired his spectacles. For her they were arguably his most important feature, lending his face a clerkly chastity and inwardness. Nothing of the foreigner's roast-beef floridity of feature about him, nor yet was he disgraced by nature in the manner of his mallet-skulled, bullet-headed, pig-visaged opponents. (When it came to chastising enemies Mam was an inspired exponent of the cephalic index.) On top of which – bonus of bonuses! – Dev's glasses made him seem kin to that other bespectacled arbiter of Mam's known world, Pius XII.

Dev came to Lismore once, electioneering. He stood on the back of Dowd's lorry and harangued a fair-sized crowd for half-an-hour. I remember it being an evening meeting, one of perhaps half a dozen whistle-stops he made in the long dusk when men were in from the fields. I remember the strange energy of a stimulated crowd dispersing, and a moon-faced labourer wearing a beret and with slight slope to his walk shouting 'Up Dev!' as he made off up Chapel Street home to Ballinaspick. I remember Dev as something all the family agreed on. So Mam was very proud of being able to claim proximity to her hero through my Uncle Seamus. It was a vindication of her politics that her eldest son married into lofty principles, gunfire and near-martyrdom, though a more gentle, mild-mannered group of people than my mother's family I find it hard to imagine.

Mam would have taken good care of it that I was proud of them too, supposing I didn't feel that way inclined. I had no problem, however, identifying with them and their romantic, obscure, triumphant past. Whatever it was they were trying to bring about – of course I knew quite well what their historical and political attainments were; what I couldn't quite grasp was that the boyish spirit of their efforts had not been sustained; their day was a lot more exciting than mine, which though intriguing I thought unfair – at least they hadn't shirked it, whereas in Lismore nobody knew what was going on until it was all over. I discriminated unfairly, irrelevantly, between Lismore and almost the whole of the rest of the country outside Dublin. But pride in my patriots also acted as another reminder that I wasn't where I should be. I should be living among the Notables and Elders of the Cause on the banks of the quick-silvery Slaney. The shadow of their history should fall, transformingly, on me.

When I visited Enniscorthy, however, I was not changed utterly. Indeed in some ways, my sense of frailty was reinforced. Granny Royce and I would be walking home from the L & N with a teatime treat when, going by the convent, a neighbour would stop and after a few pleasantries say, 'Oh, and this is Nuala's little chap,' at which Nuala's mother would blink fondly, tearfully, and I would meet myself once more as a refugee from death. 'By the gob o' man, missus, he's gone as big as a house,' Paddy Nolan might say from behind his counter in Rafter Street. And although he spoke merrily, I always felt my existence surprised him.

Paddy always treated me to a bottle of Lett's lemonade, however, which quickly made me feel again a chosen person in a positive sense, something the Donaghues accomplished much more adeptly. Whenever I was taken into their shop I was given ice-cream immediately and never felt a thing, even though just across dark, narrow Slaney Street from them stood the house I was born in. They never said a thing. Sim came out to shake hands with me, thrusting forward his red-brick, owl-oval, eyebrow-free face at me. His large wife remained behind the counter, her placid smile like a dent in a firkin of butter.

I looked upon the lemonade and ice-cream and saw that   127 they were good (and that they were no more than my due). I also saw them as being a kindly tribute to a respected local, Granny Royce. So in that way, too, I felt nearer to my desire for specialness, for recognition as a breed apart. Additional assistance came from the unfamiliar accents on the streets, flatter, with quaint usages and asseverations such as 'Ain't it' and 'Be the tear!' And of course there was a different history. The castle in Enniscorthy is on the side of the street, commanding nothing. Much more eye-catching is the statue of the man with the pike in the middle of the square. The countryside's main landmark was not some imperial implant but a place where the have-not peasantry was ruined in 1798, Vinegar Hill, a bleak bump of a place that glowered at the town below. A history consisting of the wasteful death of humble people was one with which I could identify.

The desired ratification did not take place, however. Enniscorthy did not take me to its heart. I remained a novelty passing through. While the place seemed a tissue of redactions of my history, I was the only one aware of it. Nobody else had the need, I suppose. Their need was to be absolved of history, not to claim it. This strikes me as being especially true of my two heroic uncles. Seamus had a fortification of rosés. Uncle Mike owned a hardware shop and was radio-mad. Neither of them ever offered anything of his history to me. The very thing that lent them substance, mystery, power and manhood – in my eyes – was the very thing they had effaced. I never wanted to prompt them into volunteering a tale or two. That would break the spell of desire. So they never did. There seemed to be no relief from the sense that we were all living in an aftermath, a limbo. I could be as Irish as I wanted. The degree was irrelevant. The condition of Irishness didn't apply. When I went back to Lismore I still had to try and prove myself hurling. I was the same as everyone else, after all, a person without alternatives.

Every Friday afternoon, to end the week, Brother Blake would lead most of the primary school out from the monastery, along the Tallow road, in past Dunne's lodge and along the Castle farm-track to the field (rented by the hurling club from the Castle). To him it was a great outing. Once off the main road, and out of the Brother Superior's hearing, he'd burst into

song: 'I love to go a-wandering', usually, though he had a
good 'Gipsy Rover' as well. He could croon quite well in his
thick Clare accent, and would shout at us to join in the chorus.
We'd go:

> Awdi-du, awdi-du aw day
> Awdi-du, awdi-day-dee
> He whistled and sang till the green woods rang,
> And he won the heart of a lady.

Once at the field he'd appoint captains and have them pick
teams. Captains were usually favourites; either Blakey was a
friend of the family or the lad was good in class or he was just
a pet and a good hurler. If I'd been able to hurl I'd have been
well set for captaincy, because Blakey had taught with my
father in Dublin before being shifted to Lismore, and had
come to tea one Christmas for a chat about old times with him.
And didn't Mam and all the brothers meet every morning at
convent mass? So by rights I should be given some sort of
prominence. But I was never a favourite of his. It wasn't I he
called 'ceann bán' and put his arm around, but Leonard Lyons
of Botany. The only thing he did for me was give me permission to go to the lavatory whenever I wanted to without
raising my hand. I had to go a lot.

Although there were enough of us to make a reasonable
number of seven-a-side teams, the invariable format was to
divide us into two factions, town and country. This was done
in order to foster competition, which was the thing Brother
Blake liked to do best. In class – he had the three junior
primary classes; Brother Murphy the two senior – he also
divided us up, naming the teams after parts of the town and
awarding points for scholastic attainment (in sums, spelling
and writing), while deducting them for bad behaviour and
stupid mistakes. Around three o'clock every day the schoolroom atmosphere (the three classes were in the one room) was
a fine old frenzy of nerves as the competition reached its
climax, since whichever team won couldn't be caned the
following day. Winning was a wonderful feeling, almost as
good as making a mistake next day and realizing Blakey
couldn't beat you for it.

Dividing us into town and country teams was shrewd and   129 pointed. Any other division would have struck us as weak and artificial. But nobody felt that Blakey was imposing a rivalry by having us compete along community lines. The antagonism was already there. It wasn't necessarily clear-cut, however. Most of us townies had farmers' sons as friends, and regarded some of them as just about our equals. But localized exceptions didn't affect the general outlook. We despised the country and all belonging to it, and felt ourselves immeasurably superior to everything it stood for.

Town was a world of its own, independent, aloof: no cowshit, no pig-squeals, no thatch. Town was cinemas, shops, priests and policemen. It didn't take a genius to work out where the world would be without any of them. The country was all tearing and dragging. It was weather-watching, chores at sunrise, accents sounding like gravel being shovelled. And country lads (*cabógs*, we called them) were no good in school, slow, dull, humourless, sullenly and silently objecting to book-work, sensing no doubt that they had no need of it, but were merely in attendance out of legal obligation, only to be beaten for being so obliging – well, why should they bother, wasn't there land ever before books were thought of? Most of them quit after primary school, an odd few going on to do the Intermediate Certificate, a rare one or two finishing secondary.

They, in turn, thought us weaklings, cissies, Mammies' boys, half-men who'd never pulled a teat, choked a chicken, or forked a bale of hay. They had arcane jokes. 'How d'you get down off a donkey? You don't, you get down off a duck.' Their breath smelled of buttermilk, slightly raw and unsavoury, and they had to walk miles to get anywhere. But, as tradition decreed, they had the brawn right enough. They were fitter and stronger and ran rings around us. They seemed easier to please, too. Perhaps getting together to play was a greater novelty for them, or maybe showing their paces was. At any rate, they overran us, while we stood around frustrated and complained of being fouled, the brains which tradition said we possessed as useless to us as swatches of wet straw.

Blakey loved the whole thing. He ran up and down, in a gloating, giggling gargle and roaring hoarse encouragement – always in Irish, a vain effort to bring the national tongue down to the everyday level of the national game. It wasn't that anybody objected to Blakey using such phrases. The practice lent him novelty, and therefore a certain amount of credibility, as a teacher, the way singing 'Val-de-ree, Val-de-raw' going to the field did. Gaels were not so common amongst us that we could take their behaviour for granted. Moreover, as Mam told me, being from Clare Brother Blake was not only Gaelic but 'mad Dev' as well, that was 'only natural' for a native of what Blakey himself called, proudly if obscurely, 'the Banner County'. I knew I was supposed to be impressed by the Irish-Dev connection, but if it did indeed confer an honoured place in Gaeldom on its beneficiaries, why was the Clare county team as useless at hurling as our own? This deficiency worried me: surely everything was supposed to interlock – hurling, Irish, Dev, God, the O'Briens and me?

That kind of worry was a luxury, of course, an exercise, a combination of conundrum and eye-opener. Much more pressing, and just as strange, was the way Blakey relished the country lads' triumphs. Monday morning, first thing after the prayer, he'd write the score up on the board. *An tuath 3-5, an baile 1-2. Ar aghaidh an tuath!* Oh, it was mortifying: those louts getting the best of us. Well next Friday – you could hear the intolerance seethe around the room – we'll knock 'em into kingdom come. For five or ten minutes even I felt ashamed of my inability, and I longed for nothing better than to hammer the country single-handed with unprecedented feats of stick-work.

Being a hopeless hurler made me ashamed in a more complex way too, however. It made me lie to Georgie.

'How'd you get on, Mike?' he'd ask at tea.

'Okay,' sheepishly.

'Did you score?'

'A goal and a point,' heart hammering.

'Good on you. Did ye win?'

'Naw,' with immense relief, though all disguised.

I thought to tell the truth would be a greater offence. My athletic incompetence was, I felt, a species of disloyalty to him and all he'd done for me – made me hurleys, bought me balls, brought me to matches – as well as all he stood for, his sideboard silver and his beaten leg.

And then, as well, I had to lie to protect myself. If I told him how I really was I felt sure he'd shout and carry on at me and 131 give me useless advice. 'Arra what ails you? Don't mind anyone. Wade in there. You'll do fine. And if anyone's too rough, just tell me.' It wasn't possible to say, 'I can't.' I couldn't be different from him. He loved me too much to allow it. So I lied. And he let me. Week after week I gave him a false tally. He never questioned it. Never even asked for the details for which the bare figures were such a transparent substitute. My lies were punished by his indulgent trust.

I found myself in the thick of the action once. Noel Coffey was going to strike an almighty blow for the opposition.

'Hook him. Hook him!' was the cry.

So I put my hurley in front of his as he was about to come out of his backswing, and sure enough he missed the ball.

Instead he knocked me cold for maybe as much as ten seconds. When I came to, I was 'spouting' from a cut over the eye. The sky was full of faces. There was a lot of jabbering. Nobody knew what to do. I was helped up and someone was told to escort me as far as the monastery kitchen where Nora, the housekeeper, washed me off and told me to call into Mr Hanrahan on the way home to find out if I needed a stitch. A stitch! Marvellous martyrdom by catgut and needle!

Using strips of tape, however, Mr Hanrahan deprived me, and even seemed to enjoy his ingenuity. Still, when I did get home, there was a gratifying outburst 'Oh my God!' and 'Sit down, boy', and questions galore. Mam went, 'Coffey . . . Coffey . . . ', narrowing her eyes, but she couldn't come up with anything to blacken the name of Noel or his people. So she just reassured me that 'them fellas' were all too big and rough for me, and I felt that my weakness was in a way precious to her, and that maybe I'd be sent to bed with hot lemonade.

I wasn't. Worse yet, when Georgie came home, he only threw me, 'Thing o' nothing. It'll make a man o' ya.' How much more face could my injury lose? I was looking forward to tons of attention, and I just knew I'd have to stay off school because every time I hung my head a little blood seeped from the cut. But by the Sunday I was well enough to write to my father about it, and by Monday I was back tackling vulgar fractions as though nothing had happened. In fact, the most memorable aspect of the whole affair was my father's letter back, in which he said I was becoming 'a war-scarred veteran'.

This strange phrase (he was not given to toughening me up to be his manly little soldier or anything like that) struck me as pleasantly sympathetic, with its fancy ring. It wasn't all that easy to pronounce, but it had an obvious truth to it which appealed. I had been in the wars. Then, as I savoured it, the phrase revealed a deeper meaning to me, a connection between hurling, battling and bloodshed which I was easily able to manipulate into a sense of patriotic self-congratulation. I too had suffered for my Irishness. Now I belonged with my mother's people, belonged more irrevocably than if, with open arms, they'd made me theirs.

It fell to Mam, however, to demonstrate exactly what such a sense of belonging could entail. And it came out of nowhere, that searing testament of hers, out of no more than Pa Sheehan's innocuous, light-hearted, weekly visit.

We all loved Pa. He was an agent for Royal Liver Insurance, a queer-seeming company to me, because it had a cock for a mascot. Up hill and down dale Pa travelled, collecting dues for them in his black Volks. 'Greatest car ever made,' he asserted vigorously, his Tallow accent rattling along like coal down a chute.

Pa was short, rotund, and very jolly. The adults loved him because he brought in all the news, tales of who might die next, who was on the mend, who was fighting, who was courting. He mimicked backsliding clients for us, speculated about lawsuits, overstayed his welcome by an hour or more, supping tea and sucking cigarettes.

And Mam was fond of Pa too, because he embodied pleasant memories. He had been a wonderful hurler in his day. If I'm not mistaken he won no less than an All-Ireland medal as a member of the first Waterford team to go all the way in the national championship. That was in 1948, and the twinkling pace of his manner now was reminiscent of the wit and speed that made him, as Mam said, 'like an ellet' when he played.

Anyhow, one Monday evening, in the casual drift of gossip, Pa mentioned something he'd heard about the organization of a Lismore soccer team. This had not been attempted before. The town did have a cricket team and those who turned out for it were considered by Mam to be beneath contempt, traitors to the race, 'shoneens'. The same labels were attached to anyone   133 who played any 'foreign game', licence to do so being implicitly provided by the rules of the Gaelic Athletic Association. So, I expected an outburst from Mam denouncing soccer. In fact I'd heard some of it before: soccer was a cissy's game, all tip-tap, no lavish scoring, played solely by cockney slum-dwellers and suchlike reprobates, for whom there was nothing deviant in the denial of hands. And in addition, now, those whose names Pa'd mentioned were idle *cadets*, useless articles, namby-pambies, deficient in unspecified yet definitive areas for declining to take swipes at one another with hard sticks.

'Well I don't know,' said Pa, mildly. 'I don't care what they're doing as long as it's not standing at the Red House corner waiting for something to happen.'

'Pa,' said Mam, vaguely alarmed, 'I'm surprised at you.'

'Ah, that oul' ban,' said Pa, referring to the GAA's prohibitions. 'Bad blood is all it ever caused. Of all things for people to be falling out over. They ought to get rid of it.'

'What?' cried Mam, huffily. 'After boys giving their lives, and that crowd trying everything they could to stop everything Irish, flamming the hands off in school if we spoke a word of our own language . . . .'

'I know all that, sure,' Pa said patiently. 'But listen. If Georgie or the child's father walked in the door and told you they were going to play soccer from this on, what would you do?'

'I'd show 'em the door,' said Mam harshly.

'You would not,' said Pa, gently dismissive.

'Oh, I would!' said Mam, bristling. 'I wouldn't have 'em under the same roof as me.'

'Your own flesh and blood?'

'Yes!'

'By gor,' said Pa, sighing, allowing his gaze to follow the flight of his cigarette butt to the fireplace, 'you're a hard woman.'

And she certainly looked it. Her face was as sheer and obdurate as steel, and as unflinching. It was a face that didn't have another cheek to turn. A face that was a prayer of dedication to the one true cause, to the only cause that had ever won through. Uncompromising, exalted, vindictive, extreme.

134   Irish.

I felt embarrassed. I felt sorry for Pa (he'd lost). I felt somehow weakened, confused, as though I'd been left standing bleakly alone, my hurley and its heritage reduced to a withered twig because I couldn't play.

2

As she probably knew, Mam had no reason to doubt Georgie's attachment to our national games. My father was a more likely source of concern. A nippy half-forward in his day – so I heard; as with so much about him I only have casual remarks to go on – he now spent all his free time going to foreign films. But Mam accepted as best she could that strange developments occur in cities. He hadn't stooped to foreign games, anyhow, thank God!

To call Georgie's involvement with the GAA that of a mere fan would be to misrepresent grievously its ardour. What went on between them was more like a marriage, tense, erratic, satisfying only in consummation (not in consciousness). Player, official, aspiring bureaucrat – or, if you like, lover, husband, self-styled head-of-household – there was no phase of the organization's activities in which he wasn't utterly, selflessly, critically engrossed.

He was past his prime as a player when I saw him. Full-back was his position, and no doubt he was what the papers call 'a stalwarth', often exhibiting 'tenacious defence' and 'clearing his lines with dispatch' (where did they get the pseudo-military lingo?), but more often shoving and poking and being beaten for speed. For me, too, there was an additional problem with the full-back position: it wasn't glamorous. Not for Geo the elegant overhead 'double', the point exquisitely picked off from an acute angle on the wing, the bullet scorching its way to the back of the net. Occasionally he might burst out of a ruck of enemies and deliver what the parlance called 'a long, relieving clearance'. But I wanted everything he did to be spectacular, lyrical, cheer-worthy. It was difficult to be stylish, I knew 135 that, I'd heard players being criticized for it: style was light-weight, aggression was what counted. I was disappointed, though, that Georgie couldn't, just once in a while, describe an exhilarating arabesque with his stick, or side-step musclebound intimidation, or beat an opponent to the pull with zesty speed. Why couldn't he be like Chrissy a little?

I wasn't too critical, however, because I could see what a good Gael he was in other respects, what a dutiful caretaker, loyal husband, diligent *domestique*. He could never do enough. On the day of a match he lined the pitch, which meant going around the field (110 yards by 30) with a brush and a bucket of whitewash, marking the boundary of the playing area. He painted the goal posts. He made the corner flags and the side-line flags and the flags for the umpires. He brought home the team's reeking jerseys and demanded they be washed, causing consternation among the two women, who neverthe-less scrubbed away, for all their mutinous mutterings, as though their sense of duty too was bound up in the black-and-amber of Lismore.

Georgie served unpaid, and largely unthanked, his sole reward an occasional senior county championship fixture or, more rarely, an inter-county exhibition game. The whole town feasted on the prestige and publicity of such events, and naturally George was thrilled to see the town, the club and the field recognized, though no doubt he would have slaved away regardless of whether a big match ever came to town or not.

I looked back with awe at his powers of commitment, at how fervently – and with enviable innocence – he believed that life is the possibility of total immersion. His involvement with the GAA was such that it went well beyond the narrow righteous-ness of national games. It had to do with activity as authentic-ity, with large-lifeness, with trying as hard as possible to obtain as much as possible on behalf of comradeship and community. Trying too hard, perhaps. I wouldn't be at all surprised to learn that other club members were less active than they wanted to be because of Geo's drive. But at the time it was very clear that nobody needed the outlet as badly as George. And it may be too that, thanks to being vulnerable in ways that other men his age had been able to grow out of, Georgie was best placed to appreciate what the GAA represented. It was the only secular, nationwide organization that offered a life larger than the everyday – the life of a designated, and perhaps archetypal, cultural participant, in which sinew surpassed cash-box, wind bettered prayer, body smote body playfully, and a crowd might still marvel. And a big match was not a small reward. It was wonderful to feel the streets filled with anticipation, to be borne along to the field by a garrulous throng. The sense of everyone enthusiastically united, which gave rise to the exhilarating notion that we were absolutely right to be carrying on as we were, made a match seem the thing for which mass was a rehearsal.

The Mellary Pipers Band would be in attendance. We'd all stand exuberantly to attention, face the tricolour and give out the national anthem. 'Soldiers are we . . . '. And who amongst us didn't feel that indeed he was? And just to make sure that this was an occasion, that living hallmark of the great day, the fiddler, turned up as well. Where he came from, and where he went to, nobody was able to tell me: it was as though the atmosphere had contrived him out of nowhere, in order to reproduce itself in his delirious reels. He got paid, too, I noted jealously. Not a man passed but didn't drop a copper or two into the little bag hanging from one of the tuning-pegs. (Women were stingier.) He'd nod his head thankingly, his elbow unceasing. His face was as brown as a nut.

Big matches had drawbacks, though. The crowds were so large, sometimes, and so avaricious for a glimpse of a star – Pad Stakelum of Tipperary, Philly Grimes of Mount Sion and Waterford, Duck Whelan of Abbeyside – that a nipper like me could hardly see a thing. I didn't mind that too much. The atmosphere was so charged it was hard to concentrate anyhow, and I was happier expressing my excitement by darting round the grown-ups' legs. Sometimes, too, dodging around, I'd run into Chrissy talking to some strange fellow (big matches were a fairly rare opportunity for girls to parade their finery), and I'd tug on her dress till she thrust a penny at me, scowling, 'Don't be so saucy!' and off I'd run to buy a Pixie bar or a Cough-No-More (the *jalapeño* of liquorice treats). God knows how many dates I may have ruined on her, how many hopeful swains drew back, thinking me a euphemistic nephew, thinking maybe that they had a lucky escape from the clutches of a fast woman as, after the game, they cycled 137 uphill home to milk the cattle.

The bad thing that big matches did was to reveal the field's inadequate facilities and to suggest, to me at any rate, that no matter how much Georgie might do it was never enough. The crowds showed that it was inconvenient to have a pee. What passed for a toilet was a few strips of whitewashed galvanized iron, behind which men could go. There were always too many waiting, though – predictably: who in his right mind would think of attending the centrepiece of his Sunday without a feed of porter? But I didn't like hopping from foot to foot in a thicket of hairy jackets and brown boots.

Also, the field had no changing-rooms. There was nothing unusual in that – no field had: the nearest ones were in the city of Cork. It was one thing, however, for veterans of local junior games to 'tog on' under the stand of limes behind the town goal, quite another for a luminary whose picture had been splashed in the *Independent* the previous week, especially as such demi-gods went in for new-fashioned shirts, that opened all the way down. It didn't seem right to me that they should be to the same rough-and-ready conditions as any yob from Knockanore or Gaultier.

Yet it was those very buckoes who provided the field's standard fare, barrel-chested swashbucklers from the back of beyond. Theirs was no flattery. They feelingly persuaded us what we were. If the big match embodied for us the lyric of carnival, the typical encounter enacted the drama of blood-feud. And their usages could be damn ugly. At these junior matches (junior and senior are categories of excellence, not age) the crowd was split and hostile. It generally wasn't satisfied to watch the action, it had to join in as well, invading the pitch and laying about them while club officials, among them usually a young curate, ineffectually went, 'Boys, Boys . . . '.

Some clubs were notorious. The Geraldines. Ballyduff. The Shamrocks. The rate at which they tore and slashed was simply terrifying. Nearly everyone in Lismore was too well-reared to fight, too respectable for that kind of thing. Besides, many were shopkeepers and reluctant to risk trade and reputation by allowing tempers to fray. If Lismore was too civilized to defend itself, the others (whoever they might be) were just out-and-out savages. The latter verdict kept the town honour intact. I suppose I subscribed to that outlook. Let the art of the stick prevail, not the force of the arm. And at home I received repeated cautions from both Mam and Chrissy about unseemly, ruffianly fisticuffs.

Still, people continued to get hurt. George, of course. And I remember distinctly seeing a player for Brickey Rangers with one side of his face a bright red veil of blood. And I was at the field the Sunday Wally was stretchered off. That was the incident that really frightened me, because Wally was a neighbour and he nearly died.

It happened in a game of quite commonplace vehemence. The opposition was Fourmilewater, a team from the hills north of Dungarvan. Although he lived virtually next door to us, Wally lined out for the team nearest his own townland; he came from Camphire, so he played for Tourin. Such fidelity was entirely normal. For countrymen who'd newly settled or who had jobs in town, playing with their own sort was the only conceivable choice. So there was Wally at midfield in the pink-and-white stripes of Tourin, pulling across his opposite number every time the ball came near them – overhead, on the ground, every way – with his opposite number giving as good as he got, bits of broken hurley flying furiously out from them with every contact, to the cheers of the crowd, until at length down Wally went, and the crowd kicked up blood and murder.

Wally bled. He bled all the way to the doctor. The doctor advised immediate removal to the hospital in Dungarvan. He bled, we heard, the whole of that fifteen-mile drive. They didn't like the look of him in Dungarvan, so off to Ardkeen in Waterford City he went, still bleeding, for all I know, since by the time scraps of hearsay came my way Wally was virtually a man in a legend. 'Main strong,' people said, their tones a mixture of horror and admiration. 'If that was a town-boy, now, 'tis in a box he'd be.' But box-wards Wally seemed to drift: the next thing we knew he was up in the Richmond Hospital, Dublin, to have his skull operated on. Apparently a splinter from his opponent's stick had embedded itself – so I heard, anyhow. (Or maybe so I was told to stop me asking endless questions. Or maybe that's how legend had it after-wards, registering the force of the skull-opening blow.) I remember trying to picture the big knife, and shivering.

I remember, too, Georgie's forceful reactions, mainly   139 directed against the hurling bureaucracy. Why wasn't it compulsory for clubs to insure players? Even when Wally came home he still wouldn't be fit to work: what were his wife and child supposed to live on? Geo waxed highly indignant and disgusted, as though only realizing for the first time the inadequacies of amateurism and that hurling was really only a game, not an ethic. What were *they* doing about Wally? Bugger-all! Eventually, a benefit dance was held, but it took so long to organize that Wally may even have been home for it.

He did come home, I'm delighted to say. It was strange seeing him, his shaved head and ice-coloured face. Convalescing, he'd stand for an hour outside his front door and my friend Pete and I would stop and chat with him. His scar was plain to see, a livid snake of a thing that ascended from behind his right ear. He had a slightly crackling laugh. He spoke softly and obsessively about women. Six months passed. He went back to work for Hyde the timberman, pottering about. Main strong!

Chrissy and Mam agreed that Georgie's criticism of how Gaeldom handled the injury was nothing but the truth. His judgments were as quick and as definitive as Mam's. And the object of his criticism was familiar too. On winter Sundays, as the Lismore delegate, he attended meetings of various boards and councils, and on his return insisted on regaling us with examples of their idiocies and timidities, eyes turbid with Guinness and a cigarette cocked crookedly between marshy lips.

Geo never took me to these confabulations, no doubt aware of how bored I'd be, and I didn't mind much at the time, though I'm sorry now that I never heard him denounce in public, to their faces, the sub-clergy who ran the GAA. What I was sorry and very resentful about then was not being taken to the inter-county games at which he officiated. In vain, George tried to explain that he couldn't umpire effectively and keep an eye on me at the same time. I had no use for explanations predicated on responsibility; I'd heard too many of them. Nothing could persuade me that Georgie's having a day out without me wasn't the height of injustice. And not just any old day out either. The games he inspired were of championship significance; they'd be written up in the morning's paper. He was going to see Buttevant, Thurles, Kilmallock, towns which my sulking mind translated as Isfahan, Baghdad,

Constantinople.

It was an act of rank ingratitude for me to sulk (and I'm sure I cried a time or two as well: the slightest hint of being left out or being left behind was quite enough to start me off). As Mam impatiently reminded me, I'd no right to whine, Geo did damn well by me (implying, too well) – what about all the other days out I'd had with him? And at the mention of those, though I may have added a snivel or two for form's sake, I basically shut up. Mam was absolutely right, I couldn't deny it, there wasn't a child in the town who'd had more outings than me. And of all the good times of my childhood, those small excursions were without a doubt the best.

Cappoquin (four miles to the east) was the usual venue for Lismore's away fixtures. The distance didn't matter; I already felt transported thanks to the novelty of a car-ride. And I liked Cappoquin, even though Lismore people generally thought it a hole. That was because it had no scenery, the Blackwater just made an impressively wide right-angle turn to the sea there. Instead of a castle all it could boast of was a bacon factory. On weekdays the whole west end of the town seethed with the hysteria of the condemned, while a continual stream of offal poured down a gore-striped factory wall into the river. Lismore people seemed to raise a collective eyebrow at such phenomena, as much as to say, 'Is this the way for a town to conduct itself?' Nothing disturbed Lismore's peace and purity, nothing whatever.

But Cappoquin always seemed a free-and-easy place to me, maybe because it didn't have big buildings casting long shadows on it, and instead of slightly unreal street-names like Lismore's Fernville and South Mall had Pound Lane and Mill Street. The names on the shop-fronts were delightfully different too: Uniacke, Meskil, Gillespie, Herr . . . . And I loved the orphanage, it overlooked the hurling field. Sometimes marching down with the team I'd see the orphans being taken for a walk by the Sisters of Mercy who had charge of them, their mothers, as I thought then. I only remember that they were all boys, they were all dressed alike (grey jerseys, grey flannel trousers), and they all seemed the same size – the effect, no doubt, of having to walk two abreast in a rigid column. The sight of them provided me with a bracing dose of *schadenfreude*.

141

During those Sunday outings with the team, however, I saw more of the town's pubs than I did of the town itself. The pub was our home from home. Sometimes we plumped for Conway's Hotel, rather more rarely the Toby Jug (a true piece of Cappoquin novelty, that name, I thought), but mainly Jimmy Foley's 'The Railway Bar' was where we pitched camp. Jimmy was from Lismore, and a friend of Georgie's – they used to cycle competitively together. It struck me that Jimmy must have been the better of the two. Above the bar there was a colour photograph of someone on a real racing bike, in real racing kit – black shorts, wide-striped jersey, and a crash helmet that looked like a gorilla's mitten. Photos of Georgie were few and far between. And Jimmy had a prosperous air to him, he'd retired from competition, possibly even owned a car. Business was good, and he owned a greyhound, hoping no doubt that its phenomenal haunches would replicate – or maybe improve on – the thigh-power of his own sprightlier days.

It was in that small bar that each visit perfected itself, as I sat in a corner with a tumbler of the rust-coloured fizz that was called lemonade and a bag of dusty-tasting Marietta biscuits and, rapt, revelled in the company of men. Their playful jostling before the game, their nervous teasing, the rattle of coin and key as clothes were changed. The sleeveless singlets and cotton drawers, pale freckled shoulder-blades, the surprising sight of hairy legs. The few who had watches – Michael Madden, Ronnie O'Donnell – wrapped them up carefully in their hankies. Sonny Bransfield, home from England, leaning time after time on his angled stick to test its spring, hoping that this year, maybe, he'd rediscover the touch that he'd once been able to take for granted. A murmuring, a restlessness. Vacant, undirected whoops and shouts. Everybody hopeful, boyish, unrecognizably gay.

The game didn't matter. Lismore always lost. Tourin beat us, Tallow beat us, the Geraldines regularly hammered us, as did Affane and the Brickey Rangers. And when they first stumbled back into Jimmy's, team members often looked crestfallen or sheepish. But disappointment was amazingly short-lived, and Geo considered it bad form to denounce backsliders on the spot. In a twinkling there was hearty laughter and rounds of drinks, and soon – a true test of conviviality

– morbid ballads were aired. They sang, in ragged unison:

> Goodbye Johnny dear and when you're far away
> Don't forget your dear old mother far across the sea.
> Write a letter now and then, and send her all you can.
> And don't forget where'er you go that you're an Irishman.

After each song strong cries of approval went up – 'Good man, Joe. Good man yourself!' – followed by a moment's silence while an orchard of Adam's apples wobbled with draughts of down-coursing porter. I sat amongst them with my mouth open (its inside a kind of beach from biscuit crumbs and gassy cordials), marvelling at all this ease and camaraderie, so rare, yet seemingly so accessible, unable to do wee-wee even, though I was bursting, the spell of my defeated, happy townsmen was so strong.

3

'Are you awake, Seoirse?' Chrissy called softly.

Was I what? 'Awake' was hardly the word. Since the first twitterings of dawn I'd been on full alert, charged to the hilt with electric tension. This was the day of the big one. This was the day for which those Cappoquin Sundays were a rehearsal. Geo was taking me to Dublin for the All-Ireland.

I was sybaritically aware of what an extravagant treat it was to attend the final of the national hurling championship and to travel over a hundred miles in Corny Willoughby's Ford V8 in order to do so. None of my pals had the ghost of a chance of doing half as much. Most of them hadn't been to Dublin even on an ordinary day. But there was just as much pleasure for me in the thought that I was caught up in an event whose outcome stirred the spirits of the vast majority of my fellow-countrymen, and that my heart would drum along with the pulse of thousands and that my roar would contribute to the great roar. I saw the event as an acting out of the old nationalist hymn 'A

Nation Once Again' (a temporary state, of course, but all the more precious and intense for that). And I hoped to feel more overwhelmingly and more delightfully than usual how good it was to have a self to cede to the collective.

Fuelling me further, everyone had high expectations of this particular clash. For weeks the newspapers had promised a 'classic encounter'. Would the purple-and-gold cohorts of Wexford come down 'like a wolf on the fold' on the stalwarths of Cork, the Rebel County?

In those days there wasn't a livelier question a national daily could ask. Economically, politically and every other way the country was dozing on the sideline, the national mood the inspiration of not much more than jokes. (The one about compilers of an Irish-Spanish dictionary having trouble translating *mañana* because nothing in Irish quite conveyed the same sense of urgency probably first surfaced in a Dublin pub *circa* 1952 or 1953.)

Yet in all the stagnation, hurling thrived, had its Golden Age indeed, or its Age of Ring as it should be called, since the chief igniter of interest and inspirer of purple prose was Christy Ring – superstar, genius and enemy (he played for Cork). For quick wits, speed over five to ten yards, instinct for undefended space, economy and wristiness of stroke, there never was anyone like him. He sprang into the country's torpid imagination like a flare in a fog. A damn shame, I thought, that he wasn't on our side. But at least I'd be seeing the great man. And then, think if we beat him?

As if anticipation of the game and sense of occasion weren't enough, and as though to ensure that I wouldn't be able to succumb completely to the collective, the day also promised a treat that would be all mine. (I wouldn't want it any other way, of course, but how wonderful when world collaborated with self!) I'd be seeing my Daddy at a totally unfamiliar time of the year, the first Sunday in September, when we were both in school. I'd bashfully drink in again the tanned face, the deep brown eyes, the jet-black hair swept back. I'd realize again – soon, soon! – with eye-opening, brimming confidence that I was his alone, he mine, the real thing, antecedent and superior to anything Lismore provided.

'Eat your breakfast, there,' said Mam, impatiently.

I couldn't. And every minute was an hour.

But soon we were off, stopping to pick up our last passenger, Billy Linneen, at the bridge (Geo and three or four of his pals had hired the car between them), then sliding smoothly up the mountain road, north towards Ireland.

Over the mountains with us, via the Vee, with the whole plain of Munster spread out beneath like a quilt of heaven, fertile Tipperary in green and gold, and in the shade of the Galtees the Golden Vale. On hummingly through Clogheen and Cahir, all fast asleep, and next Cashel of the Kings, with its massive, abbey-crowned rock, as isolated and lofty as the past itself, while opposite the ruin's main entrance sat the comprehensible present, the 'Rock' cinema.

The talk turned to why Tipperarymen were called 'stone-throwers', and a long and learned discussion ensued (we flew past the Horse and Jockey), featuring solemn references to Dan Breen and Sean Treacy, whose sons, it was plain, Geo and the other sojourners longed to be. We were beyond Urlingford, we were in Laois, a county nobody knew anything about, not even how to pronounce it. But there was the big jail in Portlaoise, and there was the castle in Portarlington where John McCormack lived.

'Count John.'

'I suppose he was called Count on account of all the money he made.'

'Yerra not at all,' disputatiously; 'Wasn't it the Pope made a Count of him?'

The car rocked with laughter, and to maintain the mood, someone sang a snatch of 'The Fairy Tree', breaking off when it came to the line, 'And Katie Ryan saw there' to ask, 'Is that one of them Ryans of Glenshask, I wonder?'

'The one with the crooked eyes?'

'I dunno is that all she has crooked?'

'Are you asking or telling, now?'

More explosions of laughter.

On we bowled, the increasing flatness of the land seeming to increase our speed, as though the openness made Dublin act like a magnet. We crossed the Curragh of Kildare – maledictions from a few, especially George, on the site of the political obscenity of their generation, the Curragh camp. Then the barracks at Newbridge and the wide main-street, then Naas and Mrs Lalor's fine old ivy-clad hotel. Almost 145 there. Billboards, double-decker buses, fast driving. Clondal-kin, Walkinstown, Drimnagh – and, at last, tucked into that treeless vastness of public housing, Sundrive Road, where brick uniformity turned into uplift, landfall, hope.

There he was. 'Hello John,' said everyone, crowding around the front door, and I didn't get to say hardly anything, what with the throng, and feeling shy, and because the next thing we had to do was go to mass – short twelve, at St Bernadette's, Clogher Road – and then there was a lot of garbled big-people's talk about arrangements, Geo and his pals being in a terrible hurry to get a few pints in after the rigours of the road and before the minor game, but wanting to seem concerned about my day, as though my father's presence brought out the parent in all of them, until at last 'Up Wexford!' George called out the kitchen door to me, and they were gone.

I was in the garden, attempting to slip into my other life. That was the best place to reorient myself, to reintroduce myself to city birds (gulls and pigeons), to hear the nasal Dublin voices from the soccer game in the communal field beyond the garden wall, the voices of people Peg called 'gurriers'. I'd been rigorously instructed in Lismore that while the people who lived all around us – in Clogher Road, in Stanaway Road, and on up into Kimmage – were only recently converted slum-dwellers, Sundrive Road was somehow above all that, had to be, since it housed my father the school-teacher. But the raspy, glottal shouts from the field were a delight to me, conveying, I felt, the tang of the real Dublin, beckoning me away from my familiar self.

Perhaps it was a pity that I had no Dublin playmates, but I never bewailed their absence at the time. The city itself was my true friend. In it I found the measure of my yearning. Besides, the once or twice I talked with neighbouring kids they ended up asking me why I didn't live there all the time, obliging me to explain tearfully it was because my mother was dead. Then I'd run indoors, only for Daddy to greet me with an exasperated, 'Och, what is it now?' That made me cry even more, because I thought my tears had a truer basis than his prickliness, and because 'Och' was an Enniscorthy expression.

146   Still, I did think of the people next-door as my friends. A

mother and daughter (Mam and Chrissy figures, I suppose, but distanced and made bland by the change of bailiwick). They were just my kind of people. The girl (how is it that I can remember everything except their names?) worked in the Clarnico-Murray sweet factory, as she often generously reminded me. And better yet, they were related to Shay Elliott, the famous cyclist who rode in the Tour de France, a fact which delightfully connected me with a celebrity and connected them with my father, who knew all about the Tour. He'd been to France, after all, and not just Lourdes, either, but Rocamadour, where he had a pal, Maurice. And he told me about the race, the yellow jerseys, the national mania: it was like an All-Ireland that lasted two weeks. He could pronounce the names: Babet, Fausto Coppi. He could sing 'La Vie en Rose'. I was so proud of him.

I was alone in my pride, however.

Mam wrangled with him about money, about new clothes for me, about my tearful temperament ('that child can't bear correction'). As for Peggy, I chanced to find out how she felt during one of my summer visits. My father, unusually, had gone out for the evening, and I'd been sent to bed early because of the fuss I'd created at his going. I lay there snivelling, waiting for the pink, traffic-burdened evening to go away.

Downstairs, Peg must have thought I was asleep, or probably was unfamiliar with the acoustics of the house (never having been in my position and bred to the thick-walled silences of Swiss Cottage). In any case, out poured all her resentments, Mam encouraging her – Mam summered with Daddy and me until I was ten or so. My father didn't do a stroke around the house, he treated Peg like a skivvy, he'd never have a square meal if she didn't make it for him, he didn't care tuppence for his schoolwork ('and him with his BA and Higher Dip.Ed. A School Inspector he should be, not teaching in that slum in Inchicore'). And – horror of horrors! – he drank. Brendan Tiernan puked on the stairs. 'So I said to John, if you think I'm going to clean that up, you have your wax!' Peg's voice had a touch of a turkey-gobble in it and she relished afresh her indignation.

'You were right, girl,' said Mam, solemnly.

I heard it all, appalled. My father a boozer, no better than 147 any Church Lane clown. The tears came in earnest, then, a flood of anger and shame, as I lay wondering how I would lay up this picture of a life hitherto invisible in my store of specialness.

I've often tried since to reconstruct for myself the life I was denied in Sundrive Road. Judging by the house, it can't have amounted to much. At the time, of course, it was difficult for me to see that, or even to see the place simply as a house. It was a place tinged by the strangeness of my parents having briefly lived there. But, as a dwelling, it showed itself to be completely beyond the range of that golden moment.

Take the aborted front room. This was the most spacious room in the house, the one with the bay window, the one that most people I knew would make the home's centrepiece, complete with china cabinet, sofa and holy pictures. In the home I yearned for, the front room contained my father's bike, bundles and stacks of old papers and magazines, an upturned butter box rimmed with shoe-polish, and brushes, rags and tins on the floor around it. And dust. Layers – beaches – of it. An airless, neglected, rejected space; indifferently, negligently, knowingly accommodated, making a cipher of 'home', turning the house into an address, a depot. Domesticity's grave. My mother's memorial.

Only by lending the room emblematic force can its nullity be redeemed, and I'm all the more prompted to do that knowing now my father and I never did make a family. But as a know-nothing child, the room was just one strangeness among others, one of no great magnitude either. I used to visit it off and on, despite severe cautions not to ('You'll get your shirt all dirty'), and whiled away pleasant half-hours thumbing through old copies of *The Listener*, with its close-printed pages and sober livery. Once or twice, the room even provided a discovery. One was *Feasta*: the idea of anything written in Irish for grown-ups amazed me. Another discovery was of a tea-chest containing, among bits of bike gear and played-out Travelites, four old-fashioned notebooks, real good ones, with marbled board covers and stout spines and inside – incredibly – full of my father's hand-writing. My nervous skimming revealed the contents as the story of my father's youth. I put them aside guiltily. But the next time I looked for them, they and the tea-chest were gone.

I played at being bus conductor, running up and down stairs shouting 'Any more fares?' and standing at the closed front door intoning, 'Kelly's Corner', 'Dolphin's Barn', 'Step along now, please!' in my fake Dublin accent. A busman's life was the life for me. It was solitary, standing on the platform alone. It was citified: when my time to enrol came I intended to make it quite clear that I was prepared to man double-deckers only. And it combined to a nicety service and command.

When I was ordered to stop reciting my gazetteer of inner-city landmarks – a practice which I conceded might become tiresome, without quite seeing how – I went and pitted the wooden mantelpiece in the living-room with my father's tuning-fork, echoing its hum with a long, drawn-out one of my own, in imitation of Brother Blake trying to teach us to sing. Five minutes of this, however, and I was told, 'Oh, shut up.'

I liked being in the living-room, though. It wasn't dark. The bookshelves overflowed enticingly, sometimes disgorging treasures such as a picture book of Fernandel, whose title must have been *Forty Ways to Look Ovine and Happy*, or perhaps a photograph album with snaps of me when I wasn't the height of a bee's knee. There was a Bush radio, which, in contrast to the one in Lismore, looked like a real piece of cabinet-making, and which had a broad, sea-green dial, promising reception from Frankfurt, Hilversum and AFN. And there was a picture on the wall of a man in specs and a bow-tie.

'Who's that, Daddy?'

'W. B. Yeats.'

'Who's he?'

'A poet.'

'Oh.'

The Sunday of my All-Ireland excursion, I remember, Peg did not officiate at lunch, in fact she was nowhere to be seen. She must have decided that a load of countrymen pressing in, and for all she knew expecting to be fed as well, was more than she could face on her day off. I was disappointed, though, since I'd been hoping that maybe she'd have a bit of pork ready for me. (Pork was a great novelty. The butchers of Lismore didn't stock it. And it was in a meal of Peg's that I first had it.) Peg's disinclination to serve us means, however, that I know exactly what I had for lunch that day. Bacon and cabbage, done in my father's inimitable way – the pressure cooker. This method, which I approved of on the grounds of speed and spectacle, invariably made the bacon awfully salty and reduced the cabbage to wraiths of singed steam.

I set-to with a will, however, and bolted down the meal in record time, partly to please Daddy – he disliked my finicky moods – and partly, of course, because we'd have to be getting a move on if we wanted to get to the game. Surprisingly, though, Daddy seemed in no hurry, lingering over the inevitable post-prandial cup of reddish-brown tea and drawing with relish on his John Player. Eventually, crushing the butt with exaggerated care, he said:

'Do you want to go to the match?'

Why yes of course, naturally, wasn't that what the whole day was about? What did he mean?

'Well,' he went on – 'It's a bit late now, and there'll be an awful crowd (so it'll be hard to see), and it looks like rain, so I thought we could go to the pictures, instead, if you like.'

'What's on?'

Half an hour later we were sitting in the Regal, I was scoffing a tub of HB ice-cream, and Kirk Douglas was warbling 'A Whale of a Tale'. *Twenty Thousand Leagues under the Sea*. And that was just about as far as I felt from the day's original promise.

I still don't know why I did it. Was it that I felt I had no option but to play along with whatever my father suggested, being so used to living in the shadow of his (and everybody else's) designs anyway? Was it, simply, that I just wanted to be with *him* more than anything else? Was it that I thought it smart to go to the cinema in the city, especially with a big noise from the Irish Film Society, which I believed Daddy to be.

When we were in town together (without Mam) he often took me up the three flights of tall stairs in North Earl Street to the Society's offices. I loved being able to look down on the pigeons and the roofs of double-deckers, while the names of Rossellini, De Sica and Ford ambled through the smoky air behind me. Mam attacked the whole thing as a waste of time, and said Daddy ought to be ashamed of himself for thinking more of a sideshow than of his teaching, advancing himself in his profession he should be – making more money. She never saw that the Society and its films provided most of the aesthetic pleasure and intellectual grist which my father needed in order to feel that he was living in the present, instead of in the limbo of widowerhood. So, in opting for the cinema, was I unconsciously siding with my father against Mam?

If I was, the impulse occurred at a depth of twenty thousand leagues in my psyche. The fact is, I had no sense of having deliberately done anything much at all until Geo and his mates came back, all flushed and glad-looking, and full of the game. It had been a classic, a thriller, worth going any length to see.

'A shame ye lost,' said Geo to me. That was the first I'd heard, or thought, of the result, but the news of it had no effect on me. Stimulated by my own day, I promptly blurted out, 'We didn't go. We went to the pictures.'

'The pictures!' Geo cried, and I knew then there was something wrong. 'Sure you could have done that in Lismore.'

A beam of pain irradiated a face slackened by porter and surprise.

I knew I'd betrayed him. Geo wasn't interested in me just then, however, but was glaring at my father. What was I to do now? I felt caught between them, in no-man's land.

But it was all right; we were leaving anyhow. Clumsily I threw my arms around my father and sidled out to the car. Evening was closing in. We glided away.

Soon, once the city had been forsaken, the men's talk picked up, the match was replayed blow by blow, and incident sparked memory. I listened lackadaisically, morosely. Not even the jolly stop at Mary Willy's – the half-way house – picked me up. The men let me be, imagining, no doubt, that I had Daddy on my mind. I had, of course. That tobaccoey smell, the rasp of that rough, dark cheek, that mellow voice made smooth by city usage. But what bore down on me much more heavily was the idea that I had inflicted on Georgie the worst injury of his hurling career. Just by doing nothing. Just because I was me. It was as though pain and conflict were endemic. Clash inevitable. And myself both agent and outcome. That's what I took with me down the long road home.

DANCEHALL DAYS

for Pam, who should have been there: with love

CONTENTS

DANCEHALL DAYS

You take delight not in a city's seven or seventy wonders,
but in the answer it gives to a question of yours.
Or the question it asks you, forcing you to answer . . .
— Italo Calvino, *Invisible Cities*

I
CUCKOOS

They were tigers. They were liners. They were only slightly less fabulous than jukeboxes, the new 7AS and 8s, with their sixty-four seats and automatic transmissions. And though Dublin buses and I went back a long way together, now – I had just been released by the Leaving from boarding-school in Culshiedom – they were more than ever like vessels of desire, Loreleis. Their motors palpitated as though Phil Spector had tuned them. Their familiar ads – so many welcome mats – hymned all I'd pined for: Granby's Sausages, Players Please, Mi-Wadi. The vagaries of their leaps and bounds were surely, I thought, meant to coach me in a risky but fashionable dance, whose moves I – the Chubby Checker of the Sallynoggin run – would soon tame and thrill to. When they breezed along the road beside the bay they turned me into an heroic voyager, alone, aloft, captain and master, drawing smoothly on a Player and practising smoke-rings. I assumed that the fate and soul which I supposedly commanded would present themselves at some pleasant set-down-only stop a few months down the way. How could my present life – nothing but work and family – be the real thing? Like most of my present lives before it, it had to be a missed turn, a detour from the unrocky highway to the city and the city's proper suburbs, pleasure and style, buses' only fitting destination.

For the time being, however, I was not heading into town. I was Monkstown bound. This was where my Da had his new house, his new wife, his new life, his new baby girl. This was where I was supposed to call home (I knew no other word; wished I didn't need one). Eleven d. it cost to get there. That took more than I'd bargained for from the four quid a week I was getting from the International Electronic Company, 161 thanks to my aunt and colleague, Peg. My heroically voyaging sails were in fact a pair of deflated pockets. But I was no more on speaking terms with fact then than I had ever been, so had no bother talking myself out of the high cost of elevenpence. If I couldn't increase cash, I could sustain image, and thus go on pretending that I retained control of something. Drawing on the masochism and self-deception which is mother's milk to hero-voyagers, I puffed myself up with the thought that forking out full fare at least made me a paid-up member of the general public. What I was to those at home and to those I worked with I was afraid to imagine. But the bus took me for an adult. If that cost elevenpence, fair enough. Compared to the free lifts Da gave me – the stuttering Morris Minor; our baleful silences – it was cheap at the price.

And there were the compensations of the route. Lansdowne Road. The Number One Army Band. The country spuriously and therefore happily united through the presence of foreigners. An International! Joe Linnane's crisp tones: 'Kyle to O'Meara, going left . . . . ' Tense faces crowded round the wireless in Lismore. Wasn't O'Meara something to the dentist in Fermoy? Peg used to go: 'Ah, the French were grand,' she reported. But the Welsh – 'Dirty coalminers!' I often wondered how somebody as petite as her – a regular communicant and good to her mother as well – could relish the heaving and rucking. I could only imagine that the city was in her, creator of mysteries and freedoms, of freedoms as mysteries. So when we stood revving for the light to change and I glimpsed the empty stands, I knew Lansdowne Road would do something for me too – that vague, ineffable, impossible, inevitable something which would finally confirm that I'd arrived, that I belonged.

It was only partly on the authority of Peg's experience that I knew the city could remake, enlarge and consolidate me. I had already had some twinges of such a possibility, one or two of them up the way at Lansdowne Road's big first cousin, the RDS. It was fun to see all Ireland on parade there, I supposed. The Nations Cup and the Aga Khan Trophy sounded like the big time. The Number One Army performed prodigious feats of what sounded to me like breaking wind, more impressive for its crispness than its melody; and I craved the true *kitsch* of the Artane Boys in their pink and black, and 'Kelly, the Boy from Killann'. Also disappointing was the unaccountable absence of chair-o-planes and bumpers. It showed poor taste and worse judgement to forego these mechanical analogues of equine callisthenics. But then the horses here were tame creatures, with ankle socks, braided tails, fastidious footwork; mere biological associates of the divot-spraying juggernauts of Lismore point-to-point. All I had to do was look around to see that the mechanical counterparts of these prima donnas were parasols and shooting-sticks, not the vulgar hurdy-gurdy. And Ireland always lost. Why couldn't they, I wondered impatiently, have mounted someone with cavalry in his blood, somebody like Jeff Chandler or Randolph Scott (a shame Grace Kelly was not a man . . .)?

As usual, 'they' were not taking my needs into consideration. Try as they might, however, they did not completely succeed in ignoring me, because as well as showing horses they showed machines. These static brutes were my delight. Horses were for the ancient ways; machines were monuments to the world to come. Horses were the stink and labour of down the country; these machines were of a cleanliness which, together with their power (called horsepower, but I knew it was more mysterious than that), kinned them to godliness. Fired up and roaring, they would anathematize Adam's curse in city accents. I saw myself reflected in the paintwork of their newness. I collected all the glossy brochures I could find, and found myself in them as well. The future was a forklift truck, a Lambretta with panniers. *Some day mine; some day* . . . . The world was Meccano for adults. I was good at Meccano.

I was walking to eternity through Industry Hall.

And when we sprang from the lights at Ailesbury Road, I remembered that here, too, the childish notion that my longing to be something might be satisfied, given time, found more support. This was where Da used to come to get visas for his holidays on the Continent, or to collect something for the Film Society. This was where the flags waved and the pages of my stamp album came alive, and I thought I understood what international meant. It was more than horse-prancing and scrums. It was a realization that we must amount to something if these foreigners came to live here. What that something was remained concealed for the time being amidst the rustle of 163 papers in cool vestibules, the muffled busyness of typewriters and telephones from the rooms beyond. Or rather, the something was that atmospheric *je ne sais quoi*, a combination of the air in those other places where we paid our respects and found perspective, the chapel and the bank. Oh, only let me be the equal of such exquisite establishments!

But after Ailesbury Road I was in no-man's land. By Merrion Gates, even though the houses were once more of a size I felt at home with, the world was dead, a place of names only. The sea was not a sea because it would not roar and crash. All it wanted to do was slap sulkily against the concrete wall, or withdraw to Howth, leaving a black non-beach behind. There was, of course, the giant illuminated Time Ale bottle opposite the Punch Bowl at Booterstown, so for a minute, while the busmen punched the time-clock there, it was possible to imagine that we had not left the city after all. The ad had all the witty effrontery of city style and of downtown's Bovrilorama: beer is larger than life, it said. But this was the last fizzle of bright lights; after it, no life at all was worth talking about until Dun Laoghaire, where at least there was the Top Hat. Blackrock College was a national landmark, no doubt, what with de Valera and things. But I never gave it a second look; I knew all about places like that. Besides, Dev's day was done. The cottages at Williamstown, opposite, were more interesting; they reminded me of the alms-houses in Lismore. And speaking of Lismore, there was a house at the top of the hill before the slope down to Blackrock that would not have been out of place down there, except it had a strange name – Frascati; too unEnglish to fit it properly. I suppose I should have asked Da about it – he was a teacher and would know. But sure it was only an old house. And I was not a tourist. And it was being brought home to me how much safer and simpler things would be if I pretended to be completely indifferent to them.

No *terra* was more *incognita*, though, than Monkstown itself. The bus plunged down the Monkstown Road, and I felt scared. It wasn't the speed, it was the strangeness. The road itself was unnaturally straight. Ailesbury Road was straight, too, but it was supposed to be foreign. There were no flags in Monkstown, so what business did the road have in being different? I eventually concluded that it must have been made by the British for visiting royalty, a miracle in macadam after the rigors of the Irish Sea and the squalid Kingstown waterside, with room to spare for entourage, outriders and loyal beggars cadging a sovereign. Perhaps it was in order to crowd out this last contingent that houses were built along the route. They spoiled the royals' view, but that seemed a small price to pay for such an estimable exercise in civic sanitation, all the more so since the houses were such as to make the regal guest feel that he was among his own. The lower-case 'house' grossly understates how these creations struck me. These were Lodges, Villas, Seats. It was as if all the grandeur and self-possession of the piles I knew in the Blackwater valley were condensed into this one, sheer, untypical stretch of road; into these haughty watering-holes for Wolseys and Rileys whose rooftops were crowned with cubist crucifixes tuned to the latest transmissions from across the water. Only for those aerials and the occasional sough of the mailboat hooter, you'd hardly take this for Ireland at all.

Even the churches in Monkstown were odd. Monkstown Church itself (my stop) was Protestant. I'd never been in a place where that kind of a church was the main landmark. But then I wasn't used to churches that looked like the result of a novena to St Pineapple and Blessed Jelly-mould. Our own drab place was strangely adjacent. It only had a hanky of foreground between it and the street, and so seemed oddly unwithdrawn compared to everything else around, imagining itself, apparently, to be in Westland Row or Aungier Street. Yet, like its city brethren, it seemed quite unassuming, as though it had no thought to be taken for anything more than a fairly good-class post-office. It didn't even have a graveyard. But what, only strangeness, could I expect from somewhere which, as I discovered at the top of Carrickbrennan Road, had gone to the trouble of having a castle and had then let it go till it was only a Croke Park for jackdaws; a place which, besides, had never even thought of a river. Ah, Lismore – did I ever offend you!

The reason Monkstown stonework stays with me is that the people do not. And at the time, of all the place's distance and difference from all I'd ever known, the absence of people from the streets was the greatest and most unexpected piece of modernity. It couldn't be right, I thought, surveying the 165 windswept, spotless Monkstown Road: this was the city, there had to be people. They emerged, of course, to go to church and chapel, but these appearances – like those of special guests on variety shows – only drew attention to their general unavailability. Why didn't they stop and gossip, and come over to borrow a saw, and walk up to the match together? Why did they not take to their fine avenues to savour the air of bracing Seapoint and salubrious Salthill? Every so often, the bus would shriek to a halt and an elderly lady in a tweed suit and a miniature greengrocery in her straw hat would struggle aboard with a 'Thank you *so* much' to the conductor, her voice surprisingly firm and carrying, as though formed to address people at a distance. There were hotels in the sidestreets leading to the rocky waterside, which I was glad to see at first, thinking they would bring a bit of life to the place. But they turned out to be encased in a mortifying quiet; dark, lonesome buildings that, being public, had to go by some name, there being no word for the absence of holiday their appearances connoted. Who stayed at them – widows of indigent rectors; bachelor librarians of limited means and fond of a sup; the flotsam of families and the jetsam of marriages; monks of various kinds in the right domicile at last? No trippers. Monkstown, I could see, didn't hold with trippers.

We had neighbours, of course, but I didn't have the remotest notion who they were, what they did, or where they came from. They made no introductions, nor did I. They drove by in their Wartburgs and Simcas; I walked by the wall, cursing their splashes. I cast sheep's eyes at the beautiful Miss Keegan in number 24, and dreamt of taking her to the Top Hat. But it was too far away to ask her to walk home from, and I had never seen her ride a bike (I would have remembered her legs). A taxi was out of the question. They were for turning yourself in at the hospital or, for pleasure, were the birthright of a social class superior to whatever mine was. The dances were dear enough. Not only that, but by the Top Hat ads I saw that it was an awful sophisticated place, and the kind of girls that attended – judging from the photos in 'Going Places with Terry O'Sullivan' in *The Evening Press* – were much too smart for the likes of me, who was, in the world's way, no better than a lapsed boarder, positively sodden behind the ears. What if Miss Keegan was only all amphigory and what she could get out of me? I decided I would cross over when next I saw her coming. 'Nice day,' I'd say; no need not to be adult, after all .... The words stuck in my throat when I did see her. 'Hello,' she said, and passed. Eyes widened, jaw became unhinged. Someone to talk to would have been so nice. But I never did find out her first name.

There should have been tribes of boy and girl Keegans around. The snobby convent and the hardly less classy Brothers at Monkstown Park knew them. They all hadn't left home just because I'd arrived. But they might as well have, because I couldn't lay an eye on them. It never occurred to me that, having lived in Monkstown longer than I, they had probably formed clubs, found activities to share, paired off in dates, held parties and had generally evolved a private social life. I was after the freedom of the streets: they were well beyond that. I thought social life was public: dances, sports, going to the pictures, doing the town. It was unforgiveably anti-urban of Monkstown to prove me wrong. I couldn't stand it that the streets were always empty and cars kept whizzing by. Now I was being made to feel private, estranged, unworthy of the dreams which I believed had destined me for Dublin. Longing began an insidious curdle into disenchantment.

When, a little later, I read how Gabriel Conroy lived in Monkstown, I nodded in approval: 'Right again, sir' – that's what it was all right, a world of Gabriels coping with their Gresham nights; or, if anything, a little deader – *unter*-Gabriels waiting for their never-Greshams.

It was a nice new house, nice because new, nice because I had never lived in a new house before. I was used to parlours and pantries and kitchen tables able to seat six. Now I found these were things of the past. A living-room occupied the whole of the ground-floor rear. One corner of it, just, was the kitchen, fenced off by a chest-high wall surmounted by wooden slats reaching to the ceiling. The slats were spaced so that dishes could be passed through them – dead handy. There were barstools under the kitchen counter to sit on while snacking, while waiting for the coffee to perk (they drank mostly coffee) – talk about chic .... The living-room itself was a lake of light and openness, with French windows that gave onto the 167 garden. It was the image of a simple, generous space, like something modern, like America (they'd been on holiday to America). I could easily see why Da and Kay picked it for their new start, instead of something older, more familiar, full of walls which turned space into darkness.

And it was new too because it had machines. Venetian blinds, a fridge, central heating, a garage with a door on a track (no hinges!). There was a yoke like a pocket-sized pneumatic drill for grinding coffee. Da had got himself a new wireless, a Telefunken, compared to which the Sputnik was a tricycle. It seemed the kind of thing Superman would carry in his underpants. Leave it to the Germans . . . . It was reassuring that in one respect, at least, Da identified with the sentiment so frequently repeated by Mr Franz, at work – just as at work I was pleased to hear a foreigner like Mr Franz support what so many Irishmen were saying. The only thing the house lacked was a television set. But I inferred that ownership of such an object would be a violation of Film Society principles, and besides, everything else had been done to be up to the minute; they'd earned the exception. The house even had a phone of its own. And, acme of modernity, there was no bath, just a shower, and the jax was in a separate closet.

The machines and I did not get on, though. Milk from the fridge was a dentist's needle through the bridge of my nose. I didn't know the temperature could be lowered. If it was part of the fridge's job to transfix sinuses, so be it. I felt I was in no position to challenge it. And I was always forgetting to put the shower-curtain inside the shower, so that after a sluice I could have had a swim on the bathroom floor. Since the jax was detached, I had no paper to mop up, so had to use my towel. But then I couldn't dry myself. Shaking only worked for dogs, I discovered the window was placed too awkwardly for me to lean out in the hope that the great Monkstown air would oblige; slapping water from chest and shoulders into the handbasin was also less than satisfactory. And then the inevitable rattle came on the doorknob – 'Will you be long?' – and everything yielded to that combination of cringing and bristling, embarrassment and umbrage, which laces the straitjacket of adolescence.

To prove I wasn't house-broken, there were rules. Some of these struck me as childish, such as always using the back door to get in. Maybe they thought it fun to have a back door, that it was part of the house's newness for them. Or perhaps it was more evidence of privacy, the Monkstown *malaise* of ducking in from the garage. If I were they, I thought, fairly newly-wed, still happy-acting, I would have wanted everyone to see me, and would have loudly availed of the front-door as often as possible. Then I remembered that there never was anyone about . . . . But, having never yet chanced on a contradiction that I didn't want to lance, I knew there had to be something to this back-door custom: they couldn't be doing it just because it was convenient. Had I a key, there would have been no need to think. Without one, idle speculation became an end in itself. I began attempting the insoluble acrostic of other people's lives. I, *Observer*; they Ximenes. Then there was the shoeless rule. That was one of the explicit ones. It covered the sailcloth which covered the carpet in the hall and on the bottom stair-step. The idea was that the carpet should be made to last, an innocent enough domestic ambition, as I now perceive, but which seemed the height of repression at the time. I was the thing which might not last! To preserve the carpet, no shoes were to be worn indoors. But I had no slippers and felt stupid in my socks. Shoeless I would not go, preferring to stain and scoff my way into bad looks and thunderstorms. Jesus Christ (comforter of carpet) was frequently called upon as aid and witness. What way the head was on me at all, I was often asked? What the *hell* was I thinking about?

I was thinking this is the way the world ends. I was thinking, so this is the life of the dream at last. Life with father. Why the fuck can't you live with lino? We used to. The country was covered with it . . . I was witnessing the death of lino. But I had no idea what that meant, apart from their being a connection between new carpet, domestic law and order, a way of life that was tantalizing and forbidding and for which I was unrehearsed, and a sense that all this newness amounted to a mute scream directed at me: *not yours, clear off.* 'Useless article,' 'hopeless case'; the phrases, no matter how often I heard them, hardly began to plumb the black hole of domestic dunderheadedness into which I felt my life had descended. Appalled at my incompetence, bemused by the differences between Monkstown and that future which the past's omissions surely had vouchsafed, I became a numb cuckoo in an ice-bound nest.

If Da shouted, he tried too. He tried to tell me about the holiday in America. But I was wise to that dodge. Earlier he had tried to interest me in the honeymoon, hitch-hiking in France, the ride to the south in the big Citroën with the magic-carpet suspension. Stuff it where the monkey stuffed the nuts, boy! I wasn't at the wedding; I didn't want to be anywhere else. So when he brought up how amusing the TV ads were for Rheingold's (or was it Ballantyne's?) beer – the bottles marching to Sousa, making as if they had legs to kick like cheerleaders – I just thought, bloody hypocrite: TV in Queens was fine, but here he wouldn't give it a second look. He brought home an American summer jacket. 'Feel the weight of it,' he proferred, pleased. I did a fine job of disguising my surprise at its lightness: bloody paper, a small shower would make shit of it. I asked him if he saw any blacks over there (Kennedy was in the White House, the cities were either scabs or ashes). Da explained that the blacks just wanted to be Americans, like everyone else. That'll get them nowhere, said I to myself (a fat lot integration had done for me): they'd be better off burning the whole bloody place down. That's what I wanted to do, only I couldn't find a way· I couldn't even well and truly break a silence.

He had Kay, what did he want with me? He swapped items from the paper with her: he was ignoring me. He'd betrayed the dream. It was all a dreadful mistake, as other family members encouraged me to believe. And everyone knew mistakes could not be rectified or palliated, they could only be detested. But he liked her! Unlike me, he wasn't overawed by her French-inhale smoking style, her swift movements, her knowledge of names mentioned in 'An Irishman's Diary', her mastery of maths. He called her 'hon'. On Sunday mornings they cruised together through the splendid scenery of *The Sunday Times* and *The Observer*, some of it now in colour, even, fags and coffee to hand, the scent of a Sunday lunch growing on them – meatloaf, delightfully spiked with unfamiliar capsicum, and a side of cream-style corn; the pair of them as comfortable as a couple of retired Yanks. After tea, then, the critics on the Third, a crowd of talking newspapers with accents telling how they squirmed and smarted from their own cleverness. Sometimes they got worked up: 'Oh come now – '; 'But surely – '. Why didn't they take their coats off and have at it properly? Then I'd be able to understand them.

Da laughed his flat, dry laugh, sank in his contented armchair, enthralled by vicarious controversy.

'Will you be in this evening?'

Of course I bloody will, what d'you think? If it wasn't a Tech night, where else had I to go? I glowered: 'Yeah.' But I was glad they had a good social life: it was nice being alone in the house, looking after the baby. 'We won't be late. There's a play on the radio, I think.'

'Oh?'

Well, you never know, where's the paper?

As You Fucking Like It! Sure we did that for the Inter. There were only two good bits in it. One was about the cleanliest shift is to kiss, and we all went *smack-smack-smack*. Then another day, when Rosalind said, 'What shall we do with my doublet and hose?' someone in the back in a great take-off of a Dublin accent went, 'Gethem awf ya!' But as for 'Now my co-mates and brothers in exile' and 'All the world's a stage', nothing could be more *passé* to my ears, with the possible exception of the collected works of Dickie Valentine or Guy Mitchell. So I twiddled with the Telefunken's control panel until I was sure the coast was clear, then headed straight for Luxembourg, fingers snapping, tie off, shirt-collar up. I didn't know which was more seductive 'The Wanderer' or 'Twisting the Night Away' – Dion's sax had the sound of mortal sin in it; Sam Cooke was so light and bouncy and the number's invita-tion so irresistible . . . . They were both great. And there was no choice necessary: they were all there, all the time. Radio Luxembourg, prototype of heaven, next parish to America.

But even the Station of the Stars – to which I had been faith-ful since childhood and in whose company I had planned to spend the rest of my life – let me down. Whatever it was about this ostensibly omnipotent receiver, it balked at 208. At first I thought it was because the evenings were still a bit light (soon, I believed, I would have scientific confirmation of why Lux was stronger after dark: aesthetically, the reason was obvious, rock being the language of darkness – not just of the night, but of the body, too, and the convulsions of its humours). But no,

even when the clocks changed and there were fogs that would
do justice to 'The Harry Lime Theme', I couldn't get it, though
the rest of the Continent came jabbering through in fine style,
undaunted by my profane reception.

I tried the short wave. Worse. My eyes narrowed. My jaw
clenched. Was it that Luxembourg was perceived in this house
as a species of television? I wouldn't be surprised. Did he
perhaps unscrew the one valve vital to dancing pleasure? I
wouldn't put it past him. Paranoia gripped me like a hobby:
the stamps I now collected were, I imagined, meant to douse
whatever fire I had. This outlook made home life seem real by
lending it the deliberateness of drama, whereas in reality it
was all mundane, unthinking casualness. All the head's a
stage and all the fuzzy signals and frayed circuits merely
pretexts. So that when all was said and done, I still would have
my own story, the story which had up until now kept me from
a permanent place in Dublin, and which would have a happy
ending yet when I at last secured that place. Till then, I could
cultivate paranoia for fulfillment.

I broke some rules, too, during those evenings alone with
the sleeping child. The front room was never used; that was an
implicit rule. So I went in there. This was where the good
books were – books in hard Irish; *Franny and Zooey*, *Ship of
Fools*; books in French (once upon a time he used to ask me
would I like to slit the pages for him. *Would I like* . . . !). There
was as record-player too, and I'd have played a record only I
was sure I'd break it, so I contented myself by calling the
records crap, the work of no names (Leadbelly, Tom Lehrer),
apart from *The Best of Sellers*, which I'd heard a bit of on the
Light, the – to me – brilliant and brilliantly timely mockery of
Céili music.

And there was the portrait. I suppose, looking back on
things, that this was why I bothered with that room, that
mother-and-child by Brock of Woodstock, Kay and her baby
girl. The mother, seated, inclines her head to the white bundle
resting in her arms and on her lap. Her face contains great
tenderness, rapt, serene absorption. The colours are soft pinks
of flesh, sweet greens of new beginnings. Compared to the
baby, the mother is very big, a monument, upraised, yet
deferential, to the little all-important life it cherishes. I have to
force myself to look at it. Then I can't look away. I think it is a

172

a picture of love.

I drift back aimlessly to the living-room. Or, I tip-toe up the carpeted stairs to look on the sleeping child. With luck she'll wake. I'll take her up. She'll blindly clutch my shirt, and I'll feel wanted. She'll whimper from her dream, just like a human. But I'll tell her it's okay; knowing nothing, she doesn't know how well off she is. She settles readily. I look on her with envy.

But back downstairs the bloody old square brass brazier, central to the heat, has gone out on me. Rake, rake; shovel, shovel. Not a spark. The air is filled with ash. Here's the car - 'Fire out again?' He starts in (Kay is checking upstairs): 'I swear to this and that; of all the . . . ' Who does he think he is? *Fucker*. Father!

2

We used to live in Sundrive Road, and there was a 'we' then, or at least it was easier to assume there was since, with a child's pure ego, I believed I was the centre of the family circle, that there would not have been such an entity without me and that all concerned had me to thank for the getting out of our-selves that Dublin provided. The circle may have had a sketch-ier construction than the later, ostensibly normal, nucleus of Monkstown. But sketchiness wasn't threatening then; it was the stuff of a holiday. If I lived in an improvised family, that seemed an appropriate accompaniment to the lackadaisical, please-yourself ethos of the city. And I was able to relish these arrangements all the more since they so closely resembled the permanent set-up in Lismore (the set-up that was permanent, I thought, for just as long as I wanted it to be, at which point it would be transformed into the eternal bliss of being with Daddy in Sundrive, that road named for my simple, golden dream). Mam accompanied me; Da replaced my Uncle George as my main man; I made an Aunty Chrissy substitute of Peg, who shared the house with Da, even though she worked all week and only had time to play between finishing the clean- 173 ing and starting the Sunday lunch. (Dinner was lunch; I was learning to speak Dublin.) And, adding extra excitement, Granny Royce sometimes came up to see me from Enniscorthy, her soft, indulgent presence both the ultimate confirmation of my being a person of emotional significance and the ultimate reminder of the household's makeshift integrity, as real in its temporariness as a carnival.

For there was nothing only novelty, then. In the mornings I'd wander down for the paper to Keeley's on the Crumlin Road. Waiting to cross, I'd breakfast delightedly on the sweet, unfamiliar fumes of diesel exhaust. The 50s lumbering up from the Barn looked like friendly elephants; the 22s, turning up to Drimnagh, heeled over like great green yachts. Up the way, the Moracrete plant looked so unlike the only other factories I knew – the Cappoquin bacon factory, the tannery in Dungarvan – that it seemed like what they must call monasteries on other planets: it didn't even smell. The Merville milkcarts jogged along with a christmassy jingle, adding to the pleasing music of morning bustle and reminding me again of the classy way the city did things. These carts had tyres on their wheels, not the iron rim that cracked and harshed along the patently insignificant roads of down the country. And I noticed, too, that if the city had to admit that it couldn't do without horses, then it gave them interesting work to do, and often great long drays. Not only did they bring the milk around, they worked for Guinnesses, for CIE, for such fascinating concerns as Tedcastles, McCormack and Heitons (memorialized in bus-ads and in neon signs, rather than for the coal they sold, which merely burned). No tedious ploughing here. No sloppy hauling of those casks of water from the Castle spout. Dublin even had horses drawing those strange little pleasure-hearses that stood by the railings of the Bank of Ireland, run by what I thought must be a large family of brothers, the jarveys. Ah, leave it to Dublin, a multi-horse town and no mistake . . . .

And on Thursday mornings I had an extra treat, the bin men. The palace of varieties that was the daily street became mundane when their act passed by. Their brusque banging and barking put me in mind of circus-men's behaviour. They banged bin lids brazenly, and swaggered on, indifferent to the hissed criticism such rowdiness drew forth (acrobats seemed

174

similarly indifferent to the comments elicited by their bulging crotches). They swung the bins with the lithe ease of athletes and the unerring aim of practised hands. None of them was fat. And they had a fabulous wagon, a semi-cylindrical bin on its bed, compartments with upward-sliding doors containing all the colour and mystery of a Fawcett's poster, with (for comic relief, as I saw it) tin baths dangling from hangers at the rear. In Lismore we only had a spavined man called Johnny Gorgeous with a creaky dobbin and a cruddy cart.

But in Lismore we knew Johnny, we knew his little house in Chapel Street, we knew where he took the rubbish. There was no knowing the Dublin bin men. One sure thing, though; they didn't live around our way. I had a feeling that somehow such a state of affairs would not be allowed. Distracted as I might be by their antics, I had still to bear in mind to whose family I belonged and that its city representatives would not dream of living in a locale below their station. My father (BA, HDip) was a schoolteacher with the Christian Brothers, let me not forget it. St Michael's, Inchicore, was not the school Mam would have chosen for her brainy first-born to serve. Its name could only be carved with pride on the palms of the ragamuffins it took in, and it served them right, too, Mam believed. But she knew that John had no stomach for flagellation, and she didn't know how he could stick it otherwise. Thanks be to God, however, we did not live in Ragamuffinland. As though to reassure us, there was the toney Loreto Convent at the corner; 'Oh, a very good school,' I'd heard confabulating wise old heads aver. In case that wasn't enough, weren't we well within a donkey's roar of roads named for the holy places of Ireland – Kildare, Downpatrick, Lismore itself, indeed – which could be invoked as patrons in times of class misgiving, of when what the world was coming to at all needed to be known. But what cared I for nunneries screened by lugubrious evergreens? And as far as patrons were concerned, I gathered from remarks Da passed that this office was being more than adequately discharged by the Behans of Kildare Road.

Sundrive was the real city, monument to the works of man, all the look-alike houses arranged so neatly, people living in a plan. My parents' city. These houses were the future in their time. They were built in the hinterland of history, beyond sites of ambush and executioner's courtyards. These were the 175 houses of peace, of Dublin renewing itself.

What was it like, really? The house was bigger than the labourers' cottages built in ones and twos by the County Council on the outskirts of Lismore but built to the same design. Everything is to the right of the hall and stairs. The hall ends abruptly in a doorless galley of a kitchen, too small to have two people turn at the same time in it. But then it has been made with only one person in mind, and when she's using it she'll have no time for sitting down, will she? So why make space for something for which life's too short? (People living in a plan . . . .) Upstairs, two bedrooms and a box-room. The children, whose arrival can only be prevented by taking absurd psychological and moral risks, can share. (Who ever in the 1940s heard of teenagers? Whoever thought young people might try to translate peace into freedom. They will say nothing and do as they are told, as it is written in these bricks and mortar.) There is a long garden; nobody living here will buy what they can grow. The planners themselves don't, probably. The country isn't moving that quickly. We still retain our roots. If the crop fails, someone will open a chip-shop. There is no place to store a bike, unless it's slung on top of the coal in the outside bunker. It is impossible to put up a garage. A narrow future, a claustrophobic peace. Homage to the safe side.

Except that there is no 'really'. It dissolved in the imagined presence of Seán and Nuala, brave new selves and bridal couches, blushes and giggles: the age-old story and its eternal originality. In the wedding picture his trousers are creased so sharply that they seem capable of cutting the cake and the table it stands on. He is too shy to smile, sobered by a point beyond pleasure by pride in his good fortune: a woman by his side. She, more alive to the moment, smiles candidly, as though replete, an impression confirmed by her high-waisted, tight-fitting dress. Later on, they gaze with pleasure on their sleeping child. Love in Dublin.

They think they'd like another one. But while it ripens, her toxemia festers. It's too far gone. Before she's thirty, Nuala's in her grave, he's a widower, I'm in Lismore. She's just delivered twin cuckoos. Fledgling me is borne to a different nest. Seán is cuckolded by God (the pregnant woman has to cede her life to save her foetus) and by His proxy, nature. The body is betrayed in the body's moment. Love in Dublin. For a long time I'm firmly convinced that he wrapped me up tight, put me in the fine new black-lacquered high-sprung pram they'd bought, got on his bike and pulled me behind him in the pouring rain to Kingsbridge Station. I ask about this, am told it's just a silly dream. But it remains more real to me than anything. I know I'm right. (It's the rain that clinches it.) I know that some day I'll reverse this childish funeral journey. We practise it every summer. One of these summers it'll be perfect.

Aunt Peace lived in Mount Merrion. We had to visit her. We had to visit my mother's Aunt Poll. Now and then, Mam would develop a yen to see someone from Lismore, so we'd go to Inchicore to visit Father Devine, an Oblate, one of Da's contemporaries. The best thing about these visits was the buses. The 46A to Mount Merrion even went by one of the wonders of the modern city, the Donnybrook bus garage, spouse of that more spectacular fifties confidence-builder, the Busaras (at last, I noted with pleasure, buses were getting their due), though Donnybrook had sunk somewhat in my estimation for failing to protect Billy Kelly from the fists of Ray Famechon. Kelly might have been from Derry, but he was definitely one of us – he's Spider's boy, fathered by the nickname into familiarity and fame at once. This lineage was repeated so often before the fight that I mouthed it myself, assertively authoritative, knowing nothing of its history. But it was enjoyable to realize that when I used the phrase I was joining in one of the pastimes of big men: speaking in headlines. Not that the invocation of origins and paternity helped in the event. As Billy – and the whole country – discovered, stunned (as though it had never been known before), a father is no amulet. Still, anyway, though: Fred Tiedt did well in the Olympics. But of course he, I believe, was a busman . . . .

Once beyond the garage we were in Ballyposh. The road got as broad and shady as an avenue. Few buses could be seen, nor could little of anything else: Stillorgan people seemed to have trees on the brain. The place was lousy with foliage. A low hedge ran down the middle of the road. There was a Trees Road. It was amazing to me that here were people who didn't seem interested even in pretending that they were of the city 177 and that the city was of them. They didn't even plant the odd traffic light. Thank God, I thought, for the concrete openness of Crumlin and Kimmage, where there was no doubt about where you were.

Mount Merrion, however, was better, being either above the tree line or having laid down its arboreal arms before the onslaught of new housing. Probably the latter: the ground was very broken all around. In school we had learned in Irish about the fate of Kilcash, and how the felling of trees presaged the fall of houses: *tá deire na coillte ar lár*. But killing and cash had evidently changed in meaning. Now trees were downed that houses be raised. That, I assumed, was history. And in principle I was all for it, ever a fetishist of the new, whether it was a reformed hillock or the latest from Hank Ballard and the Midnighters. When it came to it, though, I didn't much care for Mount Merrion. The houses were fine – semi-detached with white fronts, taken but unused; newlyweds. They had bigger kitchens, rooms to both left and right of hall and stairs, large gardens full of grace and gladioli and maybe a lone bed of lettuce, as though in self-conscious acknowledgement of how the great cabbage-growing tradition, to which we were all born, had become watered down, in inverse relationship to the growth of white-washed cottage into breeze block, Walpamur and mod. cons. But where was their Keeley's, their Moracrete, their big Flood's pub, their Mrs Fox, the Gospel woman (our great gossip)? No 81 snaked handily around the back roads. The air was 'great', no doubt, as the elders all agreed; and having Mount Anville so close by was a godsend, surely. How could anyone be content to live in a mere house, without the scutter of Lambrettas, or the steam and hooters of laundry chimneys, for company? I believed, too, at the time, that Peace and her neighbours thought somewhat along similar lines. That was why they gave their houses nicknames – Manresa, Avoca, St Luke's. We did the same thing at school: it was a way of being informal while acknowledging difference. Peace lived in 'Southwell'. Well, she was from the south .... But what did it *mean*? It meant the house had a name.

What were we all doing together at Southwell? Visiting – a very complex synonym for nothing. No doubt my anticlimatic and dismissive reaction to Mount Merrion's combination of exclusivity and banality was (continues to be) reinforced by

178

the same characteristics distinguishing the reception of the Sundrive deputation. The kids were stand-offish, the adults desultory. Those afternoons moved like boats on a bitumen sea. And teatime – looming like the visit's first cause and last resort – could never come quickly enough. We sat out in the famous air, bored. When the boring rain came we sat inside. I was older than my three cousins, and older was better. We had nothing in common. The older girl was quiet, the younger one too small to bother about. Their brother was a Mohawk (sc. ordinary small boy): I can picture him still crashing around, inside and out, roaring the name of his father's trade journal, 'Chemist and Druggist! Chemist and Druggist!' How extraordinarily immature, I said to myself, my nose extending itself obligingly as I looked down it. And him a Dublinman, too. My nearest and queerest. Of course I hated them all. How come they had a Mammy and a Daddy and a new house? They were so well off they didn't have to notice me. Didn't they understand that I was only there to be noticed? – not just at their place, and not just then, but in all the others (there were only others' houses), all the time. After tea, of course, there was no mistaking who was the lucky one. *I* was the one going back to town. *I* was the one who'd see the brilliant Bovril sign rainbow out its letters to the night, probably lighting up the eyes of chemists and druggists.

Yet whenever I did receive attention it was never the kind I wanted. I had high hopes of the Oblates. Granted they were missioners, and they had a grotto at the side of the road by their house and chapel, so they definitely meant business. But it pleased me to believe that their business was not the timber-shivering roar of hell-peddling Redemptorists. Order of Mary Immaculate – ah no, they'd be nice. But in Father Devine's cavernous parlour with its penumbrous paintings and holy smell of beeswax, after the rock cakes *á la* Dunlop were choked down and a temporary lull fell on Mam's exhaustive gospelling of Lismore past and present, I felt the afternoon swivel inexorably in my direction, impelled by our host's large, somewhat protruding, rather liquefactory eyes – the eyes of 'saintly man'; eyes whose hangdog melancholy could have transfixed and embarrassed me even if their owner's stupid questions hadn't. School, yes; ah, grand, grand; and did I remember my morning and night prayers? Oh, sure, I was a 179 great boy altogether. Da squirmed; but at least he was able to light another fag. Oh, geography was my favourite subject – well, wasn't that a great big word? But speaking of big words, could I tell him this: Constantinople is a very big word, but if you can't spell it you're a big dunce . . . !

'I – t;' and I could puke.

Applause! Acclaim! For unto us is born . . . . All culminating in the detested, the inevitable, intelligence conveyed by some sparrow-fart of 'a little bird', namely that I was not only the hope of the West Waterford intelligentsia but a grand little singer to boot. 'So I hope now that little bird wasn't telling a big fib.'

I baulked, of course; I pouted. I may even have believed that this was one of those battles of wills that I could win (as though I were used to winning them, or something). It wasn't a matter of will, of course, but of infinitely more inflexible manners. Quickly my resistance became 'trying to think', which wasn't easy. It would probably be a sin to do a Johnny Ray or David Whitfield. Walton's advice – 'If you feel like singing, do sing an Irish song' – was all very well, but a solemn delivery of 'Down by the Glenside' struck me as a hymn of the wrong sort (awareness of wrong, its omnipresence and many nuances, was as knee-jerk as genuflecting). So, what *gaisce* would satisfy them (meaning me)? Okay, then: let my vaunted braininess speak for me. I finched out with a finical, unconsciously cynical, sweetness: 'Oró, a bháidín, ag snámh ar an gcuan . . . . '

Yet all my compliance got me nowhere. Going home – after being unctuously (or not in a Lismore accent any more but rather in a quavery contralto) blessed – all the talk was not of me, my conspicuously being good, my musicality. Instead, Mam harped on 'Poor Father Devine, isn't he looking wretched? Oh, he's looking hunted.'

'Ah,' said Da, in his cynical drawl, 'I suppose they had him too long down in Daingean.'

Still, ordeal by infantilizing sentiment and song was considerably less tiresome than being taken seriously, the fate I suffered through Uncle Gregory and his ordeals by sums. He and Aunt Poll lived in Fairview (more great bussing: the 54A from Mount Argus) and, dread it as I might, we absolutely had to visit them, because Poll was one of the four Comerford girls,

180

Granny Royce's sister, my mother's aunt: therefore she had every right, and considered it her bounden duty, to look on me and see that I was good. Mam thought Poll was perhaps just a little bit touched, because she called Gregory 'ducky', and terms of endearment between spouses were suspect; not 'clean daft' exactly, nor yet the mark of an *óinseach*, but definitely 'simple'. Also Poll was peculiar in being childless. We didn't know too many women like that (and it was always the women who were childless, of course). It was strange to contemplate someone whom nature had entirely overlooked, apparently, and whose soft-hearted manner and roly-poly figure suggested that she had emotion and to spare to lavish but was without a place to put it, which was why she was always gaining weight.

Poll was different, too, because of Gregory. Her three sisters all had married men with whom they had grown up in Enniscorthy, but nothing would do Poll, apparently, only to marry this bald old coot from some hole in Tyrone. At least I assumed Stewartstown was a hole, because that's what I inferred the whole of the North to be, a limbo with purgatorial side-effects, a place behind an iron curtain, poorer even than the God-obliterating Commie countries because it had no Stepinac, no Mindzenty. Sure I could see fine and well what sort those Northerners were. They sent their GNR buses down here, painting them cream and blue, trying to be smart, acting like green wasn't good enough for them . . . . Of course Gregory was on the right side. I mean he was a Nationalist. That, I imagined, was how come he worked now in the General Post Office. Only people with special historical qualifications got jobs there, I assumed, particularly jobs as hard as Gregory's – he had to work all night and couldn't smoke on duty (his palms were dyed mahogany from a lifetime of concealed cigarettes). He must have been in Frongoch or Lincoln with Dev and Seamus Doyle. When he got out it was too risky to go back North, so he convalesced in Enniscorthy, was that it? Or did they meet in Dublin when victory's tide ran full? It was the era of promising proposals. A faith in consummation hung in the air like the scent of cordite, like the scent of sex. They fell in love. They plumped for Fairview because the name described how every prospect seemed then. Or something. I don't know. The past is a frozen mouth, tolerant of whatever 181 words are placed in it, most itself when mute. It reproduces itself in gargoyles known as books.

Perhaps if Gregory had not sprung his sums on me – leaping up from expostulatory converse with a smiling Da on the state of the bloody country, during which he incessantly polished his bony egg-bare head while quite as compulsively feeding Afton-ash to the fireplace – I would have been able for them. If only he could have read them out in a natural voice, instead of in his native torrent of whines and fricatives . . . . Except that he never did sneak up on me: through salad cream and shop cake I could see him coming. And he didn't have to read: the problems were all there on the exam paper, the eleven-plus, through the mindless torture of which some relative of his put children in the North (poor Billy Kelly). 'Thar, nowe,' Gregory would go. 'Take a look at that. Yer Daddy 'n' me have to go out for a wee mingute.' I saw him wink at Da; I felt the women stiffen. 'We won't be long,' pointedly to me.

I bit my pencil till the paint cracked; I would have happily died of lead poisoning. But the exam paper went on sinking its icy, sterile teeth into me, and no relief came nigh. Cruel God! I had to face the fact (again): I was the world's worst at sums. I couldn't have cared less how many men it took to cut an acre given that a square perch was accounted for in three weekends by two urchins and a greyhound (let X equal the number of wet days). Why did sums think that what went on out in the world was a problem? As any fool (or I, at least) could see – especially in Dublin – the world was fine, a sleepless system of rates and ratios, so blatantly, self-satisfyingly mechanical that the best way to live with it was by mimicking it with machines (beloved buses). Sums had it all wrong: real problems were not compound interest and decimal points. People, alien people, were the problem. Women. Quavery priests. Men who came back and it nearly ten, with grins and inclinations to be gigglesome, but only giving rise to frosty bus-rides downstairs on the 20 back to Dolphin's Barn and sullen bedtime tea.

I was, however, well rewarded for my tours of duty in the unnervingly accessible hinterlands of boredom and embarrassment. Not that being paid-off was part of a plan. There didn't have to be a plan: there was Dublin. The Museum (inseparable from wet days): the Lismore crozier and the fabulous cooperage of the great elk skeleton. Collinstown: Viscounts and Fokker Friendships. We made the pilgrimage to Glasnevin in honour of the major dead. Sundays meant Croke Park: it didn't matter who was playing – though I was glad that so often it was Wexford – because there would be some famous name on show, not to mention the somewhat more exotic, sweaty fruit-women, lugging their unwieldy baskets up and down the terracing: 'Tuppence each th' Willyum payahs!'

The best place was the Zoo. I learned things there. Mandrils came from Africa; llamas from Peru. But nobody could tell me why there were no wild animals from Japan. And it wasn't just an open-air, out-loud geography lesson, me teaching myself in the (usually disappointed) hope that teacher Da would overhear me and approve. The monkeys who pitched their shit at people passing were great gas.

Even when we went somewhere I wasn't interested in, there was some saving grace. The Botanic Gardens I considered a prime bore (apart from the jungle hot-house where at the prompting of one of my favourites, *Martin Rattler*, I sensed delicious danger in the fetid undergrowth and thrilled to see lianas as thick as a child's leg). What pleased me there was the sight of Mam pleased. Green-fingered to a degree herself, her eyes lit up at the riots of colour in their orderly beds. Here, to her eyes, I can now see, was an aesthetic of the Big Houses round Lismore brilliantly at play. But with a difference. Here the cult of property did not supervene. Beauty occupied a zone which seemed at once loftier and more natural, in which the lawns and blooms and foliage were cultivated just for the sake of their own sweet selves. I saw Mam's mouth move in minia-ture *moués*, the way she did when things affected her. Perhaps she was adjusting to the realization that this zone went by the unfamiliar, whispery name of *pleasure*. At any rate, I knew by looking at her that things now would be a little easier for a while. We might even have tea in town.

The enjoyment of inspecting these official city treasures, however, bore no comparison to that of travelling to them. This was the time when buses and I were in the first blush of our romance. Being all pattern and movement, buses defined the city. The predictability of their routes varied with their intriguing oscillations of pace. I loved how they jammed 183 together trying to cross O'Connell Bridge. I loved how they slicked along the South Circular. I loved the busmen. They had strange little battered tin boxes for squatting on. They all wore signet rings – real city stylishness. And speaking of style: what about the way they kept this balance stepping off the backs of open platforms while the bus sped on? Now there was a turn in the human circus performing night and day in the heart of Dublin. I was the only one – except Da maybe – who loved the busmen even when they went on strike for lightweight summer uniforms (which they got): if everybody hated them– 'Too well off they are,' said Mam, starting the argument – it meant all the more to me that I stay true.

But I never thought of being related to a busman, and therefore was amazed one evening when, getting off a 22 at Sundrive Road, Granny Royce began to smack the bus's mudguard and go, 'Nick!, Nick!' I knew that neither she or Mam were very quick around town. They wanted to ride inside all the time with the other women and the shopping bags. They acted as though what was freedom to me was disorientation to them. Still, beating a bus barehanded . . . . But she knew very well what she was doing. The driver slid back his side-window and shouted happily, 'Wisha, how the devil are you, ma'am.' This was Nick White, husband of one of Granny Royce's nieces, Annie, named for Granny. We had a busman in the family, and I never knew it! I often asked about him afterwards, but found nothing out. I never saw him again. He and his wife were never on our visiting list. Was this because they lived in Preston Street? There's no knowing. But there's that smiling face and delighted greeting; chance meeting of an unknown connection; romantic, enigmatic bus-world – kinder to memory than the whole story would be.

We had three ways of getting into town, though generally settled on a 50 or a 22. The 81 didn't get good until Clanbrassil Street, and was good for that street only – was very good then, the Jewish names with -stein and Gold- were wonderfully foreign: yet their butcheries and chandleries were just as dark and cluttered as our own. But both the 50 and 22 got good almost immediately. The 50 snaked around the fringe of the Liberties writhing through impossible narrowness and almost dwarfing the small, tightly-packed houses. But by the Coombe (what did Coombe mean?) – home of Donnelly's, the skinless wonder-sausage, and a strange place called St Nicholas-without-the-Walls – streets widened, as though breadth was the passport to town proper. Unlike the 22, which entered town on a suitably *très chic* note – Cassidy's, Kellett's and Pim's in South Great George's Street – the 50 ran the gauntlet of crumbling, black antiquity: St Patrick's Cathedral, Christchurch Cathedral, great wooden buttresses propagating slums on Cork Hill, the Castle that couldn't be seen. Still, I supposed that some place had to be old; that was what I'd learned in Lismore. Not every bus could be as modern as the 22, and have a synagogue, a Gold Flake factory and the Labour Court in its path. And at least the 50 tried to make a go of it in Dame Street before finally succumbing to the ancient world at its terminus by Trinity.

The main thing was that we were in town. And these were the best days of all, when we had no purpose beyond the ritual of Clerys. Shopping done we'd just spend the afternoon ambling around, taking in the show. I saw Noel Purcell once. Mayor Alfie Byrne accosted us, insisting on a handshake. He spoke in burbles; he patted me on the head. 'Did he want money, Da?' I wondered. 'No, just a vote,' Da said, with a laugh. We ate like royalty at Cafolla's: the ice-cream treats were as colourful as a jukebox's offspring. I heard the cawing of the paper-hawkers: 'Hedl-au-Praiss! He'ldee-Mai-au-Praiss!' Wouldn't it be great to be one of them, or one of their urchin sons, dashing through the buses pausing at termini, shouting? (Wouldn't it be great to be anything – full-time son, even? Oh for the freedom of the typical, of the collective? Oh to be in Dublin . . . .) We had ourselves snapped by one of the numerous street photographers, who deftly peeled a ticket from the wad inside the belt of his gaberdine. Sometimes we went to the dingy counter in Marlborough or Talbot Streets to collect the snaps. They came out grand, unposed and carefree, the city spirit in our mobile postures.

And there was always something new to enjoy in those wonderful nineteen-fifties! If it wasn't the Tóstal it was the Teddy-boys, and if not them, the Unemployed. The teddyers were all style. They were bin-men *en fête*, busmen on a fashion picnic, swaggering and shoulder-conscious, effing from their paths widow-women laden down from a visit to Todd Burns. But the Unemployed were different. They did nothing. They 185 were as fierce as the Mau-Mau. Here they came marching, roaring, the whole street black with them, buses stymied by them, dinner-time disturbed by them. I wasn't able simply to dismiss them as 'a parcel of bums', as Mam did (I felt the room cool, tighten). I dreamt about them. In the dreams the man who was shouting from the top of the Pillar jumped off. He never landed, just kept whistling through surprisingly bright space, a broad smile on his bearded face. I recognized him at once, of course: he was the devil. He was rushing to make work for idle hands, as I understood he had been mandated to do by his first fall. I wake up. It's hard to know what to think. I'm afraid to tell my dreams to anyone; it might mean the end of going downtown.

And, as we all know, nothing happens to us when we're there. We have tea at Robert Roberts or The Log Cabin (Wicklow Street), boiled eggs for the grown-ups, a bit of liver for me to thicken my blood. With luck we'll catch the 5.40 house at the Metropole. I've read that Father John A. V. Burke salutes *The Maggie*. It really is extremely good. Or, for a special treat, we try the Theatre Royal: a film and a show. Maureen Potter blurs by with Jimmy O'Dea in a mangey coat (Biddy Mulligan the Pride of the Coombe in all her moth-eaten glory: an apparition of outrageousness): Harry O'Donovan plays the part of the *amadán*. The sketches are too quick, too topical for me, but I don't care. I'm waiting for Tommy Dando. And here he is in his twice-nightly resurrection from the basement aboard the Phoebus of his electric organ, all pink winks and primrose flashes, a thing of tulle, of organdie trailing clouds of glory in its throbbing, metallic diapason.

The 81 goes *lick-lick-lick* at a fair clip along Clogher Road. I stand near the edge of the open platform to feel brave and let the bus-created breeze course over me deliciously. Here's St Bernadette's: the next stop's ours. I can see the winking-willie flashing at the Sundrive intersection. It's the city's sanctuary lamp. And the only hymn to sing is Tommy Dando's signature tune: 'Keep the Sunny Side Up' (Clap!) 'UP!'

3

But all the big houses in Dublin were wonderful. We usually seemed to end up at the Metropole; it used to have Disney movies like *The Living Desert*, and J. Arthur Rank with his enormous gong was a more or less permanent visitor. I don't remember any cinema having better pictures than the Metropole, but the Carlton had grand banana fritters and you could get a mixed-grill on the mezzanine of at least the Adelphi and the Capitol. The latter, though the least well-sited – shyly, down dead-ended Princes Street, between Metropole and GPO – was undoubtedly the most palatial: patrons went in fear of breaking their necks on the highly shiny terrazzo lobby floor.

The toniest cinema to eat at was the Savoy. That was where I went with Da when he took his French friend, Maurice, out to lunch. A shrivelled figure in a swallow-tailed coat showed us to our table. Numerous others similarly clad attended: who were they – men who'd been asked to leave the priesthood but had been allowed to keep their clerical suits? busmen at the apex of their style's evolutionary potential? Deftly, with indifferent courtesy, they plied us with various *pièces de resistance* – soup of lumber-jacker brown first, then brown-boot stew, and for afters a silver boat of ice-cream with triangular wafer sails, *trés* French. It was definitely not the kind of place where I could not eat all my carrots. And to enforce pleasure, there was a string quartet. Throughout lunch it cut and scraped its way through its Palm Court repertoire, unsmiling policers of brittle feeling, evanescent moods who, once a sitting cranked themselves up for a climatic 'Wien, du Staat meiner Träume', while the oblivious trenchermen fell to and wallowed in their no less bathetic stew.

The only cinema at which meals were not served, I believe, was the Corinthian, which Da said was called 'the ranch' because of its unvarying menu of horse operas. For most people such fare seemed to be corinthian enough, but not for us. Da's favourite cinema, The Astor, was oddly enough next-door to the ranch – in their proximity a good example to me of the city's anti-uniform, contradictory way of being. The Astor was altogether different – in size, in audience, in attractions: food for thought was all it wanted to provide. Mam and I were never taken there either. (Da had strange taste: he liked the weird American picture that had no fighting – *Marty*.) Neither Mam or I felt the loss, needless to say. Like everybody else in those days, we were in love with the silver screen, and basically felt grateful for whatever it condescended to depict for us. And it didn't always have to be the early house. We often took our place with all the rest in the huge queues that stretched up and down O'Connell Street, proud and democratic participants in that great trans-Lismore collective, modern life, which had clearly arrived at last, with people jammed in line just like buses.

And what was there not to love? It was the heyday of Alec Guinness and Kenneth More. There was even a sense of patronizing acceptance that the English could hardly be the worst in the world if they could come out with *Doctor in the House* – not to mention *The March Hare*, in which they had Irish actors to make us laugh at ourselves. Ten times better than *The Quiet Man* with its woman pulled along by the hair of the head. Lismore got its moral rag out over that: how dar' them Yanks (that Maureen O'Hara must be a fierce trollop)! And for cinemascope, the screen spread out suggestively.

I looked down on the Palladium, Lismore, from the Metropole queue, and even on its superior competitors, the Desmond, Cappoquin and the Regal, Tallow. None of them had ads *and* shorts *and* maids with trays of ice-cream *in tubs*! In Lismore, Kevi Noonan with the cleft palate tore the tickets and shone the flashlight: no burly, door-wielding officer he. And the films in Dublin never flickered or had woozy soundtracks, much less broke. So there was no need for whoever the owner was to come and castigate the gods, as Doctor Healy did when his features snapped and the lane lads in the fourpennies stamped their feet and chanted, all in rowdy unison, 'We want *Moby Dick*!' Occasionally I sensed a ripple of dissatisfaction in the Dublin audience. 'Cut,' Da explained, when I asked if their was something wrong. They didn't know how lucky they were, I thought, with such small hiccups to put up with. Perhaps queueing up does make them cranky after all.

Pictures were not just for pleasure, however: like everything else, to be any good, they had to rise above the gnawing of the moment's hunger, which, if it remains all we know on earth, must never for an instant be thought of as all we need to know. So, once every couple of years throughout the fifties, a holy picture materialized. Not just things like *The Miracle of Fatima*, in which Our Lady was represented as a streak of pink ectoplasm (a lightly modified fluorescent tube, possibly). Such pictures weren't worth the commotion they created. Doctor Healy discovered this when he moved chairs from his surgery to the Palladium's gangways because we schoolkids had spread word that the nuns – Presentation – enclosed – had received a dispensation from the Bishop to attend. That way we would be sure, we thought, to be let go by our people, permission for a picture on a school night being by no means a certainty. And we could learn from the really good ones: *Never Take No for an Answer*, *Marcellino*, were not about apparations but about something more miraculous, juvenile protagonists for whom things worked out.

Even Da liked them, particularly *Marcellino*. I was surprised, at first; he never pushed religion. But he did work in a Christian Brothers' school, so I guessed he had been asked to do a bit of overtime. Then I noticed *Film Focus* lying around the house: he must have gone to confession to Father John A. V. Burke, the *Focus* critic. It wasn't until a little time later that I realized that Da spoke well of the two films in question (and never of the *Don Camillo* series, though it pleased large Irish audiences) because movies with kids, movies for kids, were important to him.

I already knew that he thought a lot of films in general. This I discovered when he took me to Youghal for the day the summer *Moby Dick* turned the wharf there into New Bedford (hence the anthem of the Palladium anarchists). 'Go over and touch the windows,' he said – of the new façades. Gingerly, I did. They were all paint – but looked so real! I remember him telling me, disappointedly, afterwards, when he'd seen the finished product that illusion had not been perfectly sustained after all: in one scene, the sacks on the quay bore the markings of the Irish Sugar Company! He was also slightly put out that day in Youghal because we didn't see Gregory Peck, John Houston or anybody until – I'd been whining, and at last we were on our way to Perks and the bumpers – a car sped by and he cried, like Ahab: 'Look, Seoirs'; Wolf Suschitsky!' – a real-life cameraman, confirmation that there was another 189 world, and that illusionistic windows were also real.

And of course I knew he was in the Film Society.

The Film Society was in North Earl Street above Denson's shoe-shop, just where the 30s set off for Dollymount. As though to prove it was *bona fide* it had its own letterbox, and its name, in Irish as well, Cumann Scannáin na hÉireann, was on a plaque by the entrance. Up then some dusty stairs, and some dustier stairs by the shoe-shop's storeroom, until at last the narrow rise to the third-floor landing, an hallucination of lime-green woodwork, very shiny lino the colour of Savoy soup and unshaded hundred-watt bulbs. There was an office. A lady called Betty ran that. She worked briskly with phone, typewriter and tongue, and she wore black spectacles with winglets on the outside corner of each eyepiece, like those worn by the girls in 'From Nine to Five', an unfunny and unviolent cartoon that the *Independent* ran. Things seemed business-like with Betty around, but lest anyone lose sight of what the Society stood for, there was a still of that wonderful shot of Harry Lime in that Vienna doorway, the playboy of the western conscience himself. And Orson . . . I never heard his name mentioned without the speaker's tone warming to what a Dublin darling that man had been. Orson Welles, bright spark and lavish liver. Disturber of the peace. American dynamo. The youth of a different culture, familiar but fundamentally inaccessible – too quick, too bold. Unnerving combination of birth of a nation and a star is born for Dublin to do anything else but hold him dear in memory, another legend from the limitless past.

Two other rooms opened off the landing, one with projection equipment, speakers and the like; the other, looking out over the street, had a screen and a projector, almost at eye-level with Nelson, and well above bustops – now that was how having arrived felt, though I'm sure I would have felt the same way if the Society met in a Baggot Street basement. It was the people who made it all so sophisticated for me. Those Dublin names – Harper, Toner, Painter, Mulkerns, Waldron, MacLochlainn. The man with the cheroot. The lady who, hail, rain or shine, wore dark glasses. Men sauntering in after short twelve at Marlborough Street, rueing the night before and laughing. Da and me dropping in ('for a minute', he'd say, thinking of Mam and teatime, as if I cared): at the fag-end of a wet afternoon to find – surprisingly, delightfully – that there were others with the same idea, looking for someone to talk to, willing to let the talk ramble and the clock run. 'I see Myles had a good one today, comparing them yokes they have strung across Grafton Street to the lavatory pipework of a big hotel.'

That didn't seem right: 'them yokes' were model atomiums, put up because it was The World's Fair in Brussels. Important. Nuclear. Aluminium. Due to be given to these words' resonances. The new dispensation of the age demanded it. Uranium – pray for us. Thy will be done on earth. World without end. Amen. Who did this Myles think he was? (Who was he?) But I laughed anyway. Everybody else did, and I so badly wanted to be part of it, even then, even for those half-hours that brought us right to the threshold of the rush, so that we'd have to hurry away and call at the Kylemore Bakery for a slab of appeasement before hopping on a 22 for home. Because in the Film Society I saw another Da, a Da without a family, a Da who was a Dublin Seán instead of Lismore John, a Da who, somewhat unexpectedly, had a mind to speak to other grown-ups, who laughed, made others laugh – no longer a silent, chain-smoking withstander of his mother or a man of widower's sorrows. Movies meant life.

But the Film Society was not just sociable, it was social, possessing possibilities of meaning and relevance of which I had neither inkling or appreciation as a child, when I was too near it, and which I can only recollect now, from too far away, with slack jaw and star-struck eyes. Perhaps the membership did not appreciate what was going on either, since it was disguised as novelty, and since one version of the Irish fifties is that everybody was a child then, polite and more or less perpetually hungry. The novelty was that the Film Society would show movies of quality which otherwise would be denied to Irish audiences – items of such quality that they should not, I learned from Da, be referred to as movies (much less pictures), but as films.

These films were, needless to say, largely foreign. So, the first accomplishment perhaps was to get beyond the ooh-la-la, *La-Dolce Vita* barrier, and to invite the audience to take itself seriously by having a look at cinema being intimate, being analytical, being editorial, being (in a word) thoughtful. To do so – inevitably, as far as I can see – meant to make a rude 191 gesture in censorship's direction, since censorship as much as commercial canniness kept Bergman and his mordant men from our shores. And often in North Earl Street I overheard harsh words directed at the censor's office and the official himself was sometimes regarded as not being up to scratch (voices were raised, references made to the Palestine police). This was like cursing a bishop, to my ears, seeing as the censor had his own white little film, with harp and signature, which we had to witness before anything else was screened for us, and what could be more immune to attack than a celluloid seal and office? But here I was in the merry and outspoken company of Da the heretic and his boon companions, who evidently wished for nothing but (like heretics through the ages) to stir a bit of thought, to cause talk, the times being flabby.

Quite possibly, there was a slight missionary aspect to the Film Society, which may have added to its appeal. It was a missionary time, what with the Holy Year, the Marian Year, Father Peyton encircling the country with rosary rallies, the causes of local elect – Edel Quinn, Matt Talbot, Blessed O. Plunkett – forever before us, an atmosphere of expiation so exhaustive that it was impossible to go down town without being threatened by all sorts and conditions of Roman legionaries, armed with flag and rattlebox. If the Film Society were perceived to be against such a social atmosphere, in which nothing was too great to be offered up, to be against something (anything), to be – God save the mark! – in favour of pleasure and the instruction it provides, not to mention *vice versa*, then that helped it thrive. It's preferable, however, to believe that what attracted much of the membership was the presumption of privacy, responsibility and similar anti-corporatist virtues which paying a membership fee secured, identification with which the films being screened ratified. As for the uncountable numbers who may have joined to peer down the cleavage of Anna Magnani or Anita Ekberg, such tit as there was came submerged in subtitles – so they didn't count.

At any rate, and for whatever reason, thrive the Society did. It found a public, and whatever the public found in it, more joined year after year. The season, as the series of screenings was called, was forced to move from the baby Astor to the latest thing in cinema-going at the time, the State Theatre,

Phibsboro, a thousand-seater with an exotic sound system. People had to be turned away. Then down the country wanted to join in. Da went to Mullingar, to Limerick, even back to Enniscorthy (lair of patriots), to help found branches, though these often withered, to be replaced it seems by the silence out of which they had initially clamoured, and for whose existence Dublin was no doubt blamed, as so often.

They sat, the company of a thousand, including my knowledgeable Daddy and the unforgettable woman who, I heard, cried all the way through *The Seventh Seal*, without leaving and without ceasing, and saw for the most part what they already knew but what perhaps their rivals – the Pioneers, say, or the Legion of Mary – had made it difficult for them to realize. Which of them had never seen an Umberto D? And which of them had not felt moved in their familiar lives by the strange, yet recognizable, sight of him – there, at a distance, in perspective, mobile after a fashion yet touchingly lacking in elusiveness, unlike his counterpart shuffling along Dorset Street. If there was a *Bicycle Thieves* there had to be an Unemployed. But wasn't it a cheek of those Italians to make a whole opera and tragedy out of a push-bike? But wasn't it the truth, as well – as plain as day? And can that be Italy, neither religious or fascist or a nursery for tenors? There's Rome, its eternal aspect now, unnervingly, the poor – who, as our unclerical birthright shows us every day, are always with us.

This audience begins to imagine. It forsakes for a while the kiss at sunset and Max Steiner's swelling strings. Instead it forms a temporary tolerance for the black and white of dusty streets, for the ways of ordinariness and the modest yet urgent hope of surviving their humiliations. It sees that life in the mean streets only appears to be a matter of black and white. Perhaps here, over the course of an hour, sympathy is released from latency. Perhaps there's the surprise of discovering how much of life is seen through the puce-coloured spectacles of class. This audience rubs a window. It raises, for the time being, a temporary shelter against the miserable drizzle of injunctions and exhortations to black-and-whiteness, straight-and-narrowness, that befogs the brightest day. Behind their backs, the machine dreams on, its intense eye piercing dim, fog-filled confines. This audience has something to look up to.

Was it to live the different movies made that Da went to France? He went to Rocamadour to stay with Maurice, a place no less miraculous than Lourdes, not because of what had happened there, of what might happen, but because it had implausibly clung for centuries to its cliff, as though nothing could be more natural than to carve a domicile out of stone. The people ate frog's legs and snails – they found a way of eating them. They may have been (they must have been) starving; still they were stubborn enough to put a bold face on things. When all fruits fail . . . . No cuisine without famine. No cliffs without dwellings. No style without chaos.

Da heard it all in Piaf's candid, brazen larynx. *Je ne regrette rien*. He saw it in *La Grande Illusion*, where each frame is so full it looks like a cross-section, the screen itself a cell which shows constraint and implies liberty. He saw that escape can be unexpectedly rewarded with love in the mountains, and that escape is sponsored by spontaneity, and that love is the precondition of freedom. He may have relished the film's redefinition of Robert Gregory and Kiltartan Man. He may even have seen that an illusion is only as great as the human need creating it. Perhaps (since he remains the doubt I give myself the benefit of) . . .

We went in the Henry Street entrance, in itself a surprise because I never thought the GPO would have such a private-feeling doorway. It was somewhat dark. There was an air of men smoking and moving purposefully, but that may only be how I had imagined Radio Éireann would be before we got there (memory and imagination: what is the world compared to them?). There was a lift, of course, also a liftman. All the most important places had them. There was a lift and a liftman in a pillbox kind of hat in Brown Thomas's. And were we two not important people? Nothing but a smooth machine for us today. My Daddy was going to give a talk on the wireless.

Upstairs there was a lobby, with a radio in it the size of a coffin, and a man sat in a swimming pool of an armchair listening to it. Perhaps he was the man who played 'O'Donnell Abu' on the harp before the programmes proper started, just to give everyone a minute to get ready and get us in the proper holyish mood – except it was only women who ever played the harp, wasn't it? Whoever he was, he stupidly paid us no attention. But in a minute that didn't matter, as we were summoned by a beckoning man in shirt sleeves who approached from the broad hallway off the lobby. His name was Eddie, as I found out on our way down the hall with him: people were calling him, stopping him. I was impressed that somebody not wearing a suit could be so much in demand.

I was told to stay where I was and Da was led into a room. Down the way a bit, however, I saw what I took for a window – at least I would be able to watch the buses while the grown-ups went about their secret business. But it wasn't a window at all; it was a glass wall and there was Da looking at Eddie who was behind a similar glass wall. Da was mouthing sound-lessly from a paper. Eddie raised a finger to him. There was an explosion of jabberwocky playback. Then soundlessness again. Wheels of tape. Clean, artificially lit world of brain work.

I assumed all that remained was for us to return in triumph to Sundrive, turn the knob, and there, larger than life because present in an attenuated form – as though he were finally giving expression to our relationship (and, to make the moment sweeter, didn't know it) – he'd be. But we had to wait. Of course: I was dealing with grown-ups. Not too long, however: this was great Dublin, after all, where things happen – so it would surely happen. And surely happen it did: a week or two later we all – Mam, Peg, Da, me: my picture of the happy family – crowded around the Bush.

The familiar theme came through, something brassy, kinetic, I seem to remember (by Prokofiev?). 'Film Magazine,' said the voice, 'introduced by Maxwell Sweeney', who then spoke.

'Eddie,' I shouted: *I know him.* And then I thought, 'But – Janey, just like a film star: I didn't know the wireless made you that famous.' Maybe Da . . . ?

It was a strange programme – no music, just different voices looped together by clever Eddie MacS. At length Da began. He was brilliant: two solid minutes' worth about a shorts festival somewhere in the Pyrenees. It was news, it was travel, it was nicer weather, it was words in French, it was better than Bing Crosby singing 'Around the World'.

When it was over I waited for something to happen. Nothing did. (Well, Peg put the kettle on.) There was silence. 195

It felt cold, the same as it did the night Chrissy sang in the St Patrick's Night concert and I wasn't allowed to hear her. But didn't they understand? He was great. We should be going out for ice-cream. I took to whining, as usual, and as usual was sent sulking off to bed. The pink evening expired slowly beyond Clondalkin, as usual. So nothing had changed – maybe he wasn't all that great: maybe it took being on the BBC to make a difference . . .

All I'd wanted or expected was a wallow in his radio fame, but there was more: first, the Confirmation show, then 'Boy Wanted' – starring *me*! Da became a leading light in the Junior Film Society. Going to a picture was all very well, it seemed, but how about trying to make one? He found a way of being a teacher in his hobby-time, a way of making more of himself, or perhaps attempting to turn to material and active account some of what he may have seen in Truffaut and De Sica, that there was no project too humble, that there was no such thing as the culturally insignificant, that there was now available a collective recording machine – the movie camera – which could enlarge and mobilize and change forever our posed, box-camera images of ourselves, the medium shot in Sunday suit which expressed an ethos and obscured its context.

And, as I now appreciate, this commitment had to be the result of a decision, because it entailed the use of materials, money and resources, some of which were the Society's property. Da didn't have automatic access to any of it, I assume, because no Society would survive without controls, so he had to make a case for what he wanted to do, and be prepared to wrangle – not because everyone resisted him but because institutions of whatever kind seem to create wrangles (think of families). And even if all went smoothly, I must supply some tension, some drama, to remind myself of his unusual commitment, which seems, looking back on it, to be akin to desire in its normality (I hear him still speaking quietly, proudly, of staying up late helping to edit *Mise Éire*).

Of course Confirmation was going to be a big deal even without the film. For once, the Church seemed willing to cherish, rather than chastize, us. It was the last of the sacraments for a while. It meant the inauguration of long trousers and the first wrist-watch and, to make sure we knew what

such symbols connoted, we had the Pledge administered to us
– no drink till we were twenty-one, which caused confusion
in Swiss Cottage: was it proper to have the sherry in the trifle,
the great day's obligatory dessert, the secular viaticum for the
journey to manhood, now officially begun? The Bishop would
be in town, and all the clergy for miles around would turn
themselves into his altar boys for the occasion. We had to take
an extra name, to signify no doubt the extra dimension of
identity that was being conferred on us. Almost to a maneen,
we selected Joseph. Worker, donkey-driver, related to the
godhead by a happy accident of birth: he was avatar and
patron: one of ourselves.

All was exciting enough – so when Da stepped from the
twenty-past three on that Whit Saturday with the odd-looking
container slung over his shoulder it all seemed part of the
novel event, even though I had no idea what was in it. But a
ciné-camera – to make a picture! Talk about *'Veni, Creator'*! I
thought, oh leave it to him to add the city touch to the proceedings and make me marvellously different. And there he was
the following morning, tracking us as we marched up
Fernville, crouching by Parks Road to make a happy ambush
on the girls parading demurely from the Presentation. Even
more astonishingly there he was during Confirmation itself,
over in the men's aisle with one foot braced on the seat and the
other against the armrest, looking for all the world like the
heroic standard-bearing icon of labour and of progress, who
strains forever upward and forward on revolutionary posters.

How did he do it? He must have passed himself off as
someone from the Catholic Truth Society, an agent of Verismo
House; *plámásed* his way past canon and curate as a member of
the Irish Chrism Society, man-and-boy believer in a Godly
Cinema for a Saintly People. That's what I like to imagine. But
I remind myself that he didn't start shooting inside until the
proceedings were well under way and that he didn't shoot
more than five minutes' worth. So he probably just went in
and did it without anyone's permission; he had already
packed up and gone by the time the celebrants realized that
what they just heard was the whirring of a camera, not the
flutterings of the knowledge-bearing dove. Guerrilla cinema.
That's the style! (Wasn't one of the reasons I loved him
because he was a guerrilla parent?)

But, as I saw later on that summer at the premiere, the production was more provocative than the product. There was a nice shot of Pat Lyons as we boys waddled along (the dressage of Christ's Fianna), our faces and rosettes a grainy pallor against the grey of everything else. Mary Fleming had a beautiful bright smile, brighter than her dress's pure white. I don't think I'd ever seen it properly before. But for the daring raid on the chapel, religion got its revenge: it was all spectrally white with few discernible features, from unexpected sunshine flooding through the windows over the apse. And not alone that, but where was I? He seemed to have forgotten my central status, without which the whole effort seemed a complete anticlimax. Minus me, all ordinariness a gross fabrication.

My hour arrived, however (why did I doubt him?), with 'Boy Wanted'. Unlike Confirmation, which now I could forgive – a test-run to make sure he could use the thing, thus unworthy of me – 'Boy Wanted' (eight minutes) was an original. It had a story and everything (meaning me). The Phoenix Park, morning. A (borrowed) Morris Minor, one of its side windows open a chink, a camera on the passenger seat inside. A thief – yours truly – happens by, knacky-fingered, fleet of foot. Spies window of opportunity, acts, is hailed in hamfisted hieroglyphics by large member of Junior Film Society. Flees. Film Society fatty proves fleeter. Rugby tackle fells filcher. The End.

I leaned against the side of the Morris Minor, disgusted, the bitter sweetness of finding myself at the margins of his admirable efforts coursing through me. I represented the very passivity which the project was helping everybody else in it to overcome. Why did I feel like somebody's plaything? Why did Da have to spend so much time with the other lads, explaining? I should be part of that group. *Ich bin ein Dubliner!* I hated it that the teacher-pupil relationship seemed more substantial than the father-son one, being able to draw on familiarity, continuity, a group's shared goal. What I thought would be a collaboration between us turned out to be a collision.

It wasn't 'Boy Wanted' I'd call this, I said sullenly to myself, looking at the insipid, wooden allegation of me on the screen. It's – it's – But my dream (also entitled 'boy wanted') wouldn't let me. Fuck film! It was too real: it was not real enough.

4

This is what the voices said. They said:

'Only for the blasted Film Society, it would never have happened.'

'Ah, it was all that out half-the-night with that oul' *Mise Éire* business.

'She married him, anyhow. She saw her best chance – and of course John was always too soft. Wouldn't say boo to a goose.'

'Bloody fool – and she half his age: well, I wouldn't like her job trying to teach that old dog new tricks.'

'Hitch-hiking, that's what she has him at – at his age: did you ever hear the like.' That's how they spent the honeymoon. I suppose that's more what she learned in America. She was in America, y'know, tried to push in there, but the Yanks weren't having her – they were too fly for her. But sure here . . . . '

'Men are such awful eejits!'

'And of course Sundrive Road wasn't good enough for her. Nothing would do her but Monkstown. And she from Prussia Street. The cheek of her. Nothing but a social climber – going in there among them educated boys; a know-nothing. A jumped-up nothing! An able dealer' (a rhyme,, in Lismore's eighteenth-century accent).

'They go off to Donegal and places, climbing. And staying in the hostels, what d'you call the thing? *An Óige*, that's it. *An Óige* how are you?! At this hour of his life; isn't he a desperate foolah?'

'And where's this Prussia Street is?'

'In the heart of the cattle-market – and hasn't she the look of it! On the way to the Zoo, there; where them pens are.'

'Oh my God!'

'Imagine waking up to that racket every morning!'

'Sure Sundrive Road was too good for her.'

'Of course it was.'

'And did you see the oul' mother – the fallen arches of her, the dropped stomach.'

And so it came about that in these Monkstown years there was a death in the family. The victim was the institution itself, the O'Brien family, its authority and integrity. The royal we turned into Humpty-Dumpty. Not the new family in Monkstown. It went its own way regardless, persisting in the freedom and independence which originally animated it and which created such animus in others. That family increased, and if my very slender acquaintance with it is anything to go by, all concerned seemed fulfilled, secure, until eventually, though all too soon, death – the death that is not metaphor, I mean – had its way there as well. But in my time – before I brokenheartedly discovered that I would have to live my own life after all – what I saw happening, though I could hardly take it in, was the self-willed yet seemingly involuntary eclipse of the old Lismore hegemony·

The chorus elicited by Monkstown was all the more intense and unremitting because it was the swansong of a process begun years before, at the beginning of my boarding-school sojourn, when Chrissy got married and Georgie disappeared. These two events did not occur all that closely together. In my memory, though, they are welded as one: a joint presence with the immensity and force of a wrecking ball, with something too of the desolation and deliberate irreparability which that machine leaves in its wake. Not that the events were bad in themselves, and even if they had been they would not be the first to earn a stern reaction. Ours was a family like any other, after all, with rifts and banishments the order of the day. People were out with each other, then just as suddenly were not: it was all as intense and wasteful as the whirligig of fortune in a minor duchy. The difference in the case of Chris and Geo was the finality. They were consigned to moral Coventry, left severely alone, as unredeemable as sinners from the flames of hell, collaborators with an enemy identified as their own selves.

Chrissy spent her early married life in a flat above a shop in Main Street (oh how she had fallen: she didn't even have a house!). She wheeled her first-born up and down the town one summer long. I saw her every day. The lads that I hung out with all saw her, all said hello. I never did. I was told that whatever I did, I shouldn't speak. Not long after, the moral Coventry turned into a physical one: Chrissy moved to another town. I carried on at boarding school, missing her parcels of HP Sauce and cherry cake, her five-bob postal orders. By trying not to think of her, by trying not to picture her new life, her babies, I reproduced the silence that presaged her exile. That silence, Mam assured me, was for my own good, the same as everything else I hated or misunderstood, from tapioca to my mother's death. My school silence arose from having nobody to tell. I felt a loved one had been obliterated. I felt deprived of number two Mammy. There never had been a seriousness like this, as far as I could remember. I couldn't talk. I didn't know how to mourn. In the darkness from which tears might have arisen, memories took root, monstrous, slow-maturing fungi, soul food, soul hunger.

Even more mysteriously, Georgie went away. I came home from school on holiday and when he didn't show at suppertime asked idly where he was. 'Gone,' tolled the reply. Mam wasn't sure where: she thought probably to Chrissy in Cahir. A long time afterwards we heard he was in England, married. No attempt was ever made, as far as I know, to pursue him. When he came back it was in his own time, and only for a holiday, and long after it was possible to reopen the shed in which he and his father had hammered things out, in which he had tried against unarticulated odds – as all must – to give his own life a shape, finding at last that it was only possible to do so in another country, a country he had turned his back on many years before, returning to Lismore in hopes of realizing himself there . . . . So lives go through their unforeseeable, appointed rounds, lured ineluctably through the ordeal of love in exile via the ordeal of lovelessness at home.

No doubt there was much more going on then than I was aware of, more perhaps than even the participants themselves could handle properly. Who can say what's buried in the lives of people? – not the people themselves. They simply reach an awful point at which nothing more can be said. Then action blunders in, singular and irretrievable. Yet in its wake a deeper silence wells for which a gloss must needs be found if all is not to be lost, if all lives are not to be spoken of as the unexceptional mean of rage and need, if the only version of seriousness is not to be extremism, the quelled world of silence that follows explosions.

I didn't know exactly what a dropped stomach was, but I knew from the tone that it was first cousin to knocked knees, pigeon chests, fluke eyes, mallet skulls, elephant arses and all the rest. If people were belittled by their bodies, let them be mocked and denied seriousness: that was standard practice for just about everyone I was reared with. Looking down on 201

Prussia Street was also second nature, and again as much on the grounds of aesthetic connotations as of class. It was necessary to come from a place that looked right in order to be right, and Kay's bailiwick had neither a pleasing image (cattle in pens being a species of brutal materialism which cattle in fields naively disguise) nor a pleasant sound. Sound was important too. There seemed to be a diktat: never marry a girl from Ringaskiddy, keep clear of bank-clerks from Mullinahone. It was as if there could be no sense of value without a sense of sin and devilishness, no self beyond one that an enemy evinced (oh my colonized people!) . . . Prussia was foreign and ugly, a dream of enmity, pompous homeland of gutteral brass-bands and unconscionable steel which scythed down the flower of a generation (Mam's), enemy of the clever French and Dev's own strict Spaniards, old friends of Ireland, whom Da was content to visit when his head was on the right way, in the good old days, when he could still be thought a creature of circumstance – a little better off than some, no doubt, with a profession and a Dublin posting, but essentially crushed and mournful and one of ourselves . . . . Imaginations worked overtime looking for combinations in its limited index of associations and received images so that ranks could be firmly closed against the Prussian revolution, the marriage to Dublin and the totally unexpected family, Da. Every so often out of the 'phone came a barrage of resentment and frustration, blaming Kay for an image which she had not fabricated, denouncing Da for killing Sundrive. And even these thoughts, if that's what they were, would have been comprehensible if their creators had been able to acknowledge them as simply a set of possibilities, an interpretation, an attestation of strangeness knowing itself subject to the corrective of mind-opening experience. But the aim was not to deal in forms of words and hermeneutical niceties – the aim was to use weapons. And no doubt, that death hit everybody. Isolated Monkstown spawned unfamilial satellites of isolation. Now Peg saw that she and Da would not be growing old together, silently: her years of anonymity were about to receive public acknowledgement beside some bell on the front door of an apartment house (itself an aborted home) in Dartmouth Road and Garville Avenue. There, complaining of the noise made by the three typists sharing upstairs, she would discover how long ago her dancehall days had ended and turn up the volume of her TV. Now Mam would never come to live in Dublin. Old age stretched out before her in Lismore; neighbours in to see she'd eaten, to check the fire. Now, for the first time in forty years or more, she was alone and childless, the rosary beads her lifeline. And I, the common non-functioning link between them all – what now was I, or who?

Wrong, wrong, wrong. Prussia Street was very interesting. All kinds of buses made for it from the quays heading for the unknown reaches of the far north-west side, Blanchardstown of the hospital, the Navan Road. And when I visited Kay's house, I was pleasantly surprised to find it had Swiss Cottage size, damp age and huge dark furniture. It was not a hovel lapped in cowshit, and the satirical representations of its locale's variation on *rus in urbis* so confidently projected were off the mark. Since this was where Kay and her family were from, there was an easy traffic of people in and out, talk of one son overseas, and of another living on Botanic Avenue. Kay's mother was a heavy warm-hearted woman, slow, but not slow dull, slow watchful, tender, fond of putting on the kettle and of whipping up a bite. People lived there. It all struck me as disarmingly normal. Suddenly, there was nothing to think, and I didn't know what to think.

One evening, even, the household showed itself to be capable of getting above itself, of consolidating its normality by demonstrating that it wasn't enslaved to it. Kay and Da and I dropped by late – from the Film Society, no doubt – to find the front room ringing with laughter and the chime of bottle and glass. (It was, I think, the first time I'd seen drink in a house where there was not a funeral.) Everyone seemed in right form, and before long (or at any rate it didn't seem long), Da was wearing a Gregoryoid Fairview grin. The friends and neighbours standing around looked great, definitions of male careers of a certain grade and shapelessness such as are connoted by the common nouns jobber and coper, handler and runner, and by such articles of dress as ties doing the job of belts, wellingtons with the tops folded over, *cáibíns* worn back to front and similar insults to the felt millinery fraternity, the whole disarray transfigured by cast-off or mislaid gentle- 203 man's waistcoat of canary yellow. None of those present was dressed like this, needless to say: that evening they presented themselves as victims of their families' Christmas duty, each one a lino showroom of Argyle, checks, and Fairisle – but there was a certain splayed look to their features and a list to their demeanour to suggest lack of rigidity in other spheres.

When sufficient drink had been taken, voices were raised requesting turns (Father Devine, be thou my guide!), but – what a grand crowd – nobody minded when I demurred. They sang themselves and one little man soberly recited, with a swaying motion, 'The Wesleyan Chapel', about the couple who had bought a new house and wanted to know where the nearest W.C. was; so they wrote off, and received by return an elaborate prospectus for a W.C. with plush kneelers, hours of opening, sermons, baptisms and everything else necessary to salvation. The room began to reel with laughter. We became the people Brendan Behan knew, naughty and natural and knowing no harm. And to follow, Da and Kay sang a duet: 'Rickety Tickety Tin' – a fake folk-song, about blood and murder and morality's victory: the perpetrator confesses all, because 'lying she knew was a sin'. Silly, silly adults – I shrieked with laughter, slightly lightheaded, as though undreamt of weights had been lifted off my mind.

But this was not where Kay lived, not really. She had a room in her grandmother's house on the other side of the North Circular. But how could that be, I wondered. Her parents let her do this? She wished to be a cuckoo by design? She loved her grandmother, that was all. I was surprised again. There was nothing terminal about it, there was no rift – it may have even been a generous act: all concerned seemed still the best of friends! On top of which, Kay was smart. From all I'd heard she couldn't have had much schooling. There were no fine Loretos at the bottom of her road. And who belonging to her received degrees, taught school or otherwise attained the petit-bourgeois heaven of work sans dirt? But there she was, nevertheless, a genius at unendearing sums, a confidante of high-ups in insurance companies. The Monkstown living-room table became snowed under with actuarial spread-sheets. The grass-hopperish sound of the manual adding-machine chattered late into the night. What was I supposed to

make of that? Enmity spoke a language which failed to

describe accurately the world as I found it. The trouble was it spoke a language more complex and authoritative than any that world cared to speak.

The trouble was the present had a language but no words. The 'phone rang, creating a major verb. I baby-sat and generated unutterable speeches. For common nouns we had tears, flights up the stairs, doors banging, Da solemnly, ploddingly, following. So I never got to know Kay, or she me.

I squirmed to see an adult cry. I knew what tears meant: I was a gifted sprinkler as a child. Boarding-school eventually turned me off at the mains, though: surviving it meant swearing nothing ever again would make me shed a tear. Now I wanted to cry, but had no audience in Monkstown. The audience I had was the people Monkstown knew only as the enemy. But when I cried to them it merely caused the 'phone to ring. The more it rang, the greater chill I felt. Soon nobody was talking. I learned that silence, too, could be violent.

Lismore had been the first exile, inevitable but temporary. The second banishing was boarding-school, also temporary, but far less justifiable. And now, when everything seemed set, when there was no place else to send me, when finally it seemed I was on the point of becoming like everybody else – with even a mother (or at least a Chrissy substitute), and not just mother but Dubliner as well, someone at last who knew all I wanted to know about the city of my dreams, the city and my dreams – I only felt unwanted. So what was I, or who?

I was a sore thumb. I was a ghost. I was a wedding gift from ancient history. I was the homage resentment pays to impotence, an imageless irritant, a spy in the house of love.

The telephone. It's a symbol (of course . . .). Colloquy with a dark receiver. Exchange and throughput. Dialling facelessness. The film violence of cutting someone off, of being cut off. The weapon of choice for the genteel ambush. The bridging of distance which only draws attention to distance. How important language becomes without the body it's embedded in. The telephone: mortal enemy of the cup of tea . . .

That's a way of talking about that small guerrilla action, those many years ago.

Another way – the voices come lapping in, their passion and rectitude shrivelling the intervening, silent decades – would be to try to discover what those voices really meant (that slippery 'really'!).

I hear them damning Da for the sin of change. He should have stayed neutered in widowerhood (what release did he have in that body-hating culture?): he should have stayed choiceless and loveless. He had no right to start over. How dare he believe in the romance of the second chance? Look at the cut of him, upholding desire, even optimism (no wonder they thought he'd end up in America). Sure who in his right mind . . . . Didn't everybody know that marriage was either for the young and foolish – the mot tired of baking Jacob's biscuits gives herself to the plumber's apprentice; brawny wardsmaid from the Mater overwhelms bespectacled insurance clerk. Or else it was for newly orphaned middle-aged countrymen: John Joe, the acres secure at last – praise be to Death the provider – approaches in stealth and hobnailed boots the canon's housekeeper. But here, now – lo and behold! – an act of generational and cultural miscegenation in our very own midst . . .

Da and Kay had sinned against pattern. They had committed change, and had (oh horrid hubris) assumed that they were free to do so. They had caused thought. Proud things – they won't have luck! And as to her alternative destiny, considered her unentitled to the franchise of partnership, home, happiness, sex and everything else due a desire for a full life. Perhaps she seemed insufficiently self-sacrificial. Perhaps she (being in love) tactlessly neglected to sue for their *nihil obstat*. Was she so shamelessly imbued with the Dublin looseness of Prussia Street that she was sufficiently freeborn never to consider the very existence of psychic property rights? Whatever hopes of fulfillment Kay may have realized in Monkstown, in marriage, were considered to be as spurious as a successful Sweep ticket, a revelation of how life's distressing unpredictability expresses itself in dumb luck and blind fortune, gods that only pagans worship, the same base, humanoid gods that made city life a lottery and a holy show. Speaking from lofty judgment seats – apparently in some unearthly location beyond frailty, beyond desire – did these voices finally mean to say that all they could acknowledge was a marriage between opportunism and self-deception? I don't

know.

Hovering between language and silence, all I can do now is what I did then: speculate, analyze, imagine. The only life I had was an inner life. I lived off it anorectically, demanding that my resources alone could reduce my world of words and non-words to comprehensibility. The wasting cure, the hunger strike more deadly than the cause creating it. But it was all too serious to live with, too unexpectedly serious, and not at all my version of love in Dublin.

5

It was March, the sixth month of our winter; a Sunday.

'Seoirse!' Da's voice boomed up the stairs.

I don't know why I was in my room. Perhaps the storm had been already rumbling, or I knew one was going to break, having become so sensitive to atmospheric pressure.

I remember coming to the head of the stairs. I remember roaring, 'Get out! GET OUT!'

I remember walking back into the room, reaching under the bed for the suitcase – the case that used to be his, that used to bring the Christmas gifts – and beginning to pack. I had as much feeling in me as that old leather-and-metal portmanteau, as the mound of dirty shirts and underpants which I'd built up, like an image of a depression, in the cupboard of the night stand. I felt as much alive as a sheet of blotting-paper, a palimpsest in others' hands.

Then, steps on the stairs, and Kay bustled in: 'Don't. Put the bag away. He didn't mean it.' Her face was flushed.

So just as dully I put the clothes back in their festering hide, swung away the bag, and I can remember seeing grey, then, and smoke rising from the smaller, closer-together houses up the road, so I suppose I must have gone out, walked up Mounttown and around to Rochestown Avenue. The occasional 46A snaked around the little houses. There was a soccer match at TEK. The shouts from the field, the lazy Sunday bus, brought Sundrive sharply back, memory's force confirming loss's permanence. Then, later, bed: awake, unable to get warm.

Usually, Da dropped me off where Adelaide Road met the top of Harcourt Street, while he took the South Circular on to school in Inchicore. But that Monday he had to return a speaker to the Film Society and asked me to give him a hand. Of course I should have said I didn't want to, that I'd rather walk to work from Suffolk Street, fortified by the bus's companionable cigarette smoke, than have the silent ride conveniently with him. But as usual I said nothing. He could ask whatever he liked – even if it was to leave him. I could take it. (I had taken it, I thought.) Whatever he said had to be treated just like the most trivial request ('Run upstairs for my fags'), because if ever I let on that there was more to it, if ever I revealed that I was not stone, there was no telling what might happen, emotion being bad news since I'd arrived.

It had to be the Film Society, of course; the coincidence is too obvious to be anything but true. While he attended to some paperwork I stood at the office window once again. Confident pigeons still milled around the back of Clery's. Traffic's hoarse susurrus rose to me, as ever – the old, incessant, rustling voice of promise. There was a life out there – even if I didn't have it – in the dispersing mist; and down on the street inaudible, comradely morning calls of strangers. The day before I had become one of those strangers. No tears. Whatever else, no tears! Thus on we rode, locked in our sterile norms. To do other would be to express priority and choice, as though we thought each other people rather than images. Better that than being a familiar treated strangely. I took what I knew would be a last look around. Sundrive gone. North Earl Street going.

'Ready?' We turned to leave.

'Look,' said Da. 'I'm sorry I shouted at you yesterday.'

I'm sorry . . . ! But he'd never spoken so intimately to me. And I did look. Now! I heard my heart say. Tell him. Better yet, listen, let him tell you. It's the last minute of the eleventh hour. He's going to say, let's start again, let's pretend it never happened, you'll be going to UCD in the autumn – here, I brought you the scarf; we're all going to America in the summer, for good, I have a job at Frankie Avalon High, the
Bronx – no, no; it's a long way from Boston. Would you like an

electric guitar? No? A set of drums? C'mon, we'll go to Pigott's now. It's okay. I'll take the day off. Have you ever been in UCD? C'mon. Don't worry about Peg. I'll 'phone her . . . The city seemed to withdraw.

There was only silence, our own special medium.

'Aw, it's okay,' I muttered. My valedictory to childhood.

The 15 to Harcourt Street was empty. The river stank the same as ever. The man with the tall white hat was in the window of the Westmoreland Street Bewley's raking the coffee-beans in the pan of the machine that also helped Dublin smell like Dublin. I got off at the Standard, crossed over, went in.

'Oh Peg,' I said, and then at last the tears came gladly down.

But the hardest part was still to come. Still snivelling, I made my case: if I could have an extra five shillings a week I was sure I could afford digs. Would she . . . ? Could I . . . ? Peg said she'd have to ask: meanwhile I should wash my face and run out to the Monument Creamery in Camden Street for scones for the elevenses; there was a good lad.

The following Friday I got my four pounds five. Freedom! Soon afterwards, Peg found me digs – in Rathmines, no less, where digs were supposed to be. Maybe things would turn out right after all. Peg came out to Monkstown to collect me and the bag and drove me over to Mrs Luby's – back to where she had shown me my nation's tricolour – green/amber/red – at the lights by the Stella, preferring to stand in the exhaust fumes than to spend the whole afternoon visiting Peace in Leinster Square, exhibiting her first-born. Buses in Rathmines; our earliest memories of being in Dublin together. So it was possible to start over; it was possible to back to a Peg-and-I world. One childhood went, another was reclaimed.

She parked a little down the road in Monkstown but needn't have. Nobody was in.

And so I left my father's house.

There have been other dreams. Of course. But Da was the prompt and pretext of the earliest, least forgettable ones.

He was the man whose hand I held as we walked the iron roads at Christmastime around Lismore. He was the man of words, from whom I learned the names of trees – the sycamore, the silver birch – in summer sauntering through

Jacob's Wood. 'As I was sittin' by the fire / Atin' spuds 'n drinkin' pohrter': that was one of the songs he taught me. And when 'The One-Eyed Reilly' was frowned upon in Swiss Cottage, I felt glad inside because that only drew me nearer to Dublin. He was a story-teller: 'Once upon a time there were two men. One was called Lennie and the other George . . . . '

'But what about the mice?' I asked, after the unhappy ending.

'Oh . . . . ' And with his marvellous combination of eagerness and patience (what a teacher he must have been!), he tried to explain that in this case mice didn't really mean mice – well, it meant mice, all right, but not *mice*. I took his word for it, but sighed, preferring my Beatrix Potter straight.

In Sundrive Road he stuffed an old sock full of newspaper, put three sticks against the rear wall of the house and called for cricket. I with a hurley, carved his errant yorkers through the covers, which the lupins going to seed patrolled. My name was Basil Butcher. He was Typhoon Tyson. He used to imitate the wireless, making me guffaw and lose my wicket with his backward square leg and silly mid-on. When rain stopped play he would take down the Britannica and show me that Rex Alston wasn't joking: you really could invent a deep third man if you wanted him. What a quaint game, with most positions *ad hoc*, not to mention lunch, tea, and a round field. It was true: the English were the men for oddity. There seemed a freedom in it. I regaled Mam with all I learned. She said that it was oul shoneens who played cricket now: in her day when only gentlemen wielded willow, Lismore beat the Australians (Mam voted for Dev but it was in the style of the masters he supplanted that she'd been formed and which she upheld as right, visiting a moral *droit de seigneur* on her dependents, like a Kipling character, a potent mix of mixed signals).

Da stayed a playmate for as long as he could. He tried to evolve from being a playmate into being a good sort. Though as far as I was concerned boarding-school was as bad idea – particularly compared with such attractive and convenient alternatives as Synge Street, or Drimnagh Castle, plus a life together – he tried to take the sting out of it. He didn't give me hell for getting 0 in geometry (no marks, that is: zero!) from Barney in the 3B Christmas exam. I remember being dumbfounded when Bogman, one of the Lord's annointed, got particularly riled one day at my being blinded by terror to his pedagogical accomplishments (he was a fully paid-up member of the shout-and-knout method) and roared that I was nothing but a lazy little caffler and if I told that to my father would he write to complain about it too. But I never did find out what he'd complained about (wouldn't ask, wasn't told).

Even one of the dreaded conversations of teenage – the man-to-man, what-are-you-going-to-be one – didn't go too badly. It took place one day we spent at Monkstown, clearing builder's rubble from the front yard. He had just bought the house; the wedding was coming up. The job was not my idea of a good time, but I thought of it as an investment – in years to come I'd be able to lie on the lawn for which we were now preparing. The talk turned to me during the tea break, as we played under the splendid oak in the front. Ticking off, turn and turn about, the large number of occupations I was unfit for did not take very long. 'The Guards. The Army. Aer Lingus.' I waited for the Bank and Civil Service to give Da his due, but he didn't bring them up. 'I suppose the Church doesn't attract you?' he said. No, Christ! 'Well what would you like to do?' I said, 'I'd like to go to University.' But there was no money for that. Houses were dear; weddings, too, no doubt. So that was that. We filled more barrowloads of stones. Then, he asked me endearingly, at teatime, if I'd ever seen *The Magnificent Seven*? No? Well, it was on at the Ormond, Stillorgan: if we hurried. We flung aside the cups and plates, like undomesticated boys, and ran.

Mild air, tinged with salt, steamed from the darkness through the open upstairs windows of the 46A. I was still tingling from the evil Eli Wallach (Da told me his name) going 'Khwhy?' with a twist of his mad face. I practised silently saying the name Horst Bucholz. After a while I ventured, 'Da, is that the best Western ever made?' He spoke in that familiar, so reassuring, even interested way. *Stagecoach*, he thought, was the best. And had I ever heard of *The Seven Samurai*? I should see that if I got a chance. Japanese, samurai; history, you see, that makes a difference – there's a story and there's a bigger story behind it, not like in Westerns, although of course, Ford, *She Wore a Yellow Ribbon* . . . . ; *Rashomon*, that was another good one. It was like old times, that last night out

211

we had together, him telling me stories.

But the playing and the fellowship stopped. They would have had to, in any case, I suppose (though why?). Too bad that more insidious games supplanted them, though, and that they ended when they did. Da might have become more than a handful of impressions, more than the fabulous absentee, more than the longed-for solution who became perplexing silence. That morning Morris Minor could have been a UCD for me. I might have learned that fathers are not only parents but are also agents of time and perpetrators of meaning, our fateful precursors, possessors of, participants in, the bigger picture; verbs in the life sentence. Da could have told me how things were with An Fear Mór and the Irish College at Ring, to which when he was my age he used so often to cycle, and why. What about the time at Croke Park when, during half-time with Dev present, teachers ran out onto the pitch protesting and had the stuffing beat out of them by the Guards? Was that during the '46 strike? And what did he do when the strike was on? He might have told me who Frank Edwards was, and how he got to know him. It never happened. Instead we had the puttering of the car for company. That Morris Minor was our hearse. It was what the black pram of Sundrive became when it grew up.

But it was only after his funeral, and in opposition to the hostile voices' final fling, that he became the alternative reality I'd sought. I was told what a 'bloody fool' he was, him with his BA and HDip, not even ending up a school inspector, when probably the whole Department was open to him ('he was a fluent Irish speaker, you know'), and with it entry to every bishop's parlour in the country. In other words, the years at St Michael's Primary – virtually his whole working life, that is – were put in because he didn't know how to be ambitious, not because he might have had different ambitions quite at odds, perhaps (let's hope), with the *status quo*, a way of professional life which may have, in its very absence of conventional getting on, expressed rejection of the state's numerous clerisies. 'And what about the time he was offered the job with UNESCO in Spain? But oh no – he wouldn't live in Spain for God nor man. Him and his principles. He'd make you sick.'

212 Oh, the sin of self! The malevolent eccentricity of choosing not

to be dictated to . . . .

'And you know he was a terrible Red. Oh he was, yeah. He was years out of training college before he could get a steady job. Rathcormack? No, he was only subbing there. Then he was some place in Carlow for a while. Carlow! What brought him up there God only knows. But that's the truth: a Jam in trousers, that's what he was for years.' (A Jam, Junior Assistant Mistress, the staff of teaching life for many poor-paying convent schools, was the lowest form of existence in a browbeaten profession.) 'That's where being a Red got him. But you may be sure he's paying for it now . . . . Remember this, Seoirse: the Catholic religion is a hard one to live in, but a grand one to die in. Did you know he was after teaching himself Russian?'

Oh my God, he had a history. He hadn't spent his whole life bogged down in life's abysmal privacy, with widows and spinsters on the one hand, Christian Brothers on the other. He ultimately proved himself the family's version of a fifth columnist not just by what he did – or, in the voices' terms, failed to do – but by what he thought. Ingrate, liberated son of Cathleen ní Houlihan's husband, *patria o muerte*. I hope he was a Red. And kept his head. And had his happy family, too, at last.

Four people on a beach. It's in the Hampton's at Slea Head, near Quiberon. There are two little girls, playing with each other, not playing with each other, present, simply, like ponies in a paddock. The wife and mother walks briskly ahead by herself. On the edge of things, in shirt sleeves and bare feet, a middle-aged man of average height and build. Wavelets of surf tickle his toes. His face is as brown as a walnut: the weather's been great. The scene has great weather's radiance. Every so often, Da gazes up into the serene sky, peers out over the glinting, mercurial sea, as though he's seen something. It's just a habit: there's nothing there but sea and sky. There's nothing to distract. No backward looks. I see that everything here combines the uncanny closeness of a painting with a painting's uncanny distance. I see that this picture is the offspring of the mother-and-child in the off-limits parlour. Then Da resumes the serious business of eating an ice-cream.

II
BOY WANTED

1

The earpieces had to be highly polished for the sake both of presentability and painlessness of fit, and in order to achieve the height of gloss required, the brushes of the electric polisher – the coarse brushes for the initial, clarifying shine; not the buffers (Great God! was there no end to the variety of things?) – had to be loaded with a porridge of pumice powder and oil. In which I, and everything around me, regularly took a shower.

But to get the earpieces into polishable condition the surplus plastic had to be hewn from them, which required the application of different size bits in the electric drill – one would never do, oh no. The bits were always getting stuck in the drill-shaft, and I invariably grabbed them panicking: now look at what I was after breaking: therefore a regular feature of the daily grind was those buggers of bits trying to roast my fingerprints off.

So that the earpieces reach a hewable state, the plastic moulds had to be boiled. I never remembered to set the time. When the moulds were boiled they had to be extracted from the casts. It was most important to hit clearly the pins holding the two halves of the casts together. Otherwise, if dented, the pressure wouldn't work properly or something, and pressure was everything. Guess what I did? And when it came to mixing the plaster in which to set the wax impression of the client's ear in order to make the mould for the plastic to go into prior to boiling in the cast, so that eventually these would be things of hew and grind – well, there is a house in Harcourt Street which has some unique abortive *putti* and traces of moulding on the ceiling of one room which unaccountably escaped the eye of C. P. Curran.

Ah, if only Da could have seen me whipping up a storm of plaster – those foaming peaks, those gobs in the eye! – he would have thanked (might even have paid) me for being such a disenchanted stoker. If I had been as eager to please him as I was to satisfy my boss and benefactor, Mr Franz, the Monkstown home would have been ashes in no time. Stoking had been surprisingly good job-training. It had taught me that the one way to demonstrate discharge of responsibilities was to make dirt energetically. Impress through mess. And I had to impress: I had to act as though there was a future here. The International Electronic Company – meaning Mr Franz and Peg, though they had a sleeping partner, a man with a turnip face and an office in South Frederick Street – was all I had to cling to. Thus, cling I must, quoth Handy Andy, son of Uncle Podger.

Securing and validating my grip were my high hopes. I was doing well, wasn't I? At least I was not out in the mountains lectoring, exorcizing and portering with bekirtled former schoolmates, seminarians at Ballyboden. I wasn't in a muck sweat wondering if I'd got the Junior Ex. or not. I didn't have to wear a uniform; the brown coat, identical to the ones worn by Billy Power and Paddy Flynn in the Co-op in Lismore, didn't count, since I was no shop assistant. I wasn't even serving my time. A trainee, that's what I was. Besides, instead of the banality of a brown coat, what I wore was a robe of plaster-and-pumice cake-mix, modelling my work's image of itself. Looking the part, even if I couldn't play it, made me feel happy (though Peg complained about the cleaning bills). I was something in the city.

There were drawbacks, of course. Being merely a trainee I had to go to school. Go back: that was a bitter blow. But it would be at night: that was exciting. But it would be Kevin Street, the Tech: that was humiliating. Tech had analphabetic connotations. Tech was cousin-german to Manual, and to the kind of boys that were continually wanted in the evening papers – those cramped, pictureless columns containing nothing but the most urgent and anonymous kinds of news: the stark, ungraphic format that I only knew from death notices. I never thought I'd be so near to them. I tried not to think about it. The word 'trainee' helped, also 'international' and 'electronic'. Words were useful, definitely: they kept reality at bay. Reality was silence. That was the worst. Faces blotched and puffy in the aftermath of insult. Necropolitan avenues of want-ads.

Another very helpful word was 'salary'. It made four pounds a week sound a lot more than it was. Thanks to it, I already heard myself among the professionals. And, as I was told and half-believed, I wouldn't feel the time passing until I was qualified (another wonderful word); all my tomorrows a sea of jam. I too would drive a Fiat 1800, like Franz: yes, the day would come when I'd take the bus only for old times' sake. I just had to look at Peg: for years she'd worked for half-nothing. Now she was a company director, name on the letterhead and everything. And she was only a woman. There-fore, I had no trouble seeing myself quit of brown coats, not to mention the combined gradgrindery of vindictive machinery and Tech. I saw the life in a suit, on the phone, Peter Stuyves-ant in hand, and *Take a letter, Miss McGonigle. Dear Sirs. Thank you for the favour of yours of the 20th ult?* That was the style.

Better yet. *Sehr geehrter Herr*, and by all means, *Mit freundlichen Grüssen* . . . . For we certainly were international. In a year or two I would be off perhaps to Erlangen to learn the secrets of the dB and the diode from Siemens, the smartest people in the world, whose hearing-aids we sold and serviced. I would be quite safe: Bavaria was Catholic. Not like Crawley New Town where Acusticon, our American brand, had their plant. Still, I might be old enough to look after myself by then. And if I really showed promise, there might be a trip to Sheffield to don the modern halo of earphones and see the Peters Audiometer people do their stuff. That white noise was amazing. And I'd be one of the few people in Ireland to have ever heard of it, that static which sounds like the death-rattle of nature.

Yes, and not merely international but electronic as well. See: I couldn't have been more modern if I tried. And I didn't have to try: here it was, laid on like the gas – safe, secret, instantane-ous. Electronic: the sex in the head of electricity. Those *luidín*-sized hearing-aids that the clients from Booterstown and Rathgar liked so well were only the start of things. Soon they would be – I could see – no bigger than the Smartie-sized batteries that now drove them. Hearing-aids as earrings, as brooches; barettes as bone-conductors. The designers of the fake-spectacle had the right idea. And why stop at ears? I could see a day when there would be electronically-activated false teeth, when instead of hearts there would be batteries. I lay awake at night dreaming of electronically-heated shoes, of duffel coats modelled after electric blankets, their circuit made once toggles all were fastened. If you wired up a *crios* you'd probably make wheelchairs obsolete: arise, switch on thy *crios* and walk. All when I came of electronic age. And why not? Lemass was on the cover of *Time*.

And, as though in support of my fantasies, not to mention being sweet compensation for the travails of Monkstown, there was the honeymoon. Peg, Franz and I did not exactly do the town in my first few weeks with them, when they could still optimistically assume that my splatterings and breakages were just a phase, like pimples. To one but lately liberated from black cabbage and the Argosy variety of potato, however, it certainly seemed that way. I was the missing link, to be styled and polished to fit right in, so that a bright and prosperous future would be had by all.

It began with the razor.

'Do you shave, Seoirse?' Peg asked.

'No. Why?' I was on the point of telling her that I wasn't anywhere near big enough for that yet; sure it was only after I had done the Inter. Cert. for the second time that my oxters started sprouting.

'Well, it's time you did, I think,' said Peg.

'You mean – !' A man – me?!

Peg offered to be my witness and provided the operation's venue. Only she had no shaving tackle (of course – the very idea!), just a miniature plastic yoke for scraping her legs, the blade of which was about as bright as the neophyte to whose face it was about to be applied. There was no lather, either, but Cusson's Imperial Leather provided peak enough. Or so I thought.

'Oh my God! Look at the cut of you! Are you all right?!' Peg shrieked, giggling.

I had circumcized my face. I had made myself my own blood brother. I was a man: the evidence – this grotesque menstruation, a nostril, an earlobe, pimples, chin all redly wept. I ruined two terrycloth towels, which sobered Peg. She recommended electricity from now on.

I agreed: either that, I thought, or the relative safety of a knife and fork. I was embarrassed, but the soothing remedy being proposed – be incompetent, be rewarded (the honeymoon's theme, in effect) – made it all worthwhile. Someone understood me, it appeared.

By chance, the Leaving Cert. results came out soon afterwards, so my honours in Latin and English could be rewarded without it seeming that I was being ridiculously spoiled. But I almost missed getting anything more than a black look, by blithely saying how much I was looking forward to a Philishave – largely because the radio programme for them had Denis Brennan and his wonderful voice. A Philishave would never do: Philips were dirty Jews. Then, having instructed me in truth, Franz led me to a trade-counter in Lower Abbey Street, dealt huffily with the friendly brown-coated counter-hand, and handed me my Siemens (it broke soon after International Electronics and I parted company), a machine which, followed by a visit to the Waldorf, a superior-smelling haircuttery in Westmoreland Street basement, made me a presentable dining-out companion.

The Moira. Interior dim, sophistication's shade. In that lobby it was always five on a mild September afternoon. Cigar aroma; gentle, unpressing telephone bells. Double Century, Noilly Prat, Dubonnet: the vocabulary of pleasure. I watched, careful that my eye and jaw retain their usual extensions. Quiet Trinity Street bereft now of insurance drones; a shortcut into Dame Street. But the shortcut was an end in itself – oh, skittish city!

They know the barman: 'Vincent, *s'il vous plait.*' Vincent serves. He's liked. He knows his place. He tinkers with the glasses, with the cordials and *digestifs*, those ambers and amethysts, liquid birthstones, unfolders of destinies. No paper-sellers here; no traffic. We raise our glasses. 'Chin,' says Peg, adding a hearty, 'sir'. I drown my obsequious grin in a Club Orange. And to follow, rainbow trout. I have to wait and see what the lemon is for, and the strange knife. Apple pie *a la mode*: more meltings. Franz knocks back a Cognac, proffers a tawny note. '*Allez . . .* '

And then the big test came. The lake, the boat, the day's fishing at Carrickmacross. If I pleased Franz here – as Peg had 221 done: she'd been a number of times – all would certainly keep on going as merrily as a wedding bell. But even before we left town that Saturday morning I knew the day was going to be a washout. I had tried to protest that I knew nothing about fishing – a mistake, since it merely revealed me to be exactly what the occasion required, an emptiness to be filled. Peg told me with loving reassurance that there was nothing to it – look at her, she'd picked it up in no time. 'Ja, ja,' Franz corroborated proudly. And then he launched into what he'd taught her. Peg said, 'Oh, he did: he's a great teacher.' But what if someone – a hypothetical case, of course: myself – detested the whole idea of fishing, considered it a distillation not a sublimation of the tedium that is country life? But how could anyone, not to mention anybody Irish, even think along non-fishing lines. They had me hooked: I couldn't not be Irish, so I kept my mouth shut. But what, I thought, if I'm being roped in not just to the day but into others' dreams, and perhaps not dreams that they could pay for, that sharply took me in as I observed the hefty tip for Vincent. What if I was their future much more than they were mine, more investment than person? Yet, they seemed kind, the way they made a present of the present, forgiving blunders. And later (the promise was implicit) I would have a present of my own. The dream of Dublin lived, I told myself, hoping I'd be able to believe it.

Boring Meath and boring drumlins; lake like a boring sheet of steel. And it was cold too in the damn boat: too soon the splendid coffee was all gone. I put in my usual day's work, stabbing myself with the hook, casting into the rushes, half of me Laurel and the other Hardy ('a fine mess you've gotten us into'), impatience gnawing at me like a piranha. And of course a stupid fish permitted me to catch him; distressing me with the purity of his panic (*mon semblable – mon frère!*). Get back, you naked thing! I wrenched the hook ineptly from his pouting lip and crudely fired him back, as far as he would go. Now there was blood all over my fingers (shag this for sport, anyway!).

And whether it was the extraordinary lifelike quality of the blood – it seems that I'd been expecting, if anything, something like the wake of snails, silvery and thin, as though fish were nothing but slivers of tender rainbow; whether I was in that hypnotic state on the other side of cold and boredom, or subconsciously needed to retaliate against Franz's cheery commendation of my success (till then he'd been seated in the prow with his back to me, reeling in with tiresome regularity quivering entities he called disparingly 'rutt' and 'brim' – nothing apparently was going to satisfy him but perch, if possible the best and biggest perch in Monaghan. In Ireland. Ever. I blanched to see up close the sportsman's solitary greed) – in any case I discovered after a while that I had done – perpetrated the very thing that above all – and I had Franz's frequent, solemn and pedantic word on this – was a piscatorial horror and abomination.

A mare's nest. That's what he called it, anyway – I know no other name – from that day to this my rod has remained downed and – apostles and fellow-countrymen forgive me! – I have abhorred fishing as nothing more than grotesque underwater golf. A mare's nest was a getting of one's line in an inextricable tangle around the reel. I have no more idea how it came about than I have of how I hooked my misfortunate fish. Had I had sense, I would have let the line dangle in the water all day long and dreamt of pleasanter things. But an image had been proposed for me, and who was I to reject it? No wonder things got in a twist. So an hour or more was spent hacking and picking at the horrible knot. The air was filled with clots of Flemish, the splendid, oathy sound of which was the day's one bright spot, joke-vivid, though of course I didn't dare laugh. Franz threw the pliers and the knife from him enraged. Great stuff! – see, he could act the child as well. Better till, when at last the last hank of severed line had been cast into the lake, Franz peremptorily deemed the light too poor to go on fishing, and he drove like a madman, in a blazing silence, back to town. We were home before dark. The grey quays looked beautiful. Who could ask for anything more?

'Ye're early,' Peg said, carefully scanning our faces. 'How did ye do?' Franz made an immense Gallic shrug and poured himself a Tio Pepe. 'Catch anything, Seoirse?' Oh just the usual, I said silently, with a forlorn, self-pitying look: boredom, anticlimax, fear, embarrassment, futility – and probably a cold. Yet, I vaguely felt that somehow that was not the whole story.

'*Georges*, come once!' Franz peremptorily barked.

'Come at once' is what he meant, so I automatically went, 'Right, sir!' *Shit*, what is it now? As if it made any difference. It was only that I had broken something, burned something (my range with the soldering iron was awesome), forgotten something. And it was only to Franz that any of it made a difference.

The honeymoon was over.

It would have ended anyhow, of course. The year was closing-in, there would be no more fishing, Tech had started; all good things must come to an end. Even I knew that life could not consist of a series of appointments with a fish-slice at the Moira. And the Carrickmacross débâcle had some fall-out – nothing vindictive, mind; no ridicule; merely more frequent mutterings in Flemish, more expansive, resignatory shrugs. The fishing trip had undoubtedly confirmed the early intimations: I really wasn't all that smart – not a patch on Peg; certainly nothing like himself. Was I perhaps becoming an unforeseen problem? A ticklish question. But the Tech might answer it. Softly, softly, catchee monkey . . . . Yet I sensed Franz was having uncharitable second thoughts about where his charity to me was getting him.

For my part, the best I could do was make my 'sir' sound cheerful and obliging, sensing that politeness would protect me from the depredations of my hands. 'Sir' was a good word; it bespoke a sense of self-awareness on the part of the lowly which the high and mighty appreciated. After a thousand repetitions, however, I found myself wanting to experiment a little with its sound and slant. I discovered that by saying it slightly too loud and with quasi-military promptness that I was pleasing myself more than deferring to the boss. All Franz heard was a reasonably accurate echo of what Peg said. He had no need to hear more. His deafness tickled me. Besides, the more I sirred the less I had to use his proper name. This pleased me too. My diminishment in his mind was recipro-cated by his in my intonation. If I was turning, he too attained to genre. He was just the boss.

Peg, however, didn't see him like this at all. Her 'sir' was all sincerity; her 'Mr Franz', used interchangeably, was nothing if not fond. To her, it seemed, he was like a friend of the family, a big brother, more welcome in her life than certain relatives. I remember hearing her tell Mam about him, how natural he

was, how well he'd done for himself in Ireland. 'There now for
you,' Mam said, 'and there's boys down the street in Lismore
hardly making a shilling.' (Protracted discussion ensued of
the town's most economically moribund – Peg's once prospective beaux? Bottom line and remedy: a good kick up the
backside is what they needed.) When Mam and Franz met, he
kissed her hand and said '*Madame*', and insisted that she take
a glass of Dry Sack. His accent might make him sound like a
runaway washing-machine, but he was a gent, all right. And
a practising Catholic into the bargain. The combination of
classiness and the proper creed was such a rarity in Ireland
that it made for tolerance of foreignness. I doubt if Mam or Peg
had ever come across such a perfect combination of social and
cultural credentials. Any family would be proud to own him –
or, if it came to it, to be owned by him. No wonder Franz
exuded an air of self-confidence that bordered on the narcissistic. We'd never met a success like him.

To Peg, in particular, I think, Franz was an apparition of the
beau-ideal. Not amorously speaking. Franz was much older
than her; besides, his wife and children had accompanied him
on his *hegira* from Antwerp. But this was the beauty of it.
Because he was an older man he could lead by example, he
could set the tone, talk to the bank, wrestle with the responsibilities. All Peg had to do was listen and pamper, act the
helpmeet and work her fingers to the bone in managing the
day-to-day minutiae. Franz knew how to order: she knew
how to wash-up. What better ideal to look up to than the
engineer-entrepreneur. And an exile, what was more,
survivor of 'a tough old time'.

The honeymoon, in Peg's view, was seen, I think, as an apt
preliminary to a marriage of true minds between myself and
Franz. She probably made a large emotional investment in the
happy-ever-after promise of such a liaison. I can remember
how she kept encouraging me when Franz got mad, and when
I, fearful of a future without her (afraid that the world was only
a slot machine – things without people), abjectly apologized
for the day's disaster. And sensing perhaps that this marriage,
which she'd sponsored, might prove as much a torment to her
as the one she so comprehensively disapproved of (and from
which she had rescued me – how could I dispute it?), she
would talk to me of Franz, what a clever man he was, really;   225

what guts he had; how he was as honest as the day was long; how he may be hard but he was very fair. 'Stick it out, boy. You'll do all right.'

Franz himself rarely spoke about the past. He might mention Knokke or Louvain with a bland, 'Ja, very nice', meaning for stupid tourists (bloody foreigners), or remind us that, broadly speaking, all Walloons were schtinkers, a judgment he felt all the more entitled to, he implied, because of how we thought of Northerners. But I got nothing from him about Ghent or Aix or I-sprang-to-the-stirrup-and-Joris-and-he, much less about Gheel, the town for madmen founded by our own St Dympna, for which I obscurely imagined Franz, aid to the deaf, might have a feel. Once, reminded by a client's anecdote about outwitting a Guard, he passed some remark about how he used to infuriate the Germans because, although he had his shop in Antwerp, his home was outside the city, in a different jurisdiction, so could refuse their orders to man the rooftops, join the bucket-chain. He seemed nostalgic, just for a moment, then. But why? Peg told me that the war had been wicked. Nights of bombs. The port burning, the sky burning. They had no coffee, just some kind of chicory juice. So that was why he came to Ireland: it was bilingual, and we had Irel – a liquid to make coffee from that looked like a glutinous version of California Syrup of Figs. And as to what memory might wash up, there was no telling, as I knew.

It struck me as odd though that, having survived the war, Franz didn't stay home to enjoy the peace. When I asked about this, Peg, usually so good at telling all, grew vague; it was something to do with things after the war, a new Antwerp government. Politics – boring, weren't they? But (Peg hurried on) he loved Ireland. And wasn't it great, the way he built himself up? He didn't know a sinner here, couldn't even speak English. But he stuck to it. That's what the country needed, men like him. Modern, go-ahead. When you think of how well he's done, it really shows us up. A few more like him, now, and we'd be on the pig's back.

Peg was right. Franz was the Marshal Plan, the technological revolution, the signpost to rainbow trout and snazzy cars, enhancer of our neutral peace, creator of opportunity, master of plastic, terminator of the fifties. (Pray for us! Have mercy on us!) I had so much to be grateful for . . . I was lucky, really, say

226

what I like. Mr Franz might be hard, but y'know, it's a hard oul life, it's a trial. I did know indeed: he grabbed the drill, the spatula, from my hand, 'No; hold it so. So! *Gott verdamme* . . . .' It was for my own good, really, he'd make a man of me. (He owned the spatula. He owned the way to hold the spatula. I had to let him. Could I stop him? Who had a better right than he, after all? – in business for himself.

It all made sense. My problem was that the kind of sense it made did not appeal to me. It was a sense that placed one man on a pedestal. Franz was the triumph of the will, the machine rampant with quids sinister, with (for all I knew) any amount of devices at his disposal, with all of which I would be required to identify in due course. Whether it was all too modern for me (dreams notwithstanding), or whether it was because there once was a man in Monkstown whom I wanted to be and when that didn't work I declined a substitute, or whether it was something simple like knowing I couldn't get on with a man who apparently had no stories, it came to the point that when he bent over to inspect or direct what I was doing I felt strong urges to hit him with a hammer on his perfectly bald brown egg of a head. And I laughed to myself. Because I realized that, no matter what else, I was not like him – I was free to be unlike him. Was that what my inchoate post-Carrickmacross feeling of not-quite-total despondency meant? Such thoughts – the first ones of my own I can remember having – made me feel slightly giddy, the same way I felt before going on a journey.

2

But even if I'd been in the shed at home with Georgie I would have had some of the same problems, since over and above the matter of personality – all-consuming as it was to approval-needing me – there was the more basic matter (which the press of personality squeezed aside) of work, the application of self to world, the expenditure of energy and the consumption of materials (the subjugation of the fish). The sheer externality of all that was an immense strangeness to me – quite apart from the fact that this was to be done for someone, at the behest of a stranger. That strangeness never went away, and was a more unnerving source of my unhappiness than the Franz-tension, since it bore out all I had been told about my uselessness, and all that recent experiences were giving me to understand about life's essential autism.

No doubt there were aspects of what I did which exacerbated this hypersensitivity – often I was struck, in the back room at Harcourt Street, in the space between the noise of one activity and the next, of how reminiscent my self-consciousness was of the way I used to feel, as a child, in the midst of adults when they talked politics, say, or mentioned unfamiliar names (Casement, Amritsar). The materials and machines had the same vividness and impermeability. They were more specific, they possessed greater gravity and density than I felt, and believed, I did. They cost more.

Being in the back didn't help, of course. The back windows looked out on nothing: the windows in the front had 48As to Ballinteer pass by them, 62s to Goatstown. The phone was in the front. And along with Peg, there was always a secretary to talk to, a fairly rapid succession of nice girls – three in less than the two years I was there – with whom it was difficult to be properly friendly but who at least were reminders that there were aspects of the life to come that no employer need provide for. It felt lonesome sitting at the bench, oblivious until it was too late of the drill racing on its appointed rounds, mindful of nothing but the silence within me. The feelings of lonesomeness, of being less deprived than unworthy of the front because of my position (eloquently communicated by the state of my brown coat), were intermittent, however, and probably insinuated themselves when other aspects of the job were getting me down. One thing that really gnawed at me was the repetition. It was nothing except boil and grind the whole time I was there. The earpieces had names – Mr Stott, Mrs Cargill – but they seldom had faces. I was either going somewhere at an excruciatingly low rate, or getting nowhere very quickly.

But then work itself was appalling. Even more than by the conditions and character of the job, my feelings of defeat and nonentity and fearful loathing were brought on by a vision I developed of work in general. I couldn't bear the smallness of it. The minute but crucial differences that constantly occurred provided me with a distressing climax to adolescence – the general impossibility of everything. If the powder and water were not whipped together into a consistent creamy porridge, air bubbles could get trapped, causing the plaster – in which the precious earpiece-in-the-making was encased – to split when boiling under pressure. (I knew how it felt: one air-bubble could definitely ruin your whole day.) If the plastic dough to be inserted in the earpiece mould hadn't set properly, the earpiece, after boiling, would be opaque, hence visible, hence potentially embarrassing to the client. Overea-gerness with sandpaper could result in a minute looseness of the piece in the client's canal and the shrieking torment of feedback. I couldn't tolerate the notion of a world in which significance had so minute a sphere of operation, in which ratification or occlusion of self was balanced on the slender fulcrum of such tolerances. When I thought of the world – which I did a lot, since I didn't seem to be living in it, quite – I thought of sums of parts, not parts themselves. I thought of worlds within the world – books, films, cities, girls. Bubbles and dust were not my style. And there was the matter of pace, too. To work with smallness, I found, was to work slow; to work as if there were world enough and time, and that the task in hand exerted a proprietary interest over time and world. But I was seventeen-eighteen-nineteen. I didn't want time, I wanted speed. I wanted to be on my bus.

So I was a failed machine. A bored failed machine, at that. From pure forgetfulness I branded a new sheet of bakelite with the soldering iron – 'These things cost money!' 'Seoirse, how could you?' One day, no reason at all, I stuck a screw-driver into a socket on the main plug board. There was a little pop and a bluish-yellow flash, that was all. Typical, I thought: even my involuntary but evidently incurable anarchism lacked force and spectacle. A little later I heard Franz shouting at a client, then the dry hiccup of switches. Nothing worked. Franz flew out of the testing-room and towered above me: 'So!' A coal-chute of Flemish descended. Peg, vigilant of image, rushed back, rapidly shutting the testing-room's various doors, hushing, placating. 'Sure he didn't know any   229 better, sir.' 'For this we pay Tech! *Dumkopf* . . . . ' And later, much less enjoyable, a ponderous homily on the wrongness of not telling – though, digesting this, I made the agreeable discovery that secrecy was a large part of the pleasure; secrecy was always unsuspected; secrecy was something from which I could not be parted. It wasn't long before, noticing how much insulating tape there was, I was taping books inside the lavatory cistern. Many's the sweet Gold Leaf I had in the jax at the end of the hall, relishing the latest hit, *To Kill a Mockingbird*.

The afternoon of the power-cut must also have made a rare impression on the abandoned client. He must have heard some of the shouting. He probably considered us a branch of Lourdes: a foreigner asked you to take a seat, the next you heard voices. Mr Franz the thaumaturge. 'German, is he?' clients would ask hopefully.

As far as I could tell, there were three types of client. The premier class considered of referrals from Fitzwilliam Square, where, to selected and select consulting-rooms, at Christmas time, I delivered long bottles in interesting oblong boxes, tastefully wrapped. These clients belonged to Monkstown and its familiars, Orwell Road, Nutley Park, Clontarf Avenue. Not all of them were old, either; it surprised me that people in their twenties – their teens, even – lived at such addresses. Some of them were pretty girls my own age, limbs beginning to stretch and frames to fill, now, with all that tennis, all the riding lessons. On Saturday we opened until lunchtime to receive their orders for batteries. I answered the door on Saturdays: Miss Houlihan, the typist I remember best, had the day off – was, even as we sold, still a little gaga from Friday night at the Four Ps (fine for her). But please God it would be Miss Brophy from Booterstown with the sunglasses and the great legs (all Dublin dames had great legs), or Miss Brennan of Clonskeagh – still at school, just right: how about a few tips for the Leaving, Miss – this is a man of the world speaking – interesting you should mention the Babylonian Captivity, I was just thinking there the other day, if you ask me it'd make a smashing picture. *Ben Hur* – exactly! Did you like it? I liked Ben, hated her. Sometimes it would be them, but once I started to decoke the throat, they just looked me up and down severely and swept on by into reception. They could hear now; they didn't any longer have to smile when someone wanted to talk to them. Old McMullan, a commercial traveller with a Northern accent, was friendly, a good bit of gas – but who the hell asked *him*?

Other clients – the second class – came up from the country, nuns who'd come into a bit of a legacy, gristled parties with land outside Granard, steered by mannish daughters in suits of navy-blue. The watchful Daddy tried to look more helpless than he was, while daughter simpered. This was her day, really. She'd been at him for years. Deafness was not the will of God (he needn't give her that). It wasn't even natural. Didn't they have machines now above in Dublin, no bigger than a terrier's mickey (God forgive her) some of 'em. And they wouldn't hurt you at all: they do be qualified men. Back home with James she'd get herself into a state: 'Th'oul fecker: he have it all right only he's afraid to part with it. Sure will you ever forget what he gave Pascal for his confirmation? – one lousy two bob!' But now, at last, she had her day in Dublin. The foreign doctoring would soon be done; then tea at Wynn's to watch the priests.

Franz always officiated in such cases. Often, however, they defeated him. 'What?' he'd be heard to exclaim, 'you can't hear *that*?' With the audiometer's testing pitch up full it had an impact on the ears comparable to what my sinuses suffered from the Monkstown fridge. No answer. Then Franz, incredulous, a little disgusted, and totally unaware of what the victory meant to the testee, would declare, a brusque shrug in his tone, 'Then I'm sorry, I can't hallop you.'

'What's tha' fella saying, Mary Ellen?' from the victor.

'Miss O'Brien, come once': Franz on the intercom.

'Sorry, now,' from Mary Ellen, tamely.

Peg, brightly: 'Not at all, not at all. Safe home.'

But *mutter mutter*, both of them, over restorative tea. Another sale gone west.

A much more regular source of income than canny culchies was the Dublin Health Authority. It paid for aid to deaf children. Every so often Franz and I swept out to Cabra or Our Lady's Hospital for Sick Children, Crumlin, in the 1800 – he the Flying Doctor, I trying to play the part of plucky Tommy O'Donnell calling Wolamboola Base. We also went to a school in Ballyfermot. I was afraid, of course.

I was afraid of the world's blight, of nature's blind mistakes, of the schools' trapped smells of drains and cabbage, and the hospital's air of imminence (the worst has not yet happened; it's still imaginable . . .). The little boys had big black boots, grey ganzies, trousers that seemed patterned after chimney-pots. They reminded me of the inmates of the orphanage in Cappoquin, whom we would see being marched out two-by-two as we strolled onto the hurling field. When I whined I was reminded that I didn't know how well off I was – think of the orphans.

It wasn't whining that occurred to me now, but tears. The poverty. The waste. The unbright schoolrooms in outdated premises. The patient nuns, their lives a wishful, imprecise, disturbing mimicry of their charges. The little cross-eyed boy who wouldn't stay still. The passive, downcast little girl with auburn hair and green in her nostrils. Formless utterances and stammering: a kind of incontinent excitement at the visitors, wiring them for life. The vale of tears and Adam's curse. Electronics.

And above all, what my teenage mind fastened on, appalled, thinking about these visits – swiftly the Fiat flew back to the place where we imagined we belonged, leaving mere Irish drivers, Morris Minors, limping in its backwash – was what they showed me work. Not my work, or their work, but Work, the universal damnation. The gap between the inchoate and the effort was what everybody must feel, I thought. As Georgie, wherever he was, walked onto where the hole had to be before the building could be raised, or when he prepared the flawed parlour to receive paper, I knew him knowing that strangeness. Da, not many miles away in Kehoe Square, knew it, staring at perhaps the siblings of our hapless clients, and they stared back expectantly at him, knowing it intuitively themselves but believing that 'Sir', in his sirness, in his apartness at the blackboard, might talk them out of it. Their attendance in the classroom bore mute witness to an understanding that the distance was part of a primary order of things and the talk a secondary consideration. These gaps, these flaws, the silences, the daily essays in recuperation (as precisely unavailing as they are availing), the problematic of progress, the indefiniteness of action: I imagined I saw all that in the faces of deaf children. I can only assume that I was looking for

232

it, or that those marginal kids spoke the language I understood best, the language of emotional impressionability.

Thus, I went on (what a great audience I made), machines are useless. They had to be invented, of course, to distract us from, to override, what I presumed to call the truth of what I'd seen. But all they did, like any mask, was draw attention to what we hoped they would disguise (they even broke). Even money, the most wonderful world-turning invention of the lot, the original electronics, supposedly fabricated to soften the blows, only succeeded in making sure the blows fell on someone else. I was not yet nineteen. My salary was four pounds a week and change. The world was turning out to be chronic bollox, a boarding-school with translucent, shifting walls, full of sow's purses longing to be silk ears . . . .

And how then to proceed, besides, as though a nun, succumbing?

I should have been like Peg. Peg was dutiful, Peg was responsible, the right hand ever-ready and best foot always forward.

She wasn't perfect, mind – at least not by the standards I was raised to. She too had been molested by the city: she relished her Rothman's King-sized, and when it was five-thirty a splash of Cinzano did not go amiss with her. She bought *The Daily Telegraph* throughout the whole of the Profumo affair, read with bulging eyes, and told the jokes about it that were going the Dublin rounds. There was going to be a new marmalade – Keeler's little kip; Mandy Rice-Davies did better business because she gave Green Shield Stamps. Peg used to send the weekly edition of *The Daily Sketch* (the five dailies bound) to Mam. At holiday time they'd evaluate like punters Billy Wallace's chances and the fate of Captain Townsend. Ah, the odd English and their public loving: all that divorce – shocking, really: awful . . . . Weren't they shameless? Weren't they gas? Peg also sent, as regularly as clockwork, the English women's magazines whose gaudy romances, complete with the vapid splendours of the oleographer's art, seemed to mimic those in the sovereign's circle, and which had no connection whatsoever to the much more entertaining items by Mary Grant and Evelyn Home.

But as a worker, Peg was no less than the second coming of The Little Flower. And not just during my time with her,   233 when, after all, she was a director and had had the incentive to invest herself. No; she had always given one hundred percent. After the Inter. she had cycled over to the Tech in Cappoquin and in next to no time was typing and taking shorthand to beat the band. Of course there was little call in Lismore for such accomplishments which, in any case had been polished to such a pitch that Dublin was the only fitting showcase for them – Dublin being a far more desirable venue than that nebulous conurbation, England. But how to place her?

Well, as luck would have it, wasn't Peace just newly married and her husband starting up a business for himself. The very thing. Big sister would be on hand to show Peg the ropes and keep an eye on her (since as sure as God she'd be off dancing as soon as she had a few bob in her pocket). But it was a grand business, too, dealing in perfume and vitamins and related requisites for the MPSI's, while Henry – new boss, new husband – was more or less one of our own, since he was from Mitchelstown. And he could sing grand. On top of which, then, poor John – Nuala (God help us) . . . . So Peg was able to move in to Sundrive Road – sure God doesn't close one door but he opens another – where she cooked and washed and cleaned and applied the Coty before she hit the town.

I assume she had her nylons torn to flitters by stocious salesmen in the National, and that she went in style and in high hope to the Metropole's *thé dansant*, Sunday afternoon. And no doubt there were dates; a drive to The Scalp, Portmarnock, of a starry June-time, hops with loutish medicos at Bective Rangers and at Wanderers, dinner-dances at selected minor golf clubs. Dancehall days and love in Dublin . . . . (Let's hope.) What's certain is that she worked long hours, year in year out, in Liffey Street, stuck behind straw and crates, and in the course of time developed extraordinary skill in wrapping and packing and applying sealing-wax, in balancing petty cash, in keeping a weather-eye on the easy-come easy-go drift of messenger-boys who ferried talcs and unguents to Hamilton Long – no doubt for 'moddom' at Switzer's too; and by no means least in babysitting Peace's growing family, preparing the Mount Merrion home for each new arrival, scrubbing the bathroom while the angel cake rose to perfection in the oven. There never was a thing she was asked to do that Peg wasn't

able for. She'd never say no, just roll up her sleeves and pitch in without a second thought. A treasure. A godsend. And all she asked for in return – as far as anybody knew – was to have a fortnight, every third year or so (however long it took to amass enough in the Post Office), sweltering under Nivea in San Sebastian or Riccione – 'God, anything for a bit of sun!' (I hear her still.)

Then one fine day she walked. Oh, the badness of her: the saucy thing: too well off she was . . . . Another breach, another unhealed wound. Once again, silence the seal and mark of ultimate significance. She'd never said a word; nobody ever suspected how fed up she was, or even that she might have been fed up at all; sure hadn't she been given a life – job, roof, that meant – what more did she want . . . . She wanted the job she'd seen in the *Independent*. She'd discovered that, in the end, independence was as simple as that.

She was an instant and sensational success. Franz had found exactly what he wanted. Peg was obedient and obliging. She supplied the human touch to transactions with often fretful clients, teetering as they were, for the first time in their lives, on the brink of intimate newfangledness (if secret ears were becoming commonplace, somebody, somewhere must have been having the inchoate dream that would one day assume material consequence as the vasectomy). She knew, above all, all the varieties of yes – compliance, endorsement, initiative. They had amounted in her by now to a second nature, a nature which took its lead unasked, from Franz Masterful Male. She was ten times the earpiece-maker that I was – 'and I never taught her,' Franz crowed, praising her, showing me up: 'just learned by watching'. He'd taught her how to do the testing, and here too she performed immaculately. And as for keeping the office in order, the statements and invoices and correspondence and the years of training as a packer in Liffey Street coming in so handy after all . . . . She was a gem, truly. Beyond reproach. Franz relaxed, signed over day-to-day matters to her, schemed for more partners and bigger business, cast his entrepreneurial gaze on me, the all-time pig in a poke.

By the time I came on the scene, then, Peg had made it. Not only that, but she had all the appurtenances of having made it. When Franz plumped for the 1800 he bequeathed his old Fiat 1100 to her, and taught her to drive. She had a fine flat in

Garville Avenue. Only the indifferent reception on her TV prevented her from being as made for life as anyone on the Monkstown Road. And sometimes she was. Some autumn Saturday afternoons the wrestling came in as clear as anyone could wish, parodying the old, unfeeling confidence tricks of flesh. 'God, but I'd love to be flogging that Mick McManus!'

I heard again the voice that flayed the Welsh. But things seemed different, somehow. Just my imagination, I suppose, but I saw her present, larger life as a diminishment – the result of the shrinking family context perhaps. The car brought her closer to Lismore, where Mam was on her own. The television lulled and dulled the day's exhaustions: there was no need to go out – but really there was no impetus. Besides, she was so good at what she did old clients dropped by to chat (and that was tiring), so she had a social life, so she was too worn-out to have a social life. And she liked to get an early start to beat the traffic and to catch up with the paperwork.

I had seen people work like this. Her father; her brother, George. They could be absorbed to the point of self-forgetfulness. They could stay late and start early, no clock but their own vitality and interest – a species of profound amusement – to monitor them. But that, to me, was the point: those men were working for themselves, as perhaps did Da when he closed the classroom door. I began to think of Peg as though she couldn't, that all she did had to be placed at the disposal of a self not hers. And here I was, the history that was going to repeat herself. True, some of the details had been moved around, as though to suggest that no, really, this was different: I was getting my turn at the Tech now rather than sooner; the cosmetics angle had broadened and become more subtle. But I too had thought that I should serve in order to acquire a life, only to find that when I had the perfect chance to, I was unable. This was one of the strangest dislocations of all, to find I was unlike Peg, too, of whom I was so fond, who obviously was so fond of me, who had apparently done so well: so irrevocably unlike her.

It's tempting to say now that Peg was so fond of me she tolerated my boredom and disaffection with the job, and as a result of her sensitivity I became a messenger-boy. But that's the kind of tribute sentiment has a habit of neatly, retrospectively,

236

paying to the unforeseen. Peg certainly never viewed me as a messenger-boy. If I was fed up, it was my own fault and good enough for me; besides it was only through accidents and incompetence that my state of mind revealed itself, and these my mentors attributed to a state of non-mind, or stupidity (God be with the days when difficulties were thought of as no more than errors in prefabricated meaning!). So, thinking of myself as a messenger-boy was all my own work, and all my own the pleasure of the image – at once false, since I remained to all appearances Browncoat of many colours, and Trainee; and true, since I regularly was sent on messages. Whatever I was, therefore, I was in disguise. Whatever I did, I had an alternative me not doing it, a me like a suppressed giggle. Messenger was trainee's unboring, declassé twin: trainee was messenger's staid good fortune, the chance he should have wanted but for which he was unable to find the necessary need in himself. And I had glimmerings of enjoying myselves now that I could see life being fuller than I'd previously imagined. I was five again with a fantasy pal – certainly the play element struck me, even if I couldn't afford as yet to concede its childishness. But I also saw in the errand-runner something that everyone around me lacked. I was something that, being unsuspected and only of personal, or least-valued, significance, could not be taken away from me. Apparently, imagination could prompt autonomy: more important at that stage, to my mind, was the sensation of impenitence that freeingly accompanied imagination.

There was a tiny shop in Camden Place: that was a regular place to run out a minute to for Aspirin, milk, fags – the instant needs. It was run by a woman with wispy hair, 'from Wickla' she was, she told me. She had spectacles; she was flusterable in the extreme. How she must have suffered: the shop was so small that two customers filled it. That made it interesting the odd time any of the classy secretaries from Arks were present – china shops among bulls, poor things . . . . What had the poor woman inside the counter done to be cooped up in such small-ness? Perhaps she thought it freedom, compared to Wickla. It was hard to tell by her. She had a habit of lifting back her head when anyone came in, which made her look scared, averse, half-daft – the very way, indeed, that the look made at least one of her customers feel he looked. And she confided in me   237 one day: 'Oh, I do get terrible headaches. But they affect me strange, d'you know? Aye; it's in the legs I have 'em.' As messenger-boy it was possible to be a regular, a party to confidences, known. That was great.

Down to the post office past famous Arks – *The Kennedys of Castleross* was done there: I tried standing unobtrusively by the National Children's Hospital to see if I could spot any of the soap-opera's stars, but no; I was forgetting, these were not like old times: no Alfie Byrne, Noel Purcell. Then a quick dart into the second-hand bookshop, and hurriedly by The Green Tureen, the restaurant where there'd been a murder in the basement – Dublin wit had made a meal of that – to the post office. Back then by Cuffe, Wexford and Montague Streets, with a stop for a chat with the white-garbed grocer in the Wexford Street H. Williams who never failed to remind me that I could do a lot worse these evenings than tune in to Tellidew Simrew. I, still loyal to Peg in my way, politely doubted if the Welsh *bostúns* of Teledu Cymru were any better than the local ditto's in Telefís Éireann with its Friday evening prime-time offerings of Boris Karloff. But, fair dues, no, I'd never seen Criss-Cross-Quiz; so no doubt he had a point. Thus we parted friends, the elderly, old-fashioned grocer and I. He was constantly pacing up and down outside the shop, brilliant in white apron over white coat, guardian of the old ways, weather-eye out for encroaching supermarkets – Comiskey's a couple of hundred yards away in Camden Street, had turned itself into a superette, run by a young girl . . . 'There y'are,' he'd say, 'the thin end of the wedge'; mordantly straight-faced.

Quite often I had to go farther afield – sometimes even not on any old messages but on official business, to Radionics in Hatch Street or better yet to Brownlee's, Molesworth Street. It was good to have a walk, to breathe at leisure and at length familiar smells. But I wasn't happy with my destinations. Everybody else but me knew what they were doing there; I just handed over the slip of paper with the order written on it, then the money. There was no use pretending to be a messenger-boy in these stores – they were invariably packed with the real thing. And the camaraderie of the electronic cognoscenti also had me at a loss. I often left the receipt behind ('can't even do a simple message . . . . Honestly, I don't know what you're thinking of at all.').

The best of these official outings was the most regular, over to the Munster and Leinster Bank in Baggot Street every Friday. I was entrusted with the wages cheque, also the weekly 'lodgment', another of those darling words like 'salary' and 'trainee'; I loved the way it seemed to go with the bank's sanctimonious air. Four quid lost its nettling impoverishment for a while. But the best part was the walk across the Green. During those walks it was always sunny (the deaf schools I remembered as being invariably dark, with the baby-pink glow of fluorescent tubes causing a false, excessive warmth to suffuse the dank air). There were always girls in short sleeves lying stretched out alone, or in couples sitting, talking, on the grass, absently plucking at it: he loves me, he loves me not . . . I even felt close to the ducks and the flowers. Sometimes I smiled at a girl if I caught her eye, and it didn't seem to matter too much if she turned her head with a huffy flounce – the familiar, who d'you think you are? But, see, it's not all that important at the moment who . . . aw, come on. The only girls to come on, however, I didn't know how to handle, young-wans from York Street or the flats on Redmond Hill, Lowry-thin, features bleached and drawn, marmalade hair in turquoise curlers, shouting. 'Ay, mis-star, Maggie here sez . . . . . ' Then screeching. I tried to smile. I knew it was fun, but I was afraid it wasn't friendly.

And always when I was out, there was the city, motoring along with its muted roar and constant movement. It was closer, now that I was on foot. A bike would have been ideal, of course. I envied the real messenger-boys' way with the traffic, wearing in and out of jams on those special bikes of theirs with the short frames and big caged-in basket out in front. But walking did me fine. I felt I'd grown a little, since I no longer wanted to be looking down the whole time from the top deck. And this way I could drop into Combridge's on the way to Brownlee's, or cross the street to the Eblana to see if there were any new Penguins in while I was supposed to have nothing else in mind besides getting Franz the vile shag and green Rizlas from the civil gent in Kapp and Peterson's (another Friday ritual). Yes, the city was there all the time. I hadn't been giving it very much attention. Now I realized that it served my new perception of myself to perfection. What 239 better confirmation need I have that I was a couple of people than to do one thing while I was supposed to be doing something different. Of course! – as I always had believed it could, Dublin would make me up as I went along.

3

Physics was fine. I had the teaching of Bimbo and Bulganin from boarding-school to stand me, unexpectedly, in good stead. I knew how to cheat so that weight in air equalled weight of water displaced: that way the teacher doing the rounds would leave our group alone. But the calculus crucified me and applied maths turned me into a parallelogram of inertias.

The original idea in sending me to Kevin Street was to make me an AMIEE, an Associate Member of the Institute of Electrical Engineers. Franz might have known that he was misguided in this ambition for me by the difficulty he had in articulating such a mouthful. But his conception of me, and of himself, required that if I was not to have a university degree at least I would have as many letters after my name as possible. Like all conceptions (as I was finding out), this one too was blind to its own capacity for error. I still don't know exactly how someone qualified in industrial electrical engineering was supposed to have contributed to International Electronics. Franz, father of three daughters, didn't have very much experience of the educational system, particularly on the technical side. Perhaps, after all, he did go for the sound of the thing, the poet! As anyone could tell, an Institute sounded a lot more impressive than anything with the populist denomination City and Guilds.

Since the courses, the examining bodies and the qualification awarding institutions all seemed to be English – and reflected the way the energies of working people were boxed into fitters, technicians, improvers, trainee, in order that they

might earn union rates and fit in with the employers' designs (a place for everyone and everyone in his place, just like the army, just like the priesthood) – that faith in system which snobbery expresses was probably an inevitable influence on Franz's choice. I had never heard the like, of course, and was at first very vaguely, and later totally, unnerved by the way the exam system, the job system and the work system reproduced themselves so incestuously in each other, and how again, everything was premissed on the slowing down of processes and possibilities into minutiae. Here I was, a career fan of the big picture, trying to learn calculus (relative of Gregory, be thou my guide!). How the foolish commonplaces of mathematical problems – the men in fields, their holes, their productivity – became suddenly endearing. At least they spoke in English, not the foreign symbology of integration and differentiation. This was the very stuff I was wisely kept from attempting for the Leaving – and a couple of months later I taking it on to get a GCE O-level, the *rite de passage* into the kingdom of AVO. It didn't take me long to learn that I was not going to be numbered among the technocratic cherubim and seraphim, and that, even if I was the last of the breed (for look how modern things were becoming), in the phrase of Brother Murphy long ago, 'Ireland is rearing them yet.' 'Rearing what, sir?' 'Eejits – you eejit!'

Twice a week we sat from seven to nine in a lecture hall with a steep rake and long, well-worn desks, while a young man in a suit named Raymond shouted at us earnestly, nonstop, in a voice of pure Kildysart or, perhaps, Belmullet. There were arias on rates of change and ratios, vectors and forces. It was nice, I suppose, to be at school where nobody was going to beat you, but this was just about the only improvement. Kevin Street Tech, then, was as gloomy place. Red brick baked black, the front door in the far right, always shaded, corner of the bike-littered courtyard. During the day, the atmosphere was no doubt unexceptional, but in the evenings the air seemed grey and dusty, as though suffused by a steady trickle of infinitesimal particles from worn stairs and gouged benches. The house of the future had a strangely entropic air. And we were all tired, trudging in after long days and hasty teas: I felt that too. I knew my classmates were the same as me – we weren't going to school; we were being sent. Large areas of choice were already being forgone: they were forsaking the 241 present in order that the future not forsake them. They came in ties, with Conway Stewarts primed. They were older. They knew the difference this chance would make, that CIE and Pye (Ireland) had not elected them lightly to see the future through. They were on the road from Bluebell. And of course there was nothing for it but constant attendance. Absences were reported to the fee-paying employer, which in my case, at least, would lead to a real fight. Since nothing, to my mind, was worse than open criticism, I attended as regularly as clockwork.

The classes were wakes for messenger-boys, as I could see from the memorials carved into the desks: the names, the execrations against boredom and dislocation. Pats, Shels, remembered fondly from the days when all of life consisted of agonizing over a flighty ball. MUNICH, an acronym remembering the glorious dead – Manchester United Never Intended Coming Home. I declined to make my mark: I had no hankering to be remembered here, or to expend the psychic energy necessary to carving a name with pride (and resentment). Instead, after Raymond's first few numbers had made it all too clear that the best I could do was kill time, I looked around for ways of kindly putting it out of its misery.

A solution was readily to hand: the public library just next door. An excellent place it was – first cousin to the Tech in architecture and appointments but with a wonderful stock. And it was like old times in Lismore, being in love with a library again (attempts to have a library in boarding-school proved abortive: library books ran implicitly against the ethos of such places, since they require quiet time in private to be savoured to the full). So before class on Monday I'd borrow my weekly intellectual nourishment. Raymond Chandler and Peter Cheyney – those asphalt Flauberts – were what my taste ran to at the time, and I found that there was little problem swallowing whole one of their productions every two classes.

One night, however, suffering perhaps from a temporary case of calloused palate, or – more likely – experimenting with the stacks' sightlines to get a more lingering, less obtrusive ogle at my favourite check-out clerk, I found myself holding a book with a shrieking yellow cover. I know such books: Gollancz published some cracking thrillers. But this was different. This was *The Outsider*, by Colin Wilson. I opened it up. It

242

spoke eloquently of nausea, of the country of the blind. Visio-
nary Russians leapt to the eye; and there were the French
again, as unashamed as ever. *Aujourd'hui, maman est morte. Ou
peut-être hier, je ne sais pas:* this Meursault sounded like one of
the original gas men, all right. I hadn't come across a book that
seemed this important since *I Believed*, by Douglas Hyde: we
all read that during the retreat, the year before the Leaving. I
was so excited by *The Outsider* that I didn't read it in class, but
saved it up for bed. Reading Mr Wilson was like being back at
those illegal, midnight Hallowe'en parties at school, when we
sat around the locker-room telling filthy jokes and smoking,
the height of being outrageous. The lads in the book were
much the same, really. Life was their dirty joke (how true!).
And, just like us, Raskolnikov and company were desperate
thinkers, passionately indifferent to respectability, were
essentially ineducable: the psychic Unemployed. The fallen,
or rather, the falling, were great company, especially with the
blustery, ringmasterish way Wilson pushed them around, like
the Billy Cotton Band Show, in a way. All of which lounging
with intellectual riff-raff and messenger-boys did me no good
at all when GCE time came round at year's end; my secret life
of reading exposed me then, caused the trouble I'd naively
thought could be avoided.

We took the GCEs in a school on the Sandford Road,
presumably because exams had to be completed before dark
and there wasn't room to accommodate us at our normal
venue. I performed disastrously. The lowest grade was H, I
think; and I bagged an H-trick. And soon enough the firm saw
what I'd done. It was a case of from electric razors to being held
by the short-and-curlies in one brief year. The Flemish
thunder rolled and rolled. I was given an ultimatum: to say
what I intended to do now (my God – a decision!) and how I
meant to go about doing it. So I cried. But tears did not move
Franz of the stone jaw.

Peg, too, spoke quietly and slowly. I pleaded with her that
the material was too hard, and gave graphic examples of what
I meant, plus a melodramatic account of my mathematical
history ('Barney gave me nought in geometry – honest!'). But
this was received as though it was a betrayal of family honour
– no O'Brien was that stupid. In desperation, I proposed that
Eamon, a fellow-guest of Mrs Luby who was doing a degree in   243

electrical engineering (properly, as I thought) at UCD, had mentioned off-handedly. In his opinion, I'd be better off doing the City and Guilds Radio and TV Servicing course. This proposal made Franz's jaw, if not drop, move. He smiled grimly; aha, he'd thought so, when it came to it, I saw that I had no alternative but to take the future seriously and give it thought – unless I wanted to be walking the streets, that is (though, confusingly, I remembered that I liked walking the streets). 'Very well,' he agreed, with menacing forbearance; 'but remember, this is your last shonse.'

It was not his tone that made me uncomfortable but the realization that he seemed to know me. He had been thinking about me too. Perhaps we differed about the impetus and terminology of his thought. But basically he had me dead to rights. I was afraid to go. I needed International Electronics. I seemed not to be the type who'd murder to be free, convenient though the hammer was, inviting though his speckled crown might be.

So, a year later, I was back where I started. But it was nice to start all over again. There was still hope, anyhow. Maybe this time I'd get it right. I thought I knew what 'it' was. It was out there somewhere; I'd know it when I happened onto it. The dream adjusts, but not the dreaming.

Mrs Luby's helped. I had a whole summer to settle in there by myself: Eamon had to go to England to earn his keep for the year. But I felt not at all lonesome. I was well-fed. I could stroll over to Peg's whenever I wanted to watch television, could even stay up late with her to watch *That Was The Week That Was*, which, like Profumo (the two seemed to blur), I couldn't quite fathom the ins and outs of: but everyone else was laughing and saying how marvellous, so I did too. The Stella was nearby, and other cinemas only up the road a bit – the Kenilworth, the Classic, Terenure . . . . Mrs Luby had a little padlock on the 'phone, but I was hardly likely to be telephoning anybody. Apart from the regularity with which sardines on toast were served, I had no complaints. It was a strange time.

And I read. Unconsciously suspicious of sitting so prettily, perhaps, it struck me that the nicest way to spend the summer would be to sit by the Valor in the guests' living-room and 244 gorge myself on books' articulate, redemptive silences.

Reading was the most comprehensive and, it seems, most natural expression I could manage that I was living my own life. Nobody for tennis. The one club I might have joined was the Film Society, but that I thought to be off-limits. Dances were too dear. But there was a library to love: that red-brick pileen on the corner of Leinster Road was my Vatican, my Mecca, a Croke Park of the intellect, a veritable Dublin. There was also one of the Banba Books chain nearby on the opposite side, specializing in kids' novelties and second-hand paperbacks; among the latter it was possible to find some of the banned (was the name of the place a complicated pun!) – I found *Catch-22* there; also just about the only 'Irish' book besides *Borstal Boy* I read at that time, *The Ginger Man*. I didn't care for the Irish writing that Mr Dangerfield represented, it was too loose and free; besides, I was developing a nasty little prejudice against students. As for Behan – much as I enjoyed *Borstal Boy*, the man himself struck me as Sebastian in the flesh. Clean writing for the mind alone was what I desired, not laughs for the belly.

I might have found what I was looking for in other Irish writers of the day, some of whose names I'd heard. But nobody ever talked about them. I hardly ever found their books in paperback, more evidence that they weren't famous or properly modern, and so I didn't bother looking for them in the library. Camus also – later such a pebble on a dry tongue – proved elusive. Okay: Merusault shot the fella on the beach, fair enough; but then I thought there was going to be blood and murder altogether – shoot-out at the Oran corral. But no. It was too unlike a movie for me to feel at ease with it. Somerset Maugham was much more like it: *The Moon and Sixpence*, *The Razor's Edge* were great – colour applied with a sweeping-brush, problems introduced with all the chilling drama of venomous innoculations: that's the style, thought I. The trouble with Maugham, though, was that all his characters wore suits. So when Woodfall Films (I had Da's habit of noticing names) began being popular and *The Loneliness of the Long Distance Runner* came out, it was a wonderfully pleasant shock now – *this* really is the style, I thought. That lad was a real borstal boy, and ever would be, and he didn't care. I was jealous. Why couldn't I be a sonovabitch too? I concluded that this failure came from not being English.

Eamon came back and we chummed up. We went to the Stella for the worn forties' thrillers they invariably had on Sunday nights. We went for walks whenever he began to overload with bookwork, and he was an Ardnacrusha at the books. I admired him. I feared his steely diligence. His discipline, his fussy phalanx of lapel-pocket biros, his strict budgeting of time and pleasure, his girllessness, his somewhat elderly intensity of purpose made me glad I was not at Earlsfort Terrace after all, particularly now that things were going more agreeably at Kevin Street. It was strange: here was Eamon reading and calculating Irish stuff for all he was worth, and all – as he cynically conceded – in order to land a half-way decent job in Canada or South Africa, whereas I, with little or no effort, learning English stuff, was probably going to stay at home. And all the time he remained a model citizen: he neither smoked nor drank and sent a parcel of soiled clothes home weekly to his mother.

But he didn't live by bread and Mrs Luby's fries alone. Every Saturday lunchtime he went to the Universal, Wicklow Street, for a taste of sophistication. Chinese. His regular lunch partner was a B.Ag. in the making, a quiet type from Elphin called Willy; but a time or two – when Franz took a Saturday off, sometimes Peg let me go at half-twelve instead of quarter to one – I joined them for number twelve (the curried brimstone) or the Egg Too Long (number five). 'It fills you up'; it was only years later I found out that meant it wasn't a Chinese meal. You had to be early to get a table. In general, I think Eamon was relieved when I didn't turn up. He liked to keep his home life distinct from such student activities as he participated in, and didn't want to be sitting next to the only person in the room not wearing a college scarf. I'd lived long enough with Mam to accept that he was entirely justified in his attitude. I, a Tech boy, was naturally on a lower level to him, and I was glad that I now recognized and identified with that level, and was grateful for its reduced seriousness and self-denial.

But I did still feel the pangs of the original dream when Eamon went on about the L & H. Early in my walks down Hatch Street to Radionics, I'd slink crestfallen past UCD. But I'd cured myself, I thought, by telling myself they were all snobs there, all suits and ties, all aspirants to the boss class.

Now I heard they had this literary and historical thing, a kind of higher Hallowe'en party, and before lights out, too, at which perhaps I might meet a Callan Dunya, an Abbeyfeale Razumikhin, with the hope of finding something to yield to, as Roquentin did salvifically to Bessie Smith. 'Very witty fellas', he'd say in a considered manner, from the depths of a maturity unwontedly roused to enthusiasm. 'Brilliant; absolutely brilliant'; and I chafed at their namelessness, facelessness, fantasizing painfully, but only momentarily, about *semblables* and *frères*. 'You'd love it.' But when I said he ought to let me tag along, smuggle me in – didn't I look the part? ('I have longer hair than you!') it was always, 'Ah I can't. They'd catch me.'

Yet, to keep my spirits up, there was Eamon's vivid giggle, his incurious tolerance of Dublin, the willingness to suspend himself for a couple of hours before the Stella's Sunday night at the B-movies. We had the bond, too, of being together the evening Kennedy was shot. Mrs Luby stuck a head full of suds around the living-room door with the first word of it. We walked into town, hung around Earlsfort Terrace for a while (Eamon would neither let me go into college with him or leave me outside, though by now we were limp with want of news), looked at one another vacantly, vacantly regarded the stunned faces on the bus returning to Rathmines, stood at the corner, watched without seeing what we could only consider the idiocy of life as it went on its way. That brumous November sky . . . . Our uncrowned king; the fell gang of renegade Catholic, Cuban, Castroite, Commies . . . . By jasus, I'd castro his fidel for him, quick and lively, so I would. Oh, my dark Jacqueline! That evening we didn't know how or what to think, or for weeks afterwards. Prayer was urged. It was the first time it seemed crucial to have a TV set.

By this time, too, however, I had a Tech pal, Mayo Eddie, who worked in the Soil Mechanic's lab at Trinity, and who was paired with me to weigh again in water and once more in air so that I could tell my fluent scientific lies. Our rendezvous was the Theatre de Luxe, Camden Street, which had a nice wide screen, small crowds and severe-looking girls with beehive hairdos that went throughout the auditorium spraying while the ads were on. The wide screen meant all the big pictures came there – *The Longest Day*, *The Guns of Navarone*; 247

the bigger the bang the brighter the billing. Dazed by the spectacle, we would ride the 12 home, hardly talking, feeling that the challenge to have a night out had been met with honour and that such pictures were as good as six pints or a French kiss at inducing the sensory deprivation without which a night out could be considered out.

One evening, Eddie surprised me by asking did I ever go to Croke Park? I did indeed, though more for old times' sake, or to see Mick O'Connell, than because I still thought myself a Gael. It wasn't for himself Eddie wanted to go, however, but for this 'wan' at work, a Miss Kelly of Clontarf, who was always onto him about going: apparently nobody at home would be seen dead in the place - 'she's a Protestant,' said Eddie. But off we went anyway, so eager – though we didn't dare admit it – that we were in time for the minor game. Galway and some other crowd played in the big match, Galway with some of their great team of Purcell and Stockwell and Jack Mangan still going strong. What I remember above all, though, was that on the way out, squeezing through the narrow gateways behind Hill 16. I ventured to put a hand around the waist of Miss Clontarf Kelly, protective, like. She squirmed around and gave me a smile that produced instant liquefaction of the knees. All day long she'd been good cousinly gas. She paid her way, but from embarrassment we insisted on buying her an orange. She roared at the game when we roared. I don't recall if she sang the national anthem – being so at ease with her by then, I didn't notice, but I wouldn't put it past her. And she was just the right height, a head shorter than me. I remember plumpness and a clear complexion. Was she wearing a floppy hat? Did she have curls? I remember softness of softness. A girl of a sunny day . . . .

I never saw her again. This was not the plan at the time, though: at the time I was full of plans for this latest version of a lovely time forever. Confidently I squired herself and Eddie through the streets of houses that might have been transplanted direct from Church Lane, Lismore, and out at Newcomen Bridge, a way Da used to take me in years gone by. There Miss Kelly was put on a bus for home – oh, an ardent swain was I! But I thought it more important to act the gentleman. It'd be fatal if she mistook me for a pushy culchie

– hence guidance by the waist, not the peremptory *hoult* of the hardened cattleman. Besides, didn't we have the rest of our lives?

I talked about her all the way back to tea, undeterred by Eddie's grunts and his, 'Well, it was a great game, anyhow.' He became more lively when I asked him for her work number: 'Oh cripes, don't ring her at all; they're fierce down on personal calls.' So I wrote down my number and told him to give it to her. 'Be sure, now.' 'Oh I will, yeah,' Eddie said, phlegmatically. But, of course, 'I forgot.' Then the next week she had the 'flu. 'Aw jay,' I said; and I couldn't afford grapes (never thinking I hadn't a clue what her address was). The following week she was off as well: 'I think I heard them saying her grandmother is after dying,' said Eddie, poker-faced. And muggins me swallowed this one too. *Shit*, I thought; she'll be in mourning now . . . . But maybe Protestants didn't mourn: hooray! . . .

It was another couple of weeks, and I was strongly thinking of starting a vigil in Lincoln Place in order to get another sight of her, when Eddie let me in on the open secret that I never in a million years would have suspected. 'Well, fuck you!' I said. How dare he not take my dreams to heart! 'You lousy fucker.' Strange as it seems now, telling Eddie exactly what I thought of him, and then stalking off, felt at the time at least as important as Miss Clontarf bliss.

It was in the spring after Franz's operation and Brendan Behan's funeral. April, a fine day: that's how I remember the bolt from the blue.

All had been right with the world. Kevin Street was turning out to be a summer stroll. We had a nice teacher for the electricity classes, Mr Sloan, who worked at Pye, I think, and who had a nice, soft Northern accent. Physics was the same physics as ever, and I heard by way of Peg, who had heard from the teacher's mother, a client, that I was doing fine. I'd even worked out a way to fake parallax. My confidence was growing (I was beginning to see how I had never allowed it space and time enough in which to make its necessary adjustments). I won't pretend that Mr Sloan jumped out of his suit when I, alone of all the class, was able to explain how transistors worked on the basis of theory already acquired, but he did 249 remark, in quiet surprise, 'vair' guid'; oh, and didn't I beam!

Work, too, had been less burdensome of late. That was because Franz had been taken bad and had spent at least a fortnight in hospital (God's door act once more creating revolutionary justice). We mice had thrived indeed, or at least one had. And Franz's return did not immediately overshadow my good mood. He'd had a blood transfusion, and told everyone who crossed his path that he was an Irishman; oh yes, he had Irish blood in him. Yet not even the fiftieth repetition of which I normally would have considered a monstrous lie and slander – and a lousy joke, which was worse – inclined me to reach for the hammer. I was relaxed. That was the trouble.

We were having the ten o'clock scone and cuppa. Talk was desultory. I suppose Peg and Franz may have been going over what news the newspapers had while he was sick, not that Franz showed much interest in the play of man and events; they probably were doing nothing more (nothing less) than renewing the sound of their voices for each other – a pre-electronic hearing test – with news as pretext. However it was, the name of Brendan Behan came up, the size of the funeral, the amount of his will. Out of nowhere I heard Franz say: 'Ja, he was a disgrace to his country'. And out of a different nowhere I heard myself instantaneously inquire, half-shouting: 'What about you?'

Twenty years later, I still hardly know what I meant, except that I meant it as Peg and Franz immediately understood it, a xenophobic slur, a chunk from the hand that fed me. I suppose I meant that, blood transfusions notwithstanding, I thought he had no right to criticize Behan – Franz, a man who probably didn't even know where Sundrive Road was. Yet it also seems – and this is what puzzles me – that I considered Franz a disgrace to his country. Why should I think that? What exactly did I mean by it? Did I imagine him a blackmarketeer, or consci? Did I picture him sipping his chicory roast or acorn extract as he drank in the latest *Het Vlammsche Land*? Did I see him on the platform at Malines? – hardly. Or with the Rexists? Or hearing mass with that devout Catholic, Gueleiter Degrelle?

I don't know. I only knew that now the word was out. This time it was pride I'd singed, not bakelite. Silence descended.

We walked around for days as though our heads were stuck in buckets. And finally, too, it seemed, Peg gave up. She didn't approach me with suggestions about making up. She made no effort to bring together sulky victim and stunned aggressor. I caught her eye a time or two but all I saw in it was an annoyed look, saying, 'Bloody fool!' I'd blown all the circuits. The clone, through no will of his own, had refused to be born. After a couple of days, Franz said, not looking at me, 'I want some notice, you know'. So he wants me to be the one to leave, I thought: well, that was tolerant of him . . . Peg must have . . . . 'Okay,' I said, 'I'm giving you a fortnight's notice'. Steam flew from Franz's ears, and the windows rattled. 'And I give you wahn whik!' he screamed.

4

The big job of the day came first thing – leaving Mrs Luby as though everything was the same as ever. I whistled, I hummed; out I bustled, business-like. Deception seemed the better part of valour because I imagined that somebody of my landlady's age would consider sacking a shameful eventuality; I had already heard a woman of roughly her age – Mam – appraise it as moral delinquency of a particularly culpable nature on the part of the sackee. Also, there was the question of rent. I had some holiday money – the final pay-off was punctilious – so was set for a couple of weeks. But from Eamon's absence the previous summer, not to mention long conversations over motherly cups of tea about Vincent and Brendan and Finbar and other predecessors – their pecadilloes, their careers, the speed with which they had discharged themselves from her tightly-run ship – I was fully aware of the stock Mrs Luby put on continuity of tenure. And since she seemed pleased with me – or at least she had made a point of telling me I was clean – I knew she expected a lot of me; two or three years at least, if not more – I was young, not a student, not a drinker, not a phoner, not a bit of trouble: oh, I was a 251 landlady's delight (not alive).

In all other respects, however, my high spirits in the early morning were not fake. 'The bullet', 'the boot', which I had received seemed merely to have elevated me into a pleasant and lofty trajectory, all the more pleasant since there was no landfall immediately in sight. My cards were a passport to an undiscovered, yet surely very pleasant country. So I thought, sauntering down to Belgrave Square for a 12 to town – very handy, that 12 (I was upstairs; the day's first Gold Leaf was doing a grand, insidious job of mollifying the aftertaste of black pudding and red tea): it brought me through the good parts of the life I'd lately left – past the Bleeding Horse, and Cavey's, past MacDonald's, the newsagent near the corner of Pleasant Street – without letting me see the sight of my confinement, as I very promptly thought it. I even thought of older days, except that I was now taking myself by the hand to do the town. I was even one of the Unemployed, and (I understood them now, I thought) I felt no fear at all. I could lie down in the middle of O'Connell Bridge, if I really wanted to: who was to stop me?

For perhaps my first three days of furlough, I wallowed. I walked the quays. How pleasant to linger by the book-troughs outside Webb's and its cousin on Bachelor's Walk, opposite, The Dublin Bookshop. How charming to wander dusty back-streets at dusty hours, half-two on a Wednesday afternoon; a quarter to eleven on Tuesdays. I tended to avoid thoroughfares. I'd seen them before. (I wasn't able to afford them.) The city became a place of short-cuts and laneways, the sites of jute warehouses and idle loading docks, places suspended in the long moment between the dying echo of the last harness-clink and hoof-clop and the incipient rumble of the juggernaut truck. Empty bays, mild mote-filled air . . . .

Poor places. I began to see this, for the first time. Because I was on foot I saw a Dublin new to me. The oul-lads sitting in the little park near Saint Patrick's and Iveagh House struck me as less lucky, now that I could see their caved-in faces and their addled body language, instead of passing them on the Sundrive bus and envying them for being Dubliners. The urchins scampering in the black hallways of Sean MacDermott Street and Summerhill were not superior versions of the shoeless gamins, my playmates in Church Lane. Instead, I found, they were foreign and frightening in their raucous intensity. I saw them, in their quickness and knowledge of the streets, as capable of committing crime, just as I'd heard grown-ups continually allege of them. I realized they lived where there were crimes to commit. They weren't picturesque at all, suddenly. I seemed to see their futurelessness: I began to be afraid. I'd heard that Sean MacDermott Street was where whores lived. I dreamt I was approached by one, a hefty piece, tight-fitting dress of shocking pink, strange feathery accessories. A ludicrous conversation ensued, me pleading poverty, she smirkingly identifying herself as the charity that begins at home. Uncannily bright, daylit streets, and a twisting, turning, rapid forced march through them. Then I vertiginously plummet down a hallway black as sin . . . I thought I had discovered why city people walk quickly, and with a style of quickness. I began to walk quickly, but that only revealed to me the sooner that I didn't know where I was going, that I had nowhere to go.

And on the other side of town, in the purlieu of the Castle, I also started seeing things I'd never seen before. This was Dublin's old raddled body, stripped of the dressed-stone façades, grey, withering places belying their colourful names – Winetavern Street; The Liberties. Streets not broad, but narrow. Images from schoolbooks: Silken Thomas's head on a spike, Lord Edward weltering in his blood, Emmet swinging while their ladyships looked on. Gore and failure; crumbling laneways and sunless precincts. It would be better not to have to look at this, the meeting of a non-future with a past that clanked its chains around places that seemed made of frozen dust. It would be better had I bitten my tongue and stayed in Harcourt Street, which at least I knew. I walked down Francis Street and foresaw a history of poverty for myself. In Meath Street I thought I'd surely go to the dogs. Rain was a problem: my cardboard shoes of elegant cut began to leak. I was afraid to face Mrs Luby with a drowned-rat look. I wondered how the sandwich-board men got their interesting, airy positions; what patronage provided the parking attendants with their appointments, which I knew had to be official since they wore caps. Sheltering under a Dame Street awning, I gazed with envy at the man propping (being propped by) a bespectacled sign pointing towards the opticians in Fownes Street. 253

I suppose I should have prayed. When I was small, I'd once asked Chrissy what would I be, prompted perhaps by Doris Day's 'Que sera, sera', though obviously expecting a more definitive response than the frankly pagan doctrine espoused in that chartbuster's chorus. Wise Chrissy said to pray: Holy God would tell me. I pressed her, but she was firm. Yes, He'd told Uncle Frankie to be an engineer and Aunt Kathleen to be a scientist. 'And what did He tell you to do?' I persisted. 'He told me I'd be at home looking after me mother,' Chrissy said. That settled it. But she didn't stay, she went away. She and Da – my two great loves – had gone and made out lives for themselves, and didn't seem to give a damn if that was sin or not.

Yet, it did not occur to me that with those two life-supports cut off I now was left with God. For one thing, I found His presence much less persuasive in the city. Now that I was paying rent, the Church's spiritual landlordism lost its appeal. Twelve mass in the green-domed hanger of Rathmines parish church was largely a yawn. There was no hurling club news. The charity of our prayers was requested for the repose of the souls of total strangers. There was the customary fashion show, of course: but what it gained in novelty and sophistication over its counterpart at second mass in Lismore was offset by the girls remaining unknown and placeless – and anyhow, the twelve was always packed, so I never could get a proper eyeful. Confession was like going to the post office. 'Bless me Father for I have two letters, three postcards and a registered package.' The items were franked, the toll exacted: 'Okay, two decades of the Joyful Mysteries – thank you – Next!' But then, I wasn't alive enough to make confession interesting.

I began to question what else I had going for me, religiously speaking. Not a whole lot, it seemed. I never had much time for the various prostrations and time-surrendering supplications – novenas, First Fridays, sodalities, confraternities – identification with which secured one an address on the *via dolorosa* which, by all accounts, life was. I did not cultivate devotion to recommended patrons and intermediaries. If I was interested in saints at all it was in the marginal lads: St Swithin the rainmaker, St Joseph of Cupertino (a sovereign at exam time), or St Vitus the twitcher. The best thing I'd discovered in old Dublin was a church to St Audoen, whom I identified immediately as the patron of cinema chains.

It began to dawn on me that my religion was my culture, not a relationship with a deity. And when I found that culture's institution, the Church, seemed banal and unilluminating – as grey and friable and redolent of denial as the walls of ancient history – then I didn't know exactly what was left. I didn't think I could meet man-to-man with God; that was what Protestants thought themselves good enough to do. And I knew I wasn't one of them. So what was I? And where was I, who sidled past St Michan's on the other side: And what to do, now that prayer, the only form of serious thinking I'd ever come across, no longer seemed the very thing?

It must have been raining, and I must have been on my way to Hanna's, Nassau Street. Otherwise I don't know what would have brought me to Creation Arcade, Brown Thomas's and such snootiness. Even the accident of weather, however, does not explain why I went into that place of silks and unguents, much less why, once there, I went to see if the Little Theatre was still in it. I remembered from the old days that Da sometimes would march us through a show of paintings or photos in the Little Theatre, his ten-minute reward for dawdling through the store people, aisles spiced with fabrics in jade and sandalwood which Mam fondled absently, tweed suits which she inspected with an ex-seamstress's hawkish eye, dreaming perhaps of what a Sybil Connolly was lost in her. (Mam dreaming. Mam on holiday: Mam young, years condense, years expand . . . .)

Whether or not the old days were guiding me, here I was, and sure enough some low-voiced, well-heeled types were in the theatre doorway. An easel with a sign announced a show of some kind – I hardly took it in before I entered, thinking that least it would let my poor shoes relax. There were some photos on the wall, but much more unexpectedly on tables underneath them were machines. I didn't know what kind they were but they looked as if they were on speaking tems with electricity because they had knobs and dials and were dressed in the shiny plastic of new technology. I didn't recognize any of their names – Lumière, Kindermann – but at least they were bigger than hearing aids, and therefore – for all their exhibition-abject, Sunday-suited shyness – struck me as a vaguely positive step in some direction or other.

A man approached. He looked young – his brown eyes glistened; his somewhat swarthy face was unlined. He asked if he could help me. His tone was outgoing, interested, nothing like the icy discriminating way that shop-help had been lately asking me the same thing. I invited him to explain the yokes. And behold, they were electric! One was as photo-copier, the other a dry mounter – whatever that was, but it didn't matter: at the sight of something new the world enlarged for me again. The streets grew broad, the Bovril sign lit up. So when the man's spiel was done, I heard myself say, as bold as brass (emboldened both by novelty and my brasslessness), 'Well, I suppose you'll be looking for a good man to service these?' The man cocked his head at me, whether in suppressed laughter or genuine appraisal I wasn't able to make out. But then he said, 'I might, if I sell any'; and I knew he was a good sort; it wasn't often I came across such candour – even youngish men like him were often apparently unable to afford it. Again made bold, I matched his directness with my own: 'Well, I'm your man!' said I.

This time he might well have smiled, but I was too busy telling him about my excellent qualifications, my years of experience, my Kevin-Street sojourn (did he know I got first in the class in the Christmas test?); no doubt about it, he'd be doing himself a favour by letting someone like me into the business. 'Well, actually,' he said, 'the main business is photo-finishing'. But this was great as well, as I gave him to understand by mentioning that my father was a member of the Irish Film Society. 'Well, we'll see,' the man said, and gave me his hand. 'My name is Ken. I'll be in touch. And when I wrote my address down for him: 'That's very near us; we're in Upper Rathmines Road'. There, see! That was definitely a sign; somebody up there likes me after all; God looks after his lodgers.

I don't know what I did then. If it had been raining I'd have sung in it, and swung from the lamp-posts too; if dry, my every follicle and nerve-end must just have gone *doo-dee-doo-doo* to themselves. What an extremely nice man; what a most interesting and enjoyable conversation! And those machines were clearly the cat's pajamas, obviously the last word – in what, though? Ken had explained, but of course I wasn't able to remember. One thing copied photos, didn't it, and wasn't the other a kind of oven in which the mounting of your photos could be finished dryly? It looked like a little oven. Or possibly a TV set. Well, anyway; sure I'd pick it up as I went along. What mattered at the moment was that a man had spoken to me, a stranger.

At this remove, of course, I see that I must have struck Ken less as Beau Soudreur, technician *extraordinaire*, than as an ill-kempt youngster, who still hadn't managed gash-free shaving, whose Siemens razor had gone the way of all his machines from the Hornby clockwork train onwards (not to mention all the machines unlucky enough to make his acquaintance); someone for whom interviews took place on the radio – not in real life; someone to whom the term 'application form' had no meaning; a fooleen who believed that 'I'll be in touch' could only be meant insincerely in a movie. And yet he'd spoken.

And of course I knew I'd have a letter from him. Probably before the year was out I'd have a little van, like the green-and-white RenTel vans that some of my ex-classmates from Kevin Street drove; except from now on they would be the jealous ones. Those oven things would sell like hotcakes in Foxrock and Greystones, where, I imagined, there were women with all the time in the world for such figaries. 'Will I hook it up for you, missus? (heh-heh-heh). Where would you like it?' Surely it wasn't too much to ask that one of these fine, isolated ladies with sensibly small families off in school, and little left to do but wait for *Mrs Dale's Diary* to come on, would catch my drift?

In the New Year, then (all out of ovens after the Christmas rush), I'd probably be promoted to camera-work – someone had to make the photos so they could be finished, couldn't they? I remembered Da proudly sporting his Agfa Isolette on summer holiday in Lismore, posing me at the miniature beach called the Bark Yard made by the Owbeg running low. 'F16 at a 20th,' he'd mutter, worrisomely, staring into the delicate rainbow and strange bat's-wing fabric that somehow made the whole thing work. He used to let me do the winding on. So I knew my way around a camera, right enough . . . . Soon I'd be able to show that Da of mine a thing or two. Then he'd be proud. Then he would recognize in me a coming man, and I'd at last know who I was. And this time no mistakes. This time the instantaneity and minutiae of work would be mine to command. This time, I swore, the appropriate chemistry would definitely, once and for all, coax forth an agreeable image.

Still, when the letter came, I had to read it a couple of times before properly taking it in. All it said was that Ken had decided to take me on, would I start on so-and-so date, but to me my first business letter, the first envelope that mistered me in type, had more poetry in it than even 'The Destruction of Sennacherib' (a favourite since first I'd looked into it in second-year, because the Assyrians had cohorts who 'were gleaming in purple and gold', the Wexford colours). I had, it seemed, done something all by myself. And I was going to get six quid a week for it, too. Damn decent of Ken, that. It didn't surprise me one bit to learn a little later that he was a Protestant. I'd always heard at home what decent types they were when it came to money matters. And when, that June Monday, I turned up at Findlater's in Rathmines – we worked in rooms above the shop – and climbed the stairs and caught the tang of onions and tomatoes and bananas and thought of Dowd's, the fruit distributors in Lismore, Protestants too, but true-blue Fianna Fáils, givers of steady work to the town, providers of lifts to Dublin in their trucks or to friends of Tony, my contemporary, to the seaside at Clonea or Stradbally in their Nash Rambler with the horn that was a rim inside the steering-wheel, I knew then that happy days were here again and that once more I could be comfortably at home with strangers.

There was Anne, Frances, Margaret, June and Chris, all girls except Anne, who was a woman: she swore at things and people when they didn't work and smoked Churchman No. 1, which even then were not sold everywhere, a strong, fat smoke, mannishly untipped. For any woman to light up one of those – and Anne's Ronson was well cared for; it had hair-trigger ignition – was a fifteen-minute exhibition of hard neck and brazen cheek. In Lismore she would have been known as a strap, if not a virago, and I was half-afraid of her in case I forgot myself when she had cause to shout at me and landed one of those soubriquets on her. I need not have feared. After watching me closely the first morning when, with that technical aplomb which was mine alone to command and deploy, I caused greenish smoke to ooze sadly and unstoppably out of a Lumière, Anne sighed expresively and thereafter held her peace.

Which was fine, because the other girls were grand gas. I got on with them so easily that I didn't even care that they looked more like people's sisters than they did dames: one or two of them may conceivably have been sufficiently sisterly to have spots, enabling me to see them as no better off than me and myself as no worse off than them, for which relief much thanks. They were all Protestants, as well, and Chris, as though to define the delightful strangeness of it all, was English, the first person I had met who had come from there to Ireland to work.

They all helped relieve the aftershocks of my mornings' disasters when we trooped off for elevenses to that fair-sized room, fronted by plastic fascia and all formica inside, near the Cecil Fine on Rathmines Road. Not that the coffee itself was not a diversion. It was made to a home recipe whose main ingredients seemed to be nutmeg, Horlicks and Scott's Emulsion, all estimable items in their own right (who, of my generation, dare cast a stone at Horlicks, sponsors – on Luxembourg, no less – of Dan Dare, Pilot of the Future), but in combination . . . . As far as I could make out, this blend was deliberately interfered with by scorched milk, American unseemliness which took place inside a latter-day descendant of the iron horse, a sort of aluminium pony, through whose nether orifices the fluid eventually seeped, gasping and frothing. A not-young-man with thinning hair and wizening phizzog placed the cups on the counter for us, wordlessly accepting our shilling pieces in exchange. It beat all. Previously, coffee was something a woman – a waitress or a relative – would provide; it usually went in my mind along with treats and I'd assumed its existence depended on boiling water. Come home, Irel; all is forgiven! Later I regretted that I hadn't paid more attention to the place: it must have been somewhere like it that Tommy Steele was discovered.

Of course I had no idea then that there soon would come a time when I'd find things English coming in handy. England had been a dark cloud east of the Customs House during my ten-day walkabout, admittedly. But those days were gone; from now on, nothing but blue skies and plain sailing. Ken's business mainly was colour processing: I felt the metaphorical 259 possibilities of a career in it – every man his own Bovril sign. Colour was being discovered wholesale – in people, in ads. Colour was a rhetoric of unsameness and of possibility. *A White Sportcoat and a Pink Carnation.* Another novelty with which I could immediately identify. *Cherry Pink and Apple-Blossom White* – cha-cha-cha! I *was* starting over. Breaking for coffee, lunching sensibly on meat and two veg in the crammed parlour above Ferguson's cake-shop, lounging by the sinks in the back room waiting for the photos to finish themself, all I felt was acceptance and relief.

I was a boy. I didn't kiss the girls, so I had a chance to make them laugh. Ken himself contributed to the boyish mood. 'Hell's bells and buckets of blood!' he'd exclaim. 'Jolly hockey sticks.' He had a thousand ways of saying splendid. He lunched with us. He went to the coffee-bar with us, and sometimes stood a round, even rising to a Jacob's Club if anyone wanted one. Knowing I lived near, he'd ask me to stay an extra hour an odd evening and afterwards he'd buy me chop and chips at Dinky Snacks, opposite the start of Leinster Road, and talk about his plans, ask me what I thought: his myriad plans, and how he seemed to effervesce with love for every one of them. I'd never come across a superior as open and as lively, had never seen work considered a pleasure not a burden, had never thought to find outside of books and banners equality and fraternity. Here, I thought, was someone to be like at last, someone obviously at liberty to believe in his own energy, for whom the world as he found it was right enough. My own version of that liberty – that's what I need.

Work, alas, did not provide it. Improvement in pay, atmosphere and conditions did not mean that I was less good-for-nothing now than I had ever been. Once more, machines, as soon as I had responsibility for them, ceased to be instruments of wonder and futurity and became agents of repressive tedious fact. Aesthetic distance disappeared; the essential, impenetrable difference of things rose up to pull me by the nose and boot me on the behind. It was as though my conscience wouldn't let me get things right, as if to snick the shutter freely or remove the lens cap, not to mention the whole presumptuous process of converting thing to image (the image becoming, as a result, a thing in itself as well as a substitute for the real thing, which in turn seemed to possess a

merely inept, potentially obsolescent reality) – all this instinc-
tively seemed to me to imply identification with the sin of
pride, puny pride, Adam's pathetic self-rehabilitation . . . .
How could I, my own mind inchoate and unratified, presume
to know the mind of an it? Little me: no confidence in the
confidence trick of making do, no confidence to do the trick,
and tricked by lack of confidence . . . .

Ken saw all this, or at least as much of it as he needed to, and
cut his losses. I became the boy. This was fun when we tooled
about in Ken's Rover 90 with walnut and leather inside, like a
parish priest's parlour. Ken was still a photographer; I carried
the Balcar flash through Jury's and the Hammond Lane
Foundry, pitched the special dove-grey umbrellas, checked
the connections like authentic Electrical Man (in case anyone
was watching). But such jaunts were few, and I was surprised
to find how little I got from them, once the novelty of the car
wore off, compared with the more difficult and, as I vaguely
thought, less fashionable Cabra trips with Franz. Most of the
time, the carrying I did was of rolls of film up and down the
Rathmines Road from the Kodak trade counter near Portobello
– a real messenger-boy, balancing long boxes on my shoulder,
labouring by the chapel without saluting it, past the Swastika
Laundry, and the tall, blank-looking houses that seemed to
have no roofs, their doorjambs peppered with white bell-
presses, all belonging to people more interesting than I,
members of the Monaghanmen's Association, past pupils of
St Jarlath's or some other school that had won something,
done something, denoted a prominent diocese or a strange-
sounding place (oh for affiliation with St Nathy's,
Ballaghaderreen . . . .). Here dwelt the sisters of inter-county
hurlers, people with the right connections due to their
exposure at an early age to networking Muintir na Tíre-style.
Hearth-warmer of the year, Horseleap branch, Irish
Countrywomen's Association. Knitter of the month:
crocheteuse of the half-century. My mouth watered at the
thought of their barm brack. I'd hail their brothers heartily as
they came throbbing through the haggard on th'oul Fordson
Major. I thought of them and lost track of my counting in the
darkroom (we developed reels by hand, the creels of them had
to be agitated, lifted and drained in each of the three solutions
every so often: say *a thousand and one*, that's a second . . .). 261

Now that I was the boy I'd fantasized about in Harcourt Street, I once more wanted something else, pined for difference all over again – would nothing ever change me? Was there some devil in me making me impervious to the present? How about scones with raisins in them, plump and moist as a frog's belly, and to follow, Madeira cake the yellow of May sunshine: tea at four on Sunday, served on a lace tablecloth her sister the nun made . . . ?

So there seemed nothing for it but to leave Mrs Luby for life, liberty and the pursuit of happiness in bedsitterland, the other that is the eternal future seducing me again: one more small leaving, what odds could it make among so many? I didn't realize, however, that I had got myself caught up in my first clear-cut autonomous decision, until, quite unexpectedly, I was called upon to defend it. Mrs L. somberly predicted ruin and starvation would instantly attend me in the wake of such a headstrong, foolhardy move: what was I thinking of at all, at all. She offered to do lunch for me. Alternatively, 'Well I can see you won't be said by someone who's only thinking of your own good' ('I know that, ma'am'); 'But I won't stand in your way. I only hope you won't regret it.' That moral sandbag, more substantial and more winning than a year of lunches. In the end, I told her some lie. The lie was in the service of a higher truth, of which I was persuaded: by resembling my culchie compatriots in domestic circumstances, I might meet some of them. I didn't dare say – to Mrs Luby, much less to myself – was that I had no future with Ken, either; all I could do there now was watch for the time when he started letting me down less gently whenever I let him down. I couldn't bear the thought that perhaps the bedsit was the last resort. I just availed myself of the efficient machinery of moving – a trip one lunchtime to *The Evening Press* small ads. So it was official now: I'd enlisted in the columns of need . . . . Closing doors, opening others . . . . But I deflected those kind of thoughts as well.

The wording of the ad gave me a lot of trouble. I wanted mine to be among the first to catch the eye, but could come up with nothing alphabetically pre-eminent, deciding that 'A bastard about cleanliness' would probably not go down too well. I didn't know until I collected the replies to the box number how effective banalities communicate. They came from Drumcondra, though I'd specified south side; a woman from Walkinstown wrote on baby-blue paper offering the room of a first child who would never arrive or who had lately died. And I was 'Dear Sir' to landladies across the city, ones with teeth and without, with whiskers and without, with schooling and barely able to sign their names. The palm of my three-pound weekly payment, however, I awarded to Mrs O'Connell of Leinster Road. In exchange I received the back room in her first floor. She retained the whole ground floor for herself, though I could hang my Bri-Nylon drip-dry shirts on her line if I liked (I'd have to get some): the flash of her porcelain dentures when she said that reminded me of the way the tabs with figures appeared on a cash register.

It was a dark room with a poor aspect. The wallpaper was brown on brown, November leaves at rest on mulch. It seemed welded to the wall, and had a sheen, possibly of the hair-oil of former tenants who'd banged their head against it. The large sink was the colour and consistency of the landlady's teeth; the bed had a hammock middle; a broken electric fire hid in the wardrobe, to save its blushes; the gas cooker looked like it saw action in the cockpit of Stephenson's rocket. 'An awful quiet fella (Leitrim I think he is),' lived on the second floor, Mrs O'Connell confided to me at the top of her voice. Awful invisible, too, he was. Some evenings there'd be a whiff of Brylcreem on the stairs, but that was as close as I came to the kind I was, in theory, seeking. He was off to a dance, probably.

The lady in the room next door to me was almost as invisible but more intriguing. Mrs Gamage was an unlined Englishwoman – still with a shy, girlish simper; still with a wardrobe of flounces, of a little lace at throat and wrists – who had spent her working life on stage all summer in Blackpool, Morecombe, Stockport, Douglas, Rhyl. 'She knew 'em all,' said Mrs O'Connell. 'Go on, tell him.' The ex-soubrette would simply smile and murmur, 'Happy days,' and continue staring out Mrs O's parlour window, waiting for her landlady to resume commentary on all the passing 'tramps'. For Mrs O'Connell spoke for everyone: she knew them all, seed, breed and generation, the cut of their gib and their gait of going. And if her English p.g. had retired her vocal chords, Mrs O. remained a veritable land of song, not to mention, when the kettle piped and the saucepans clashed, a warrior bard. Her 263 performances reached a weekly climacteric on Sunday mornings, when they prevented the house from sleeping past half-nine. Yet, she continually roared, God help her, she was to be pitied; and when that mood befell her, her vulpine face would stiffen and a faraway cast would come to her eye, as though tormented still by hurts from long ago, and she would screech her history out. They owned the finest hotel in either Nenagh or Bunclody, I can't remember. Her own man died in the rats of drink, 'the tramp'. And we were all tramps – to our faces, at that – Mrs Gamage no less than myself, no less than the lipstick-and-stiletto brigade from the square opposite: birds of passage, men of no furniture, concocters of midnight mixed grills, a desperate crowd entirely.

I sat on the bed, wondering . . . . At last the final strands of the umbilicus had been untidily hacked away. Who I was now rested in a stiff wardrobe drawer. A tramp . . . . Yes, well tramps went by themselves: the cap fit to that extent, the bed my own to lie on (cliché preserve me, *et nunc et semper*). But any tramps I'd seen seemed prone to having a bit of gas, and they always seemed to keep going. And, as the upstairs neighbour's scent reminded me, I was free to keep my own hours, to go out at bedtime and return with the milk, to go dancing even! (Do I have the confidence to be a solitary dance-goer? Well, it's about time to find out.) So maybe, after all, this – whatever it is – will be fine, when I get used to it. The best always must be yet: From downstairs, in a voice that sounded like tearing paper, I heard Mrs O. intone one of her reliables, 'Lonely, I wander the scenes of my childhood'. Not that, whatever else, I thought. Not that!

5

If Chris was in the darkroom, I'd be at the sink mixing up a vat of developer. If I was loading the reels for developing, she'd be

finishing off the ektachrome plates outside. So, because we

had the back room and the boring stuff to ourselves we got to talking: soon we were taking walks through Ranelagh where she had a room near the railway bridge, down Appian Way and Waterloo Road and back again along the vegetating, somnolent canal. Sundays on a bench along Mespil Road. Talking, talking. She too was just a boy at Ken's, the same as myself. Chris of Chingford. Walking out. Summer and shade on Wilton Terrace. Perhaps life could be simple after all. A slow waltz. What matter if I had rickets, I was in no hurry. Or so I thought whenever, without meaning to, we fell silent and unembarrassedly lingered on the passing moment, though very rarely did I savour moments for themselves: that seemed a recipe for anonymity, silence's synonym. I couldn't stay quiet: I was a broken lock, foaming and gushing.

At first it was, 'But enough of me, let's talk about you: do *you* think I need a haircut?' Chris – my God! – listened. I told her about Lismore, and school, and Monkstown and Harcourt Street, and as I spoke (as Chris tactfully clucked and t'ched and sighed appropriately) I began to hear again that I had a story of my own, a recitation of experiences which resembled none I'd ever heard, experiences which even seemed worth having since I could interest this tall, placid stranger in them, experiences which seemed almost tolerable because remembering them so clearly gave a kind of voyeuristic pleasure. I felt special again, through this naming of parts of myself. And not just by simply the naming, since I had done this off and on, vaguely and silently, when I thought I was reading *The Razor's Edge* or was effing and blinding Mrs O'Connell's interminable recitatives in the doric ('Flo-ho on laffly ri-vuhr'). It was naming to another that made the difference – better yet, an innocent other, who could neither contradict nor expropriate anything I said, but instead could only (made in England) politely accept it for whatever it was, unjudging. She was given to civil softly-spoken utternaces of, 'Oh, dear'; to giggles similarly well-bred, not the fearsome secret satire of those wans in the Green and their screeching skitting. What a desperate bore I must have been! But I could not conceivably have thought myself one at the time. It wasn't long-suffering Chris I had in mind but the silence that at last I was scattering to the four winds, and the strange sense of reintegration that I felt, hearing myself being listened to.

Yet even when I was at my most stifling, Chris and I still usually managed to tread out a measure or two of common ground. Our ground was books. Did you read this? Have you read so-and-so? Chris taught me how to pronounce the phenomenon, the concept, Sartre, and solemn as a missioner, informed me that *The Age of Reason* was, 'very important'. I replied that I had been living in it since I was seven, but the crack misfired and I felt obliged to cash in my intellectual's widow's mite by way of explanation, a rigmarole about what confession meant and how right could be told from wrong by seven. All news to Chris, who responded mildly and probably there were a lot of different explanations for things; she tried to keep an open mind, herself, personally . . . . Nothing daunted, I went: 'Pubs are about all you can keep open here, and you need a licence for that.' Wise, laughless Chris ignored me and went blithely on: 'Take Kafka, for example . . . . ' Another time she mentioned a certain Beckett, and communication breakdown. 'Silence is *so* important,' she declared. She was a real intellectual! My mouth hung open like a silly cow's. Evenings turned to dusk while we enthused. Dostoyevsky was the greatest. It was as if we had a Film Society for two.

Chris knew all about writers not just because she was a couple of years older than me and the beneficiary of an English education. The latter meant that she probably knew off by heart the servings of Bacon, Lamb and Hazlitt that we tried to digest – 'Of Simulation and Dissimulation'; spare us, O Lord – in the Leaving Cert. reader; on top of which, she'd passed through that pair of needle-eyes, the Eleven Plus and the O-levels, without a scratch to her hump. But that was not all. She was a writer herself, at present learning by what sounded an ideal method, a correspondence course. 'Cripes,' I exclaimed, 'that's powerful altogether,' thinking at once, in awed admiration, now there's a proper double life; look! – she's living her dreams and she's not a bit afraid . . . .

It was writing, 'in fact', said Chris that had brought her to Dublin. Here I had to laugh. Hadn't she heard that writers here were all dead? But Chris turned on me, ringingly affirming that the place was lousy with live ones. 'Where are they?' I demanded. 'Oh, pubs'; Chris waved a vague hand. 'Oh, chancers,' said I, surer in my denial than she in her rather more reasonable belief. 'One should travel, I think,' Chris said mildly, then, as though in self-justification. 'Oh, absolutely!' I agreed, and spoke at length about my supposition that Dublin was as good a place as any to finish a course with the London School of Journalism. 'You make it sound like a slightly superior Grimsby,' said Chris, huffily. She herself saw it as the Petersburg or Prague of the British Isles, historical and grey, with a Haymarket (Moore Street) and desperate, homeless minds. No murders, I objected, wistfully recalling my Franz-and-hammer moments. But what really stuck me in what she'd said was my attitude to Dublin. I was stunned. I had never for a minute suspected that Dublin might not be all I had imagined. Where had such a thought originated?

Whatever its origins, however, it led nowhere, the same as the inspiration about dances suggested by my neighbour, the invisible Leitrim-man. As I told Chris the next time we met, I had something else on my mind: 'Hey, y'know what I'm after thinking? I'm a writer, too!' My image of Chris has her replying at this point, 'Oh, you're a deep one,' politely coy: something like that. She may even have done so; I wasn't listening. I was too busy listing credentials. What I said was gospel truth. Didn't I get an Honour in English in the Leaving? Didn't I writre the monologue which was the *sine qua non* and *pièce de resistance* of the Fifth Year Concert, the school's valediction to the Leaving Cert. class. The deathless opening lines came flooding back to bear me out: 'D-Day is the fifth of June / The days come quickly on / And Fifth Year now salutes the Sixth / Who next year will be gone.' (No wonder when it came to our turn, the following year, Jacko – Father O'Donnell, that is; that Fifth Year had to have it done for them – wrote, 'Lismore gave us Seoirse, composer of songs'!) And thanks to Chris I'd been brought back to this true – or, better, extremely enjoyable – version of myself. What was more, I told her, on my way to Kodak the other day I stepped in for a minute to Baggot's there at the corner of Castlewood Avenue – 'Don't tell Ken, sure you won't?' – and she'd never guess what I saw there: an Irish paperback (a Corkman called Mercier did it) by someone called Francis MacManus who was reported in the bio on the back to like helping young writers! Wouldn't this father-to-be be knocked sideways when he heard from me! 'Oh, you're writing something at the moment?' Chris eagerly enquired. With a fine show of reluctance, I eventually conceded cagily that I was working on a little thing, crafting the lie like a born storyteller, availing at once of the new identity, the new start, Chris had unwittingly midwifed. But what was I saying? I'd not put pen to paper. I tried to weasel out: 'The only trouble is, it'll have to be typed if I'm to send it in.' 'Let me do it,' said Chris. 'Great.' I said, curtly. Now I would have to write something, blast it.

The story, about four pages of typescript, was called 'Evening of the Star' and was a treatise on a louse/pop star whose surname was Glick ('Irish for clever', I explained to Chris, who, inexplicably had thought he was meant to be Jewish), and who was in his off-stage or, as I preferred to say in those days, 'real' life made a highly successful career as a biter of hands that never tired of feeding him. At this remove, it's the theme that leaps first and foremost to the guilty eye: at the time what was exciting was blackening all those pages, with never a thought that I seemed to be creating a character with just two distinguishing features, one that he lived in a glitzy fantasy land in which money was your only Bovril, the other that he possessed an ego and didn't care who knew it, two features as complementary, evidently, as evening and star.

Chris did an impeccable job of typing, and an even more remarkable one of keeping her opinions to herself. I bought an envelope at Baggot's and bore it with exaggerated vigilance, sitting inside on an 18, down the couple of hundred yards to her immaculate room in Ranelagh. It was a Sunday afternoon. The house was quiet. I remember how white the room seemed compared to mine: the acreage of lilies on her wallpaper, their cups voluptuous and wistful; Chris's scent of linen freshly pressed. 'Thanks a lot, Chris.' I placed my vesperal treasure in its pale postal sheath. Then – how I remember! – gorm and gormette stared at each other, suddenly expectant though as tentative as ever, and above all befuddled by the revelation that all our words had somehow managed not to utter what, unspeakably, was uppermost in our minds and which, as we both turned it down, deliberately, abashed, made future trysts perfunctory and intermittent, as we recognized, though from politeness never said, what a couple of painful cases we were.

Despite the eye-opening realization that it was not an evening of the star I needed but of some more corporeal entity, and that the appropriate place to apply for same was the Four Provinces or the Olympic, all energy remained directed at the pen which, as we'd learned in school, being mightier than the sword, was bound to be – here I was espousing a logic of things! – superior to the embarrassing (as we'd learned in school) mutton dagger. Now hopes rode high; I was full of plans again.

Even before Francis MacManus replied, I was already talking to Chris about the London School of Journalism, strangely enthusiastic now about further school, presumably because I was choosing this one. Since Chris had first mentioned the place I had indeed noticed its advertisement in the posh weeklies which on Saturday afternoons I leafed through in Eason's. It definitely seemed to be keeping proper company right enough, and I imagined that when the schoolers in journalism discovered what an exceptional student I was they'd open doors for me to *The Listener, John Bull, Time and Tide*, possibly with my picture cameo-style, like Mary Grant's used to be in *Woman's Own*. I had not only talent, memory reminded me (when memory's in the mood it can do anything, shape and reshape personality with the mercy that indefinitely connotes). I had tradition. Grandfather Royce had been associated with the Enniscorthy *Echo*. Aunt Chris had penned the 'Lismore Notes' for the Dungarvan *Observer*, once, for six weeks or so.

So off I wrote – trenchant and flowery; prolix and puerile – for full particulars, which eventually came back – weren't they wicked teasers not to be in as big a hurry as I expressly divulged to their good selves that their faithful servant (which I remained, needless to say) was! (It was the same years before, dealing with Philatelic services of Goole, Yorks, in order to build the biggest and best stamp album that tips from relations could buy: waiting for orders to be filled was lilke sitting through a Sunday sermon with a full bladder). The English seemed to be like that, not ones to make much of things. Take Chris, now, and my grand story – not a peep, really. 'Very intersting,' when we spoke later; sure couldn't she tell how little nourishment that was? The Chris of the white room and unsisterly melting mood I ruthlessly suppressed, concluding obscurely that non-intellectual camaraderie would be hypocritical, as, I believed, all bonds based on feeling were.

And then, when the letter did come, with all the intriguing paraphernalia, it turned out they wanted not my genius, but money! Oh, a two-faced crowd of tricksters, them English. I thanked my lucky stars that I had kept my wits about me while waiting for that London letter, and had been able to bethink myself, who I was and where I'd come from, head swelled, resembling bladder of yore, all due to my second mister letter, from F. MacManus. It was obvious from the word go that he would write, of course, not because, or not only because, of my stellar performance, but because I still lived in a world where things happened because I expected them to – not as many things as I wanted, perhaps; but still, enough to keep me nervous and unsettled, hence as I thought, alive. Stone grey paper; Radio Éireann at its head. I stupidly hadn't thought of that when I wrote my covering note, but of course, it struck me immediately now: a job *in radio* as a writer. He'd probably start me off small, something like 'This Week's Appeal', then after a month or two I'd be promoted to *The Foley Family* – Tom and Alice the gas newly weds: the Huggetts of Marino, the Burns and Allen of Bulfin Road. They were still on, of course (I had hardly heard a radio since leaving Monkstown), waiting for me to help them have the whole country doubled-up in stitches. This MacManus probably hadn't done his homework, didn't know my radio credentials went way back. But I'd be telling him.

As it happened, Radio Éireann chose not to pursue my services at that time. But the letter was sweetness itself. (Its unlilkelihood makes it sweeter with each passing year.) I could be a writer, I was told, 'a lyrical writer, a satirical writer' (I quote, with ease, from memory), but I would have to write about what I knew, 'even if it's only a swim in the canal'. At which advice I expostulated with Chris. Maybe this fellow had written books and had a cushy job, but he didn't know the first thing about being a writer, because what being a writer means is writing about what you don't know, using the oul' imagination, living the secret, independent life of the mind within. Ideas. Murders. The Moon. The Sixpence. I knew so little I didn't even know what I knew. I didn't know – although I very well might have, given recent experiences – that it was not a matter of mind against the world. It was a lot more confusing and demoralizing than that: mind in the world.

I had the good grace not to communicate any of this to my well-disposed but all too temporary mentor. And I had the ill-grace not to thank him for his startling generosity, deciding that I would wait to write again until I had another slab of prose to impose upon those conscientious shoulders of his. So, we never met, and Chris was needlessly deprived of a chance to meet an Irish writer, about whom she might have written, earned a few bob, paid off a pressing instalment of the debt to her more sophisticated, much less personal, tutelage, gone on a skite (she often wanted me to go to a pub with her – she couldn't go alone – but I wouldn't: 'Pubs are for country mugs – now, what's this you were saying about Camus?') . . . .

One reason why I was so remiss in giving thanks was that Francis MacManus's authenticating words, combined with Chris's devotion to, at all costs, learning journalism, had given me my greatest brainwave yet, an idea which was a dead cert and which I considered proof positive of the not-always-obvious virtues of being out on my own and having to think for myself. I wrote to Uncle Seamus. (Actually, I wrote to Granny Royce first to see if it would be okay to contact him. I knew she would read accurately between the lines and butter him up for me.) My plan was, I considered, both the simplest and most perfect embodiment yet of my genius. Uncle Seamus had fought in 1916, right? *The Irish Press* was Dev's paper, right? *Ergo*, what could be more natural than for my grand-uncle to get me a job in his old pal's business? Across this *pons asinorum* I was prepared to be pulled, head high – not snoot-cockingly high, mind, since I had heard severe denunciations of pull, in my time: just high enough to let the inevitable gaggle of begrudging onlookers know that I, for one, was not ashamed of my past or of the rewards rightly accruing to it. Where would any of us be without the likes of Seamus Doyle? Wherever it was, it occurred to me that it might not be too far away from my present station: I didn't want to go there. (Might it not bear the nebulously, though incontrovertibly, inimical name of England?)

The old school ties (Lincoln Gaol, class of '17) had become perhaps a little moth-eaten and musty over the years for want of an air, but their fabric and pattern came from a stern weave and before long ('they took their bloody time,' I muttered) here I was with another mistered letter, pewtery notepaper 271

this time – one of the more obscure of the forty shades of green
– the company's symbol, with the large scaly thing, presiding
over the title (the eagle of truth or some similar monstrosity
from the comic-book times before Christ). And would I be so
kind as to come for an interview; please telephone Mr Trainor
in the Personnel Department. That was a famous name, too,
Trainor, and wasn't personnel a beautiful, modern word – just
like electronics, really, in its way. This was it, surely to God: let
rainbow now disperse and Bovril lights go dark, my hands
were stretching towards the crock of gold, and words, and all
the mythic tools of life (O Eagle!).

I was so confident that made-man would henceforth be my
middle name that I told Ken what I was doing. 'Good idea,'
Ken said. 'I'm afraid there really isn't much of a future for you
here. In fact, to be honest, I'm thinking of letting you go at
Christmas.' 'Damn good of you, Ken,' I said complacently; I'd
just been given three months' notice; Santa was coming early
this year. 'And for goodness sake,' said Ken, 'spruce yourself
up; wear a tie, get that white shirt washed.' I only laughed,
tickled by his mother-hennishness (I prefer now not to recall
what I must have looked like – just like a messenger-boy, I
suppose); didn't he believe me that it was in the bag? But,
because I would be going back to work after the interview, I
did have the Swastika do the shirt, and I put my school tie on,
hoping that Mr Trainor would recognise it and introduce
school as a conversation piece, so I could give him an earful of
my editorial style – oh, wouldn't I thunder!

Nothing of the sort took place of course. Mr Trainor was a
soft-spoken man: no plaid jacket, no cigar, more inclined to
teach than tyrannize. He listened, without remark, to what I
had to say, prodding me along (quite needlessly, I thought,
needled) with a question or two. What sort of reporting was I
interstd in? I told him eagerly that book-reviewing appealed
– or no, reviewing pictures, make that – my father's in the Film
Society! At the moment I was working for? Oh, and what did
I think of? – a competitor's name came up. 'Rubbish,' said I: it
was, too; sloughed through weak developer, run off on a dirty
glazer, 'that glazer should be Brillo'd every day if you don't
want spotty snaps.' I mouthed Ken's charge to me, his attempt
to justify a very tiresome chore. Later, when I told Ken my
remarks about the competition, his jaw dropped and his eyes

narrowed: 'Oh God, you didn't, did you?' 'But it's true,' I said: and wasn't that what the *Press* on its masthead said it stood for, *The Truth in the News*? 'I know,' Ken said. 'But they'll think you heard it from me.' 'But I didn't!' Ken sighed, 'I know . . . Shit, anyway.'

Another inner meaning – well *fuck* it, anyhow – it was as bad as religion with its accidents and essences. And this time I knew what I meant by 'it', the whole, dumbfounding, autonomous, institutional, impersonal machinery of man and affairs – the world of work, the world of business, the world of buildings, the immense and indifferent world of the not-me. I wasn't going to be even a messenger-boy for the *Press*. Mr Trainor had explained it all to me. The phrase 'Manning agreement' came into it; the word 'union': he mentioned in passing a bright young fellow fresh out of Coláiste Mhuire who had just been taken on. I understood there never had been a job. But hadn't he heard what Francis MacManus said? 'Of course there will be an opening again next year,' said Mr Trainor, meaning to be kind. 'I'm not sure I'll be around,' I said, not sure what I meant. I saw Christmas, then a wall of snow: I wasn't getting through.

So, I couldn't write. Antonioni could sleep sound. No pen of mine would patronize *La Notte*. Not that I expected to appear on the arts page right away. I'd imagined that they'd test me on the mean streets first, where the drunk and disorderly had their daily sabbath; where the ambulances raced to Jervis Street and cars plunged into the river. I knew the world was a terrible place. But I would make a different world of it (the pen is mightier than the sword). I might even get to like that kind of work: 'Streetwalker – Blood is my Beat'. I could go in for a bit of sleuthing on the side. I could change my name to Cheyney Chandler. Brother of Nancy Drew. The third Hardy boy, the older one, tortured to death by Commies on assignment. Instead, as brooding made me understand, it was goodbye to the free ticket and the big event, goodbye to novelty and fashion and everything the city stood for. Whichever way I stuck a cigarette in my face would never, I knew now, be the city desk way. And why was it that the longer I lived in Dublin the farther away from me it seemed? That must be, I thought, from being on foot so much: I never should have left the buses. 273

And all the room in Leinster Road had come to mean was that I now lived a private life, and I never had done that before – life had always been something on the outside, on Lismore's streets, in school, even in the family. That outside had somehow been misplaced – with work, I thought (bad luck to it!). I was appalled to realize that here I was in Dublin and there was no swim of things. Failed son of Sundrive!

Failed heir of Enniscorthy, too, this squabble of contents answering to my name, longing for a rectifying image to be imposed on them . . . . This, too, I understood myself to be, in the post-*Press* bout of uncomfortable, unfamiliar introspection. But then, I'd found no thrill on Vinegar Hill. That outcrop of miserable historical associations stood bleak and bare above the pleasant town, a reminder that no matter how nice a time I was having, it was being had against a melancholy background. It wasn't only that in this town my mother was buried, and where her father (also at an early age) had died, and that for an hour every summer as a child I became a graveside mourner, provider of sweet pea and impatiens from Uncle Seamus's garden, exterminator of disrespectful dandelions. Such bitterness, such failures, being final, seemed somehow acceptable. They were, after all, what the past was all about. They made me think that I was right to want to live – to laugh and turn on Luxembourg; to play the piano half the night at dances like my Aunt Chrissy. But there was nobody in Enniscorthy like her. That was what preyed on me, particularly since – heroes and patriots all – who better had the right to vital life than they, and who lacked one more?

In the forty years since his glorious incarceration, all Uncle Seamus had done, it seemed, was cultivate flowers and disappointment. His wife, Aunt Gret, taught school in outlying areas – Taghmon, Tombrack. Seamus read the *Press* and growled and shook his fine white mane. Why was he so unhappy? He didn't have a care in the world; a good woman waited on him hand and foot; though childless, couldn't he rejoice in the little boys and girls in school around, his wife's life? Cultivating roses was his passion. Perhaps he had no faith in ordinary life, its daily pageant pale compared to the historical extravaganza to which he had given his youth. I hesitate to say. What comes to mind is nothing so fanciful as an explanation. Rather it's something sterile, iceberg-silent . . .

it's a cultural hunger-strike It's the solemn kitsch of the prayerbook he gave me for Confirmation with its snow-white plastic cover and elaborate inscription in Irish. It's the niece he more or less adopted and educated for nunhood. It's the visit he paid in his declining years to his old comrade Dev, now President, and far gone in age. I hear them discuss crops, the numerous recent deaths among the old guard. But very soon they kneel – it's the Glorious Mysteries today. Not very far away, an urchin pries open the side-window of a Morris Minor, reaches in, takes the camera . . . The old men shudder ('what was that?'), clutch their rosary beads with renewed tenacity: 'is now and ever shall be,' the quavery voices conclude. Faith of our fathers, purging and purging . . . .

There were no other men. Seamus had a comrade, and a brother-in-law, Mike Moran, but I don't remember him, except he seemed more energetic, more forward-looking, had a hardware and electrical business in Castle Street – and a family, too, unlike Seamus and Gret. Mrs Moran was Auntie Nell. She had a soft, white face. Her voice was soft and low; contralto. When I climbed the stairs up from the shop and opened the living-room door, she leapt up with gleaming eyes, as though proclaiming, 'Ah it's fondness that's the true history!' Yet she, too, in her time, like her three sisters, had done her bit for the cause, was a woman, or at least a volunteer in the name of freedom. The four Comerfords – Gret, Nell, Poll and Annie: an extraordinary quartet of high-thinking, risk-taking, God-fearing, Erin-loving girls.

And of course Nell also knew – as who could not – that their day had not quite lasted, the body's destiny too had to be lived out, not just (alas?) the spirit's. There was family, there was the different freedom children have to claim, more fundamental, less idealistic, finally perhaps assuming ideological shape (a language; an unfamiliar, disconcering language, pronouncing 'Jesus Christ' differently, also 'let' and 'go') in order to receive a hearing. Jim was at sea, radio officer. Willy worked in Wexford town. He had a large family. Eily lived up the street, near the Duffrey. She had a large family, the Askins. They went to Dagenham when the Mac Smile blade factory was shut down. Dispersal. Uprootedness. Jim came back, then went away again. Willy, with family, returned to Enniscorthy: I wasn't able to see why. The wife of Nick White the busman   275 lived in Dublin. May, the nun, professed in Broadstairs. (Uncle Seamus paddled in the English Channel, glowering at the prospect of being snapped. He did not wear the bottom of his trousers rolled.) Michael Moran, youngest son, became an Augustinian, vowing poverty. He was ordained in Valladollid. That was how it went in those days: sunderings and surrenders. Restlessness. No different from ourselves in Lismore. Family life a tunneling through to exits.

Except that in Lismore I was aware of the exertions: I heard the slamming doors, the inadmissable language. In Enniscorthy all I met was sweet gentleness and generosity. It was as if the women who stayed were happy accepting all that came their way without complaint, living in an Ireland masked by the other cheek, incurious legatees of a two-faced heritage. Why weren't they nurses, teachers, barmaids, actresses? Why hadn't the world made of them what they so clearly were entitled to be? It bothered me. Their natures were richer than their lives. It weighed on me, that row-free passive tolerance which seemed as close to happiness as anything I'd seen adults manage: why did it make me sad? (Impossible questions. Impossible to reconstruct and deconstruct those far-off atmospheres and auras. And equally impossible to forget. Impressions all the more indelible for being inchoate, resistant to all prompts towards meaning; watery sunbeams in the eternal parlour of those endless afternoons . . . . Hauntings.)

And Anne, Granny Royce, embodying it all. She was about five feet, with thin blonde hair. She married William. He died. They named their one child Nuala. She died. Granny owned a house in town where I was born. She had to let it go. She lived in Pullinstown on the farm with her uncle, fierce whiskey Joe. We fed the hens, we picked the winesaps in the orchard. Andy Doolin at the end of the boreen brought honeycombs (they looked as brains should look). When we could see Mount Leinster in the distance it was as good sign. In the evenings the cards for spoil fifteen; the oil-lamp's mellow light. Joe died. The farm went, so back to town. Declining years. She lodged with able Gret and grumpy Seamus, drew her pension, kept forgetfully putting smouldering fag-butts in her handbag 'for after', became a risky visitor. She never saw enough of her darling grandson – the stranger, the survivor, all she had to show, poor thing. Her life of loss· Her sunniness.

After the *Press* episode, she contrived an invitation for us both to some old friends. I did enough overtime for a five-day weekend. The friends lived in south County Wexford, less than thirty miles from Enniscorthy; of course we could have got there, but she insisted on breakisng the journey to them and staying the night at White's Hotel in Wexford town. We sat up late talking, smoking. I carried on loud and long that nothing was going right. Everything was rotten. Nobody gave a damn. I was sick of it. Musha, musha, she, as ever, soothed, not wanting to hear my crass goodbye to Enniscorthy, home of grand deeds, and useless articles. My loss her greater loss; my hurt to her more painful than to me. Eventually I shut up, submitting with ill-grace to her mild insistance that it was a shame, and hard to understand, but these things are sent to try us, but please God, next year . . . . As I had in the *Press* office, however, I had an unsettling inkling that there was no next year. Suddenly it seemed that I was in this impersonal room not to regroup but to part. In one lengthening silence, where only wreaths of smoke expressed our transitory presence, I saw that we had been attending each other's wake.

III

A SWIM IN THE CANAL

1

It was from no less an authority than Mam I had it that dancing defined pleasure. There were no Paul Jones's now, of course, she sighed, no Lancers. But God be with the days when the Courthouse was a flood of frocks and polish. The army band came down from Fermoy (I had seen the shell of its burned barracks from the train: the barrack square had made a fine foundation for the hurling field . . .). The military two-step was executed to perfection: 'Now everybody "Sing bum ta-ra-ra", it's that ever-popular polka, "Roll Out the Barrel".' Miss O'Shea's workroom, where Mam was a seamstress, was agog with muslin ruffs and furbelows. God be with the days. All you found now at dances, she lamented, were clowns in blue suits and brown shoes, people who were crippled from lifetimes in wellingtons and showing off in court shoes with masochistic cuban heels ('what possessed her – wasn't her mother a martyr to fallen arches?'), not to mention the trollops who attended just to be noticed – there seemed to be heinzery of them, if not more than fifty-seven varieties. They sounded especially interesting to me: it was a fine, fat, dirty word, trollop.

Even if standards had declined, however, there was still no mistaking dances' importance. There was one for every important day of the year – Cappoquin Regatta, Tallow Horse Fair, Race night, Stephen's night, the night of the gymkhana. They were the equal and opposite, it seemed, of holy days of obligation, secular sabbaths, responding with licence and late hours to the duties of observance, a reciprocity seemingly confirmed by the fact that the same clothes were worn to kneel and to do the Highland fling. Not that the occasion need be so formal. Outside Lismore, at the Araglen crossroad, there was 281 an open-air stage. On summer evenings, in the gloaming, town lads would glide with country lasses, Tom Keating obliging on the button accordeon. But a stop was put to it. I remember the talk it caused at the time. My uncle Georgie foamed, but I thought the priests were right: you could get your death of cold, staying out like that. It was only a lot later I found out the stage was an occasion of sin, and I was already in Dublin with pretensions to paycocking my way around the Four Provinces Ballroom, Harcourt Street, before I found myself, like George no doubt, in furious pursuit of that same great sin.

The dances which took place at big events were not the only opportunities to shake a leg and show a tail feather. As I knew from Aunt Chrissy, who played for the Marino, the Lismore band, there were dances of all shapes and sizes. They were held in galvanized-iron sheds, in concrete blockhouses known as Parish Halls and frequently named after some attribute of the Blessed Virgin. The Marino played Conna, Knockanore, Ballycotter, Kilworth: once I remember Chrissy saying the following morning – she was up to get our breakfasts as usual – they'd got lost en route the night before, stopped for directions, were told merely to follow the electricity poles: where they ended the band was supposed to be. They'd play from nine to one, nine to two, or just a hop, till midnight. Then pack the car and again home in darkness by roads that weaved with hallucinatory, lightless bicycles. Sometimes, if the dance was an all-out effort to raise money for the hurling-club, say, sisters of the committee-members would be recruited to make sandwiches, slice Swiss-roll and serve tea. Chrissy, too busy playing to take the floor much, appraised the evenings in terms of the patrons' drunkenness and the lavishness of the spread, the latter a code for *two* kinds of sandwiches (ham and corned beef), the former secret lingo for whether she'd met anybody she wouldn't mind meeting again – maybe he'd cycle over to a hurling match some Sunday soon . . . .

At least I assumed her pleasure could not be solely governed by eating and non-drinking, much less by her share of the band's take (a pair of shoes and a large Gold Flake is probably as much as that amounted to). There had to be romance as well, though it wasn't Chris but Sally, a Church Lane neighbour, who best bore that necessity in mind. Wherever the band went, Sal went too, emerging – a cumulo-nimbus in her early thirties; a woman for whom the word 'blouse' was designed – from her little house into the promise of evenings in whatever the feminine was of 'all Gilette and heel-ball', Mam's phrase for freshly shaved, brilliantined, date-conscious men, a phrase applied ironically to people for whose state of mind irony was instant deflation and death. So here she came in American regalia – she had relatives in Massashootus, as she said: ensembles of fuchsia, turquoise, tangerine; of salmon, cinnamon, heliotrope – the nosegay that ate Boston. And always given to having a superb good time. Each outing kept her talking until the identical next one. Each time she danced the whole night through with a series of smashing fellas, every man of whom was a creamery manager. A faraway look would enter her small eyes, her face would sag a little (revealing incipient flabbiness), as she pictured herself once more in the capable arms of a stocky citizen hitting forty – he lied, of course, but Sal could tell; she simpered from being lied to; she loved his comforting scent of evaporated milk . . . . She came to tell it all to Chrissy. I stood apart, humming and pretending not to hear her, but secretly exulting in the news of this dancing life. So grown-ups did have fun, it seemed: their always seeming fraught became less distressing – an act put on for children, probably, so that we would be good.

At school there was dancing too – apart from the Irish kind, that is, which wasn't worth bothering about because it failed to feature partners in the personal, modern, accessible sense of the term. There was non-traditional as well: a woman with wattles taught me to tango. I was nothing loth, being at this point in Fourth Year and able to boast, in the idiom of the inmates, that I knew I didn't have it for stirring me tay: dancing was going to be awful handy one of these fine summers . . . . The lessons, however, were lacking. Music, for one thing. Rather than turn our heads with the wrong translation altogether of Latin, the powers that were evidently, and correctly, concluded that counting would never make us prey to passion. So it was a quick one-two-three up and down the clearing provided for us at the back of the assembly hall, a space so devoid of atmosphere that it would have quelled the call of any and all concupiscence. I was told I had good rhythm. 283

I wondered if I'd recognize the compliment in Spanish – clearly the object of the 'extra' was to ensure we would behave like gentlemen if ever invited to an embassy do in Buenos Aires.

Tangos has no relevance to our Saturday-night school hops, that was plain. But then those hops bore no very clear relation to what we thought a dance was, particularly with just each other or a priest as partner, an arrangement all the more ridiculous since the boarders of the Mercy Convent were no more than the height of a wall away. (This wall was like all the others, of course, topped with either spikes or broken glass whose ugliness kept fresh thoughts of world, flesh and devil, while inhibiting actions that might relieve thought's burdens.) So instead of lurching daintily with a heifer in a gymslip – it was safer, broadly speaking, to disdain what could not be attained – we scraped the floor together, released the odd roar together. Stubbles, ace accordeonist of Kildysart, did his best to satisfy all tastes, from Bridie Gallagher's blockbuster, 'The Boys from County Armagh', to Slim Dusty's great epic, 'A Pub With No Beer', while for the modern set (whom nothing would satisfy, according to the glares of their keepers), 'Wooden Heart' and 'Blueberry Hill'. He refused to give us 'Lipstick on Your Collar'.

The priests spun round sedately, prefects firmly in tow, giving good example. The rest of us fell over one another, giggling, cursing, talking dirty to our dirty-talking dates; the few man-and-wife couples, as we called them, turned into wallflowers and ardently conversed; Rock Sullivan looked in vain for someone to jive with; Stubbles caught us unawares by throwing in, out of the blue, 'The Lion Sleeps Tonight', or bored out of his mind, a stave or two of a reel or a jig. Which was great. It reminded us that dancing was one of the faiths of our fathers. Gaels did it. Priests did it. We would do it too, properly, indelibly, to the tune of 'Here Comes Summer', 'A White Sportcoat and a Pink Carnation', the revised lyric of 'Peggy Sue' never far from our minds.

> Oh Peggy Sue, I do love you,
> Especially in your nightie.
> When moonlight flits across your tits –
> Oh, Jesus Christ Almighty!

Refreshed by renewed resolve – there could only be a future –
we trooped off to night prayers.

Like a lot of other things in my life, however, dancing at first
turned out to be only in theory: when it came to the real thing,
I was missing. At least that was what happened when the first
dance for which I was eligible took place, a dance that was a
must for everyone, the victory céilí.

The novelty was not only in having the céilí but in having
something to celebrate. But we did indeed, and we knew how
to be grateful for it. We would dance. The whole town would
dance. The Courthouse floor would never be the same. It was
the summer I was fifteen, when Da and Kay vacationed in
America for the first time and the Lismore minor hurling team
won the Western division of the country championship,
crushing Tallow, hammering Ballinameela. . . We had all
suddenly come together as a generation, had laid claim to our
bodies, were history in the making. I was allowed to come
along to carry the bottle and the spare sticks, to roar myself
hoarse, a kind of outsize, overzealous mascot, the team's
unicomical version of romancing, dancing Sally from Church
Lane. Oh, was I happy!

We beat Fourmilewater in the final, which was played in the
Fraher Field, Dungarvan, no less – a prestigious venue
particularly since it was the first pitch we'd played on that
wasn't let for grazing between fixtures, thus was neither
covered with cowcakes or riddled with sheep's raisins, so
players could run and fall without circumspection and
without risking what parents greatly feared, lockjaw. And
every man among us played a blinder: Tommy Heffernan,
Gunner Brady, Paddy Farrell, John O'Connor, Peter Hickey . .
. lithely skipping through the twilight, pale forms amid the
lengthening shadows, light failing beyond the homes of the
Colligan Rockies and Brickey Rangers, a coaster's masts
framing Maloney's warehouse – inscriptions of an evening
that has yet to end.

And famous warriors, guests of honour at the dance, that
other way of saying the body was temporarily okay. The three
beautiful daughters of Johnny Jawsus Murphy were there.
Martha Dunne was there too. The Fleming girls, as well, no
doubt. And who knows what went on. The lads tipped one   285

another winks next day; the more they did so, the more credulous I became. So it wasn't called the Courthouse for nothing. All I knew was that I hadn't been allowed to go. It was bad enough, apparently, that I was smoking: now I wanted five shillings for a dance. Wasn't I turning into the right little maneen . . . ? I prowled the streets. I heard the old accordeons playing . . . . 'The Rose of Mooncoin', 'Red Sails in the Sunset'. Latecomers passed me hurrying, their people having finally relented, calling 'Are you going?' to me. I was used to feeling strange, to offering explanations of myself, at school, in Dublin. But I never had felt strange in Lismore till then. The feeling was a victory of sorts, I suppose, though not for me.

It wasn't until some time later (I may have already been in Dublin and long-weekending in Lismore with Peg to lick my Monkstown wounds) that I discovered that strange was how dances were supposed to feel. One of the lads still at home, whom I didn't know drove, much less had a car, borrowed a relative's old Anglia – and here was I arriving back in a Fiat whose front I could barely tell from its back: was it possible that there was someone in Lismore freer and more trusted than I (shades of the céilí flapped unsettlingly before me)? But such thoughts didn't linger. I was too taken with the forty-five m.p.h. dash along familiar roads, familiar figures on familiar bikes waving in the dust after us. By the time we reached that failed but welcome Courthouse, Dungarvan Town Hall, I was racing as fast as the car, plonked down with lordly (citified, I thought) aplomb my six-and-a-tanner – which meant that it was not the greatest event on West Waterford's social calendar that year: big dances cost at least seven-and-six – and made like a sheep through a gap for the dark place where the saxes wailed.

Oh, what a night that was. At one point I was in a ring of six or eight skipping to a Johnny and the Hurricanes medley. The floor was a burning trampoline. The body was a pogo stick. I had never sweated so much in my life before. Oh, what delicious hell was this? And though the circling and the skipping seemed to go on for a long time, when it ended all I wanted was the same thing over again. But the music slowed. Then that was all right too, though. The singer poured himself into the mike, doing Ruby and the Romantics' 'Our Day Will Come'. It was then I learned how to move without making

286

forward progress, without caring if there never was progress again, because all that mattered was the sandy shuffle of the brushes on the snare drum, the girl's hair like a tickling breeze about my face. I saw now why dances had to be crowded; from a full heart I silently thanked the strangers all around me for creating for me, for everyone, this inspirational heat, this fabulous undulance in which we bobbed and dipped, bubbles forming, breaking, forming in richly seething stirabout.

And I found out what 'shift' meant. This was what dates were called in school, and I could never imagine why, since all the word meant was move. I realized that on a date one might well be moved, but the way the term was used suggested more the adventures of the hand than the palpitations of the heart. I supposed it must, like everything else, be a double meaning – connected, perhaps, to mickey muscle rising to the occasion, though (and this was not easy to figure out either) there was no need to be on a date for that to happen. But that evening, as soon as the girl I was dancing with said 'How about a breath of fresh air; I'm stifling', I realized at once that that was my line, except that the way to say it was, 'Will we shift?' disguising in laconic lacking confidence.

There was a bandstand in a little park beyond the dog-legged street. We went there and watched the idle water of the bay, and the moon over the Cunnigar, the sandbank that was silting up the bay but which now seemed as exotic and unthreatening as a sleeping whale. She shivered. She was wearing a cotton blouse, a skirt of navy blue. She was very thin, pinched face that spread just like a child's whenever she smiled (and she liked to smile), arms and legs that looked as though they were just the shoots of real limbs. Her name, she said, was Bríd. She lived in Wolfe Tone Street – did I know where that was? Yes, on the fringe of Loughmore, the poor part, out by the County Home. I asked her who her favourite singer was. She said Cliff Richard. I pretended not to mind. Soon I was more interested in how it was that while her arm was cold and goose-bumped she otherwise felt very warm. I noticed that her lips tasted at first of peppermint, then after a while of strong tea. Lips clung, noses didn't seem to matter: that too seemed to go with the stranger, with the strangeness. And strangest of all: here I was with a girl who'd let me dance most of the night with her without minding one bit the number of times I had to say 'Sorry!' for trampling her.

But I couldn't miss my lift. We danced the evening's last slow waltz, stood with arms around each other for the ragged valediction of the national anthem's final bars, always played at dances and cinemas then to make endings official. How much more pleasant it felt to loll irreverently together . . . it was as though our bodies had finally found the nerve to tell us the good news – you've been solo, uptight at attention, long enough. A last squeeze; her final, goodbye smile. In the glare of the full houselights she looked very white and wan. I didn't care. She was the one. The lads were calling though. (Did life have to go on?) I know: I'll get 'My Happiness' by Connie Francis played for her on Irish Requests on Luxembourg. No – it'd take too long. What, so? 'I'll write to you!' I blurted. I could think of no higher compliment . . . .

And I did write, care of the Dungarvan postmaster, which obtuse Cupid replied re my communication of 2nd inst . . . directed to state . . . *le meas* . . . I waited and waited, but nothing from Bríd. Then, perhaps six months or more later, I got a letter from the Isle of Man. She was a chambermaid in a hotel there: did I remember her . . . ? I saw in her ill-formed hand a thin frame, loneliness, a gruelling slog and screaming bosses, no dancing. The romance of travel: the impoverishment of work. She too now knew, like me, the history of the world. But I didn't know how to write back. I didn't have either the words or the nerve to tell her that if she remembered the dance, that was all that mattered.

I remembered. I went over every step of it often, though not as often as I would have liked, because the distractions of the job, of family, of ambition, of wondering if Dublin was the larger life to addle me, kept falling like so many shadows between the dance and me, supplying a wrong, lugubrious kind of darkness. If only those nuisances would stop putting years on me . . . .

Yet sometimes when I relived the Bríd evening it vaguely struck me as peculiar that I had found it such an eye-opener, or rather, languorous eye-closer – lotus and hookah in the shadow of Helvick. Hadn't I known all about this kind of thing from the time I was a small boy? The dance was unfamiliar rustling and urgent steps upstairs. It was shaving cream on

Sunday night, and scent in the middle of the week. It was Mick Delahunty's twenty-one piece orchestra: Mick Del from Clonmel, as big and brassy as Geraldo or Joe Loss. He even played a Hunt Ball at Lismore Castle – next thing we knew he'd be on the wireless. There wasn't a hall in Munster that band didn't pack, including our very own, the monstrosity clad in russet galvanized iron, the Happydrome (whoever called it that must have thought Hippo-ditto an obscure English joke which he was determined not to fall for: *if it sounds like a zoo they'll turn it into one . . .*). This was what I understood the dance to mean – not understanding anything: peculiar venues, foreign (Tipperary) musicians.

Not only that, the dance meant the morning after, too. While Mam heard Mass at the convent, Chrissy and George would go over every inch of it again, exhausted but, clearly, delightedly at peace. They kept telling me to eat my egg, but I always made a point of listening to this legendary stuff of grown-ups' night-time. The tone was so agreeable – it often was when something shared outside was brought back home. Not that the events were particularly exotic. The footwork of some Ballysaggart bostoon had nearly crippled Chrissy. Geo thought he was going to break his neck at first, the floor had been that heavily massaged with Glideezi. But Andy Ahearne was still a gorgeous dance. Mona, the new girl at the hairdresser's, was found to be 'pleasant, like, y'know, no airs and graces; a natural being' – said wistfully (the workday loomed). For a while, the familiar had ceased to be contemptible. Neighbour met neighbour on an equal footing. There was the harmless lottery of pairing off with partners. Life was both reduced and elevated to a grand game, and all were free to play, all – as far as I could tell – seemed mollified having played, having lapsed, both male and female, indiscriminately, publicly, though without usurping privacy, just once in a way, together, imagining they could share, into the culture of the body. There were faraway looks in early-morning eyes, and absent-minded silences: they told me that the dancers felt they never wanted to feel freer than they did dancing.

And sometimes for a while after a dance, Chris and Geo would try behaving in that freedom's name. Geo would stop going to the library and would hurry off as though he had something better to do. Coming from school I'd see Chris making off down Ferry Lane on her own. I'd run after her, calling: it wasn't fair of her to go walking without me. It was shocking to hear she didn't want me with her – nobody went anywhere alone; who better than I for company? She was being so bad that she was sometimes late for tea. Then – equally shocking – it turned out Geo was doing a strong line with a girl from Tallow. I happened on them, talking earnestly, as I rounded the corner going home one Sunday evening after benediction. I greeted him effusively. He was less than friendly. I hung around, thinking he might give me money, but I was wasting my time. Then, just as I was heading on, he called me. 'Don't tell,' he told me, seriously: 'Don't say you saw me.' But what was there not to tell? He was doing nothing. Not long afterwards he returned to normal, reading Westerns by the dozen, staggering after midnight on the stairs: we knew where we were with him again then. A good thing he'd given up trying to have a private life, a life beyond the family: that kind of thing only happened in pictures, and they weren't real. Didn't Geo know no dance went on forever?

He would have only got in trouble by carrying on. Priest trouble – there was always that. Every so often the chapel would resound with denunciations of immorality, late nights, motor cars, modern ways that forgot God, but let those selfish enough to think of nothing but pleasure take care in case God forgot them! I understood the bit about the cars. Priests were very nearly the only unmarried people who owned them. Naturally they didn't want anyone going the roads to have one and that way start getting it into their heads that they were as well off as the clergy . . . . As for the rest, the roaring could sometimes be exhilarating.

True trouble, though, and what I was really afraid of was that my erring uncle and my wayward aunt would be mentioned in Pot Pourri, the paragraph of rumour and innuendo that appeared in the 'Lismore Notes' carried weekly by the *Dungarvan Leader* (the pot was pronounced pott, as though to underline the fact that the paragraph's intention was to stew certain reputations in gossipers' acidulous salivations). Full names were never used, just first name initials or identification by means of place. 'The Chapel Street colleen wouldn't be pleased if she saw the couple that went up the

Green Road Thursday evening . . . . A little bird told me that Paddy F – is off his grub on account of the new employee at the Hotel . . . . ' All good clean fun; mostly made up, perhaps, to cause a stir or give reluctant swains encouragement. It was all so much trouble – meeting someone, finding enough time for them, finding a place to be with them. But I remember, too, that people got upset if a scenario could be said to frame them. Talk of this kind – Miss Emptyhearts speaks the language of love, unsweet nothings – would be awful if it came our way. We'd die of shame. Safer by far to dance and have done.

2

There was the Crystal in South Anne Street. I won a spot prize there. The singer stopped the music suddenly and called 'Who recorded that one?' Quick as a flash I called back, 'Cliff Richard'. (Easy – 'The Young Ones'). Two tickets to the Wednesday hop was my reward. My dancing partner was so impressed she almost let me date her.

There was the Town and Country Club in Parnell Square, but it was too far to walk back from. So was the National, which was also somewhere thereabouts. I didn't go there either. I'd heard it was a home-on-the-range kind of place with quare culchie cowboys and the quickstep a thundering herd, or perhaps I read as much in the raw redness of its neon sign. Dancehall signs should be pink, the delicacy in red's desire: they should be green, the colour of hope in the liturgy.

Mainly, though the Four Provinces in Harcourt Street was my delight and especially the Sivilkems of a Friday night. That was the easiest to walk home from. If you clicked it would more than likely be with some bird from southside flatland, so taxiing her back would not break the bank. And it was best to score on Friday night, obviously, since there would still be cash enough for Sunday night at the pictures, if she was interested, and of course she would be interested in getting something for nothing, who wouldn't? Even I, prone to regard myself as the Lazarus of Leinster Road (compared to the large family of civil servant Dives I saw around me), took care to have spondulix for the weekend. Dining off a small tin of, for preference, Crosse & Blackwell spaghetti greatly helped the cause, I found, and if on the toasted rounds of O'Rourke's Vienna I was able to shed temporarily the Lazarine for the Lucullan – there had to be an image always, something that the world poured into me to salve all the hungers.

The Sivilkems was best, too, because it was a student dance – put on by prospective civil and chemical engineers. The Ags – the civil-chems' agricultural equivalents in academe – probably had the better dances; they usually had all the big-name bands, anyway, and a more exalted-sounding venue, the Olympic. But that hall was obscurely located somewhere off the upper reaches of Heytesbury Street, the dances were dearer, and in any case were mid-week events, suggesting that their public was the student élite, lazy buggers all, privileged to stay in bed as late as they liked all the live-long week. Dances existed to eliminate distinctions between their patrons, or at least to make the jeopardy of difference negotiable – a rehearsal for the dutiful sublimations of parochial whist drives in later life: Mrs V. Mooney all night upping the ante on biddable Mr Tommy Dunne. But it was hard not to be aware of the distinctions.

Why dances were the remit of students, I don't know. I suppose it helped the dancehall owner identify a clientele. But I doubt he hired students to run dances for him. And I don't remember any talk about what happened to proceeds and profits. Was something of the take used to help fund scholarships for scholars barred by poverty rather than by brainlessness from college? Was the whole business nothing more than a handy grind in the entrepreneurship without which success in later life would be inconceivable? I don't know. Money, presumably, came into it somewhere. Anyone with only public spirit could try doing the St Vincent de Paul Society's sober cakewalk.

The main point about student dances, however, was that they had the best women, drawn by career prospects for themselves – good catches, that is; well-educated, well-paid professionals. Why else would they go? Therefore, certain vital steps had to be taken in order to compete with bestness.

A brisk rubdown, first. Bathing would have been better, of course, but a bath cost a shilling, the price of a mineral later on, and a mineral was essential because you had to have something to sweat; besides, if negotiations were going so poorly as to recommend sleep before midnight, at least a shilling would have been saved towards the cigarettes essential to easing the empty stomach from Thursday lunch to Friday pay. Then, after Matt-Talbotizing myself with a towel that felt like a luge along a course of pebble-dashing, came the ticklish part: the shave. Even if it took half the evening, the shave had to be perfect. I still was far from shaving nick-free, so was unable to shave without smoking, which caused problems of its own, but smoke did manage to impart the cool within which its more gelid cousin, lather, was supposed to produce on the outside. With a fag going I at least had an image of the way things should go. The slightest sign of blood meant trouble, though, because since the *Press* episode I'd boycotted newspapers, hence had nothing to plug a leak (Mrs O'Connell's jax-paper was non-staunching, shiny Izal), and it was most unwise to let the damage congeal by itself since standing, watching, waiting, wondering, foot-tapping, made it all too easy (I could vouch for it) absently, fretfully to pick the cicatrice and find yourself B.D. (bloodied dimple), much more objectionable – much less deniable (I could vouch for it) – than the mentionable social scourge – B.O. Thus, I scrupulously shaved.

Ditto quiffed. But this I knew from primary school, when Brother Blake used to give points for neat writing, good sumsmanship and tidy appearance in which smart hairdo rated highly. Whoever got points had no slaps next day, at least we could more or less completely take charge of the hair-control component of our destiny. When it came to quiffs, therefore, I knew exactly which way the wind blew. Ignoring, though with difficulty, the insipid displays of hispidity on chest, in oxter, and in any case knowing of no lubricant which would increase and multiply same, I devoted assiduous attention to the mane that mattered, the visible one. Here again, as with the fickle blade, great care, or to give care its proper name, Brylcreem, was called for: too much and it might run when the hall began to swelter, ruining the shirt not worn since Sunday, and worse, causing excessive use of hanky 293 which risked making the partner think she was dancing with a cosmetic cripple suffering from a progressive and evidently degenerative attack of leaky pores and semaphores. (Partners were invariably, irresistibly, maddeningly impeccable.)

No blood anywhere; no soap in ear folds? Okay. Tie; jacket; pat of pocket for key and smokes. Right. Time to take the floor (please God, tonight's the night . . .). Time to hit the high spots, where- and whatever they were. Time to enter real time. The preparations had to climax in the front door being slammed, that irrevocable moment, point of no return, a subconscious rehearsal of the emergences and turning points which, it was hoped, the evening would present, which indeed the preparations – *pas seul*, Narcissus and his porcelain trough – were intended to excite, that sole self a dance of possibility, leading (being led by) that machine which called dreams to test, the dancehall, where with luck and timing leg might inadvertently slide along anonymous leg, and give rise to the thrilling little kick and tingle.

Sweet mystery of life! I'd found at last what it was all about: people not being people, but being girls. Birds, dames, wimmin, dolls, dishes, bikes, cushy pushers with dainty dairies, quims, gowls, fans, and diddies. Pleasure machines. Hot. Fast. There were girt about with hooks and hawsers, but they wouldn't be long shifting your gears for you, and their arses were upholstered like Rolls-Royces, the better, it was said, to give a good ride. I was more surprised than disappointed, however, when I discovered that many girls seemed to wear cardboard covers over their behinds. These inhibitors – were they corsets? – meant as little to me as the placards outside black churches in Leeson Park and Adelaide Road, roaring in big letters about the wages of sin and judgment that is at hand. At hand: but I only knew those rears in reverse, from dancefloor collisions.

The female and the feminine were a lingo all their own, and were only known by what was said of them, the jokes, the slang. One whore says to the other, 'D'ya smoke after it?' The other one says, 'I dunno: I never looked.' I'd heard lads in school say that the reason our tubby matron, Miss Dooley, was in a bad mood was because she had the rags on. But I was afraid to ask what they were (better pretend to know it all than to be laughed at). And even if I knew I still didn't know it all, I was at least beyond the stage of sneaking up to the library in Lismore to check the big dictionary for the meaning of spermatoza. I knew a fair few of the facts. It was life that was still a little obscure.

A girlfriend, though, would surely help me in all respects. Dublin could hardly deny me that much: with all the gorgeous girls there were, wasn't there a Molly Malone for me(where are you, sweet Miss Kelly?). There had better be. I was the one just about dying of a fever. It wouldn't have particularly bothered me if girls really were dolls, devoid of crankcases and headlights. I'd respect them, I'd renounce for life all the passionate kissing and close embracing that Catholic Truth Society pamphlets warned against, I'd make a weekly confession of my non-sins to their experts on such matters, Daniel Lord, S.J., I'd do anythng (meaning nothing) just for a friendly face and merry eyes.

I had plenty of time to wonder about the everything and nothing of my dancehall days, to wonder: was it my imagination or did Chris and George have a springier step after their long rewarding walks without me; and about the night with Bríd, when everything seemed so casually happy (what had casualness to do with happiness, tell me?). Bríd – I should have stayed in Dungarvan with her: now the girls I danced with never had names. I never knew what to say after 'Fierce crowd. Great band.' If I asked them where they were from, it only led to greater silence: what did I know of Edenderry or Bennettsbridge? And I knew girls were not supposed to talk first. There now, verbal me, who'd virtually talked Chris into needing hearing aid . . . . Wasn't it terrible, I said to myself, that Camus, smart as he was, and calm, and George Orwell, so brusque and clean, had nothing to offer me in this line? Was that how it had to be though – Chris for talk and a pretty kisser for dancenights?

So all too often, when it came time for 'He'll Have to Go', I was in the balcony sucking fiercely on yet another cigarette, feeling that I was the one who had to go, that the whole thing was a dead loss – Jim Reeves, for God's sake! Couldn't they do any better than that President of the Unctious Schmaltz of America? Yes! – not only were the girls not forthcoming, the bands didn't give a damn. They played the popular, pure-in-heart dead man; made him one of our own. Didn't they know there was a dance revolution going on? As Johnny Tillotson had so eloquently reminded the free peoples of the world, it was the age of 'Poetry in Motion' (the motion being a girl's, the poetry being her motion) or, to put it another way, like Chubby Checker, 'It's Pony Time!' But if it wasn't the twist – idiot, passé offspring of the hoolahoop – it wasn't anything at all: 'We'd like to pick the tempo up now, ladies and gentlemen, boys and girls, with the latest from Helen Shapiro: 'Walking Back to Happiness'. *Walking*! Where was the Fly, the Mashed Potato, the Madison, the Hitchhiker, the Locomotion, the Watusi – 'Let's do the wa-wa-tusi!' – by the exciting Watusis?

Not that rickety me required the latest dance fad to appreciate a band. Even without a radio, I was still more hip, more cool than anyone else – I knew that for a fact (not knowing very many people). Nobody had my awe and admiration for Santo and Johnny's 'Sleep Walk'; The Teddybears' 'To Know Him Is to Love Him' (now that was how a holy anthem should sound, instead of lapsed marches like as 'Faith of Our Fathers'); and breathed there a man with soul so dead who never to himself had said 'This is fucking beautiful', about Maxine Brown's 'All in My Mind'? It didn't matter which band it was – Rebel Cork's own Dixielanders; the Clipper Carlton of Strabane, who took the country completely unawares by coming over the border and playing like men possessed – were they invaders to be suspicious of or escaped prisoners of conscience (minor musical Mindzentys to be welcomed)? Even the Royal itself: nobody knew more than me, felt more than me. Too good is what I was (probably): signs on I was being kept to the sideline. But the fools, the fools! . . . the bands, by not giving me my due, were only drawing attention to themselves.

I pitied them, really. They weren't even young. How could they be? No Mammy would allow a son to travel and be out late unless he was well into his twenties. Their taste had to be formed by different dancing, perhaps even by pre-teen ditties from Guy Mitchell and Max Bygraves. And they hardly believed in electricity at all: reed and horn still basically ruled their roost. They seemingly disdained the perfection of the blessed plastic wafer created by the grace of electronics. They

rejected the high calling of being human radios. They only
played the tunes. They didn't mean them. It never occurred to
them that they shouldn't be so innocent. They should have
paid more attention to Messiah Kennedy, to his prophets Elvis
and Jerry Lee. Ask not what your jukeboxes can do for you but
what you can do for your jukeboxes. They should have got to
know me. I'd sing. My name is Frankie Avalon (open-neck
white shirt, collar up). I'm going to do my new song, 'Venus'.
I want to sing it as though Villon wrote it ('Tant crie l'on Noel
qu'il vient' . . .), but I don't know how. Besides, I really don't
want to be Avalon-sweet. I want to be city-burning mad. I
want to go *I'm free / let me play / let me play / I'm free*, like an
angry jazzman (the man that rock forgot) shouting out the
crime of his frustrations. Put your sweet lips, ooh-whee
honey, do-it do-it, a little, just a little, little – Ho! tickles, umm
nice; tickles – haha-hohoho-HEE! Whoa! Is that the phone –
god *damn* that pho-o-no-o-no-one . . . !

Oh well, here we go again. Friday night, it's better than being
on my own isn't it (but I *am* on my own). Fierce crowd, d'you
like the band?

'I'm from Tallow,' she said.

'What?!' I bawled, screeching to a halt in the middle of 'Are
You Lonesome Tonight?' (or perhaps 'Poor Shep'), causing a
chain of skidding and weaving and muttering, though did I
care whose sails I was taking the wind out of? Not with – This
was –

And there was more. She was not really from the next town
west of Lismore but from a townland in between whose name
was inseparable from a couple of lads I knew from there; 'You
don't know Paddy and Willy – ?' I shouted. When she told me
she was their sister I nearly went through the floor first, then
the ceiling. *I believe in God, the Father Almighty* . . . I should
have shamed us both by throwing my arms around her and
hugging her till surgery us part. This was somebody who
knew me! But unabashedly staring at her as though daring her
to disappear, as though waiting for myself to wake up, was all
I could manage for the time being – though I might readily
have realized she was certainly all there from the virtually
continual presence of her insteps beneath my feet. I assumed
she didn't mind, however, because she said nothing when I, 297

being too distracted, forgot 'Sorry'. Instead, after a while, she disengaged herself from my omnivorous, moronic eyes, and began to giggle.

I came to: be serious, I told myself.

'What's your name?' I gasped.

'Maura.'

I'd never heard a nicer. Simple, yes, but not common; definitely not common . . . Irish, but not off-puttingly so, as Seoirse was. Kind of like Bríd in a way, but nicer, really; much nicer. A name with shape and firmness to it. Not a thin name. A name for a Ritchie Valens hymn.

Now, all of a sudden, the world had become a very small place, consisting simply of merry eyes and unbitten nails. There were well-tended teeth, too, which let me know she was special (not everybody had them). There was a gorgeous globe of chestnut hair. And I could live in the small confines of this world, I thought. Its slow time would be a boon, its minute graduations would never intimidate. I had no need any more to play the secret-life, alternative-self game. I had come home to Tallow. We perpetrated certain phrases to me as we congealed and unglued in the slow, deliriously slow melée. ('Yes,' I said stupidly, 'I love The Cadets'; 'Yes,' Maura said charmingly, 'I do come here fairly often'.) We were Mr and Mrs Crysostomos. 'We'd like to liven it up a little bit, now, with 'Way Down Yonder in New Orleans'. We were Freddy Cannon's *Whoo!*

Then, though, just as my heart was turning into a toasted marshmallow (on fire with sweetness), Maura muttered something apologetic and headed for the sidelines for earnest hugger-mugger with a blonde girl, and at once I greatly feared. Silly me: be *serious*, can't you, I told myself: how can anything go wrong? The whole thing is a miracle: it can't turn out typically. She knows me, I told myself; I know her. We can place each other, we can see each other in lives the opposite of this (she carries a bucket to the hens, I lounge at the Red House corner like a man of the town), our talk is anchored to familiar never-mentioned roads and the bark of saucy mongrels from cottages. She can't leave me down. She knew I was somebody, because she knew the someplace I was from. She couldn't let me down. Yet – damn it to hell and blast it – what was keeping her!

Of course the dance saved me (how could I have doubted it?). A ladies' choice was announced and, promptly, forward Maura came smiling. It was the first time I'd been saved from the ignominy of self-banishment to the balcony, the usual choice that ladies gave me. Now we danced closer. *Put Your Sweet Lips* . . . I didn't have a nerve the soppy number failed to hit. I was captain and master. Plain sailing now. Steady as she goes . . . Aye, aye, sir! Oh *fuck*! the first mate was saluting: down, boy; *down*, sir! (*He'll* have to go.) But the mutinous flesh would not be still. What now?

'It's fierce warm,' I blurted; 'would you like a glass or orange or something?'

'Yes,' said Maura, 'It's close all right.'

(Oh, so *that* was why I used to see couples on the balcony . . . .)

'That was Carrie,' Maura said when we were sitting with our glasses of C & C. The blonde girl, one of her flatmates. She just had to talk to her about meeting up later: 'Sorry.' I waved that aside, more interested in what 'later' meant. Was Maura thinking what I was thinking, that there would be no parting us now, and later was a synonym for never? She and Carrie had been at Mercy together –

'You went to the Mercy?!' I was shouting again. You mean, I meant, that you were one of those girls we used to pass so snidely on our walks out Duckspool and Ballyneety, with the cerise uniforms and silly soup-plate hats – that you were on the far side of that cutting wall all that time? She and Carrie had probably been sizing me up for years (if they had any sense, they had)! She'd thought of me during night prayers, in domestic science. And here we were at last. Blessed smallness of the world! Wasn't life very simple after all? A mere matter of gales of giggling and lots of dancing. Oh Angel of God, my Guardian dear, keep nether man stowed safe below for me! Oh don't let me (him) spoil it. I vow and swear to you, Father Chaste Ukase of Veritas House, respect is all I have in my heart for her. (Pray for me.)

But she had to go, she really had to go; it was gone half-twelve. 'Ah don't.' I was far from ready for life to revert to cinders. But Carrie – oh that was it: the pal was an escape clause. (Yeah, I knew pals were great, I brooded nastily: Eddy is probably up against Miss Kelly in some doorway this very minute . . . .) And the lie of the land around the Four Proivnces was so good, a shame to waste it; the porch of the old Harcourt Street station had to be designed with dancehall trysting in mind. And now she wanted to go to the cloakroom – well Jesus Christ! – leaving me feeling a right fool waiting for her. If the floor was thronged, the scene around the ladies' cloaks was a proper post-horn gallop. Gusts of powder, shrieks of laughter, hissed admonitions, lethal-sounding 'Excuse me's' filled the air. Flatfuls of disappointment stampeded out and towards the taxi-rank, handbags wheeling like Boadicean blades. Surprisingly cool-looking girls on their own emerged and, bums arcing in disdainful sway, went out to meet their swains (how come them lads knew enough to wait out on the street?).

At last! (Her smile immediately made me feel a fool no longer.)

'Listen,' I began, but synonyms for shift did not suggest themselves. Besides, Maura was a lot quicker. 'How about Sunday?' she said, reading my mind so well that she could let on, with a straight face, to be misreading it. She hurried out the address of the flat, the 'phone number (she had a 'phone!): 'About two?'

'No, but listen – '

Carrie had slipped by us to the street door, was pretending not to look.

'Goodnight, love,' said Maura simply, and reaching up, pecked me on the cheek.

I rocked. I rolled.

I had just received my first spontaneous kiss since First Communion Day, when the women who were in my life than, Mam and Chrissy, were momentarily overcome at the sight of puny me having reached the age of reason. It was only now, though, that I was really a hero. I'd got the girl.

3

The flat was in one of those solid, vaguely holy-looking houses in Sandymount Avenue, just beyond the railway gates on the left; an expensive, brownish, leathery, red-brick house in a much sedater part of the world than Leinster Road. I was afraid. Up until I'd got off the 18 and faced into that Sunday silence I felt fine. The various items that required attention had been attended to. My dinner of incinerated rashers, which I had more or less swallowed as soon as I got up, just in case the clock was slow or broke down somehow without my noticing (I didn't own a watch), was evidently not going to repeat on me. My tie was noose-straight. I'd aired the shirt I'd danced in by flapping it out the window for a few minutes – the act of a thorough-going tramp, I knew, but it was a rear window, so what harm? I may have even brushed my teeth, although it was the middle of the day.

The 18 dozed along. I had yet one more life-sustaining post-prandial cigarette and cleaned my nails with the spent match-stick – women were sticklers, you couldn't be too careful: and this was more important than a dance, this was broad daylight (this was my first date). I noticed that the sun was coming back for another of its little visits and I found myself nodding at the passing streets in a state of stupefied homage. World, world. Life, life. So good, so kind. Sweet Appian Way. Old RDS, by memory blessed. The cardboard (concrete?) nurse with the Sweep ticket held aloft, encouraging us all to chance our arm, was right, she was so right. I was approximately an hour and a half too early. By two, I was a wreck, and sweating smellily from walking to kill time.

And I was right to be afraid, I thought, when I saw the house up close. It was more ecclesiastical than at first sight. The door was flanked by stained-glass sidewindows depicting nothing except a pattern, which made me superstitious. The pattern did signify, yet remained a pattern, panes of blood and bile joined and disjoined by veins of lead, armorial bearing of the uncertain body, of which we are all scions, now and at the hour of our death – Get a grip on yourself, for the love of God! I stepped into the porch. The house engulfed me. I stood close to the door, as beggars tend to. The bell screeched. This is it. Throw the cigarette away – crisp footsteps on the cool tiled hall, mottled with pools of pale colour. Check the fly. This is it
. . . .

But what, exactly, was it? I would have been quite happy to sit and smoke and have a cup of tea and jaw and have another cup of tea, as I might in the frontroom of my aunt or cousin I was visiting. But whether it was Maura saying, 'Won't be a tick, I'll just get my jacket', or one of the flatmates asking where were we going, in a tone that sounded barely on the polite side of ironical, it suddenly dawned on me that there was supposed to be a plan here. I was the man, wasn't I? What had I masterfully in mind? And tea out, no doubt, I thought uncomfortably, hearing the ghastly flap of empty pockets – and tomorrow's only Monday! I gave the flatmates an idiot grin, and shifted the weight on my feet. 'Oh, sit down!' they cried, which was not what I meant at all. I sat down. I offered around my cigarettes – clean me out altogether, why don't ye? But of course they didn't smoke. Instead their tense, wrinkle-resistant noses said, Filthy habit. They found a flowery saucer for my ash, which I by now was wishing I could deposit in my socks. It's the small things, I swear to God: they're the true crucifixional nails.

So we got the bus. That immediately made a big difference. The last time I was on a 7A or 8 going the Merrion Road, going in the wrong direction – well, at least that was behind me. We got into town. So far, so good. We got off at Suffolk Street. We walked around. Maura talked. I talked much more. She was a clerk/typist in a big insurance office. She earned seven quid a week. I winced. Retaliating, I wondered, patronizingly, if she liked the work, this *career*? It was a job, she said. I'd been told that girls were like this: tolerant, incurious, accepting. Mature. (How would I ever get anywhere with them?) 'Yes,' I said, impulsively, 'and it only cost five years of secondary school – of boarding-school – to get it.' There was a silence after that. I paused to admire my unexpected cynicism: it, I thought, made me sound older. I liked that. Must remember it. Thank you, Maura, I said silently, sincerely; you've already helped me see that there are images I've barely even glimpsed yet, never mind tried on. Helping me was the whole point, of course (amazing how quickly she'd got it – without seeming to think about it, really: oh, they were rare and fine indeed in their maturity, girls . . .).

We walked – what with that and my dancing, she must have thought I didn't like her legs. But I never noticed her legs. Now that I think of it, I don't believe she was a body for me at all. Just a presence: when I embraced her it was the 'my own' that was the one I held. I remember that Sunday we sat in Stephen's Green for a while, and I put my arm around her shoulders. I noticed she, though still looking straight ahead at the ducks in the lake, seemed also a little more attentive, as though waiting. What for? I'd hardly thought I'd ever do more than dream of freedom I was now exercising, my arm mainly on the back of the bench, just respectfully resting across her shoulders, sun playing on the back of my hand, hair mildly tickling the back of my hand, sun turning the tendrils of her red hair to gold. This was it. The rest of the city was stretched out in couples all around us. I was happy, too. This was Chris plus feeling. Did Maura want more?

'Come on,' I said at length, realizing I had to make some kind of move. 'I'll show you the statue of Clarence Mangan. He was a right quare fella. Did ye do 'The Time of the Barmecides'? There was a lad a year ahead of me who used to call that 'The Time of the Bare Backsides'! But Mangan – he had something to do with Meath Street, I think. Were you ever up there around the Liberties? It's strange – different. I'll show you – '

Yes! – I could be Da and Maura me!

But, strange to say, she had a distant, somewhat tight-lipped look.

We went to the Crystal, we had a second honeymoon at the Four Provinces, we went to the Adelphi, the Carlton, the Regal and the Ritz, Ballsbridge, which had a great pong of Jeyes fluid, worth enduring only because I thought it of vital importance that Maura see *The Magnificent Seven*. She said she liked it. I think she pretty much liked everything we did, up to a point, but I can't be sure about this because I never gave her a chance to have her proper say. What can she have been thinking – what novenas she must have made to St Francis de Sales, patron of the deaf – as I told her that of course *The Magnificent Seven* was all Japanese, and that basically I knew everything about the cinema – 'they're not just pictures, you know' – because my father . . . . All I was trying to say was didn't she, like me, think it was great, that culture let us talk to each other. But I no more knew then that was what I meant, than I did with Chris. I didn't have to know it. Talk to me was its own justification, a freedom and delight synonymous with taking Maura

303

out. If girls were supposed to be pleasure machines, Maura was my microphone.

And it wasn't just for helping me break my silence that I treasured her. She was also turning me into a born-again Dubliner. Going by bus was an adventure again. Being downtown when the last house of the Metropole got out was the same old childish blare of bright lights and hoarse motors in the dark. And I had this little short-cut to show her and this little anecdote – 'Daddy used to take me to Alexandra Basin to see the big ships'; 'There's The Moira . . . ' – so that I began to see again that the city was as big as I'd originally thought. I saw myself as somebody with memories (would she never tire of giving me new images of myself?): therefore I was somebody – even if memories were only stains left by dried-up desires. But I might desire again, mightn't I? After all, I was only finding this out because I had been right about dancing, whose life of atmosphere and accident, music and mutuality, of the personal filtered through a public show to become at once more personal and less isolating, had proved itself by this person being beside me – this radiant window, this chance to pretend I could start all over again one more time.

What can I do? What can I do? I wanted us to be able to do something to show I was grateful and appreciative, something in the name of my memories and in the spirit of my desires. Dickie Rock and the Miami were all very fine and *King of Kings* profound. But they weren't new experiences. And I didn't want to turn us into tourists by suggesting, say, the National Gallery. To be mere sight-seers in one's own capital seemed awfully infra-dig; if there were sights they'd have to be my unexpected selections (besides, I knew nothing about paintings). Rainbow trout and chips at The Moira would have been ideal, but the memory of Franz flashing his wad reminded me that I was now, and always had been, paid in singles.

I don't know how it was I hit on the theatre. It may have been that *Philadelphia, Here I Come!* was the talk of the town; a strange phenomenon, a home-made hit, by someone who seemed – on the basis of our not knowing the first thing about him – not a bit like Brendan Behan. So, we went to see it at The Olympia, and that was strange too; the façade that seemed made of almond paste, the glass awning leading from street to 304 box office, the atmosphere inside which was much more opulent and cathedralish than that of cinemas (which in comparison were merely parish churches). Yes, this was what I had in mind, something rich and strange – the naked stage an altar, the text's inviolable words, the whole production like the facts of life with its confidence tricks of tragicomic puppetry. And this play itself was gas; it was under our noses, not over our heads, not like that tongue-twisting, roller-coastering, larger-than-life Shakespeare (the world's only playwright, bar Behan). We all knew the hero Gar O'Donnell. We knew him so well that, at the end, we weren't laughing half as much as squirming, yet that was pleasure, too, kind of – or at least there was pleasure of a sort in not being entirely sure, in thinking . . . .

In any case, I'd found it (oh wasn't Dublin great for still hanging onto things for me to discover): the theatre, pictures for grown-ups, pictures sans machine – that's why it was Big Church . . . . I started taking Maura to the Abbey, at that time playing at the Queens in Pearse Street near the railway bridge, a step or two below the Olympia as to façade and appointments, though this was only to be expected in something so historical. Being part of our heritage it was as entitled to look dilapidated as any of the other parts. The Olympia, on the other hand, was only a theatre. The Abbey wasn't dependent on appearance: like all our, and my, most exigent and worshipful realities, it was an idea. It was exciting to ring reserving tickets, to dash in by bus during lunchtime to buy tickets, to push to the cowpat green glass doors to the foyer. It was as though much mundanities were really expressions of faith in and visible allegiance to this small vatican of art. Weren't their posters virtually the Pope's yellow (especially when wet with rain)? Wasn't the woman and hound only a more militant Virgin and Child?

There was a musty smell. A string trio (refugees from the Savoy) played thin but spirited music, a sound like that old ladies with a bit of go in them might make after a schooner of Christmas port. Bizet's *l'Arlesienne Suite* was top of the pops, with Grieg's *Peer Gynt* at number two; they never could get poor Anitra to dance right. Then the traditional knocks, the swish of curtain – and action! We saw a John B. Keane, a Louis D'Alton or two, and the three O'Caseys. There was Eileen Crowe looking down her nose at all around her, there was

Philip O'Flynn playing Fluther, flapping his arms as if indeed
he had a feather to flutter; there was Harry Brogan sounding
very like the resonant reciter who advertised cakes by Gate-
'ux on the wireless, Saturday afternoon at two. And standing
behind them all was this O'Casey. I'd heard his name before.
I explained to Maura: 'He had his name in the paper the time
of the Tóstal.' 'What for?' she reasonably inquired, drawing
out the Uncle Pether in me. Thwarted, I retorted, 'Something
about a play, what else?' Still he seemed fascinating, in spite of
notoriety – different from Behan, that way. His plays were a
great laugh, spoiled sometimes, but not for long, by bombs
and bullets. He was a slumster. He was a Protestant. I went to
Rathmines Library and read up on him. He was a Communist.
He lived in England. All this, I reported back to Maura,
explained the Tóstal business. 'He must be a hell of a man,' I
said, 'living with all them contradictions.'

Maura smiled wanly.

I came to at once. 'Cripes! – sorry!' I took her hand.

'What?' she seemed surprised.

'I said a curse,' I said: was that the right thing to call "hell"?'

'It's not that,' Maura said.

Well, that's good, I said to myself. I wouldn't for the world
defile her presence with a dirty word. The only way to keep
her was to maintain the respect mode, wasn't it?

'See you Friday?'

'Yes, okay.'

A quick hug in the porch, then off with me, whistling,
hoping the last 18 hadn't gone, happy as a lark after another
grand night out.

I had to talk to her even when I couldn't see her. Maura
didn't like being called at work, and Mrs O'Connell reserved
the 'phone in the house for her exclusive use. But there was a
'phone box at the bottom of Leinster Road, by the library, and
thither I'd repair after my dinner of baked beans and white
pudding, say, on the Mondays, Tuesdays and Thursdays that
we agreed to wash our hair and have an early night, because
we wanted to keep our jobs, didn't we? – naturally, I hadn't
told Maura that I had more or less lost mine, in case she
thought I couldn't afford the fabulous excursions into culture
that were our love life.

There was always a line of people outside that 'phone box. We were penitents with downcast eyes. We were supplicants, waiting impatiently for our fortunes to be told. We were drunkards, craving to be slaked, jigging from foot to foot, scrounging cigarettes from each other. Inside it was sweaty and smokey. The receiver was hot and slippery. There were names and numbers all over the place, some in frail, hurried script, like the smoke from votice candles, more in confident strokes like the ads in the papers thanking St Anthony, St Jude, St Maria Goretti 'for favours received (publication promised)'. This atmosphere, these scribblings, suggested to me why others used the 'phone box ('put your sweet lips'). But I just called to see how Maura was getting on, to confirm the – to me – unforgettable arrangements for our next meeting for fear I forgot them; to be, as embarrassing hindsight makes all too clear, a bloody nuisance. I remember once standing for half an hour to call and ask her how to wash a shirt. 'I have to have it for Wednesday night.' I anxiously explained. 'Wear the one you're wearing,' Maura laughed, exasperated. But didn't she understand? – I was trying to do the right thing. Didn't she see? – I wanted to be with her all the time. Didn't she realize? – her job was to make me feel good about myself, so that I could ignore the things that hadn't gone, and weren't going, according to childish longing.

She should have taken all that in by now: I'd spent enough time regaling her with it. Not with what I considered her duty to be. She would know that automatically, I imagined, when she heard the tale of my recent woe. I assumed that anybody who was prepared to listen would be prepared to enter into my version of the story. And because Maura let me talk – being too good natured to stop me in the first instance, then latterly I daresay too bombarded by my angst and dreams of a happy Dublin for myself to know exactly what to do – I found I had a story once again and applied myself with renewed interest to all its ins and outs, the silences, the inscrutable motives, the strange searing that lingers from hurt feelings and inhibits being touched. The more I went into it, the more lost Maura became, the more necessary she seemed, the more inclined I became to think that she could anchor me, like aunts of yore. I was doing the one thing that, I had heard, was absolutely fatal with wimmin, I was trying to be serious. 307

Maura broke it off. We were on her porch after another fascinating foray into theatreland, fresh from cutting capers on the floor of the Four P's, something madly sophisticated and disembodied anyhow, I'm sure. No, no; Maura was not being critical of the evening, or of any of the evenings, really; and indeed it was difficult not to agree that Harry Brogan was 'a darlin' man' (and laugh); undoubtedly, as I'd averred, the country was still maggoty with the likes of Donal Davoren, 'poet and poltroon', neither of us knowing the name of a living Irish, or any other, poet. Still, there I was, the perplexed milquetoast in the Thurber cartoon, trying to find words for what the caption put so well: 'With you Lydia, I have known happiness, and now you say you're going crazy.' Or so I see it when old enough to find anticlimax funny.

At the time, all I saw was a foundry of nails being slammed into a forest of coffins. She had pushed me out on an ocean of wormwood and gall without a paddle. I fucked culture for being unnatural (it was nothing but the city's piss-proud erection). I double-fucked respect. I should have remembered what we'd taught ourselves at school – the Four F's: find 'em, feel 'em, fuck 'em and forget 'em. I should have made her bed and got her to lie in it and not be turning myself into the horn of a dilemma. But I wasn't like that! Oh, what *mí-ádh* was on me at all that I couldn't see what the fuck was in front of me, that one talent which is death to hide . . . . Too fucking true. They also serve who only stand and wait – well, shit on that.

I swore I wouldn't 'phone, but of course I had to. Maura was out, though (a big lie: where did she have to go?): this was Carrie. 'She's after meeting a medical student,' I think.' Aha, I might have known class would raise its ugly head. Of course, I wasn't good enough for her (Tallow – worse, Tallowish – turns down Lismore – of all the cheek!). So she was just like the rest of them, after all; chasing the oul' college scarf, girls' equivalent of a bit of skirt. But what I found myself saying was, 'She ought to introduce me; maybe he could have a look at my leg.'

'Why? What's up with it?' I could hear Carrie's ears begin to stiffen with the hint of news.

Where my story came from I have no idea, but what emerged was that I had spilled acid on my leg at work and that now it was a kind of festering greenish colour, and sore, not that it mattered a whole lot (stoically) – the implication being that I was going to hang up my dancing shoes in any case (wherever that load of cock-and-bull came from it clearly dates from before my discovery that real life can give rise to symbols!). Good Carrie condoled. The conversation limped on a minute or two more; then we had to go.

'I suppose ye're going to the Ags tomorrow night?' I swear – I didn't know that was what I'd called about!

The Capitol were playing, it'd be dear, but there was nothing else for it. And there they were, Maura looking as sweet and dapper as if she didn't have a care in the world. Hello! Surprise! Look, not even limping! I saw her jaw faint, and *oh shit!* was written all over her face. 'I thought,' she began, grimly; 'your leg – '

'Aw c'mon,' I interrupted, plaintively, hand out.

But no. Suddenly there was nothing else for what, exactly?

I watched from the balcony for a while. I saw her stand and smooth her skirt down, give her hand and take to the anonymous, teeming floor, I realized that I'd been strangely mistaken: Maura was not me and I was not my father.

4

'God, no,' said the white girl, taking exception to the first thing out of my mouth. 'I *never* come here;' then, suspiciously, 'Do you?'

'Very seldom,' I lied suavely.

It was a pleasure to lie about the Sivilkems. The Sivilkems was a dead loss, a wash-out: enticing only to disappoint, pretending it could supplant anticlimax, only to reproduce it. And I hated it all the more because I seemed tied to it. That is, the belief persisted that I had to go out somewhere, and the Four P's Friday night was my lazy non-choice. Going further would only reward my forlorn hope of faring better with a longer walk home. Anyhow, anything, even a lie, to keep the conversation going. That was the main point, I now realized, 309 keep the ballroom ball rolling, play the game. That was the mistake I'd made with Maura: I'd acted like we were supposed to be more than dancing partners. Well, I wasn't going to make that mistake again. From now on I was going to go whichever way the wind blew. If the white girl had told me that she was the niece of Archbishop John Charles McQuaid and that after this, her first dance, her uncle was going to have the hall burned to the ground and everyone in it sent straight to hell, I probably would have replied, 'The blessings of God on the pair of ye.'

She said nothing, however, and we went on for a while with her putting me through her paces. I was a bad dancer, but she beat the band. And what was more, she didn't seem to care. There was I trying to disguise my expertise in the Bunion Boogie while she, quite detached (though in fact – *ouch!* – not detached enough), swung around in a vaguely satirical hobble, by which turkeyoid gait she expresed assent to the mechanics of foxtrot. I caught her meaning right enough; she was doing the henhouse when the fox is nigh. It was just that my brains didn't reach my feet. This was the Funky Chicken ahead of its time (I was the one laying the egg).

Nothing would do me, of course, but to find out if her idea was to show me personally up, to shame me before a putative rude and scoffing multitude (of what were wimmin not capable?), so I asked her out again for the slowing of the tempo right down, now ladies and gentlemen boys, etc. This time she did an exaggerated but technically proficient waltz (at least by my rickety standards), holding me sternly at arms' length and looking me up and down with a quizzical frown – milady nonplussed by the appearance of an uncalled-for servant. Clearly some kind of lunatic . . . . Just my luck . . . . Yet, after the slow set, when she announced abruptly that she was going home, I found myself saying, 'Hang on; I'll come with you.' A lunatic was better than nothing – much!

'It's okay,' she said; 'I live in Harrington Street,' as if the point was whether her place was just a hundred yards away or not. But as she spoke she stared stonily at me, so that I saw she wasn't being stupid, therefore neither should I be. Except now I was blowing in the wind. This new approach of mine, whereby I was not to reason why and thereby be in full command of the nothing I was doing was just as confusing as my earlier flying blind. It had somehow failed to occur to me that whenever I perpetrated passivity, proceedings would grind to a halt just as they'd always done. So I said, 'Can I see you again?' I could if I wanted, came the sceptical reply, and she strode through the rim of lads around the back of the hall, firming the day with arrangements thrown over her shoulder. A bit of a character, wasn't she? (Was I supposed to laugh, or what?) I would if she liked. But of course now that I was, if only on the strength of my perplexity and low-grade desperation, willing to play, *she* was deadly serious.

I called her the white girl because of her flour-and-margarine complexion, acquired because she ate nothing (she was saving up) and slept less. But I might just as well have called her the black girl. She wore black tops I'd never seen the like of, they being neither shirts nor blouses but half-baked chemises or singlets with sleeves. She wore them tucked in tight to her black or navy-blue skirt. Her black hair came unfashionably lanky down her shoulders. I'd never seen a woman dress so indifferently, so strikingly, so obviously in a way that neither nun or man commended. She often went without stockings. Her legs were strong – bold, naked, white. Legs that spoke volumes. Outspoken, strident legs. What have I here at all? I wondered – some sort of new breed of Teddy Girl? She was nobody's machine, I could see that. She never wore make-up. She lived on coffee. She was saving to go to Paris.

That flouting walk of hers, which made her body seem to utter; her sense of image which seemed to denounce image; the way she knew her mind and spoke it: she was Dublin, I was convinced. Yet in some ways she was more ordinary than I was. She worked at the tax office in O'Connell Street, a job which smacked of pull to me, or brains, or luck, or whatever it was I lacked, the very sort of niche that parents prayed for, and with good pay, too, and benefits. She was from Cavan. I said I'd never been there; was it like Carrickmacross at all? 'Much too much,' said Mary sourly. But she had a large family of brothers there and liked to hitchhike back at weekends. I wondered if it wasn't dangerous, cadging lifts, a girl alone? Mary sneered as though I'd belittled her: 'Only for the drivers,' she growled, adding if there was one thing she really hated it was stupid statements.

311

She talked a lot about what she hated. I wasn't used to hearing someone being *against* things. (Had I been wrong all this time in wanting to be for?) She spoke with power. I was enthralled. Her performance on the Sivilkems floor, which I had labelled foolery or worse, had been the height of seriousness, I now learned: she hated dancehalls. 'It's nothing but a big cattle market,' she complained; 'fellas spitting on their hands at the thought of you – don't they even call us heifers. That's why I dance like an *óinseach*. It makes them mad, and they leave me alone, which is where I'd rather be in the first place, if gropers like them are the best I can do.' And this reminded her. 'Don't you be getting any ideas either,' she went on severely; 'none of that stuff; no involvement; I'm not interested, okay?' Grand, grand, I agreed; cards on the table, much better that way, mine not to reason why . . . . And I noted, with a vague sense of relief, that she found it difficult to talk about; it really was a hateful subject.

And Mary hated the job as well, pushing papers, answering 'phones, making tea, doing a bit of shopping for the boss at lunchtime (while he went to the Parnell Street Mooney's); and there were little hutches to which people could come in off the street and be rude to you. Besides which, tax was boring, tax was stupid, the whole country was tax-mad – punitive Church and weary family, hopeless government and boarding-schools: each took its toll. It was hard to believe she'd given two years of her life to it. Except, of course, what choice was there in this balls of a country? Well, anyhow, she'd soon be well out of it. Paris for Christmas. Ring out the bells!

The no-ness of her overawed me. How wonderfully black and white she was. How splendidly unconfused. (Saying no: what a simple way to avoid confusion!) What wouldn't I give to be as definite as her, to quit as being unworthy of me a probably pensionable clerkship. 'Do you speak French?' Mary just laughed, and her long hair swung like an arc of water. '*Non!*' She didn't care. I thought of people from my previous life for whom there also had to be a France, a different place to learn from, where perhaps (was that why Da went?) the present might be full enough to allay the rest. And now there goes that brazen Mary. She's made of herself a flag to follow. I looked up to her, cringing with jealousy and hunger.

And a little fear. She was too tough, I thought. She forced herself. (She should have been more like me . . . .) She didn't sleep. The room in Harrington Street had no light. She was turning her stomach into a coffee-grounds mine. It was the dark room I found preying on me, probably because I never saw it, never would see it, could only try to picture it. (It looked chilling and fascinating, like Mary herself. I suppose I also saw in it an image of my own vague feelings of lostness and hapless groping, feelings made a little more insistent by dancehalls' unrewarding gloom and the heavy, unaccommodating shadows of Maura's porch.) The darkness didn't bother Mary one bit, however. It saved money. 'I won't be living there long,' she said, 'and I'm never there now.'

If she wanted to read she went to the reading-room at Kevin Street library. With all the smells and snoring? That unnerved me too. 'Well, what about them?' Mary demanded contentiously. Those shelterers with nothing only time to call their own were, she'd have me know, a lot better company than others she could name: they did less harm, they never made to paw her, they didn't pretend to be anything they weren't, their lapel pockets weren't lined with fountain pens and propelling pencils. 'Read George Orwell,' she commanded.

'Ah, *Animal Farm*,' I said, assuming this to be a relevant title, though really I was fleeing for cover: I wasn't used to someone taking me on, to someone who had an active, challenging code of face values.

'No, no,' she went impatiently, and loaned me *Down and Out in Paris and London*, though this only caused another little flare-up and for me more intellectual discomfort. I liked the story fine. The only thing, I complained, was that I couldn't tell if it was true or false, fiction or real life story. 'What does it matter?' Mary demanded disdainfully. 'Everything is true in its own way.' I blanched at this novel gospel. I'd always thought everything was true in a pre-ordinaed way, a way which was controlled by something that was both in, and alien to, its nature: father and son, work and worker, God and man . . . . What kind of person was this Cavanite at all, who made me feel so woefully conventional? I had to know: it was as though I hoped her fearlessness, her restlessness, would prove contagious and would sponsor me, somehow, in hard manhood and loveless venturing. And for all my backward- 313 ness, she let me stay in tow.

I was so grateful for her grand bad company I even joined her in sleeplessness, otherwise known as the Studio Club, one or two small dank rooms upstairs in Dawson Lane, where you could go at any time, it seemed, as long as it was way late, to see strange people and drink watery Maxwell House or sometimes cider. Strange women roared with laughter here and went in holey stockings, flat-heeled shoes. Strange men gave out choruses of songs that seemed familiar in principle but were, once I paid attention, totally unknown to me. Strange Mary stood in the midst of all, an impious candle in her black garb and bright white face, at home at last and animated in her proud difference.

Of course I had seen people like this before. These were members of the maimed fraternity who played in public places, appealed to the charity of cinema queues, stared vaguely heavenward with eyes like flawed glass marbles, singing uncontrollably some *passé* song. I was, it seemed, in the company of such fixtures' sons, the pre-maimed, whose turn at immobility would surely come and who were assembling now to pass on parental tips and train each other for the rocky road. Tramps. How knowledgeable Mrs O'Connell was after all; how clearly she'd discerned the lie of the land, the shape of things to come. Had she felt in the air the ousting of her repertoire, her dreadful crooning acting like some crone-like antennae?

Some of the lads seemed to be disabled already, with mouth-organs strapped prosthetically to their guitars. But they were happy. Their clothing might be as dun as dirt, but as long as they could twiddle out the notes, ignore the barber and act like life was a prolonged fair day, what care they? I couldn't make head or tail of them. They could be a resurrection of the Unemployed. They could be what happened to a Film Society that had been forced to hock all its machinery. Once again, though there was no balcony, I took to doing what I had always done so well. I watched from a distance, wondering.

But were these people proper folk-singers? I daren't ask Mary, needless to say; my ignorance continually offended her, and the nicest thing she could think of to do was introduce me to men up to their eyes in turf-mould (mere beard is understatement), to whom I couldn't possibly open my mouth, having too much to say. It was disturbing, though, never to hear 'Master McGrath' (the national anthem of West Water-ford). And how about 'Kevin Barry'? It confused me greatly that the songs being sung were clearly Irish yet were most obscure. And in any case, hadn't Irish stuff had its day? We were in the age of Pelvic Man and 'Jailhouse Rock' now. Irish had served its purpose – fair dues to it: *de moturis nil nisi bonum* (unless you wanted seven years' bad luck). We were well shut of the English, which nobody would deny. And lest we forget, the language was compulsory at school: if you failed it you failed everything. But everybody knew that the life under-written by the language belonged to the time of the bare backsides. Didn't we wear the *crios* and Aran ganzy, paupers' chic, to prove we were a different breed, complete now with rural electrification? Yet, folk was modern too. The Clancy Brothers were the latest thing. The broadsides they belted out spoke of an unfamiliar nation, a loose young nation not afraid to stamp its feet on the holy ground and roar, 'Fine girl y'are', the girl who had (did they mean? was it possible?) sanctified the sod by stretching herself out on it in lively and obliging fashion – the very opposite in type and temperament to tuber-cular Noreen Bawn, lying stretched cold ('There's a graveyard in Tirconnell'), whose obsequies were conducted in slow waltz time.

What if the music at the Studio Club owed nothing to electricity – thought impressionable me – it rattled away with spunk and verve all the same. Nobody danced to it: but I was getting tired of dancing anyhow. I'd try singing, which made the brain dance. I listened, drinking down copious quantities of intoxicating *fol-de-dol-day* with *toorle-aye* chasers. The message to Jim Reeves seemed plain: he'd have to go.

We went to a hall somewhere around Capel Street behind the Four Courts. There were forms scattered around and thin young men and thin older men and freckled young women who wore their buttoned-up overcoats all evening long sat on them. Every so often, after a few desultory words together, one of the men would get up and take a flute or tin-whistle from inside his jacket and bend his face to it to moan a slow air or trill a jig. Sometimes fiddlers and melodeonists turned up. 315

They were nondescript too, clean-shaven and quiet-spoken. Decent skins. Respectable young men. Anonymous. They too sank themselves into their playing, submerging self so the tunes might have life, eyes closed, sharing their secret lives with small audiences in a cold hall. Nothing else in life, their playing said, evinces or encourages this rapture.

During the day, perhaps, they served at Dockrells, they were links in the Civil Service paper chain, they unobtrusively supervised the Mauras and the Marys, were subject merely to the customary quotas of paranoia, misanthrophy, dyspepsia, despair. They had a pint and a half-one before the Kimmage bus; made the First Fridays. But secret lives would out, evenings once a month or so in the city gave way to hauntings of stone and heather and empty strands, dancing firelight and the curlew's cry. It was good the youngsters were coming along. Maybe some of them would team up together (*together*, that's the ticket), keep out of the mouse race, stay away from the sullenness of women bored at home. The times they were a-changing – please God. They might manage to fall in with Ó Riada.

There wasn't any singing at Capel Street, or perhaps it was drowned out, because as soon as we began going there, it seemed, the whole town was at it, and anyone who had a loft or a back room had a folk club. After closing time on Friday nights, Ronnie Drew and his merry men held forth like heroes at the Grafton News and Cartoon Cinema, songs from O'Casey (I thought, not to mention Prussia Street) and the common tongue. How the audience roared and rollicked, singlets saturated with sweated booze, primed expectantly by the occasion's evanescent anarchism. Mary always hoped Luke Kelly would be there. He often was. She loved Luke Kelly. The raw passion of his voice could start a free-for-all or stop a train. Everyone loved Luke Kelly.

It was at the Grafton, too, that I first heard the singing of Joe Heaney. That oboe: that voice of quartz. And for the first time I tried to take in the *via dolorosa* paced out by his repertoire. He didn't supply *folderols*, which made it hard: there was no joining in. He sang in our native language (the one not taught at school, the one he lived through). That made it hard, too: he was a stranger. And I knew some of the words, because we'd done 'Caoineadh na dTrí Muire' and 'Anach Cuain' for the

Leaving. Why that made listening to Joe Heaney hard was that I never knew these works were songs. I only knew them as tortuous demonstrations of syntax and vocabulary which had to be mastered 'for the exam', an exercise which was the intellectual equivalent of Uncle Seamus sitting on his arse swatting green-fly. Only now did I learn that these poem-songs were part of a man's life, and that he thought them worth denoting to life at large (the audience). Every time he performed them, a notion of the people filled the air, permitting harmony. At the end of every song Joe Heaney sang there was a small moment of silence while we reckoned, flinching slightly (I felt vaguely cheated), with the nerve he touched, the something missing in us that had been laid bare (language and silence attaining synonymity), while we returned from the uplifting, windswept territory of the artist and his work.

So, this is why, I thought, Mary is a folkster. She loves the people. The city doesn't offer what she knows – or rather feels – of age and rootedness. She can't take the hurry and the flesh (it's only late, when that's all over, that she comes into her own). She knows she hates the not-them – the Medical Students, the Institutes' Associate Members. If Paris, mother of liberty, is the name she gives to all she loves, that's certainly as good a name as anyone can invent. But it's on the stage I'll find her one of these fine times, the Juliette Greco of Usher's Island, war to the death against nine-to-fivery and all its works and pomps in the green glint of her eyes, in her every posture.

I was dead wrong, of course. One evening she just didn't turn up. I slunk unconfidently to the Studio Club. No sign. I hung around outside her place in Harrington Street a time or two. It was uncomfortable looking up at the windows from the steps of the CYMS opposite: the windows were opaque, like sea under cloudy sky, like the pupils of the blind. The evenings were drawing in. It was getting cold. (Besides, I didn't know her window.) At last I went one lunchtime to the tax office. A clerk my own age, her age, in be-dandruffed blazer and Pioneer pin, huffily gave me the official word. 'Mary's gone.' Now here I was with something much simpler and more provocative than my image of her – her power of decision.

5

It seemed a fine idea, though, the people, so I spent that October going after them. I pursued them to The Long Hall and The Palace Bar. I saw them in various Mooneys, in Rice's on the Green, in Lloyd's, North Earl Street. My pubbing was a Mary-substitute, no doubt, at least to begin with. She had introduced me to a new style of going out, and going drinking, apart from its humanistic dimension, seemed an agreeable modification of that style, a combination of doing the town and being an insider, of joining the general public and minding one's own business, a kind of date with oneself.

It wasn't long, however, before I learned that drink provided its own rationale. Mary was quite unnecessary. Everywhere I went there were strangers eager to teach me all about it. The grail of a good pint was much discussed and a civil house – 'Quiet, y'know; you can get on with the serious business of drinking in it' – was considered a boon surely. Grey-faced men in suits gave me elaborate specifications and explicit directions. There was a pub in Chatham Street that served a decent pint, ditto an establishment in Granby Row. And I suppose I tried them, avoiding betimes the purveyors of cat's piss and similar emollients whose name was evidently legion in the town and who sucked up to tourists – 'For the love o' God, son, steer clear of that shower.' Let nothing but familiarity ring, seemed to be the old soaks' watchword. As for myself, to drink became an opportunity merely to hide in plain sight.

'The usual, Mr O?' The barman rarely has to lift his eyes from the Limerick Junction returns. I am an old reliable, and he has the tipple served before I settle to the bar. My hand shakes, greeting my old, old friend. Its cool kiss enters me, tang of mud, tang of salt, tang of cleansing; my bitter-sweet preservative. But it would take years to get to that stage. (I know it's sacrilegeous to speak of time and pubs together, but I knew no better, being young and hurried, a temporary state, mercifully.) Even more so than I had found before, drink was all slowness and minute gradations. The drawing of the pint. The pint's sluggish surge to form a head. The pint must sit. The head is capped. The glass must have its bottom wiped. The glass has to be slowly elevated, and the 'ah' slowly exhaled. And grey-faced men in greasy suits of navy-blue would tell me about cellarage and temperature, lingering on obscure points of environmental nicety in the manner of a loving father who only wants his favourite child to spoil him (it'd be only fair). All too often, however, numb from the application of minutiae, I would omit to pay my interlocutor his fee. When he at length formally brought his dissertation to a close by raising his glass with a flourish and lowering in one draught his remaining third of beer, all I could think to do was watch the fluttering Adam's apple and listen to the glottal gulping (ever the spectator). This caused the other – so friendly so recently – to move off, muttering, and made me conclude that people were strange.

If there were pubs where young people went, they went to them together, and without me. I never saw anyone my own age drinking on his own. And of course there never ever were solo drinking girls – the very idea! If there were pubs with people on their own in them, the people looked old no matter what their age, and down at heel, looked as though life had forgotten them and that they weren't too surprised it had. But I could have seen these people anywhere, there were broken men wherever I'd been; my past was peopled with victims of narcoleptic consciences, stunned consciousnesses (the population of Lismore). I couldn't think of anything to say to them, and usually they took no notice of me, since I was just as nondescript as themselves – more noticeably so, if anything, not being a regular. Only if you were real hard up would you think of bumming a pint of me. I added to the counter's age the ringed imprint of my glass and went on my way.

And never a hint of folk. I wasn't looking for songs and singers: they were easy to find. What I was after was a bit of the Grafton buzz, the flavour of carousel and relaxation. Weren't pubs places where such moods were rehearsed, their air loud with O'Caseyish remonstration, Behanish bonhomie; where the Prussia Street pantomime found permanent form and the binman's circus was forever on parade. But all pubs gave unginger me the scrape of chairs and the stench of gents. Was it that folk and people were not the same at all? – another dirty trick of culture.

I sat upstairs in Doran's, Marlborough Street, with its lounges along the walls and good class ashtrays and string of 319 fairy lights fringing the shelf above the till. I was looking at my future in a pint of Spatenbrau, but could see nothing. (Well, maybe in the next one.) For the time being, I told myself that I liked this beer's blondeness. I liked its foreignness. And I hadn't yet met anyone wanting to tell me all about it. Early evening. There was a couple in a corner, he in a crumpled suit, her hair *en bouffant*. I heard low laughter, glasses clinking. I heard new banknotes speak like a fortune-teller's cards being turned, like crisp tongues of flame. All around were appointments in plastic and off-red. I felt depressed.

But I had high hopes of Jo Locke's. These were based not so much on the proprietor's musical accomplishments. Frequent regurgitations of his 'Goodbye' from *The White Horse Inn* on Radio Éireann's Hospitals Requests had made me think that he was to vocalizing what Jack Doyle was to the noble art of self-defence. But Ruritanian connotations were nowhere to be found here: the pub was plainly named 'Jo Locke's Singing Pub'. Well now, thought I, here's something being put on by someone who's seen the world a bit. This should be good. And I made straight for that upstairs on Aston Quay. There was a microphone and a piano. You gave your name to an M.C., who was also the pianist, and sat until your number came up, drinking. Drink came via waiter, so all there was to do was wait. Talk was dangerous. People were loudly shushed for trying to spoil the granny's birthday or Johnny's return with Luton Vauxhall money. The Johnnys mainly put their sweet lips, or sometimes remembered the Red River valley, very slow and low. All concerned had as politely passive a time as possible. Did I sing? I was, rather, to be found heading as quickly in the opposite direction as three pints on an empty stomach would permit.

The opposite direction was the one taken by the empty mid-evening bus, and more memorable than my attempt to blend beer and the milk of human kindness is what happened in the aftermath of the abortive blur. Still teetering a little, I got off the bus and made for the Leinster Chalet, or rather chalet-not, since the place bore no resemblance to matters Swiss or skiful, except perhaps in the sense of being a last resort – it stayed open till midnight. There, however, I could make plans to satisfy the fierce hunger created by the drink. I'd buy two eggs, three sausages, three rashers, a turd of black pudding, which raw material I would clutch to my shirt, appetitiously and greasily, while at the same time (no easy feat) negotiating the Leinster Road and the rapidity with which railings, gateways, steps and keyholes thrust themselves at the tipsy, egg-bearing traveller.

Everything went in the pan at once and was immediately set fire to. Giant eructations of smoke filled the room (a tricky business, bending over boozed to adjust the gas jet). Steam from the saucepan befogged the drapeless window – quick! rinse out the mug under the cold tap, wipe sodden hands down leg of trousers, shovel dust of Maxwell House in. A smell of singeing rose where fag had slipped from rim of old spaghetti-tin ashtray onto the tablecloth of *Sunday Times*. But lovely grub – muck in! muck in!

But this orgy of bedsitterland *gemütlichheit* had its toll, once I toppled into bed. I was all for repose, being sated, but the bed rejected me, and turned into a disorienting engine. Round and round it spun me, petrified and paralysed (perhaps it was too many years of suchlike dislocation which had my greasy-suited pubmen the way they were). It was like my childhood nightmares when the terroristic imagination cut off legs and had me frighteningly wrong way round in bed, unable to straighten up and fly right. Or was I being punished for culinary overconfidence, as my addresses in spate to the sink suggested? Weakened and quivering, I'd clutch the side of the polluted trough like the thin figures in the middle distance at Dolphin's Barn long ago after their canal swim. Except that they had immersed themselves, whereas I had been evacuated. Was Dublin now merely an emetic, reducing me to merely being a body? I felt empty.

The clock ticked. It was November. Leaves slapped soggily against the window. Wind did its doleful number in the wires. Snatches of 'Friday Night Is Music Night' came from the Home Service of the retired *chanteuse* in the room next door. Doors banged downstairs, doors of cars outside, cars raced away to pleasure. I wasn't going out: I knew there was nothing to go out to. Only one bar of the electric fire worked. Seven-thirty. Eight. I went to bed.

To get warm, of course. But I let on I went to bed to read. I would have preferred a radio. But I couldn't have one and buy   321 books as well, and I had to buy books, otherwise life would have been just a tissue of necessities, a holding operation for the body only. I wanted to tell myself that things hadn't come to that yet.

Perhaps because I didn't have a radio, I went through a bout of reading American books. They had great titles – *For Whom the Bell Tolls*, *The Sound and the Fury* . . . . But Faulkner was unlike any America I'd ever seen, and besides was tumultuous and broody. As for the Hemingway, it obscenetied in the milk of my impatience and I couldn't be bothered to finish it (the Stella was bound to have the movie of it, anyhow, some Sunday night). I wanted every book to be George choking the Lenny in me, to be Rose of Sharon unbuttoning to nurse me. Yet when I tried other Steinbecks, they seemed somehow both ponderous and thin. James Dean was better than *East of Eden*.

No book would have satisfied me. Once upon a time (eighteen months previously, that is), I had taken to books as I might have to kept promises. They had involved me in desires. They'd shown ideas, images. Those days were gone. My mind was a leaden cloud. Nothing could hold it. Nothing held me now. Outsiders might be interesting to read about, I told myself, but in reality they're nothings. If there's nothing outside there's only an emptiness within. And there was nothing new in Dublin. I went to see *Billy Liar*. It was only funny. They should have made it true (but they never did in pictures, did they?). So I still didn't know what I was going to do after Christmas, when Ken let me go. All thought kept turning to the past. Failed boyfriend, failed drunkard. And behind those two loomed earlier ones, Monkstown, Harcourt Street, which I'd considered deliverances at the time, but could only see now as larger, more decisive failures. Book propped unattended against raised knees covered by ratty quilt, I stared off into the space that was my nothingness. I was going to have to make my mind up. I was going to have to act as though there was a mind to be made up (there had to be more than feelings to be hurt in there). I was going to have to be a Mary, and decide. I never had done that before. I never thought that I would have to pass this Leaving.

I was reduced to a bone, the bone that pointed arrogantly at nothing, the miniature 'I' that dominated a father who only wanted to reject it, who beat it till it cried.

The machine that revved and revved and overheated and coughed up oil.

That body which, quivering, caused more distress and shame than even Guinness-puke.

The surge of novelty, that banal repetition. Loving Dublin, the oul' rag and bone shop itself.

'Fog is a good sign,' said Peg, brightly. 'Looks like you'll have a smooth crossing, anyway.'

The North Wall, 4 January, 1965. I'd been thirty months in Dublin, and this was the anticlimactic climax: I was leaving.

We stood on the ferry deck, waiting for Da to arrive. We had come early, I'd already stowed the bag in the cabin. All around us exciting clanks and bangs rang out in the viscous, diesel-laden air. Latecomers hurried aboard out of the raw evening, dragging Dunne's Stores bags full of the husks of Xmas back to their lives 'over', their real lives. Behind Peg, the city was a rumour in the mist, a remote settlement in some non-milky way. 'Still no sign of him,' Peg said every so often. 'No,' I replied. There seemed nothing else to say.

It was Peg who told me to book a berth, and who had rung Da to tell him I was going. That was about as much talk as my decision caused. When I announced it, I assumed my audience (Peg and Mam, up from Lismore for Christmas) would be taken aback by the boldness of the move, a leap into the unknown worthy of a moral Tarzan. They would protest, I thought (hoped). I would insist. I'd inform them that they'd had their chance. I'd say with gleeful callousness that they should stop their gobs by inserting money in them: 'How about this?' I planned to say, swaggering a little, having them for once where I wanted them; 'send me for a year to do First Arts.' There would be tears. Their patent crocodility I'd repudiate with stony silence. I'd press my point. No faller for Christmas spirit I: they needn't try that. Goodwill, my hole! The only good was -bye. (I just hoped Mam would not start litanizing my mistakes to me. Just let not that happen.) But opportunities arose for neither.

To my great surprise, I found that my announcement caused no great surprise. I would be as well off, if not better, I was told. It was as though I had only just found out what they had known for years: Ireland was a banjaxed country and Dublin a slough of despond. The difference between us was that I was not prepared to offer up being Irish for the Holy Souls or otherwise accept it as an expression of God's recognizable yet inscrutable sense of humour (all kings had clowns: thus the King of Kings had a countryful of favourite dwarfs and suchlike, blessed imps of innocence and back-chat). If to live was, willy-nilly, what I'd chosen to do (God help me), then I'd have to go. Besides, O'Briens who had crossed before me had all done well. There was the example of Uncle Frank, the engineer, to spur me on. He'd gone to England but hadn't stopped, went on to Africa, to Canada, saw awesome Holy Week in Seville while stationed with the Air Ministry in Gibraltar, was at that very moment off to Australia (keep the sunny side up).

Still, Mam was sad at parting. She gave me a fiver. I gave her a perfunctory hug, impatient, accepting that impatience as confirmation of the stranger I had become. And I knew enough (had seen enough movies) to realize that strangers kept on moving. Even in Ireland, looking back on it (and I liked looking back), I hadn't been able to stop. School, Lismore, Enniscorthy, Dublin. Up and down and over and back. Welcome everywhere, belonging nowhere: the welcome a preamble to just another leaving: the human *Rawhide* theme, that's me.

Come on, come on. Let's go, let's go. I felt bound for Treasure Ireland. I kept politely suggesting to Peg that there was no need for her to stay, she'd only get pneumonia standing out here. 'Ah no, no,' she protested. Had my going to be seen to be believed? No: it was just Peg being dutiful again, being beside the point practically speaking, being ritualistically crucial. I wished she'd stop muttering about Da's delay, though. It uncharitably occurred to me that she was staying to see if he did turn up. He did. The three of us stood around in silence, pressing cigarettes on each other.

The hooter sounded, saving us from ourselves. We shook hands. Between Da's hand and mine, a note.

'Sorry it can't be more,' he said.

Sorry!

'That's all right,' I said.

All right!

324   I went below and lay on the bunk. The *Hispaniola* pulled

away. I shared the cabin with a stocky Scotsman who fetched tea for us and laced it with Johnny Walker. I slept a dreamless sleep. At Birkenhead I woke in panic to nightmarish pounding. But it was nothing to do with me: they were letting off the cattle. Then we drifted, a strange motion between movement proper and genuine purpose. But it had nothing to do with me.

There was the Royal Liver building with the cock on top. That was on the cover of the insurance book we had in Lismore. Then Lime Street (Mallow) and the London (Dublin) train. Cows ran away from us. Crewe was Limerick Junction with a swelled head. Dank green, in forty shades, flashed by. We cantered through Nuneaton, or was that Portlaoise? The air at Euston was smashing, everything I wanted it to be – frying, coffee and exhaust fumes. And look at all those beautiful red buses . . . .